"BOUND BY BLOOD"

NAILBITER

VOLUME FIVE

Story by
JOSHUA WILLIAMSON

Art by
MIKE HENDERSON

Colors by
ADAM GUZOWSKI

Letters & Book Design by
JOHN J. HILL

Edited by
ROB LEVIN

NAILBITER Created by
**JOSHUA WILLIAMSON &
MIKE HENDERSON**

IMAGE COMICS, INC.

Robert Kirkman - Chief Operating Officer
Erik Larsen - Chief Financial Officer
Todd McFarlane - President
Marc Silvestri - Chief Executive Officer
Jim Valentino - Vice-President
Eric Stephenson - Publisher
Corey Murphy - Director of Sales
Jeff Boison - Director of Publishing Planning & Book Trade Sales
Jeremy Sullivan - Director of Digital Sales
Kat Salazar - Director of PR & Marketing
Branwyn Bigglestone - Controller
Drew Gill - Art Director
Jonathan Chan - Production Manager
Meredith Wallace - Print Manager
Briah Skelly - Publicist
Sasha Head - Sales & Marketing Production Designer
Randy Okamura - Digital Production Designer
David Brothers - Branding Manager
Olivia Ngai - Content Manager
Addison Duke - Production Artist
Vincent Kukua - Production Artist
Tricia Ramos - Production Artist
Jeff Stang - Direct Market Sales Representative
Emilio Bautista - Digital Sales Associate
Leanna Caunter - Accounting Assistant
Chloe Ramos-Peterson - Library Market Sales Representative

IMAGECOMICS.COM

N A I L B I T E R
VOL. 5: BOUND BY BLOOD.
First printing. NOVEMBER 2016. Copyright
© 2016 Joshua Williamson and Mike Henderson.
All rights reserved. Published by Image Comics,
Inc. Office of publication: 2001 Center Street, Sixth
Floor, Berkeley, CA 94704. Originally published in
single magazine form as NAILBITER #21-25 and
NAILBITER/HACK/SLASH (one-shot), by Image
Comics. "Nailbiter," its logos, and the likenesses
of all characters herein are trademarks of Joshua
Williamson and Mike Henderson, unless otherwise
noted. HACK/SLASH Copyright © Hack/Slash
Inc 2016. "Image" and the Image Comics logos
are registered trademarks of Image Comics, Inc.
No part of this publication may be reproduced
or transmitted, in any form or by any means
(except for short excerpts for journalistic or review
purposes), without the express written permission
of Joshua Williamson, Mike Henderson or Image
Comics, Inc. All names, characters, events, and
locales in this publication are entirely fictional.
Any resemblance to actual persons (living or
dead), events, or places, without satiric intent, is
coincidental. Printed in the USA. For information
regarding the CPSIA on this printed material
call: 203-595-3636 and provide reference
#RICH—711962. For international rights, contact:
foreignlicensing@imagecomics.com.
ISBN: 978-1-63215-892-5

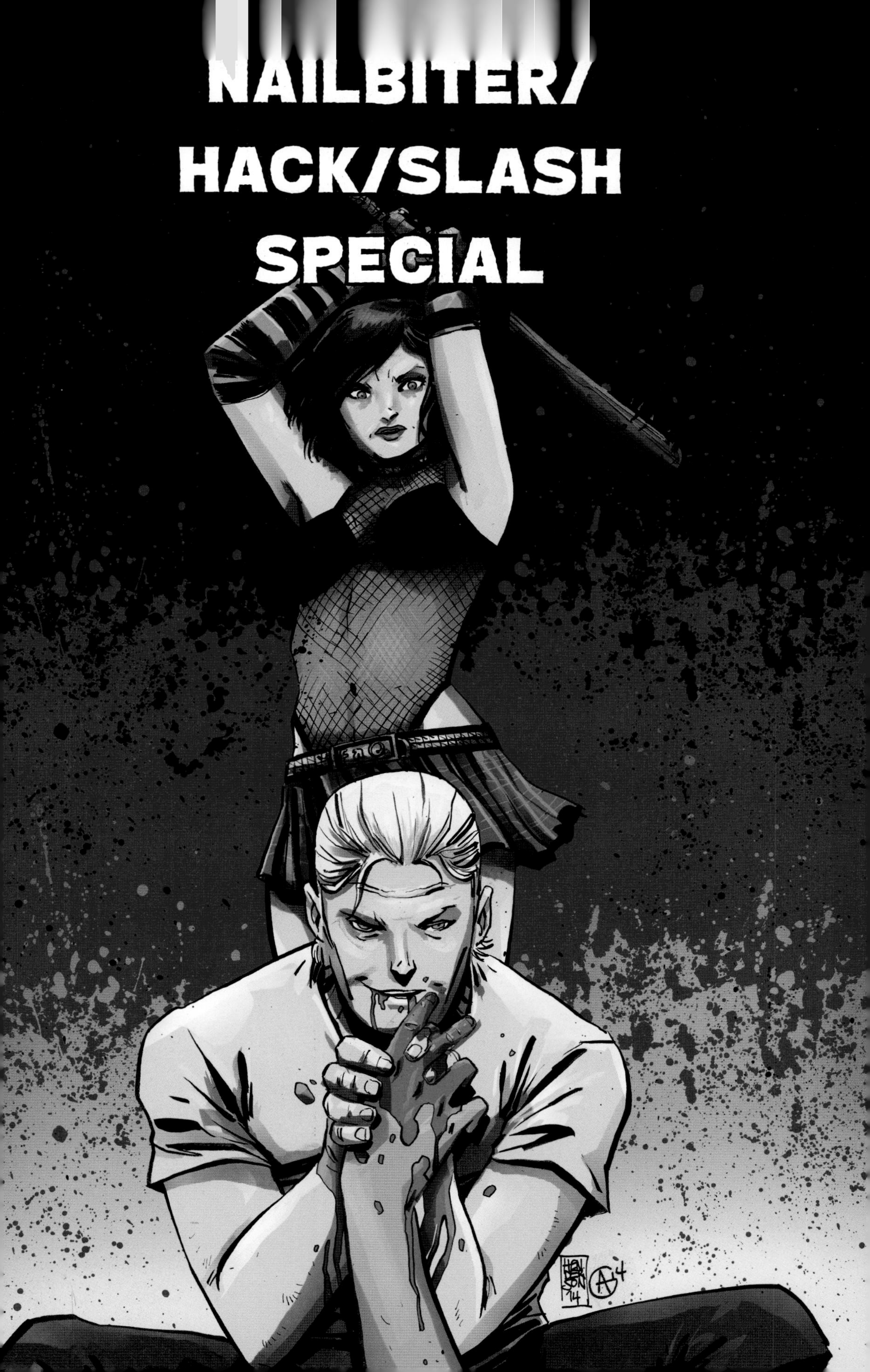
NAILBITER/
HACK/SLASH
SPECIAL

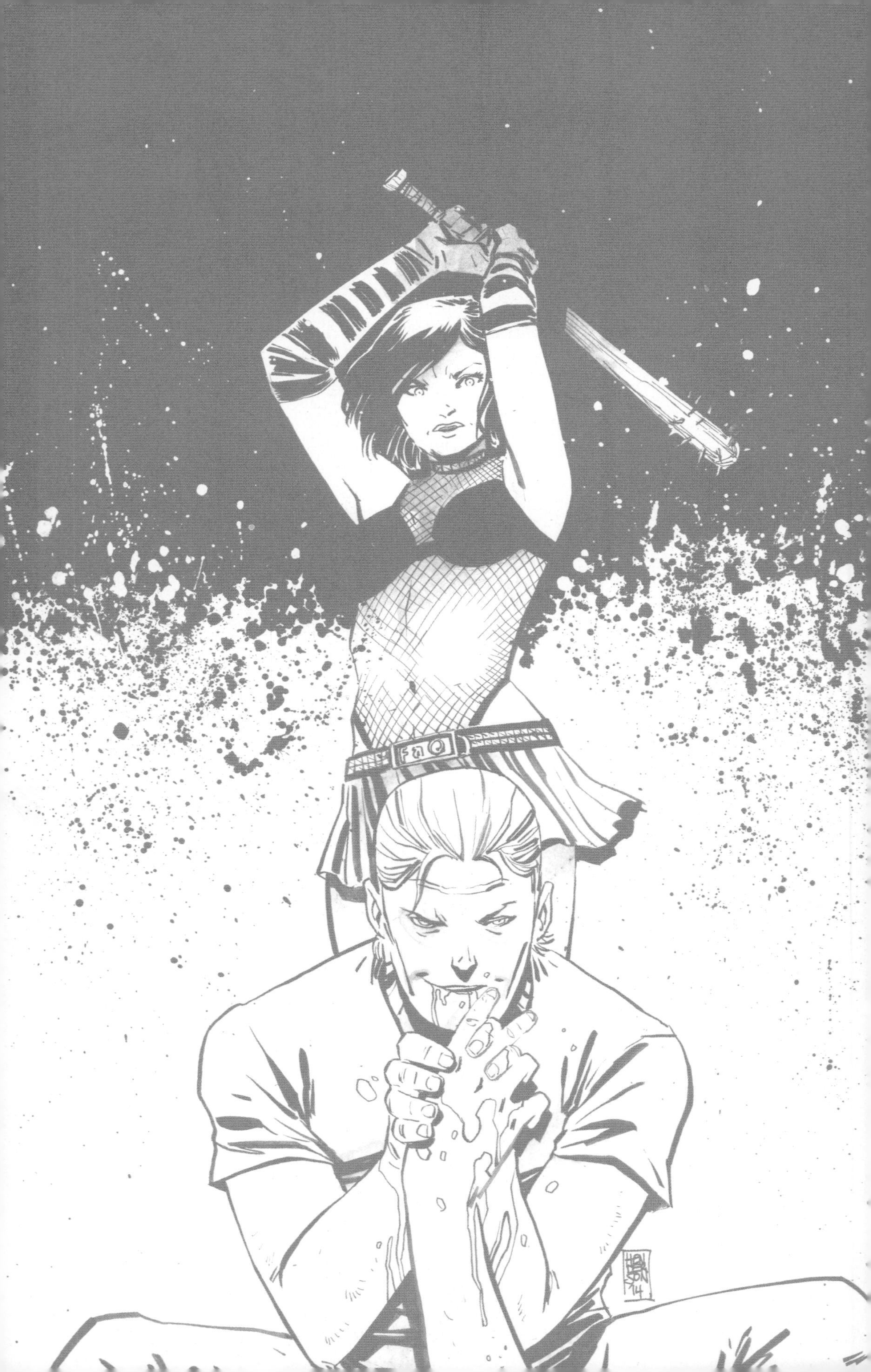

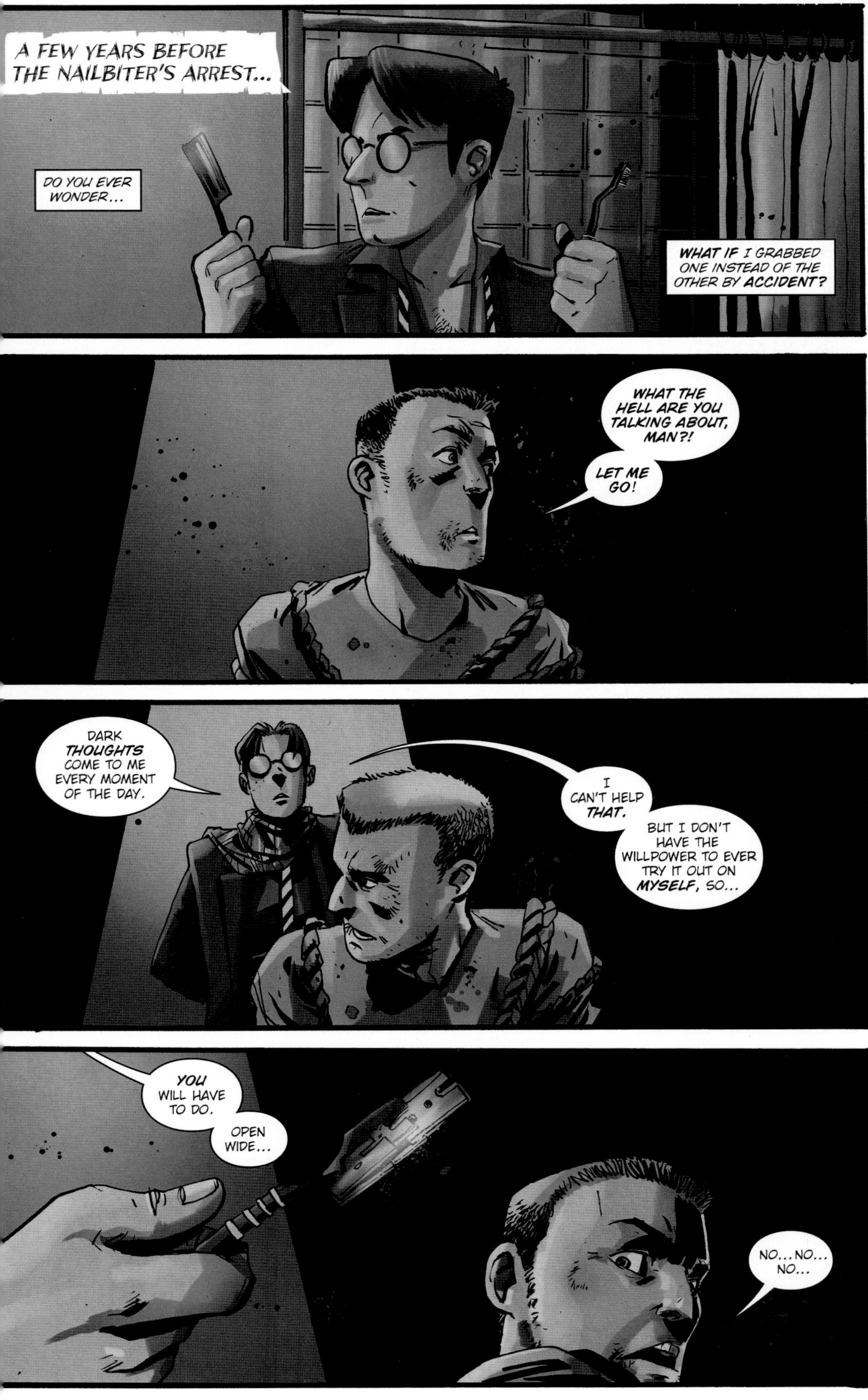
A FEW YEARS BEFORE THE NAILBITER'S ARREST...
DO YOU EVER WONDER...
WHAT IF I GRABBED ONE INSTEAD OF THE OTHER BY ACCIDENT?
WHAT THE HELL ARE YOU TALKING ABOUT, MAN?!
LET ME GO!
DARK THOUGHTS COME TO ME EVERY MOMENT OF THE DAY.
I CAN'T HELP THAT.
BUT I DON'T HAVE THE WILLPOWER TO EVER TRY IT OUT ON MYSELF, SO...
YOU WILL HAVE TO DO.
OPEN WIDE...
NO...NO... NO...

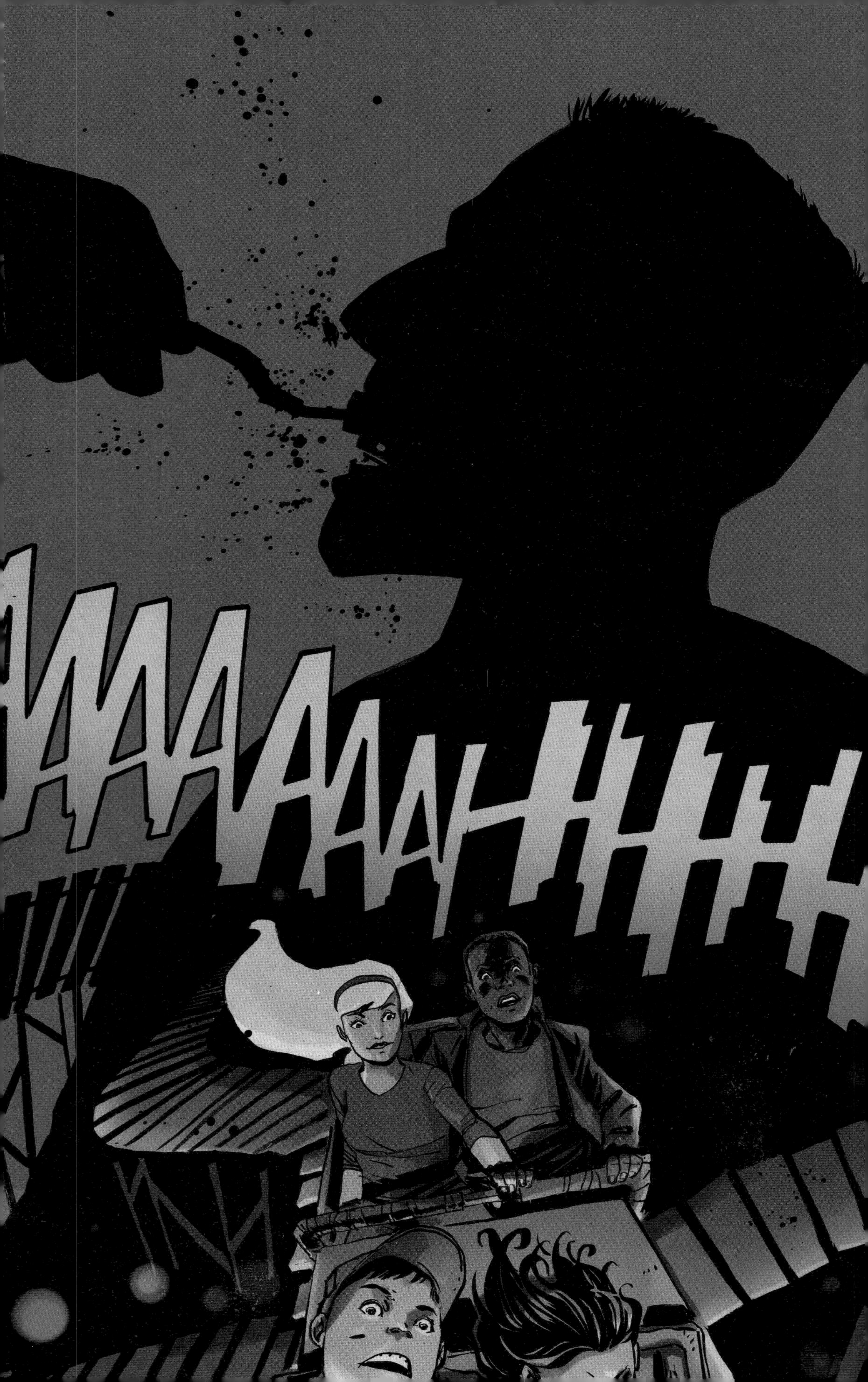
AAAAAAAHHHHH

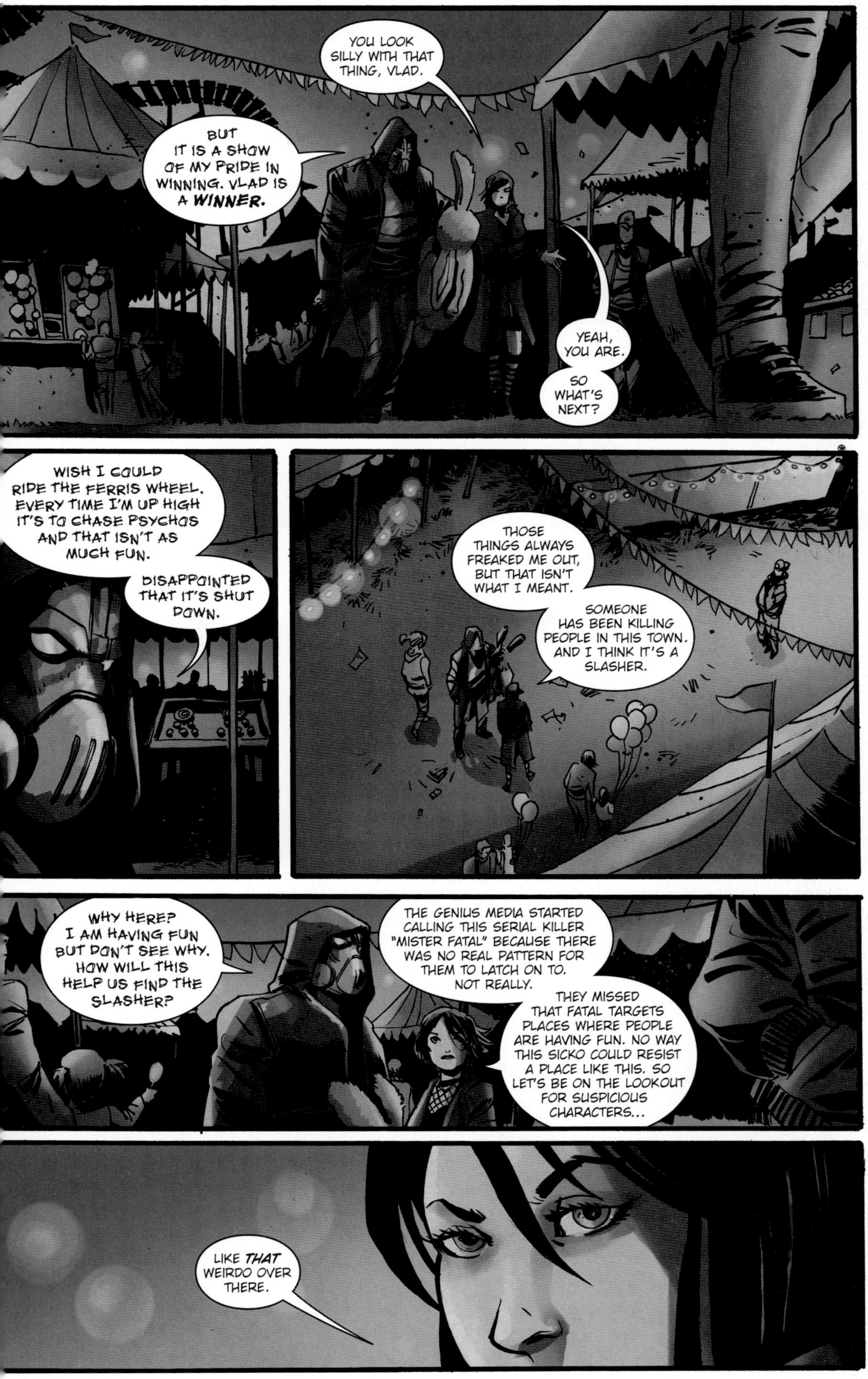
YOU LOOK SILLY WITH THAT THING, VLAD.
BUT IT IS A SHOW OF MY PRIDE IN WINNING. VLAD IS A **WINNER.**
YEAH, YOU ARE.
SO WHAT'S NEXT?
WISH I COULD RIDE THE FERRIS WHEEL. EVERY TIME I'M UP HIGH IT'S TO CHASE PSYCHOS AND THAT ISN'T AS MUCH FUN.
DISAPPOINTED THAT IT'S SHUT DOWN.
THOSE THINGS ALWAYS FREAKED ME OUT, BUT THAT ISN'T WHAT I MEANT.
SOMEONE HAS BEEN KILLING PEOPLE IN THIS TOWN. AND I THINK IT'S A SLASHER.
WHY HERE? I AM HAVING FUN BUT DON'T SEE WHY. HOW WILL THIS HELP US FIND THE SLASHER?
THE GENIUS MEDIA STARTED CALLING THIS SERIAL KILLER "MISTER FATAL" BECAUSE THERE WAS NO REAL PATTERN FOR THEM TO LATCH ON TO. NOT REALLY.
THEY MISSED THAT FATAL TARGETS PLACES WHERE PEOPLE ARE HAVING FUN. NO WAY THIS SICKO COULD RESIST A PLACE LIKE THIS. SO LET'S BE ON THE LOOKOUT FOR SUSPICIOUS CHARACTERS...
LIKE *THAT* WEIRDO OVER THERE.

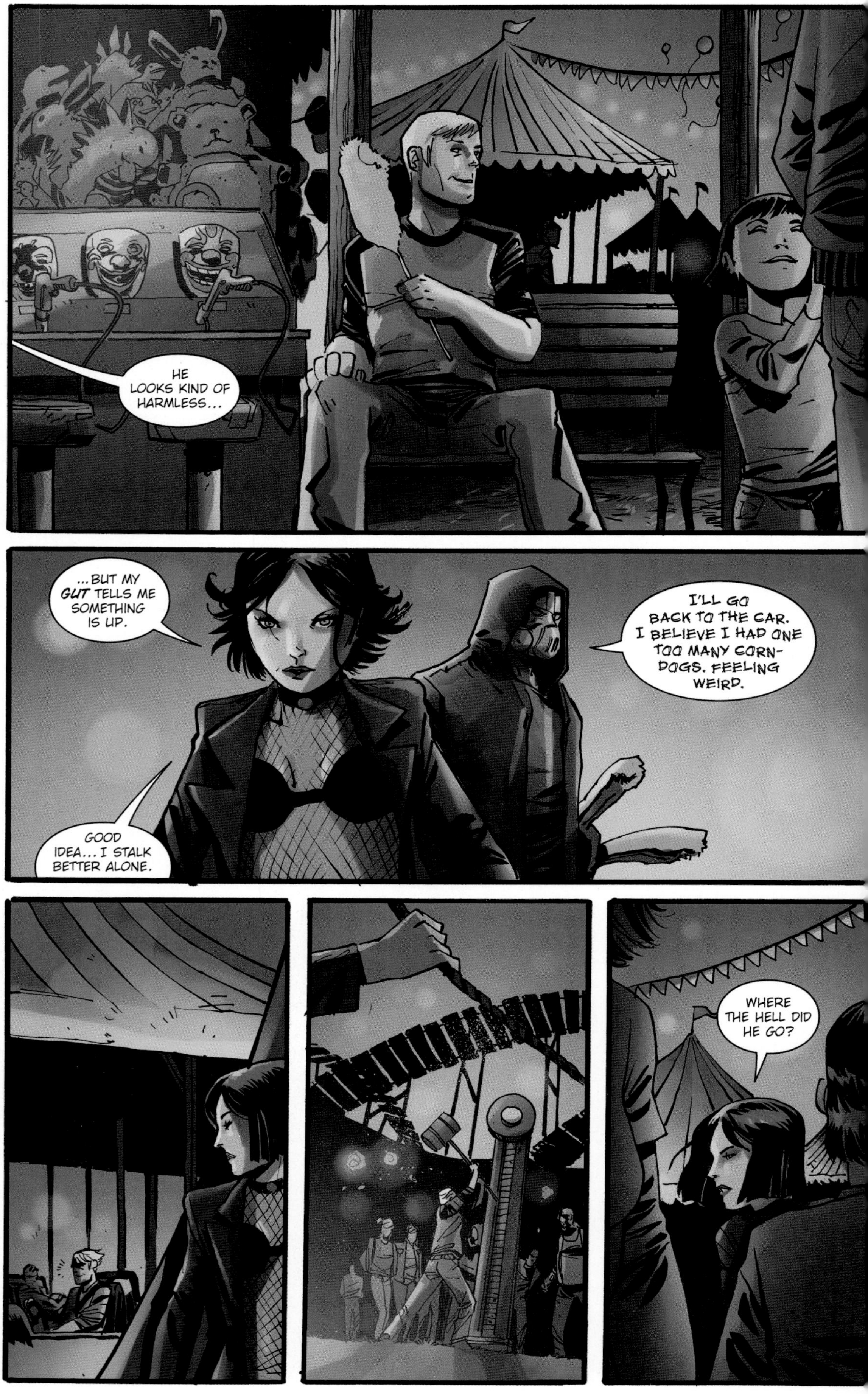
HE LOOKS KIND OF HARMLESS...
...BUT MY GUT TELLS ME SOMETHING IS UP.
I'LL GO BACK TO THE CAR. I BELIEVE I HAD ONE TOO MANY CORN-DOGS. FEELING WEIRD.
GOOD IDEA... I STALK BETTER ALONE.
WHERE THE HELL DID HE GO?

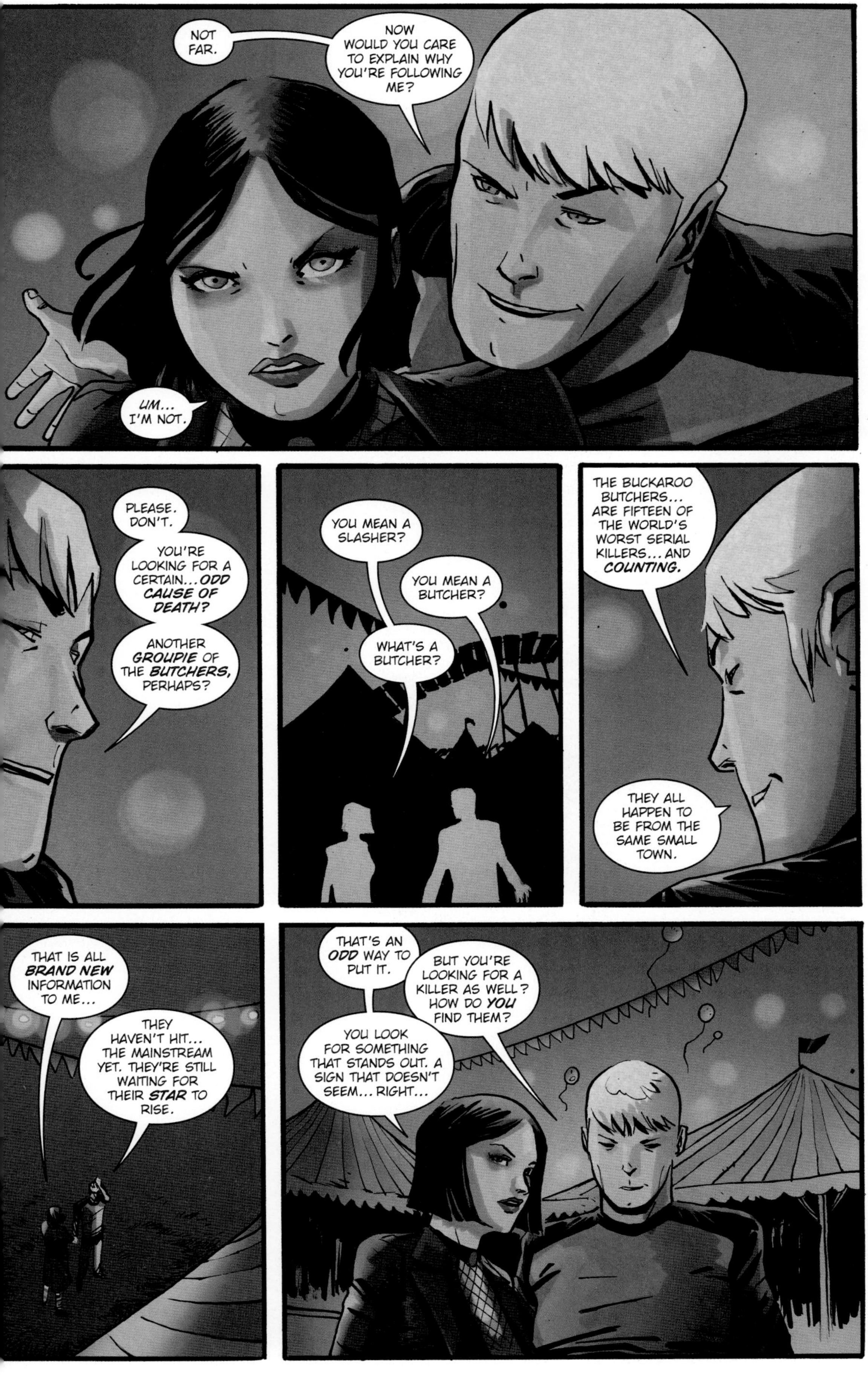
NOT FAR.
NOW WOULD YOU CARE TO EXPLAIN WHY YOU'RE FOLLOWING ME?
UM... I'M NOT.
PLEASE. DON'T.
YOU'RE LOOKING FOR A CERTAIN... ODD CAUSE OF DEATH?
ANOTHER GROUPIE OF THE BUTCHERS, PERHAPS?
YOU MEAN A SLASHER?
YOU MEAN A BUTCHER?
WHAT'S A BUTCHER?
THE BUCKAROO BUTCHERS... ARE FIFTEEN OF THE WORLD'S WORST SERIAL KILLERS... AND COUNTING.
THEY ALL HAPPEN TO BE FROM THE SAME SMALL TOWN.
THAT IS ALL BRAND NEW INFORMATION TO ME...
THEY HAVEN'T HIT... THE MAINSTREAM YET. THEY'RE STILL WAITING FOR THEIR STAR TO RISE.
THAT'S AN ODD WAY TO PUT IT.
BUT YOU'RE LOOKING FOR A KILLER AS WELL? HOW DO YOU FIND THEM?
YOU LOOK FOR SOMETHING THAT STANDS OUT. A SIGN THAT DOESN'T SEEM... RIGHT...

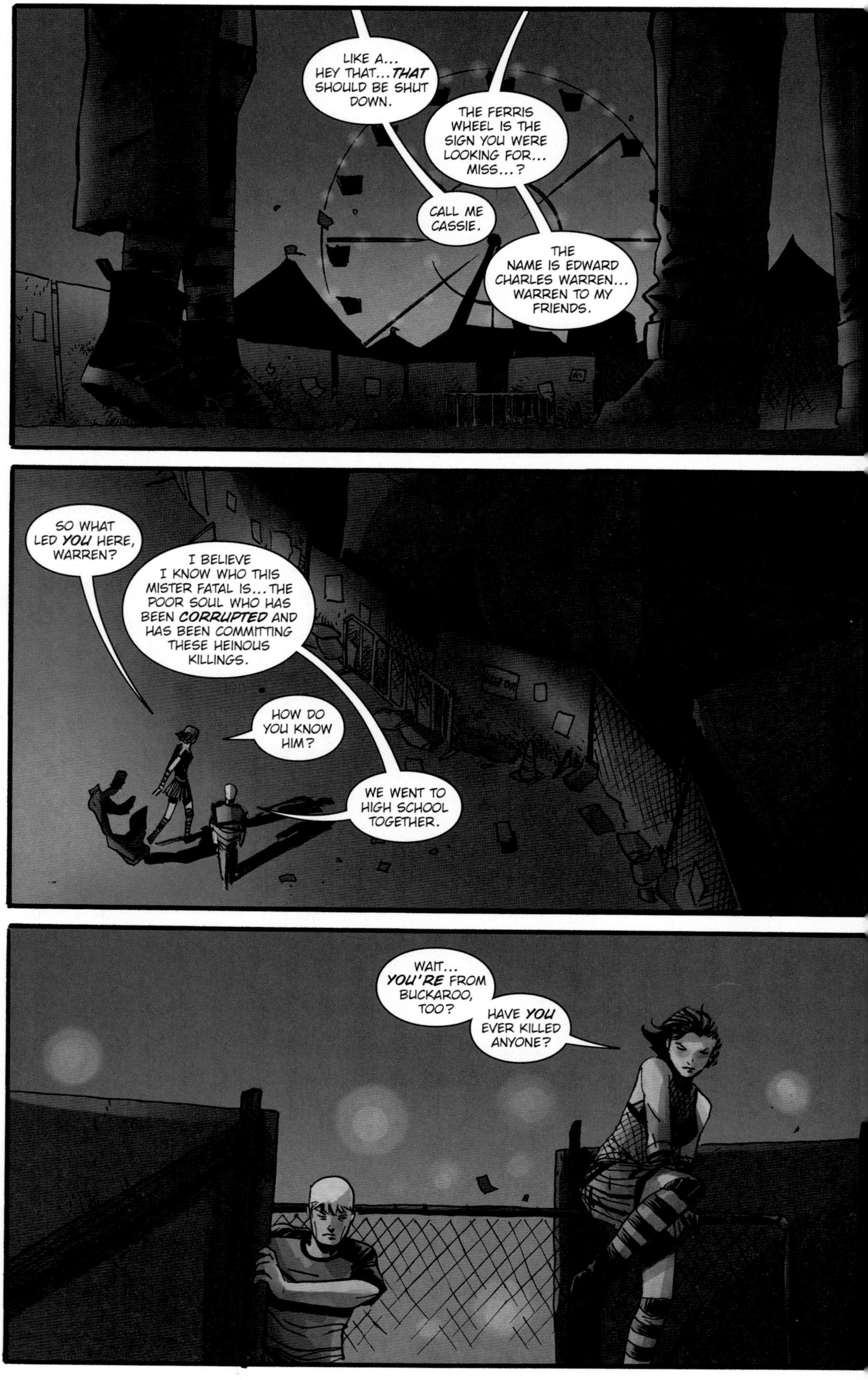
LIKE A... HEY THAT...THAT SHOULD BE SHUT DOWN.
THE FERRIS WHEEL IS THE SIGN YOU WERE LOOKING FOR... MISS...?
CALL ME CASSIE.
THE NAME IS EDWARD CHARLES WARREN... WARREN TO MY FRIENDS.
SO WHAT LED YOU HERE, WARREN?
I BELIEVE I KNOW WHO THIS MISTER FATAL IS...THE POOR SOUL WHO HAS BEEN CORRUPTED AND HAS BEEN COMMITTING THESE HEINOUS KILLINGS.
HOW DO YOU KNOW HIM?
WE WENT TO HIGH SCHOOL TOGETHER.
WAIT... YOU'RE FROM BUCKAROO, TOO?
HAVE YOU EVER KILLED ANYONE?

ME? A KILLER...?

THAT'LL *NEVER* HAPPEN.

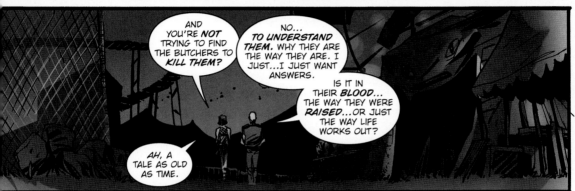

AND YOU'RE *NOT* TRYING TO FIND THE BUTCHERS TO *KILL THEM?*

NO... *TO UNDERSTAND THEM.* WHY THEY ARE THE WAY THEY ARE. I JUST...I JUST WANT ANSWERS.

IS IT IN THEIR *BLOOD*... THE WAY THEY WERE *RAISED*...OR JUST THE WAY LIFE WORKS OUT?

AH, A TALE AS OLD AS TIME.

WAS I BORN THIS WAY OR *MADE* THIS WAY? I'VE...HAD SOME PAST RELATIONS WITH SERIAL KILLERS...

BUT... IT'S NOT IN YOUR BLOOD... *TRUST ME ON THAT.*

HOW CAN YOU BE SO SURE?

HOW CAN YOU EVER TRULY *KNOW?*

YOU HAVE LOVELY *NAILS* BY THE WAY...

YOU NEED TO WATCH IT WITH YOUR CREEP FACTOR, BUDDY.

I DON'T WANT TO HAVE TO--

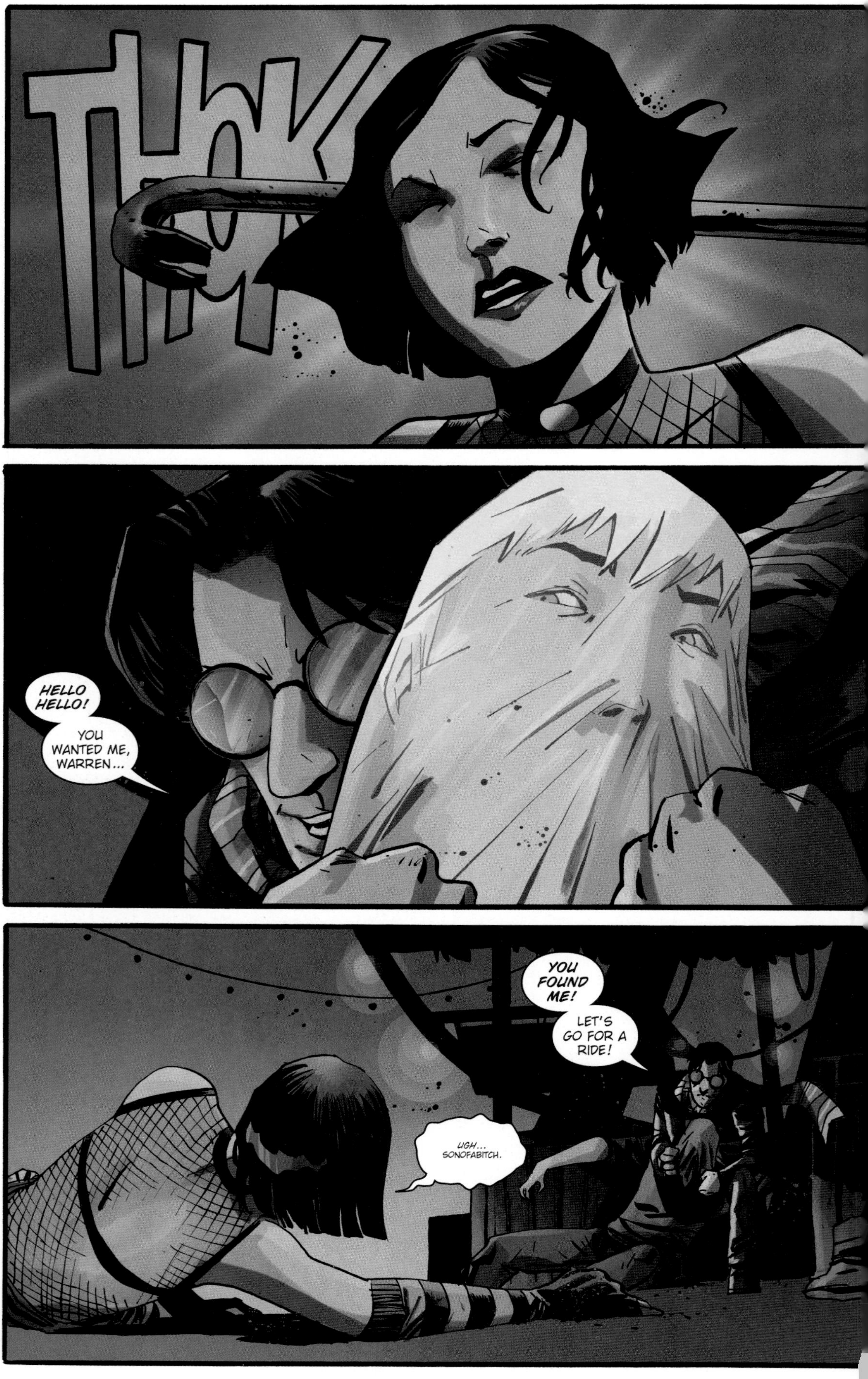
THUK
HELLO HELLO!
YOU WANTED ME, WARREN...
YOU FOUND ME!
LET'S GO FOR A RIDE!
UGH... SONOFABITCH.

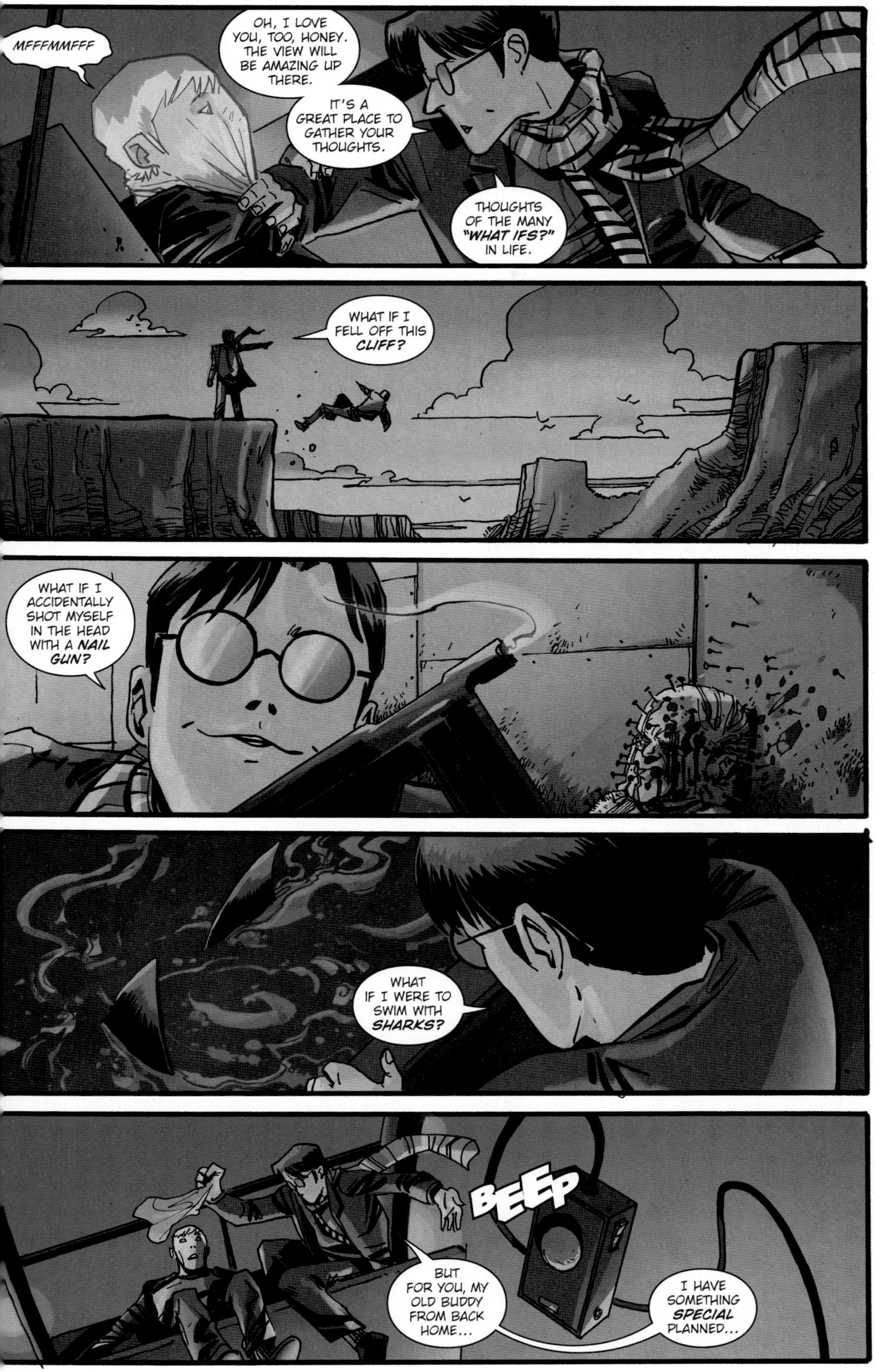
MFFFMMFFF
OH, I LOVE YOU, TOO, HONEY. THE VIEW WILL BE AMAZING UP THERE.
IT'S A GREAT PLACE TO GATHER YOUR THOUGHTS.
THOUGHTS OF THE MANY "WHAT IFS?" IN LIFE.
WHAT IF I FELL OFF THIS CLIFF?
WHAT IF I ACCIDENTALLY SHOT MYSELF IN THE HEAD WITH A NAIL GUN?
WHAT IF I WERE TO SWIM WITH SHARKS?
BEEP
BUT FOR YOU, MY OLD BUDDY FROM BACK HOME...
I HAVE SOMETHING SPECIAL PLANNED...

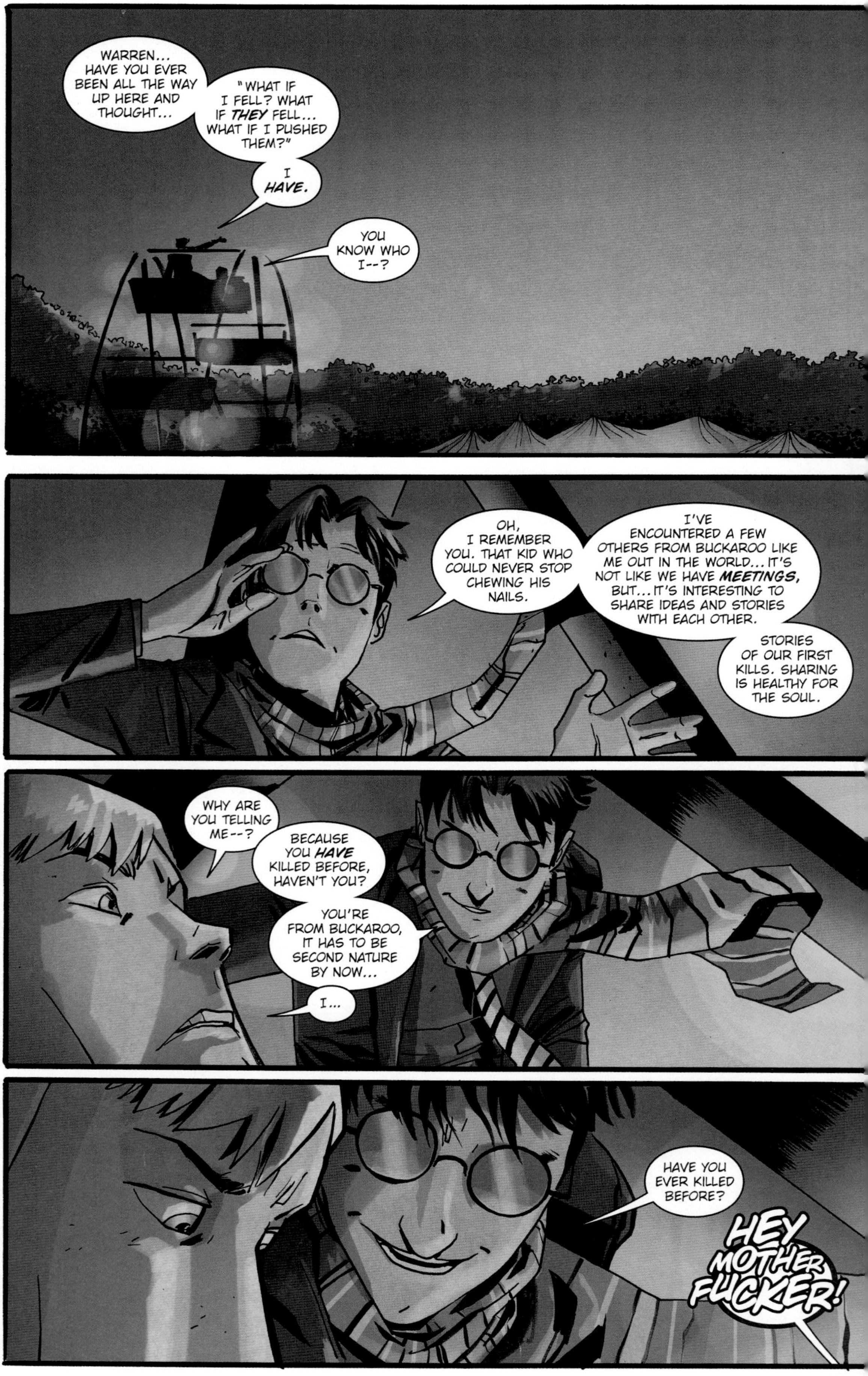
WARREN... HAVE YOU EVER BEEN ALL THE WAY UP HERE AND THOUGHT...
"WHAT IF I FELL? WHAT IF *THEY* FELL... WHAT IF I PUSHED THEM?"
I *HAVE.*
YOU KNOW WHO I--?
OH, I REMEMBER YOU. THAT KID WHO COULD NEVER STOP CHEWING HIS NAILS.
I'VE ENCOUNTERED A FEW OTHERS FROM BUCKAROO LIKE ME OUT IN THE WORLD... IT'S NOT LIKE WE HAVE *MEETINGS,* BUT... IT'S INTERESTING TO SHARE IDEAS AND STORIES WITH EACH OTHER.
STORIES OF OUR FIRST KILLS. SHARING IS HEALTHY FOR THE SOUL.
WHY ARE YOU TELLING ME--?
BECAUSE YOU *HAVE* KILLED BEFORE, HAVEN'T YOU?
YOU'RE FROM BUCKAROO, IT HAS TO BE SECOND NATURE BY NOW...
I...
HAVE YOU EVER KILLED BEFORE?
HEY MOTHER FUCKER!

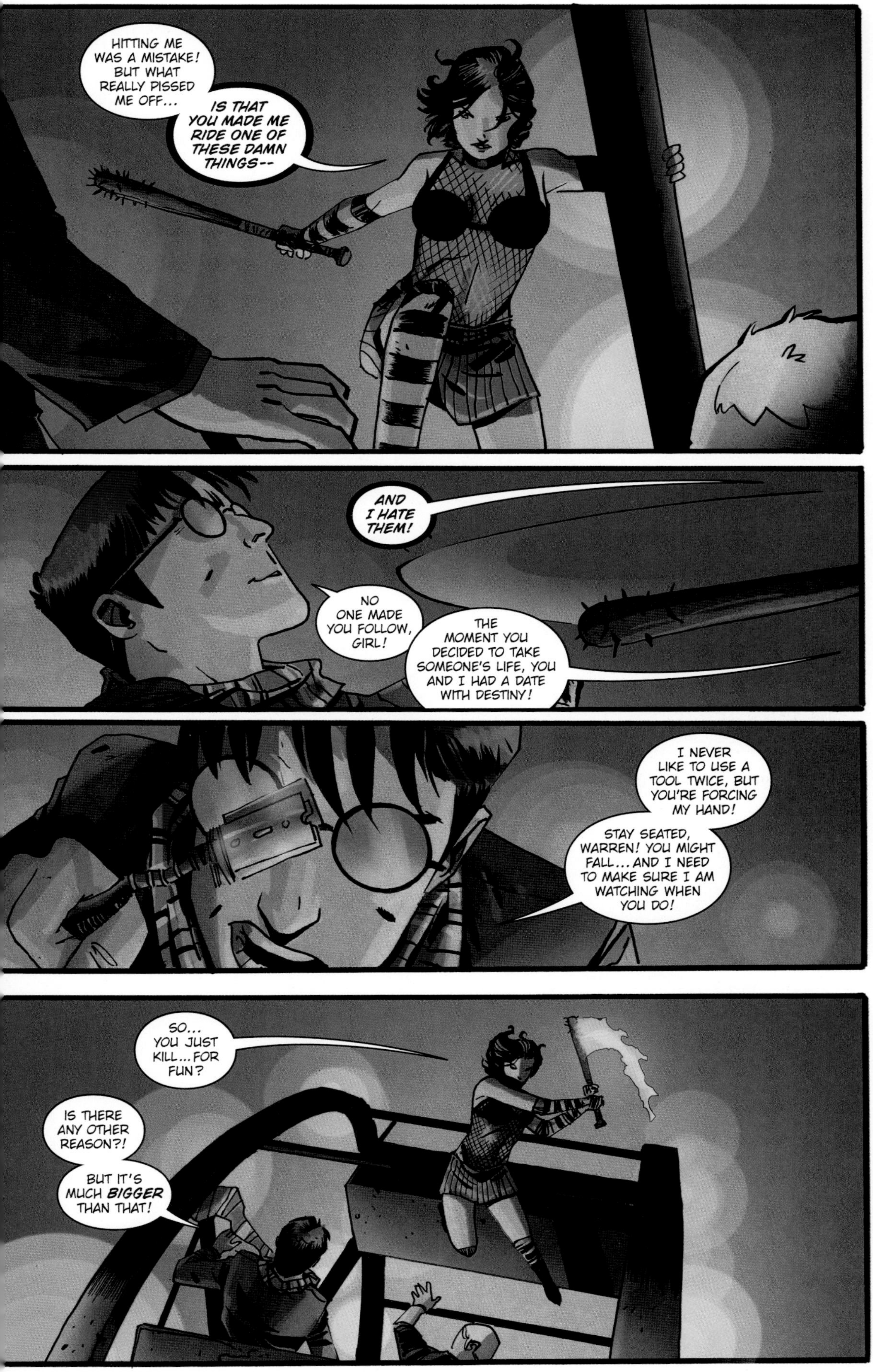
HITTING ME WAS A MISTAKE! BUT WHAT REALLY PISSED ME OFF...
IS THAT YOU MADE ME RIDE ONE OF THESE DAMN THINGS--
AND I HATE THEM!
NO ONE MADE YOU FOLLOW, GIRL!
THE MOMENT YOU DECIDED TO TAKE SOMEONE'S LIFE, YOU AND I HAD A DATE WITH DESTINY!
I NEVER LIKE TO USE A TOOL TWICE, BUT YOU'RE FORCING MY HAND!
STAY SEATED, WARREN! YOU MIGHT FALL... AND I NEED TO MAKE SURE I AM WATCHING WHEN YOU DO!
SO... YOU JUST KILL... FOR FUN?
IS THERE ANY OTHER REASON?!
BUT IT'S MUCH BIGGER THAN THAT!

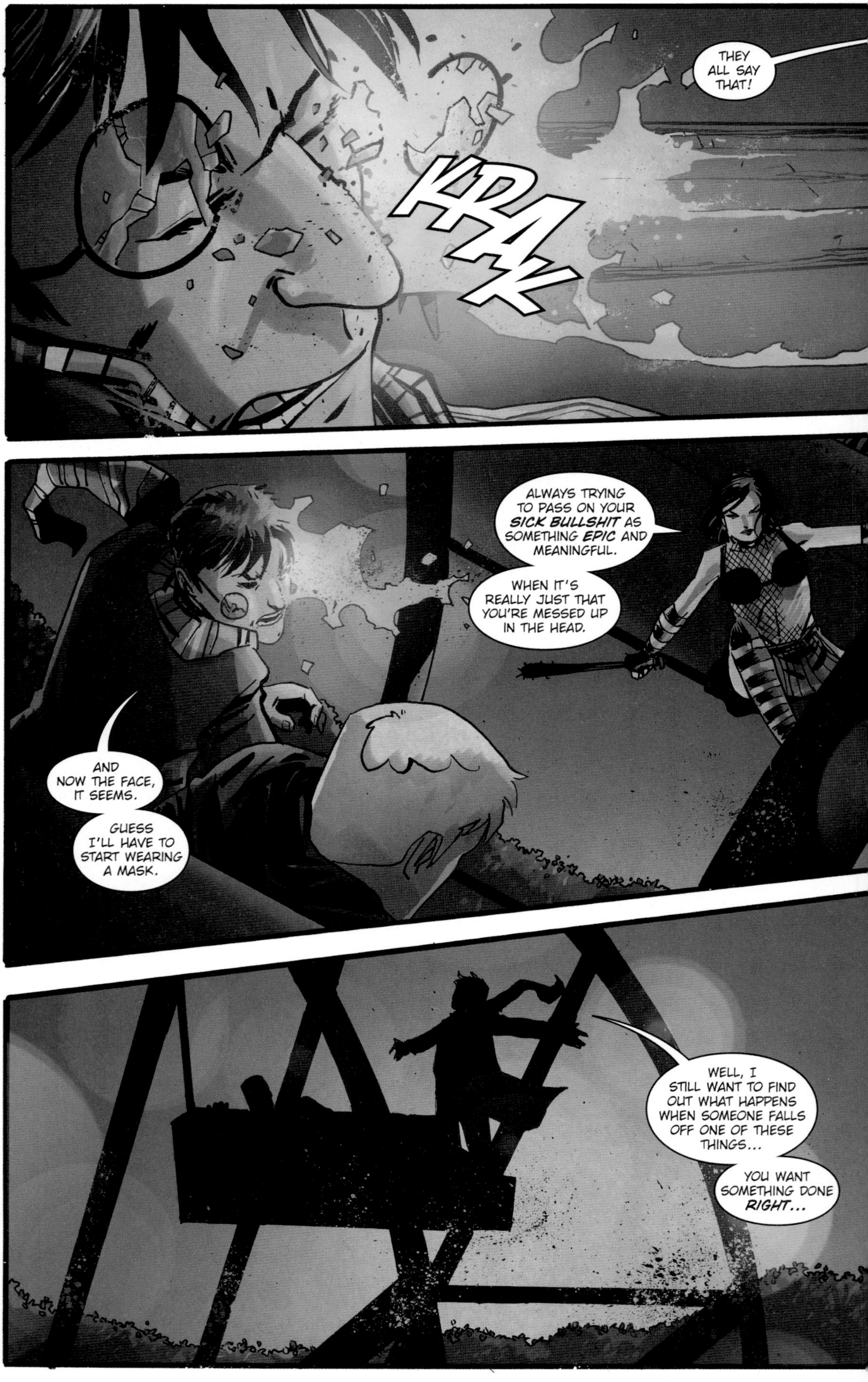
THEY ALL SAY THAT!
KRAK
ALWAYS TRYING TO PASS ON YOUR SICK BULLSHIT AS SOMETHING EPIC AND MEANINGFUL.
WHEN IT'S REALLY JUST THAT YOU'RE MESSED UP IN THE HEAD.
AND NOW THE FACE, IT SEEMS.
GUESS I'LL HAVE TO START WEARING A MASK.
WELL, I STILL WANT TO FIND OUT WHAT HAPPENS WHEN SOMEONE FALLS OFF ONE OF THESE THINGS...
YOU WANT SOMETHING DONE RIGHT...

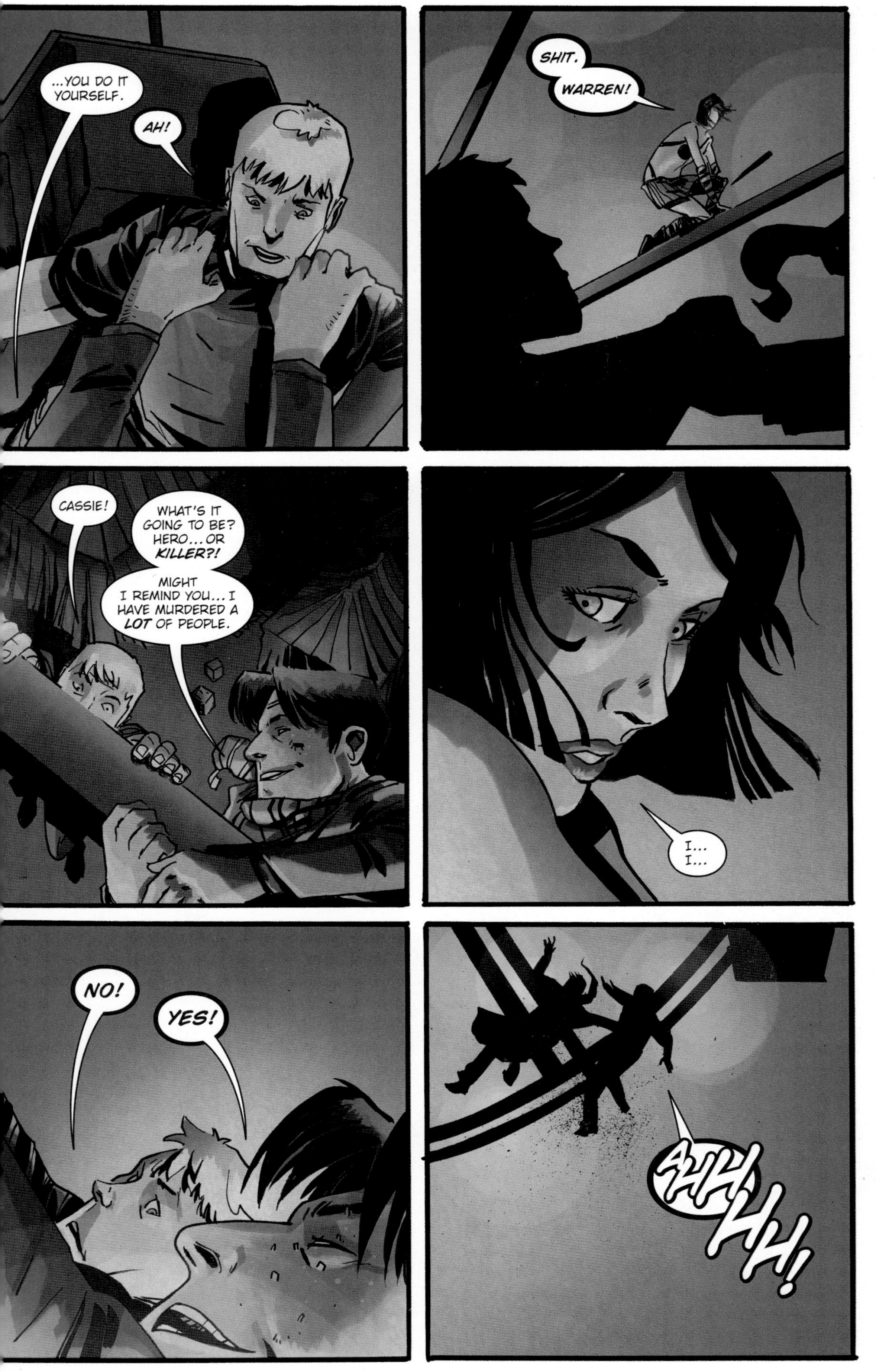
...YOU DO IT YOURSELF.
AH!
SHIT.
WARREN!
CASSIE!
WHAT'S IT GOING TO BE? HERO... OR KILLER?!
MIGHT I REMIND YOU... I HAVE MURDERED A LOT OF PEOPLE.
I... I...
NO!
YES!
AHHHHH!

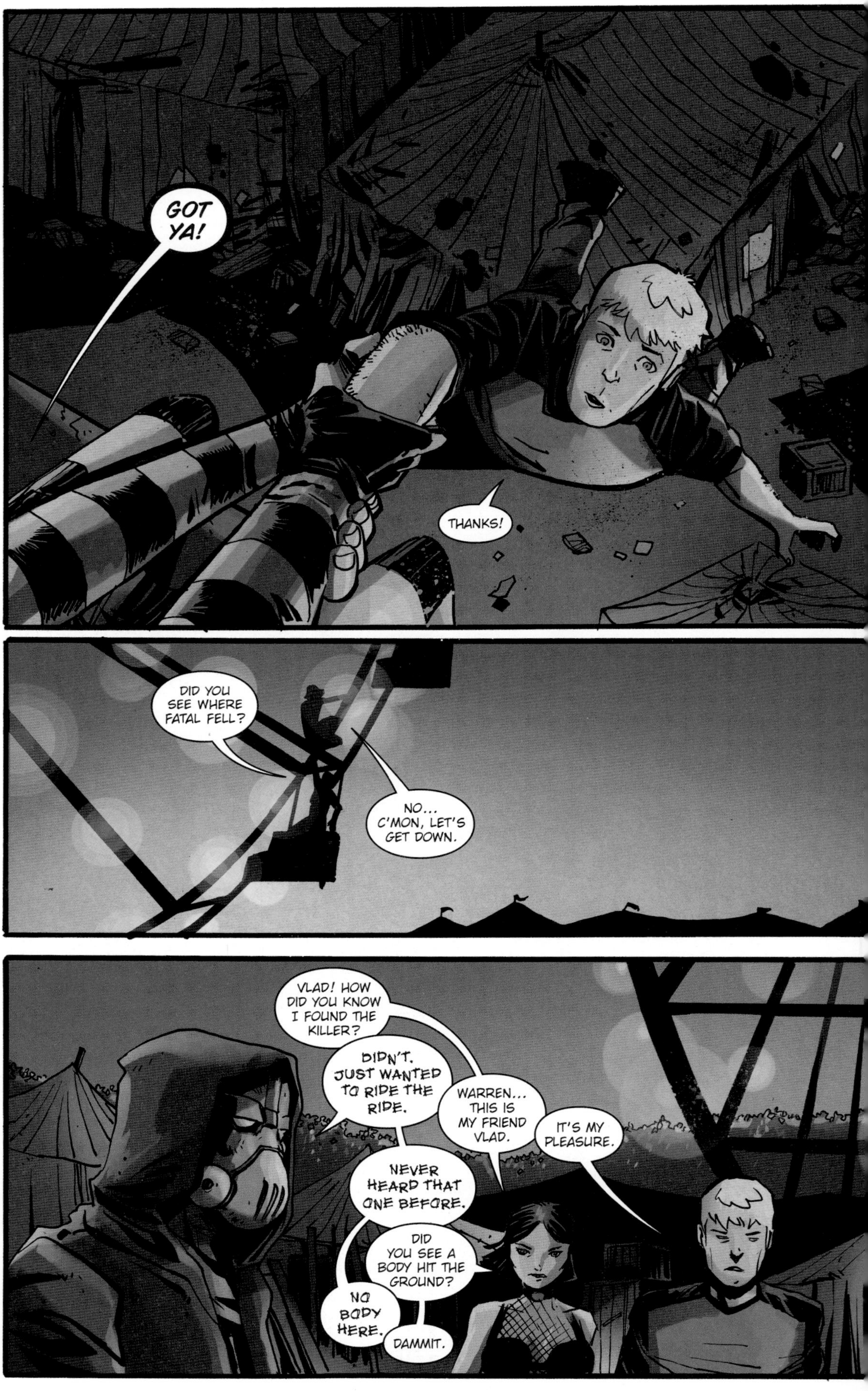
GOT YA!
THANKS!
DID YOU SEE WHERE FATAL FELL?
NO... C'MON, LET'S GET DOWN.
VLAD! HOW DID YOU KNOW I FOUND THE KILLER?
DIDN'T. JUST WANTED TO RIDE THE RIDE.
WARREN... THIS IS MY FRIEND VLAD.
IT'S MY PLEASURE.
NEVER HEARD THAT ONE BEFORE.
DID YOU SEE A BODY HIT THE GROUND?
NO BODY HERE.
DAMMIT.

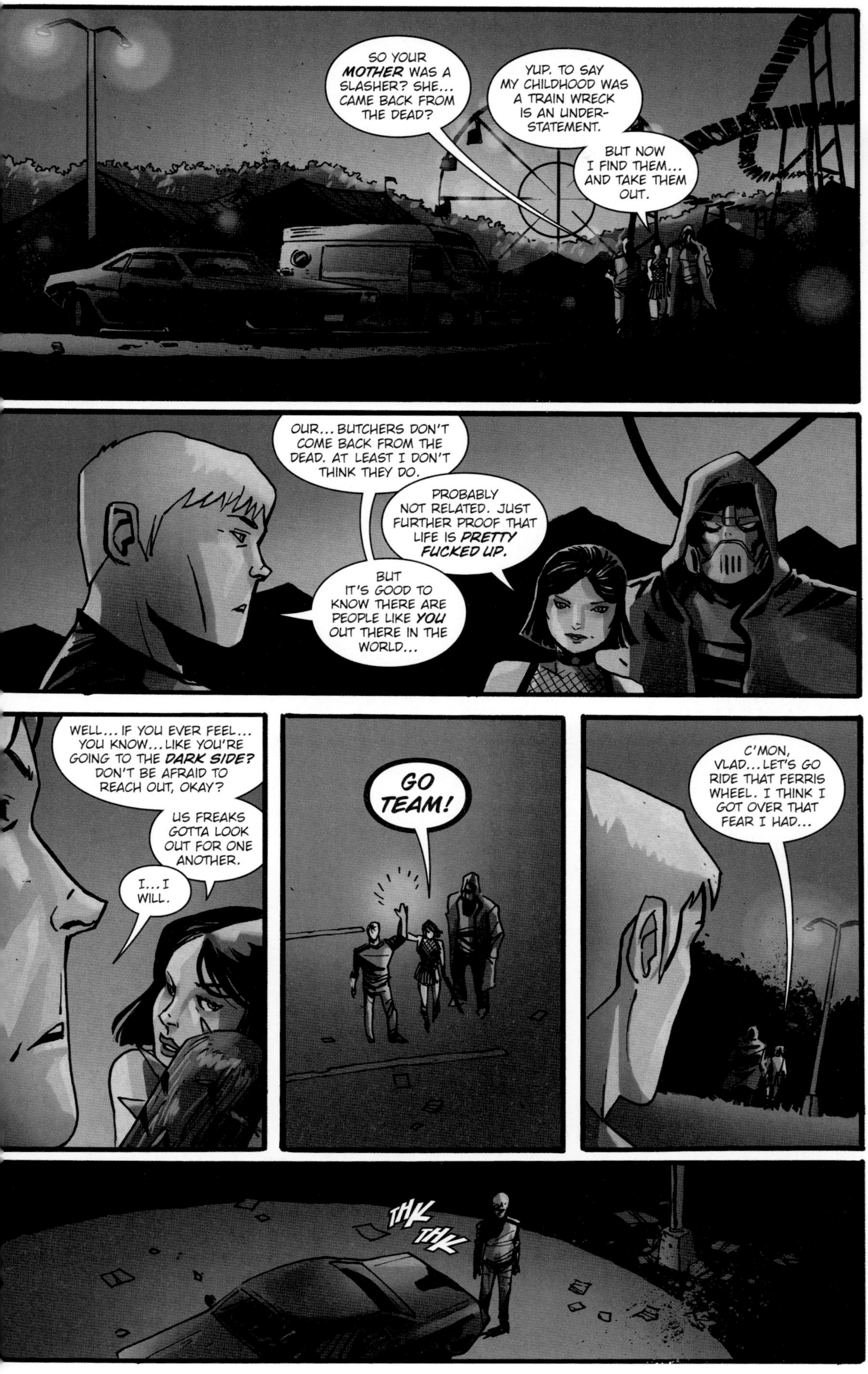
SO YOUR MOTHER WAS A SLASHER? SHE... CAME BACK FROM THE DEAD?
YUP. TO SAY MY CHILDHOOD WAS A TRAIN WRECK IS AN UNDER-STATEMENT.
BUT NOW I FIND THEM... AND TAKE THEM OUT.
OUR... BUTCHERS DON'T COME BACK FROM THE DEAD. AT LEAST I DON'T THINK THEY DO.
PROBABLY NOT RELATED. JUST FURTHER PROOF THAT LIFE IS PRETTY FUCKED UP.
BUT IT'S GOOD TO KNOW THERE ARE PEOPLE LIKE YOU OUT THERE IN THE WORLD...
WELL... IF YOU EVER FEEL... YOU KNOW... LIKE YOU'RE GOING TO THE DARK SIDE? DON'T BE AFRAID TO REACH OUT, OKAY?
US FREAKS GOTTA LOOK OUT FOR ONE ANOTHER.
I... I WILL.
GO TEAM!
C'MON, VLAD... LET'S GO RIDE THAT FERRIS WHEEL. I THINK I GOT OVER THAT FEAR I HAD...
THK
THK

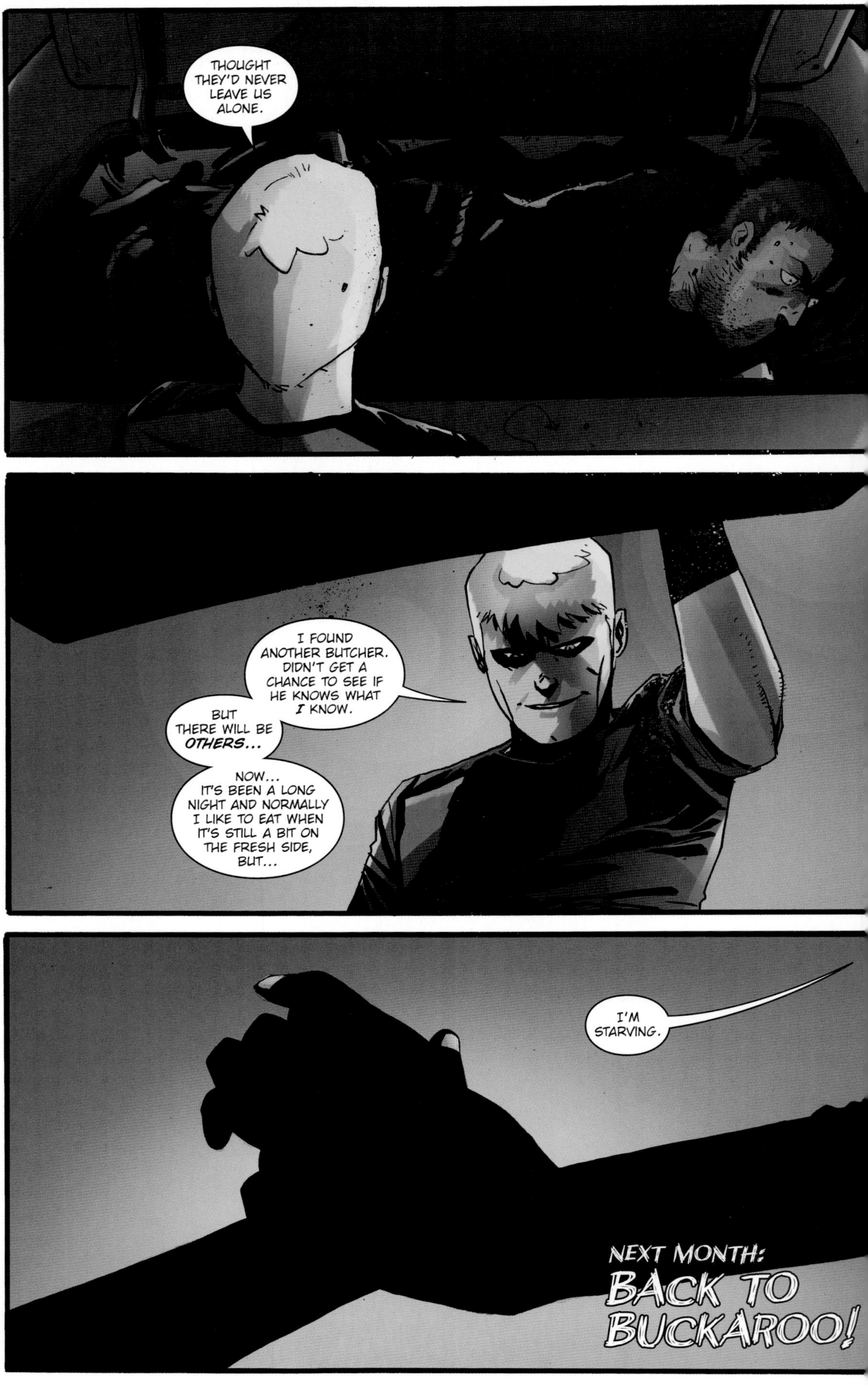
THOUGHT THEY'D NEVER LEAVE US ALONE.
I FOUND ANOTHER BUTCHER. DIDN'T GET A CHANCE TO SEE IF HE KNOWS WHAT *I* KNOW.
BUT THERE WILL BE ***OTHERS...***
NOW... IT'S BEEN A LONG NIGHT AND NORMALLY I LIKE TO EAT WHEN IT'S STILL A BIT ON THE FRESH SIDE, BUT...
I'M STARVING.
NEXT MONTH:
BACK TO BUCKAROO!

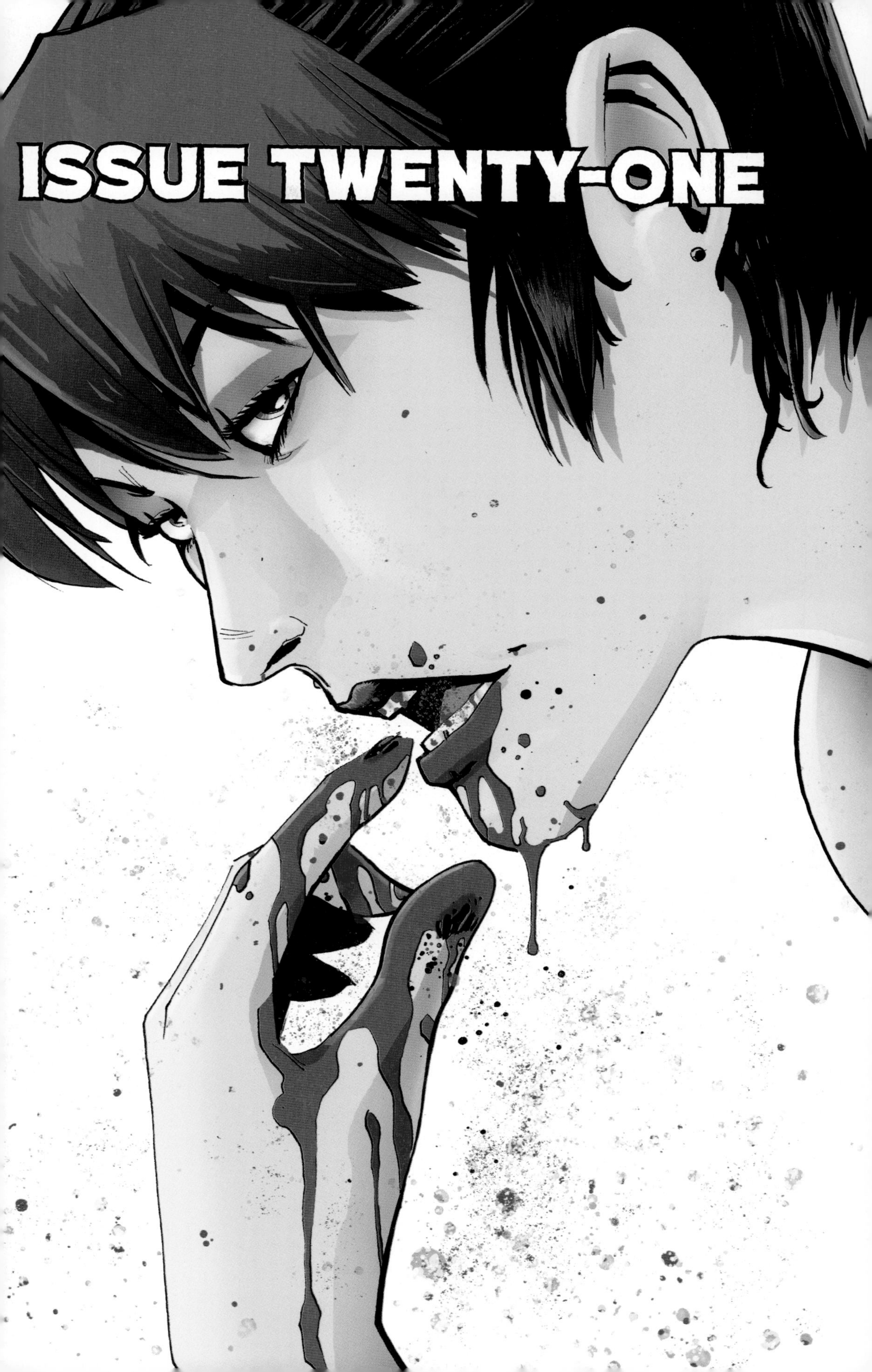
ISSUE TWENTY-ONE

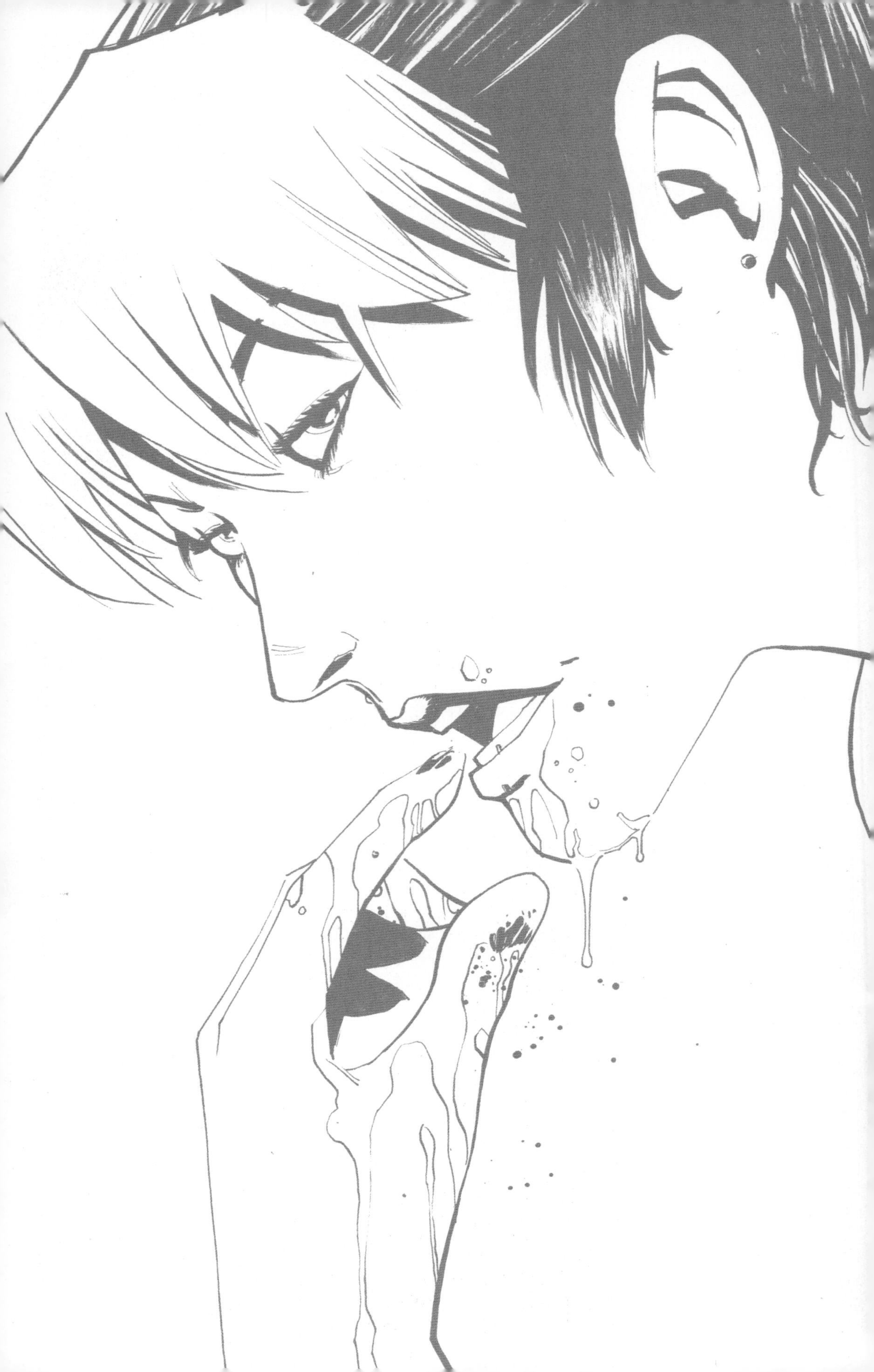

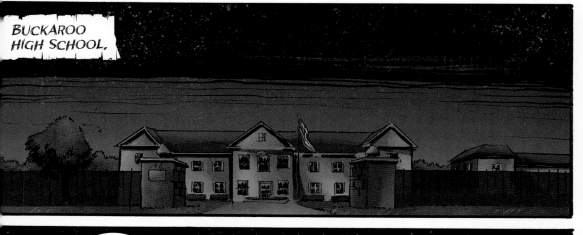

WE'RE GONNA GET **BUSTED.**

SO?

SO I'D RATHER NOT HAVE BREAKING INTO SCHOOL GROUNDS ON MY PERMANENT RECORD.

WE'RE FROM BUCKAROO... NO COLLEGE IS GOING TO WANT TO TAKE US ANYWAY.

YOU HAVE NOTHING TO--

OH MY GOD!

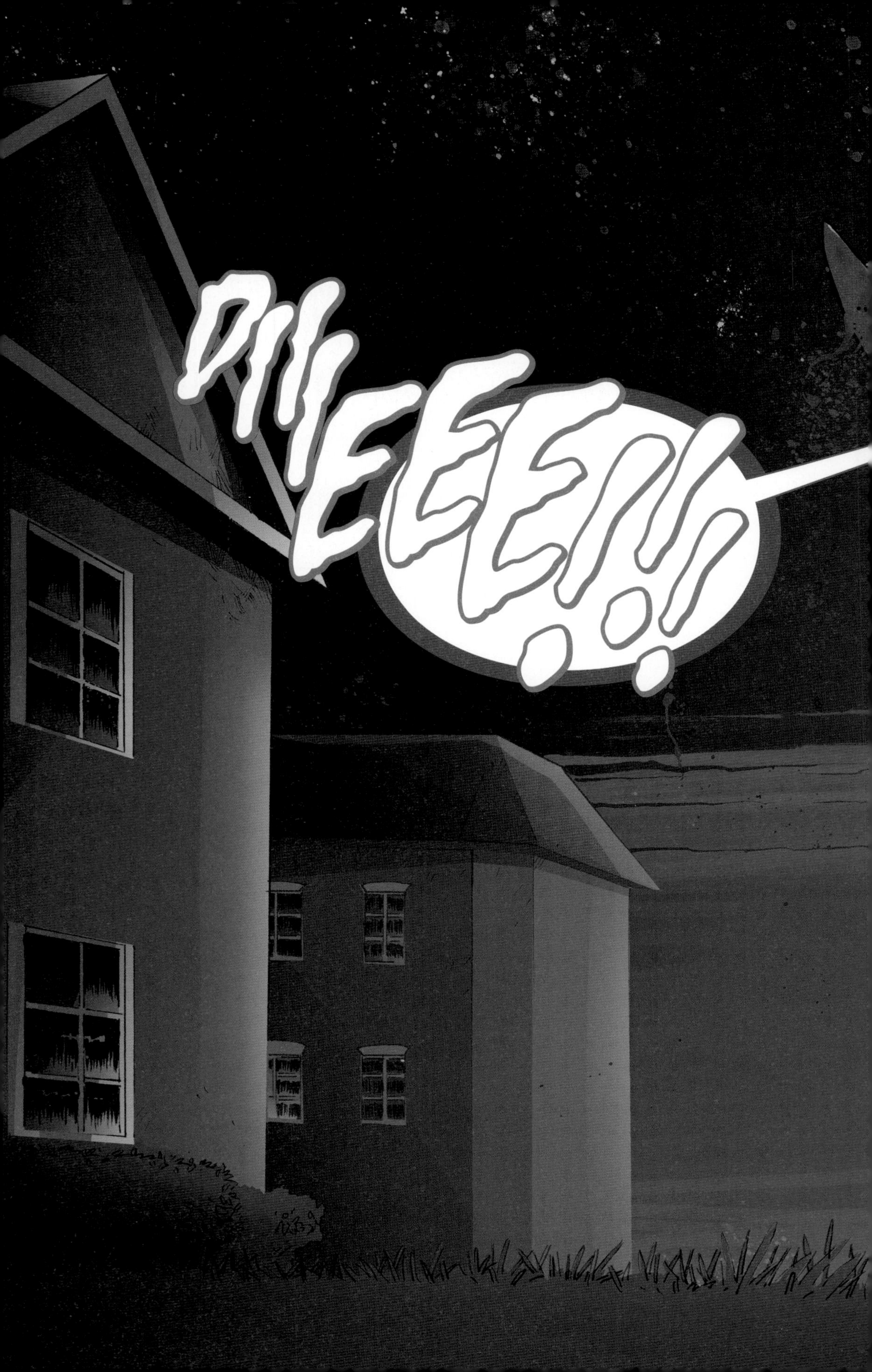
DIIIEEE!!!

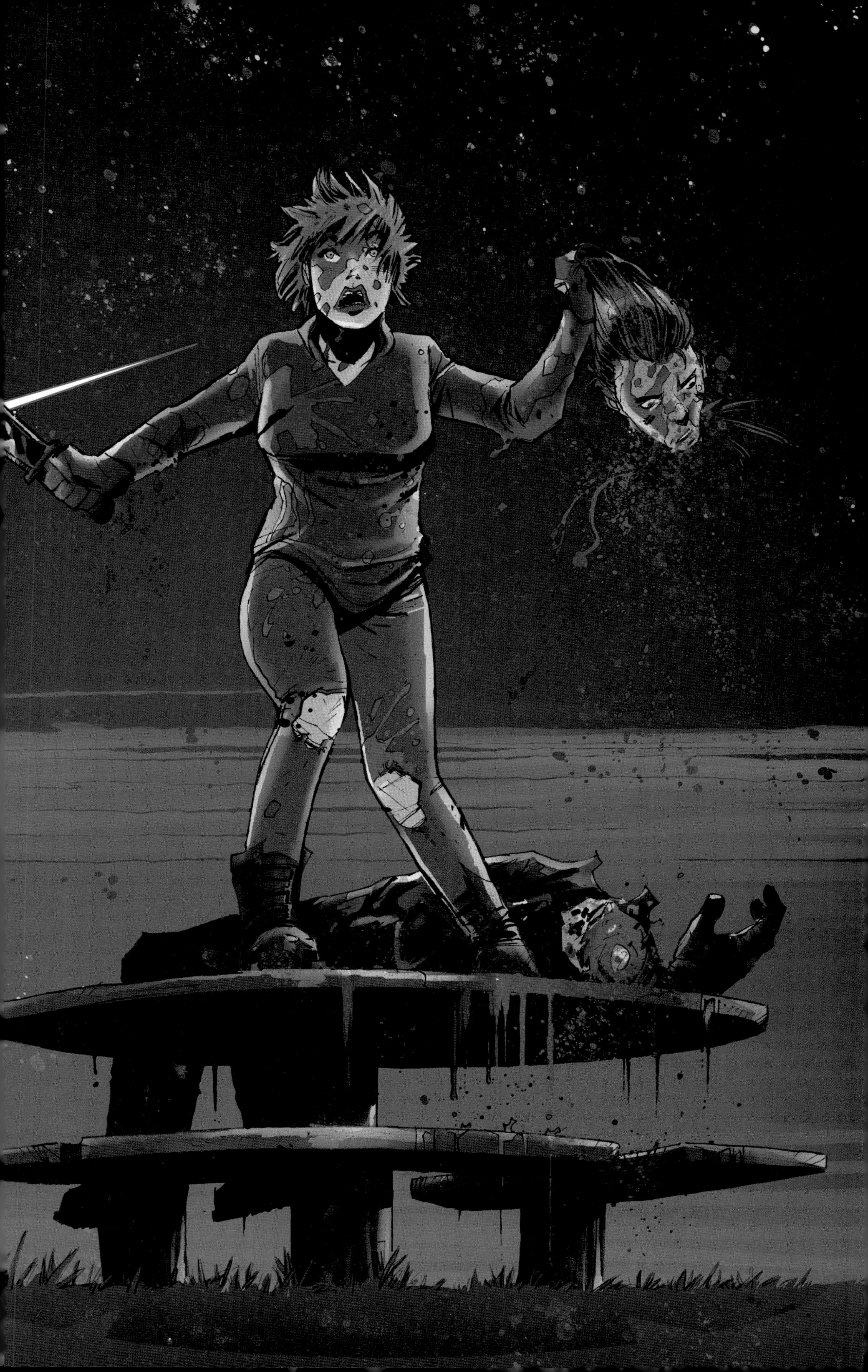

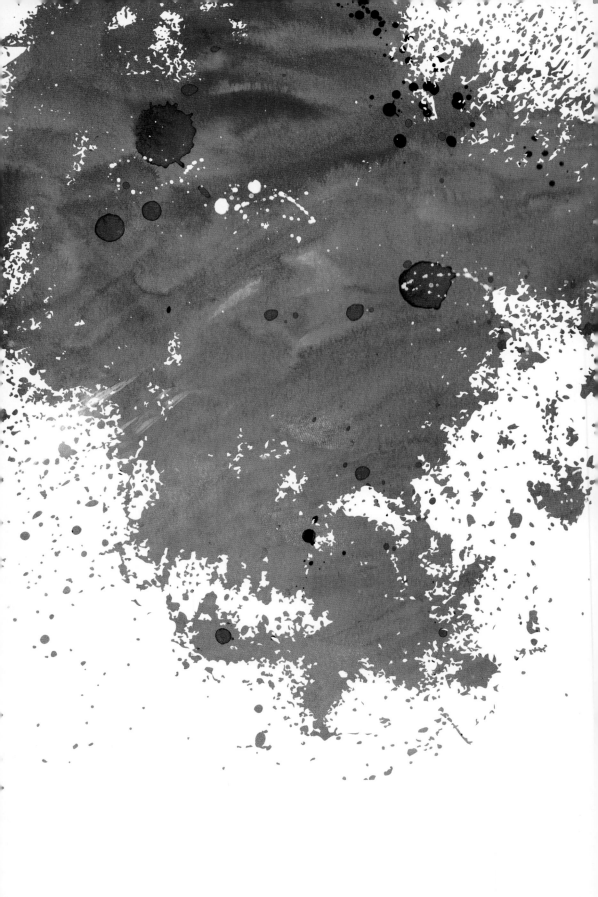

NAILBITER

BOUND BY BLOOD

CHAPTER

1

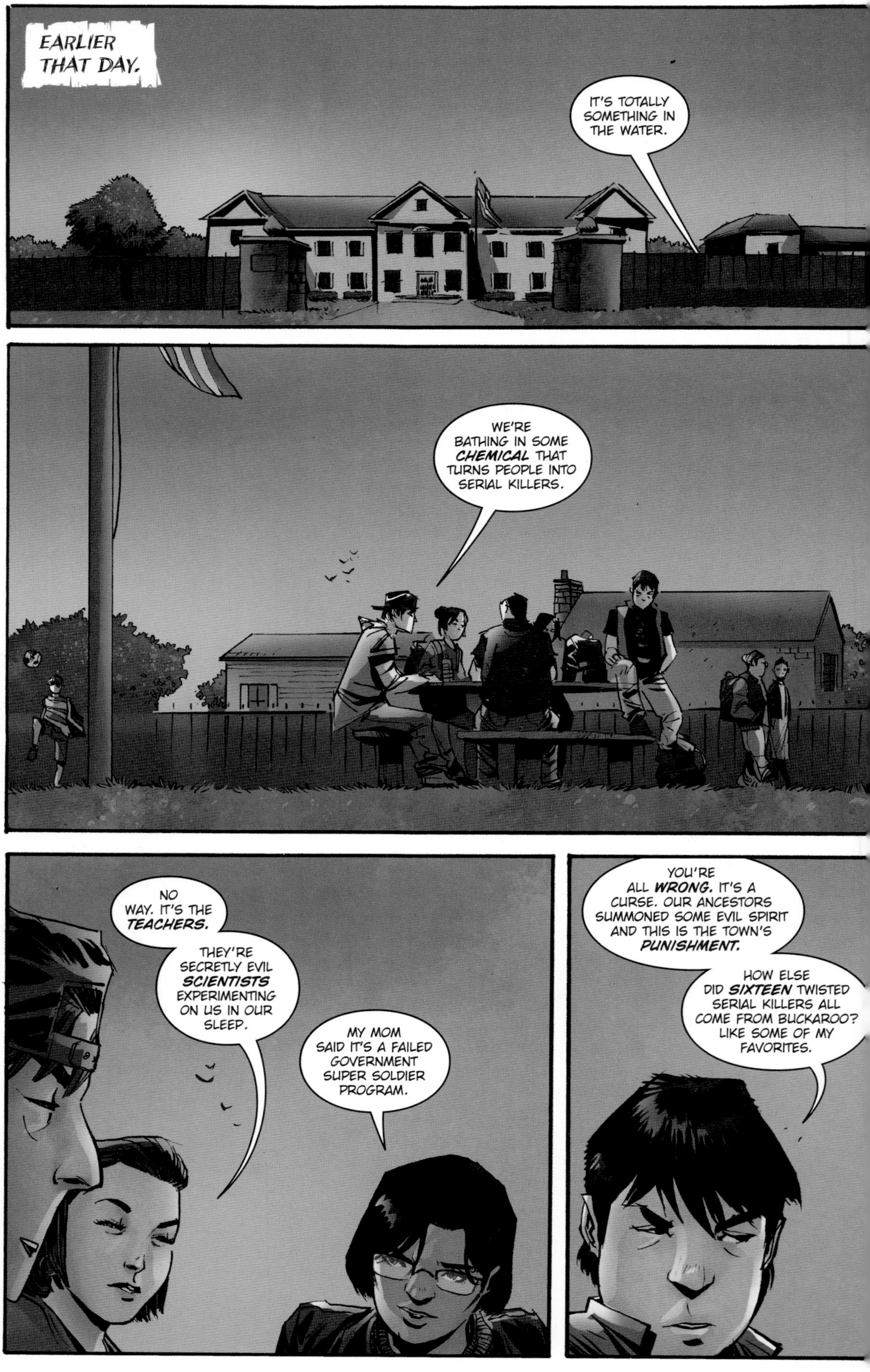
EARLIER THAT DAY.
IT'S TOTALLY SOMETHING IN THE WATER.
WE'RE BATHING IN SOME CHEMICAL THAT TURNS PEOPLE INTO SERIAL KILLERS.
NO WAY. IT'S THE TEACHERS.
THEY'RE SECRETLY EVIL SCIENTISTS EXPERIMENTING ON US IN OUR SLEEP.
MY MOM SAID IT'S A FAILED GOVERNMENT SUPER SOLDIER PROGRAM.
YOU'RE ALL WRONG. IT'S A CURSE. OUR ANCESTORS SUMMONED SOME EVIL SPIRIT AND THIS IS THE TOWN'S PUNISHMENT.
HOW ELSE DID SIXTEEN TWISTED SERIAL KILLERS ALL COME FROM BUCKAROO? LIKE SOME OF MY FAVORITES.

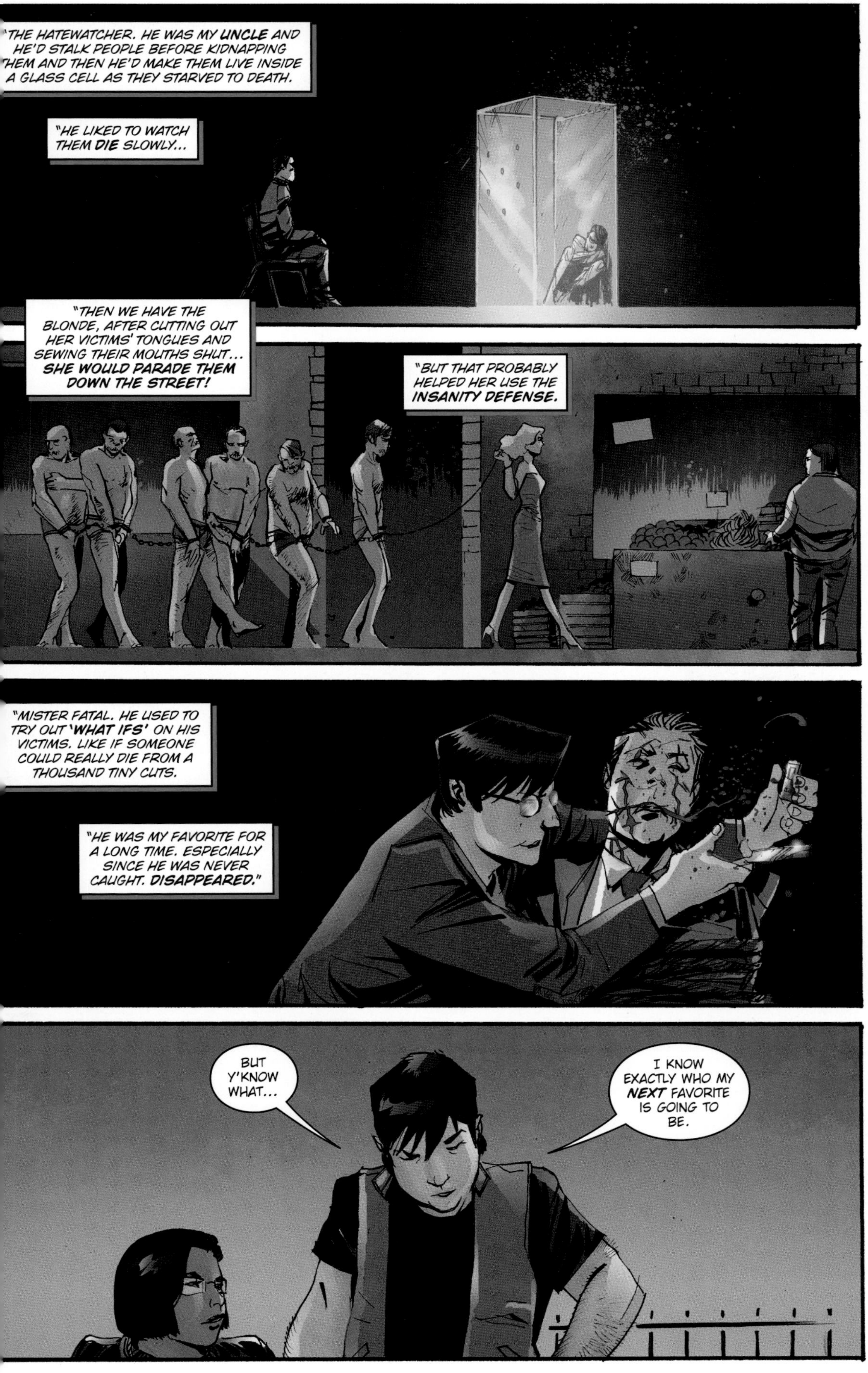
"THE HATEWATCHER. HE WAS MY UNCLE AND HE'D STALK PEOPLE BEFORE KIDNAPPING THEM AND THEN HE'D MAKE THEM LIVE INSIDE A GLASS CELL AS THEY STARVED TO DEATH.
"HE LIKED TO WATCH THEM DIE SLOWLY...
"THEN WE HAVE THE BLONDE, AFTER CUTTING OUT HER VICTIMS' TONGUES AND SEWING THEIR MOUTHS SHUT... SHE WOULD PARADE THEM DOWN THE STREET!
"BUT THAT PROBABLY HELPED HER USE THE INSANITY DEFENSE.
"MISTER FATAL. HE USED TO TRY OUT 'WHAT IFS' ON HIS VICTIMS. LIKE IF SOMEONE COULD REALLY DIE FROM A THOUSAND TINY CUTS.
"HE WAS MY FAVORITE FOR A LONG TIME. ESPECIALLY SINCE HE WAS NEVER CAUGHT. DISAPPEARED."
BUT Y'KNOW WHAT...
I KNOW EXACTLY WHO MY NEXT FAVORITE IS GOING TO BE.

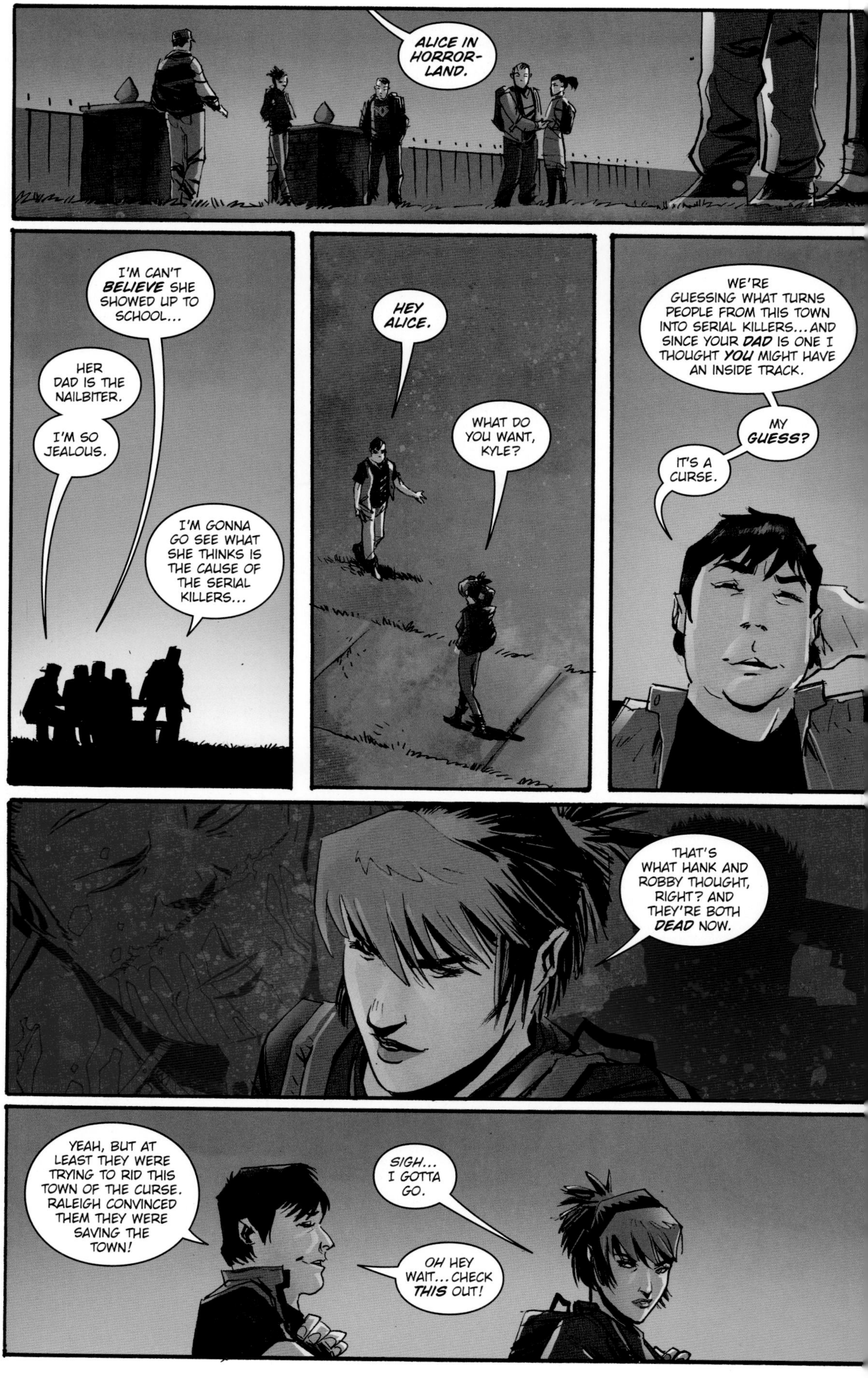
ALICE IN HORROR-LAND.
I'M CAN'T BELIEVE SHE SHOWED UP TO SCHOOL...
HER DAD IS THE NAILBITER.
I'M SO JEALOUS.
I'M GONNA GO SEE WHAT SHE THINKS IS THE CAUSE OF THE SERIAL KILLERS...
HEY ALICE.
WHAT DO YOU WANT, KYLE?
WE'RE GUESSING WHAT TURNS PEOPLE FROM THIS TOWN INTO SERIAL KILLERS...AND SINCE YOUR DAD IS ONE I THOUGHT YOU MIGHT HAVE AN INSIDE TRACK.
MY GUESS?
IT'S A CURSE.
THAT'S WHAT HANK AND ROBBY THOUGHT, RIGHT? AND THEY'RE BOTH DEAD NOW.
YEAH, BUT AT LEAST THEY WERE TRYING TO RID THIS TOWN OF THE CURSE. RALEIGH CONVINCED THEM THEY WERE SAVING THE TOWN!
SIGH... I GOTTA GO.
OH HEY WAIT...CHECK THIS OUT!

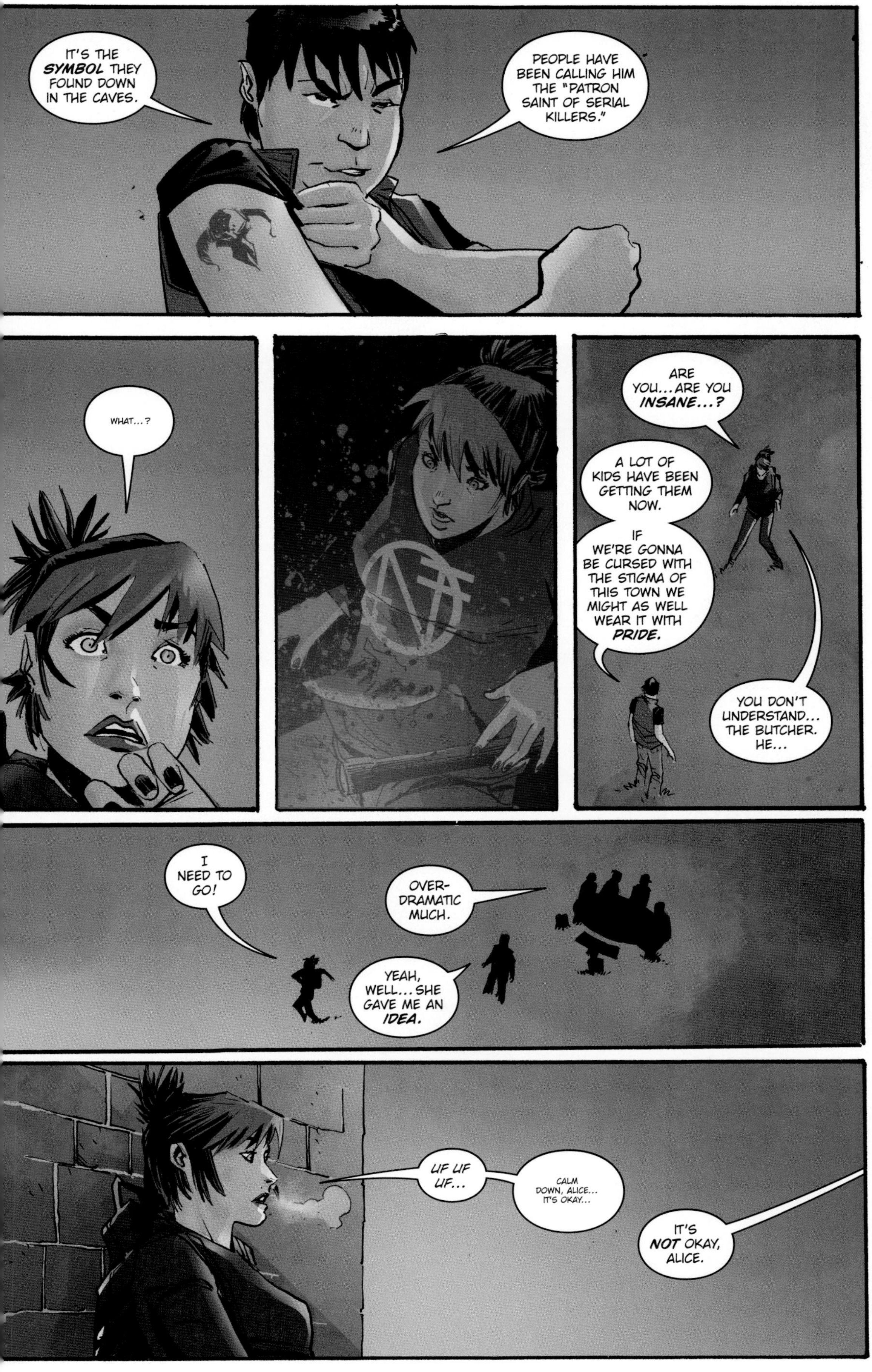
IT'S THE SYMBOL THEY FOUND DOWN IN THE CAVES.
PEOPLE HAVE BEEN CALLING HIM THE "PATRON SAINT OF SERIAL KILLERS."
WHAT...?
ARE YOU...ARE YOU INSANE...?
A LOT OF KIDS HAVE BEEN GETTING THEM NOW.
IF WE'RE GONNA BE CURSED WITH THE STIGMA OF THIS TOWN WE MIGHT AS WELL WEAR IT WITH PRIDE.
YOU DON'T UNDERSTAND... THE BUTCHER. HE...
I NEED TO GO!
OVER-DRAMATIC MUCH.
YEAH, WELL... SHE GAVE ME AN IDEA.
UF UF UF...
CALM DOWN, ALICE... IT'S OKAY...
IT'S NOT OKAY, ALICE.

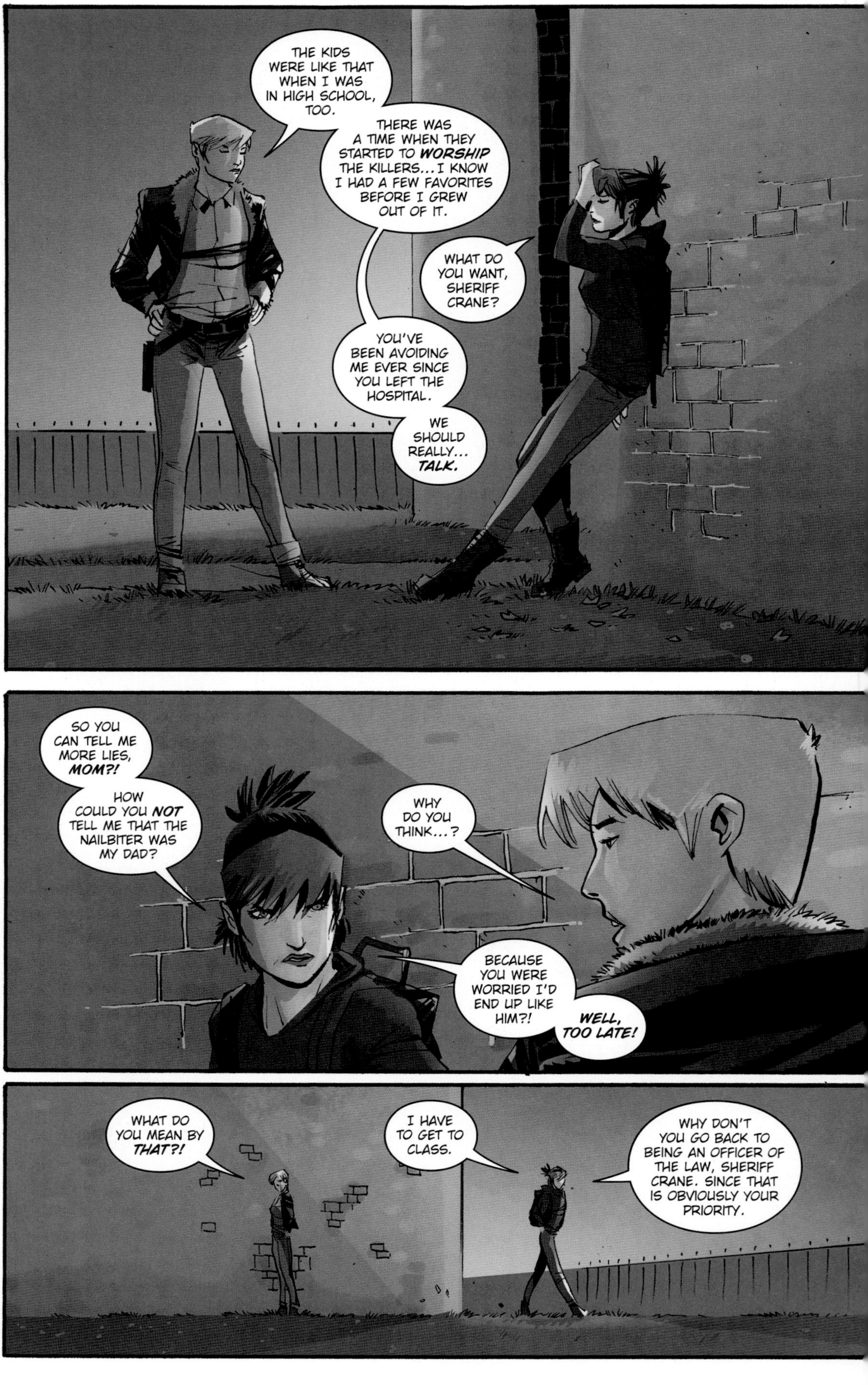
THE KIDS WERE LIKE THAT WHEN I WAS IN HIGH SCHOOL, TOO.
THERE WAS A TIME WHEN THEY STARTED TO *WORSHIP* THE KILLERS... I KNOW I HAD A FEW FAVORITES BEFORE I GREW OUT OF IT.
WHAT DO YOU WANT, SHERIFF CRANE?
YOU'VE BEEN AVOIDING ME EVER SINCE YOU LEFT THE HOSPITAL.
WE SHOULD REALLY... *TALK.*
SO YOU CAN TELL ME MORE LIES, *MOM?!*
HOW COULD YOU *NOT* TELL ME THAT THE NAILBITER WAS MY DAD?
WHY DO YOU THINK...?
BECAUSE YOU WERE WORRIED I'D END UP LIKE HIM?!
WELL, TOO LATE!
WHAT DO YOU MEAN BY *THAT?!*
I HAVE TO GET TO CLASS.
WHY DON'T YOU GO BACK TO BEING AN OFFICER OF THE LAW, SHERIFF CRANE. SINCE THAT IS OBVIOUSLY YOUR PRIORITY.

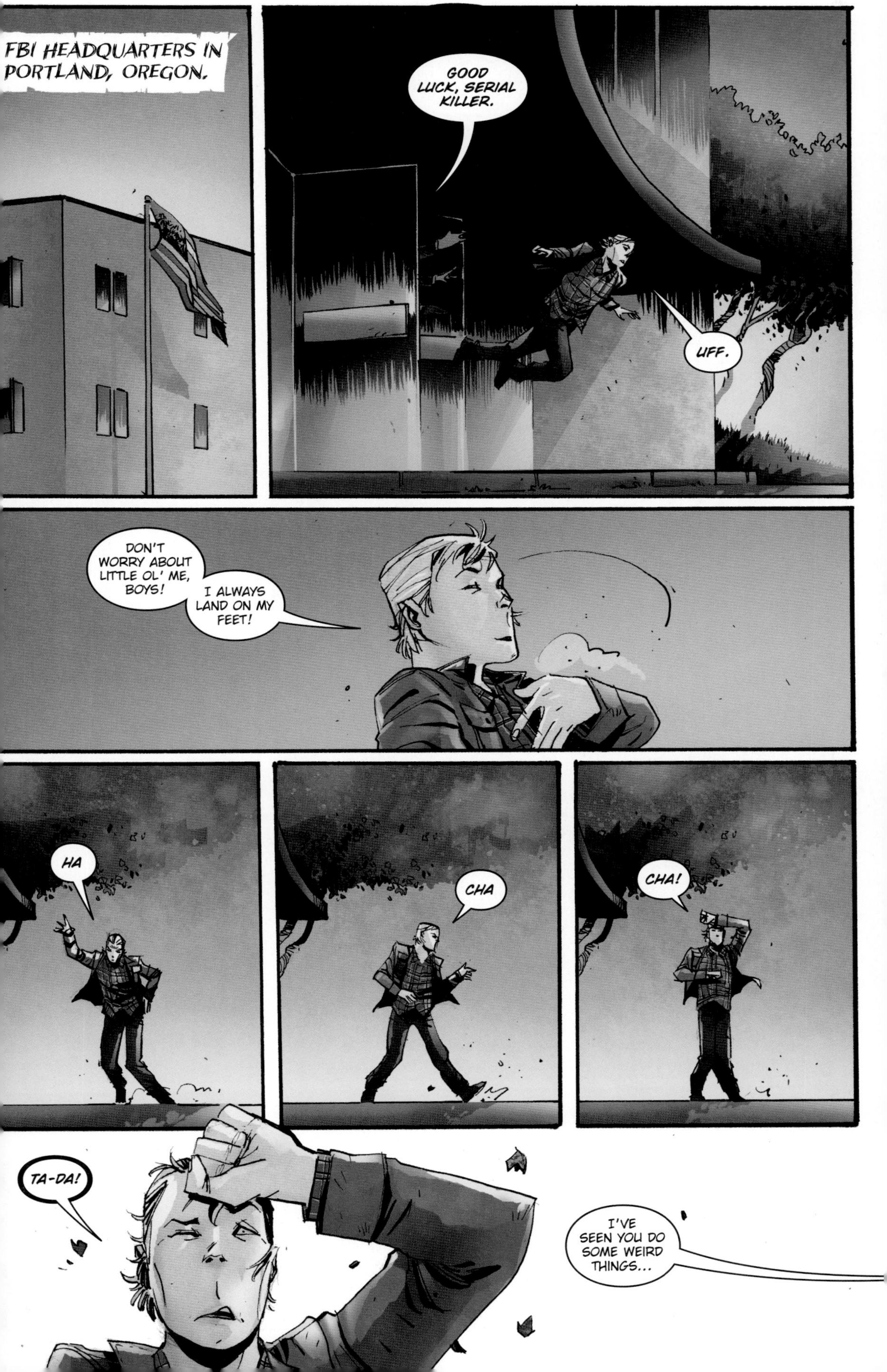
FBI HEADQUARTERS IN PORTLAND, OREGON.
GOOD LUCK, SERIAL KILLER.
UFF.
DON'T WORRY ABOUT LITTLE OL' ME, BOYS!
I ALWAYS LAND ON MY FEET!
HA
CHA
CHA!
TA-DA!
I'VE SEEN YOU DO SOME WEIRD THINGS...

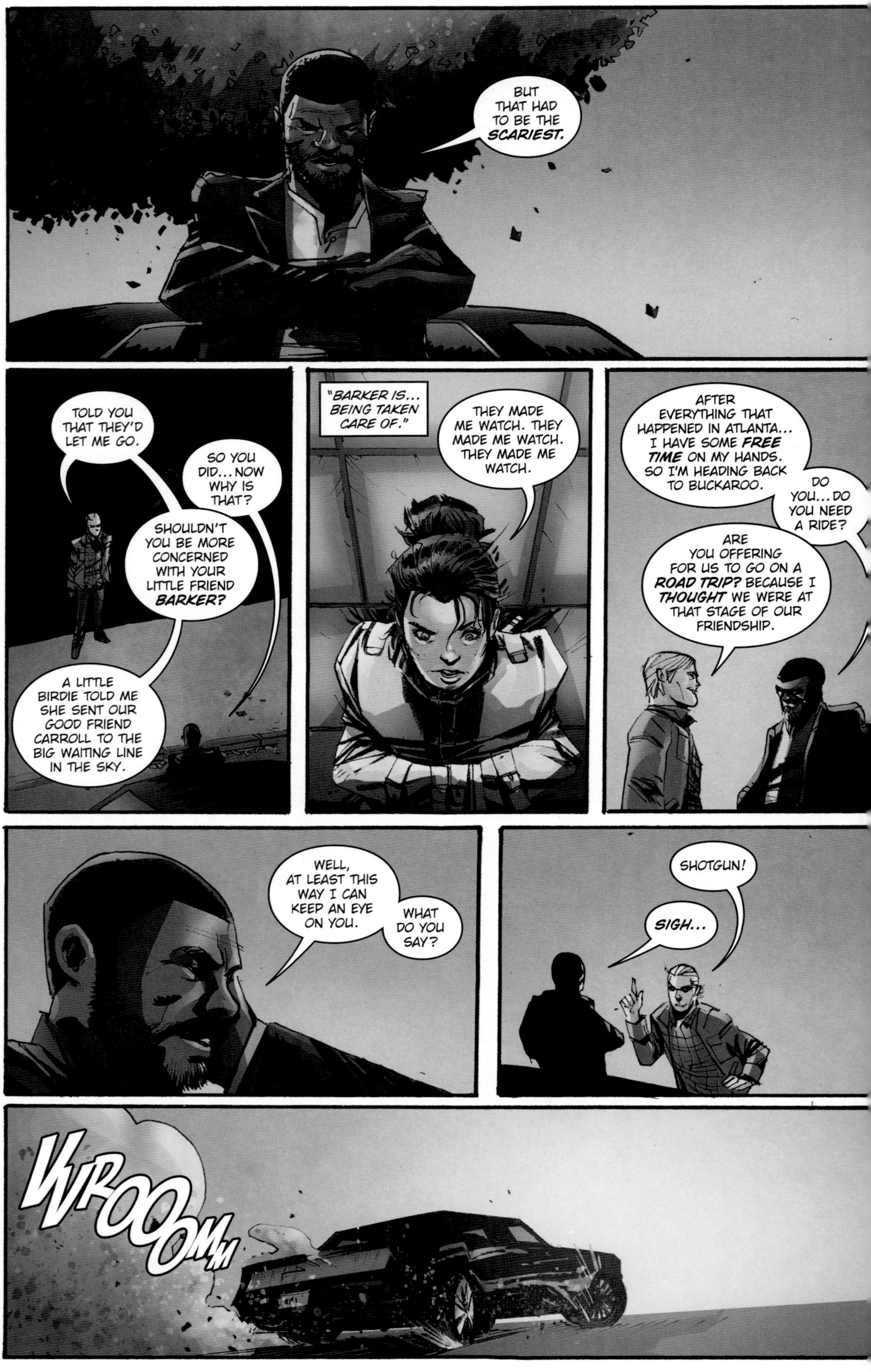
BUT THAT HAD TO BE THE SCARIEST.
TOLD YOU THAT THEY'D LET ME GO.
SO YOU DID... NOW WHY IS THAT?
SHOULDN'T YOU BE MORE CONCERNED WITH YOUR LITTLE FRIEND BARKER?
A LITTLE BIRDIE TOLD ME SHE SENT OUR GOOD FRIEND CARROLL TO THE BIG WAITING LINE IN THE SKY.
"BARKER IS... BEING TAKEN CARE OF."
THEY MADE ME WATCH. THEY MADE ME WATCH. THEY MADE ME WATCH.
AFTER EVERYTHING THAT HAPPENED IN ATLANTA... I HAVE SOME FREE TIME ON MY HANDS. SO I'M HEADING BACK TO BUCKAROO.
DO YOU... DO YOU NEED A RIDE?
ARE YOU OFFERING FOR US TO GO ON A ROAD TRIP? BECAUSE I THOUGHT WE WERE AT THAT STAGE OF OUR FRIENDSHIP.
WELL, AT LEAST THIS WAY I CAN KEEP AN EYE ON YOU.
WHAT DO YOU SAY?
SHOTGUN!
SIGH...
VVROOOMM

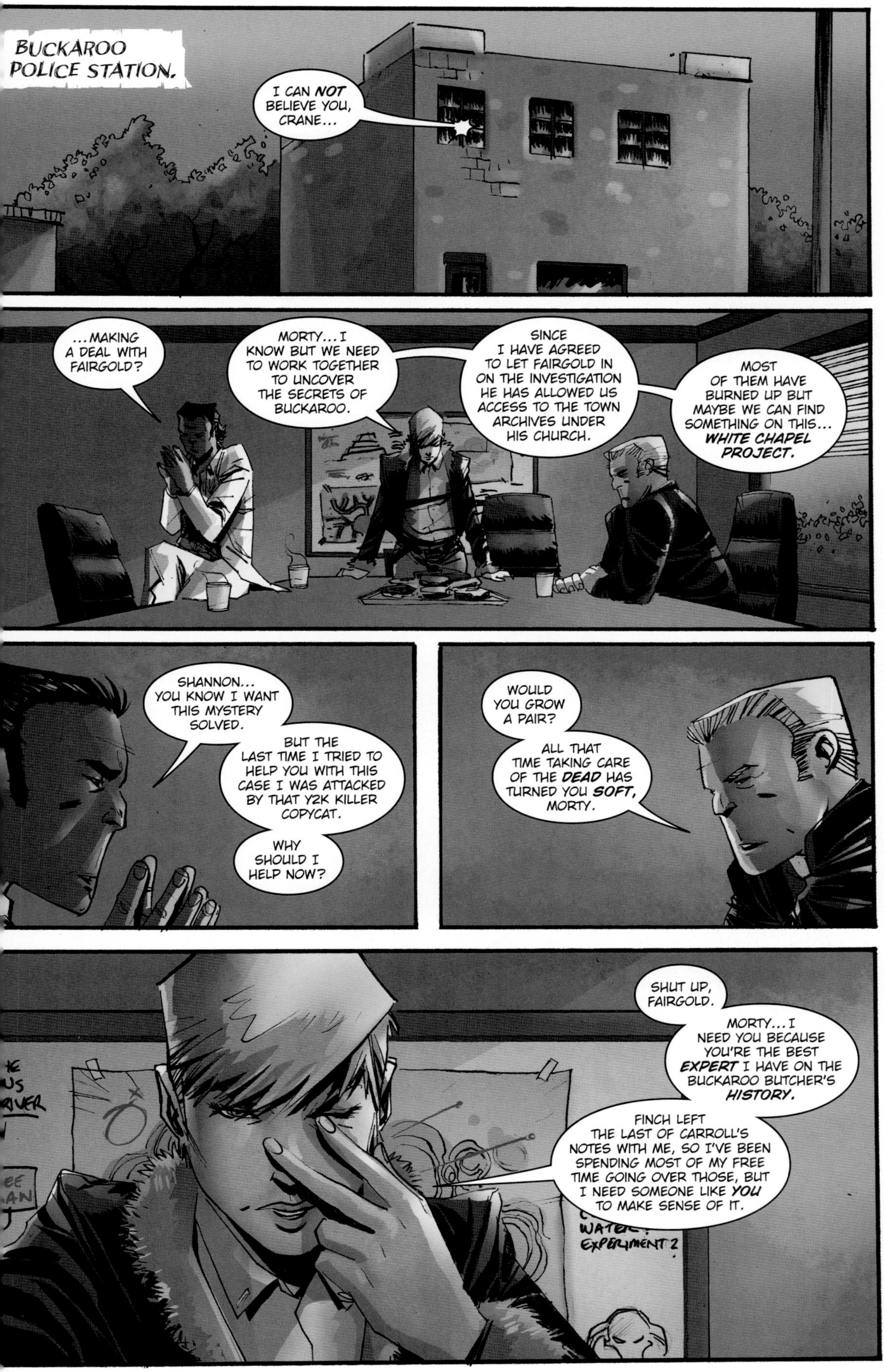
BUCKAROO POLICE STATION.
I CAN NOT BELIEVE YOU, CRANE...
...MAKING A DEAL WITH FAIRGOLD?
MORTY...I KNOW BUT WE NEED TO WORK TOGETHER TO UNCOVER THE SECRETS OF BUCKAROO.
SINCE I HAVE AGREED TO LET FAIRGOLD IN ON THE INVESTIGATION HE HAS ALLOWED US ACCESS TO THE TOWN ARCHIVES UNDER HIS CHURCH.
MOST OF THEM HAVE BURNED UP BUT MAYBE WE CAN FIND SOMETHING ON THIS... WHITE CHAPEL PROJECT.
SHANNON... YOU KNOW I WANT THIS MYSTERY SOLVED.
BUT THE LAST TIME I TRIED TO HELP YOU WITH THIS CASE I WAS ATTACKED BY THAT Y2K KILLER COPYCAT.
WHY SHOULD I HELP NOW?
WOULD YOU GROW A PAIR?
ALL THAT TIME TAKING CARE OF THE DEAD HAS TURNED YOU SOFT, MORTY.
SHUT UP, FAIRGOLD.
MORTY...I NEED YOU BECAUSE YOU'RE THE BEST EXPERT I HAVE ON THE BUCKAROO BUTCHER'S HISTORY.
FINCH LEFT THE LAST OF CARROLL'S NOTES WITH ME, SO I'VE BEEN SPENDING MOST OF MY FREE TIME GOING OVER THOSE, BUT I NEED SOMEONE LIKE YOU TO MAKE SENSE OF IT.
EXPERIMENT 2

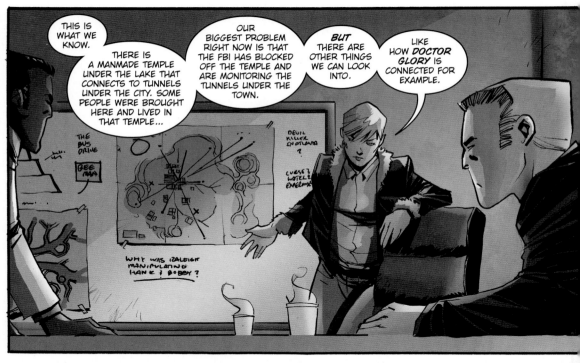

THIS IS WHAT WE KNOW.

THERE IS A MANMADE TEMPLE UNDER THE LAKE THAT CONNECTS TO TUNNELS UNDER THE CITY. SOME PEOPLE WERE BROUGHT HERE AND LIVED IN THAT TEMPLE...

OUR BIGGEST PROBLEM RIGHT NOW IS THAT THE FBI HAS BLOCKED OFF THE TEMPLE AND ARE MONITORING THE TUNNELS UNDER THE TOWN.

BUT THERE ARE OTHER THINGS WE CAN LOOK INTO.

LIKE HOW *DOCTOR GLORY* IS CONNECTED FOR EXAMPLE.

WHAT MAKES YOU THINK *GLORY* IS INVOLVED?

BECAUSE WARREN TOLD ME.

AND WE'RE JUST TAKING THE WORD OF A SERIAL KILLER NOW?

I BROKE INTO GLORY'S HOUSE AND DID SOME RESEARCH ALREADY.

YOU DID *WHAT?*

WHILE I WAS SUSPENDED I--

HEY SHERIFF CRANE... THERE IS SOMETHING YOU NEED TO *SEE.*

CAN IT WAIT?

UH, I FEEL LIKE WE HAVE A TICKING TIME BOMB ON OUR HANDS...

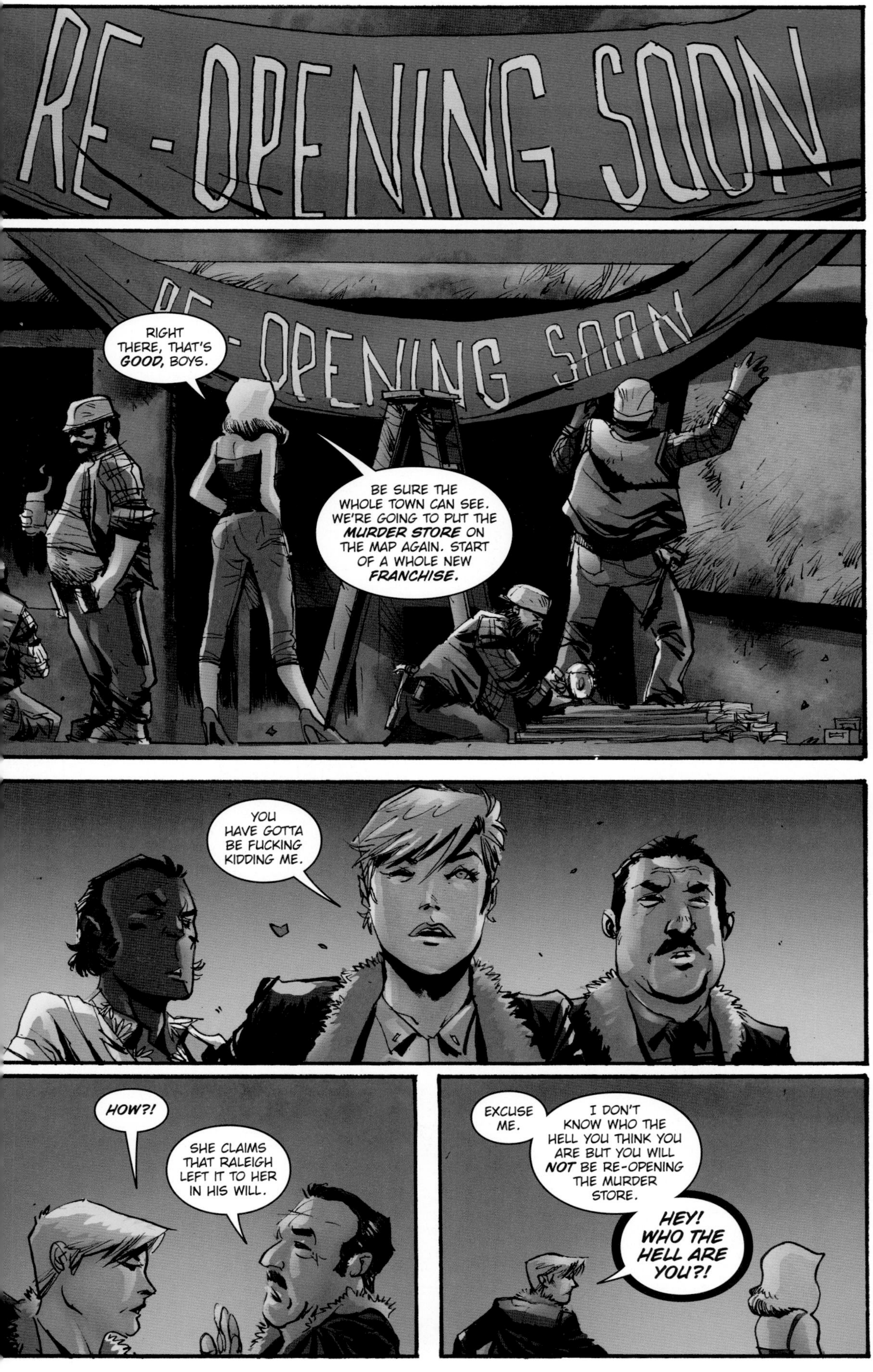
RE-OPENING SOON
RE-OPENING SOON
RIGHT THERE, THAT'S GOOD, BOYS.
BE SURE THE WHOLE TOWN CAN SEE. WE'RE GOING TO PUT THE MURDER STORE ON THE MAP AGAIN. START OF A WHOLE NEW FRANCHISE.
YOU HAVE GOTTA BE FUCKING KIDDING ME.
HOW?!
SHE CLAIMS THAT RALEIGH LEFT IT TO HER IN HIS WILL.
EXCUSE ME.
I DON'T KNOW WHO THE HELL YOU THINK YOU ARE BUT YOU WILL NOT BE RE-OPENING THE MURDER STORE.
HEY! WHO THE HELL ARE YOU?!

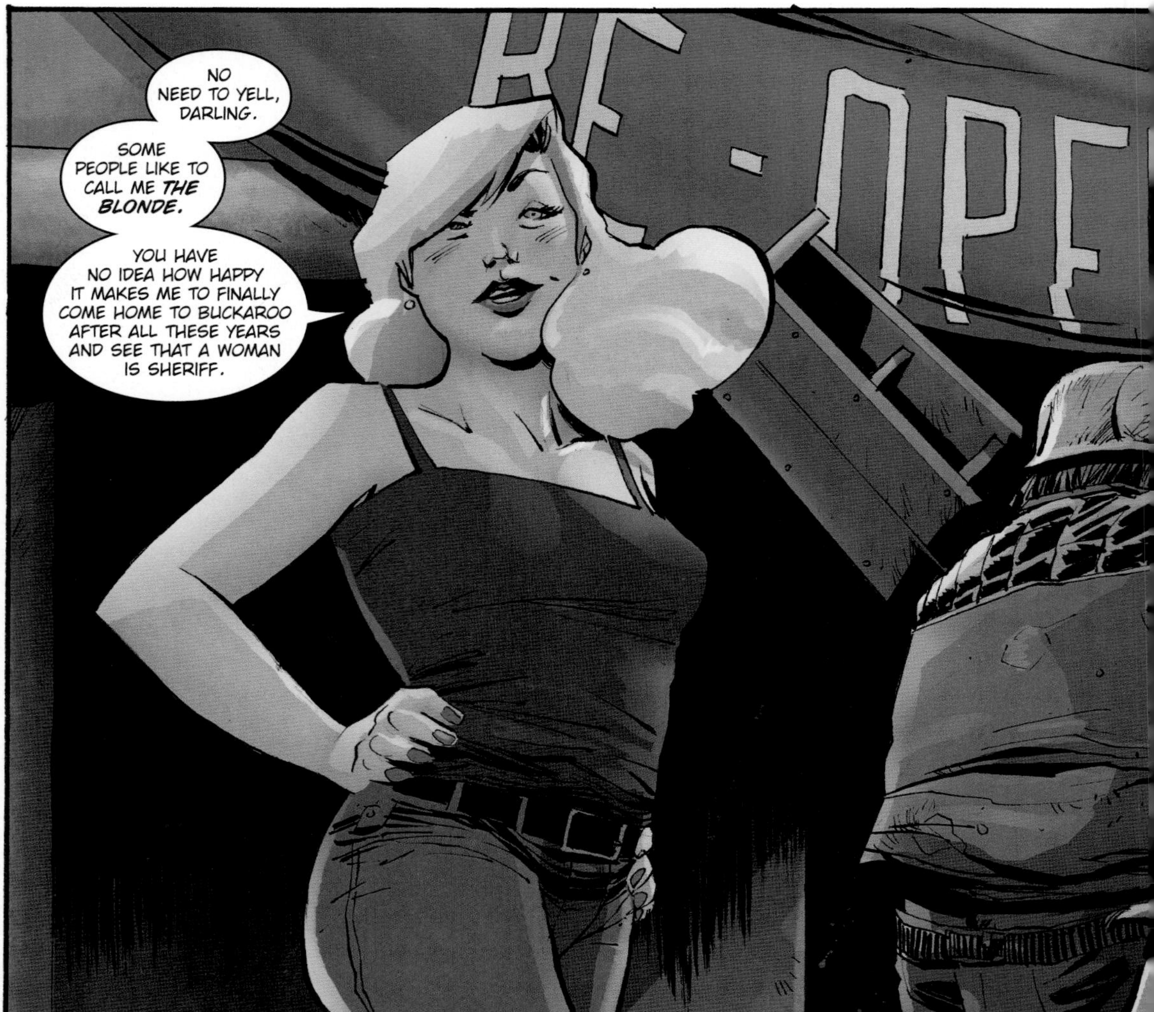
NO NEED TO YELL, DARLING.
SOME PEOPLE LIKE TO CALL ME *THE BLONDE.*
YOU HAVE NO IDEA HOW HAPPY IT MAKES ME TO FINALLY COME HOME TO BUCKAROO AFTER ALL THESE YEARS AND SEE THAT A WOMAN IS SHERIFF.

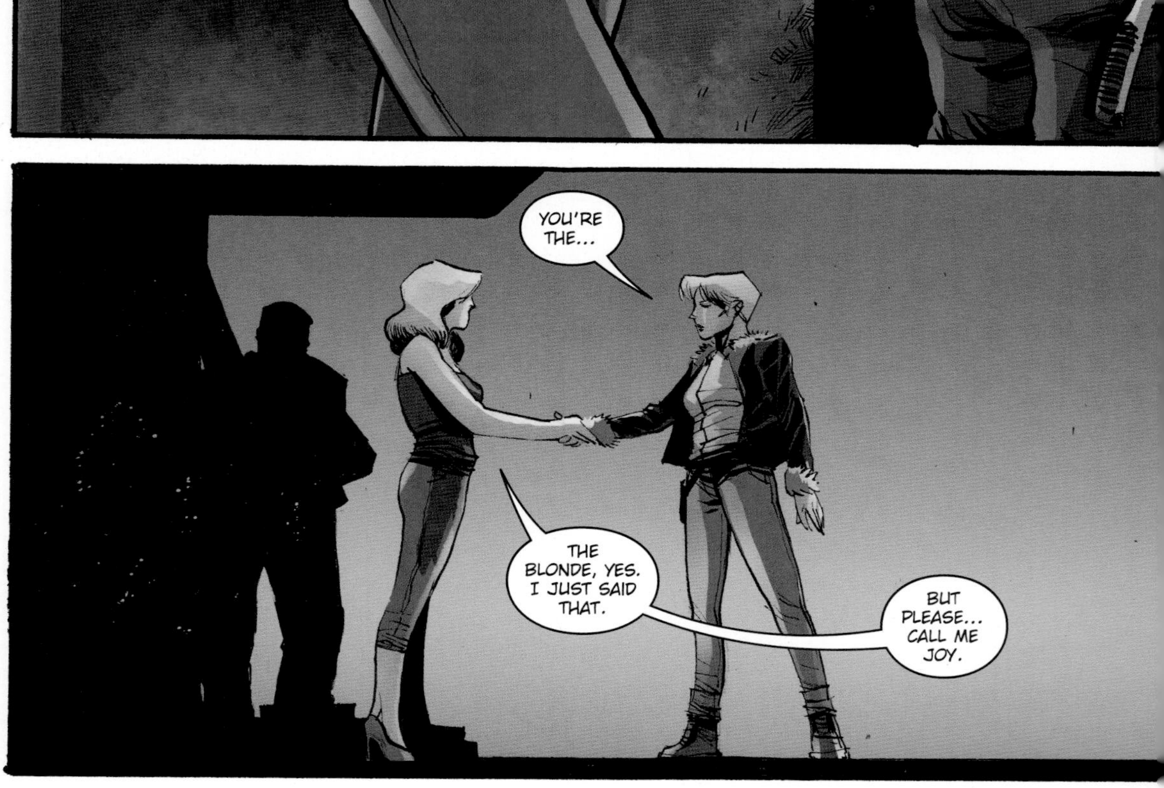
YOU'RE THE...
THE BLONDE, YES. I JUST SAID THAT.
BUT PLEASE... CALL ME JOY.

UM...

WHY ARE MY THINGS OUTSIDE?

BECAUSE THAT'S WHERE IT BELONGS, ALICE.

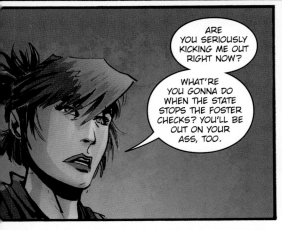

ARE YOU SERIOUSLY KICKING ME OUT RIGHT NOW?

WHAT'RE YOU GONNA DO WHEN THE STATE STOPS THE FOSTER CHECKS? YOU'LL BE OUT ON YOUR ASS, TOO.

NO AMOUNT OF SCRATCH IS WORTH HAVING SOME *SERIAL KILLER-IN-TRAINING* LIVING IN MY BASEMENT.

THIS ISN'T EVEN CLOSE TO ALL MY STUFF!

WE PAWNED OFF THE REST WHILE YOU WERE AT SCHOOL.

YOU DID WHAT?!

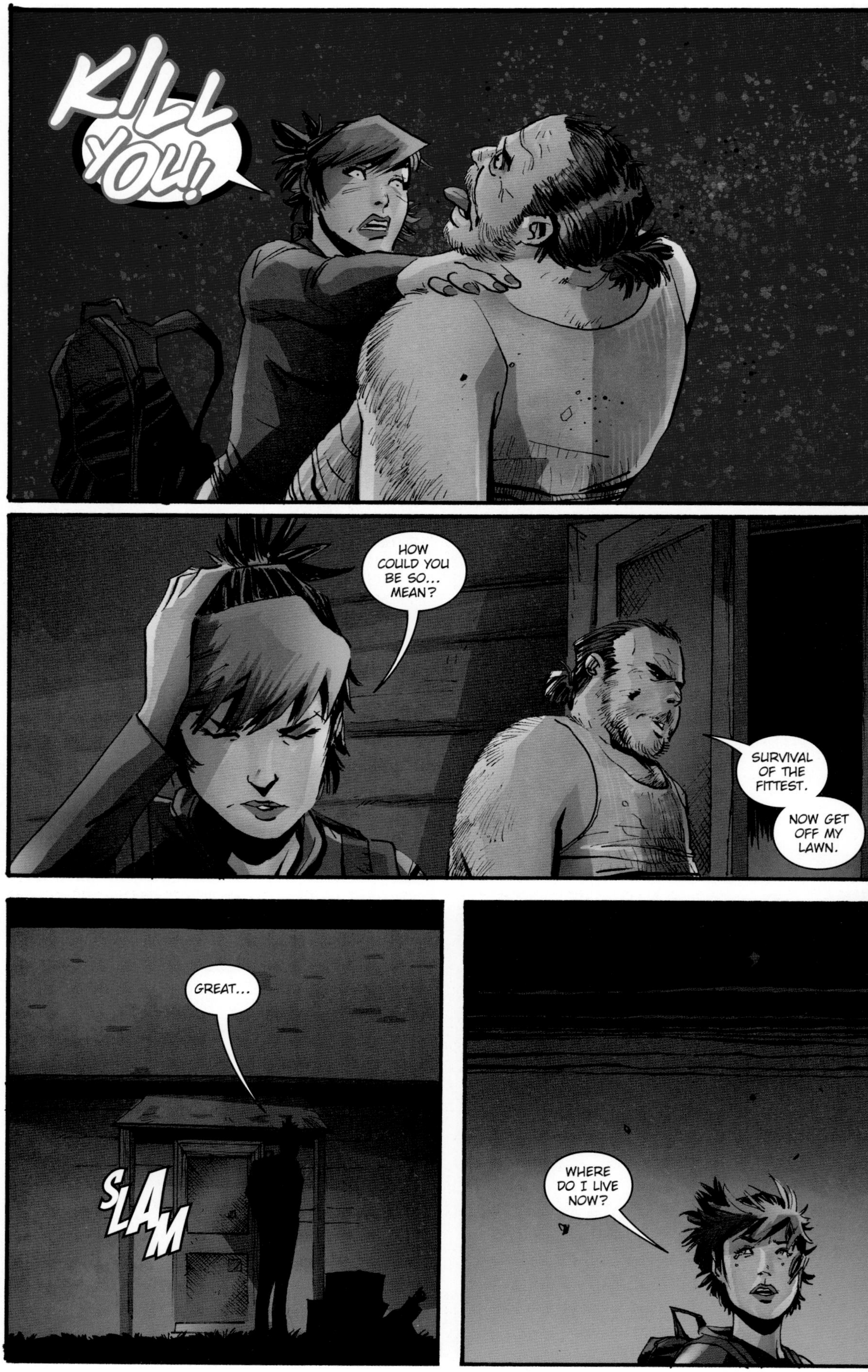
KILL YOU!
HOW COULD YOU BE SO... MEAN?
SURVIVAL OF THE FITTEST.
NOW GET OFF MY LAWN.
GREAT...
SLAM
WHERE DO I LIVE NOW?

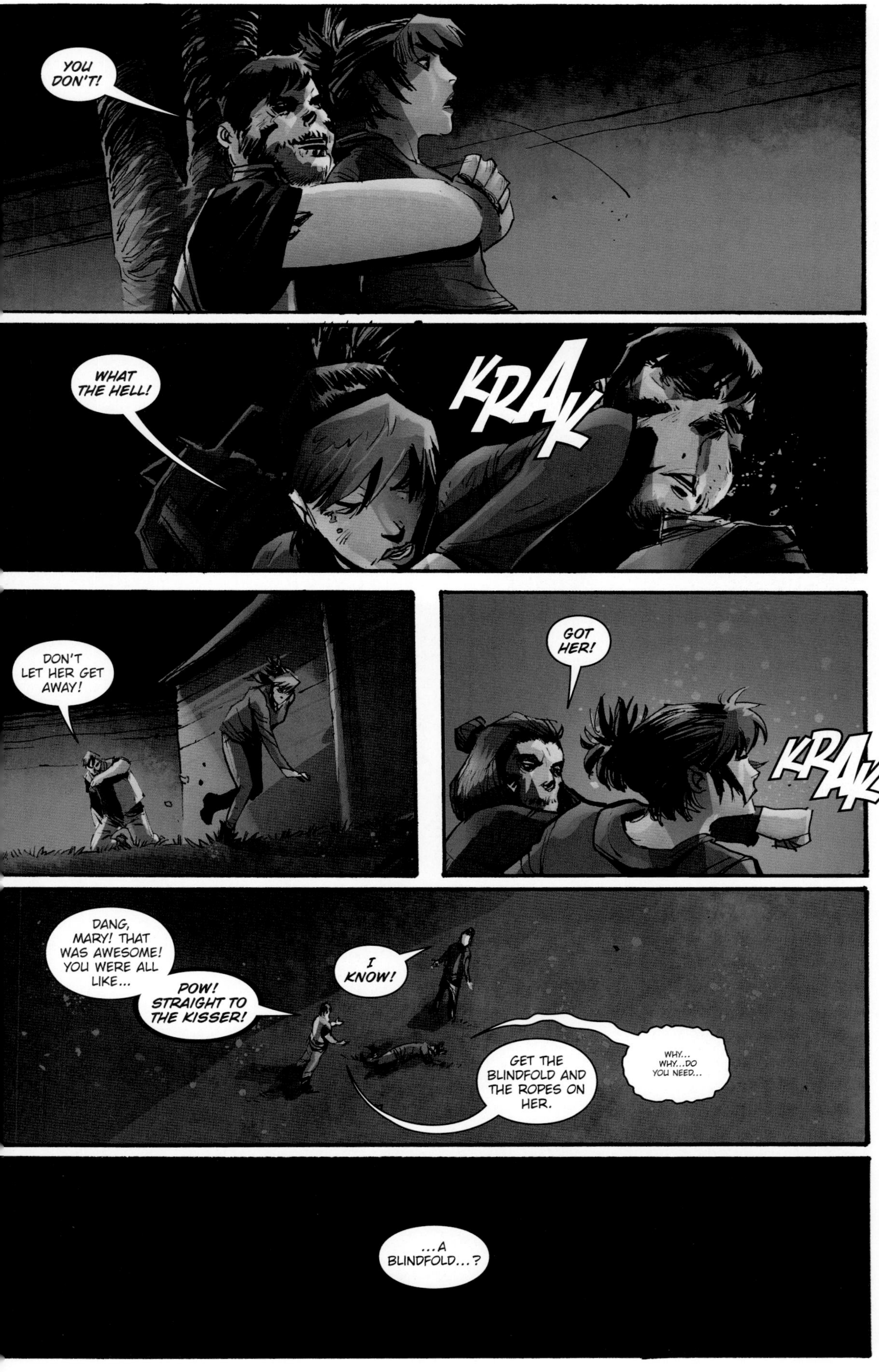

YOU DON'T!
WHAT THE HELL!
KRAK
DON'T LET HER GET AWAY!
GOT HER!
KRAK
DANG, MARY! THAT WAS AWESOME! YOU WERE ALL LIKE...
POW! STRAIGHT TO THE KISSER!
I KNOW!
GET THE BLINDFOLD AND THE ROPES ON HER.
WHY... WHY...DO YOU NEED...
...A BLINDFOLD...?

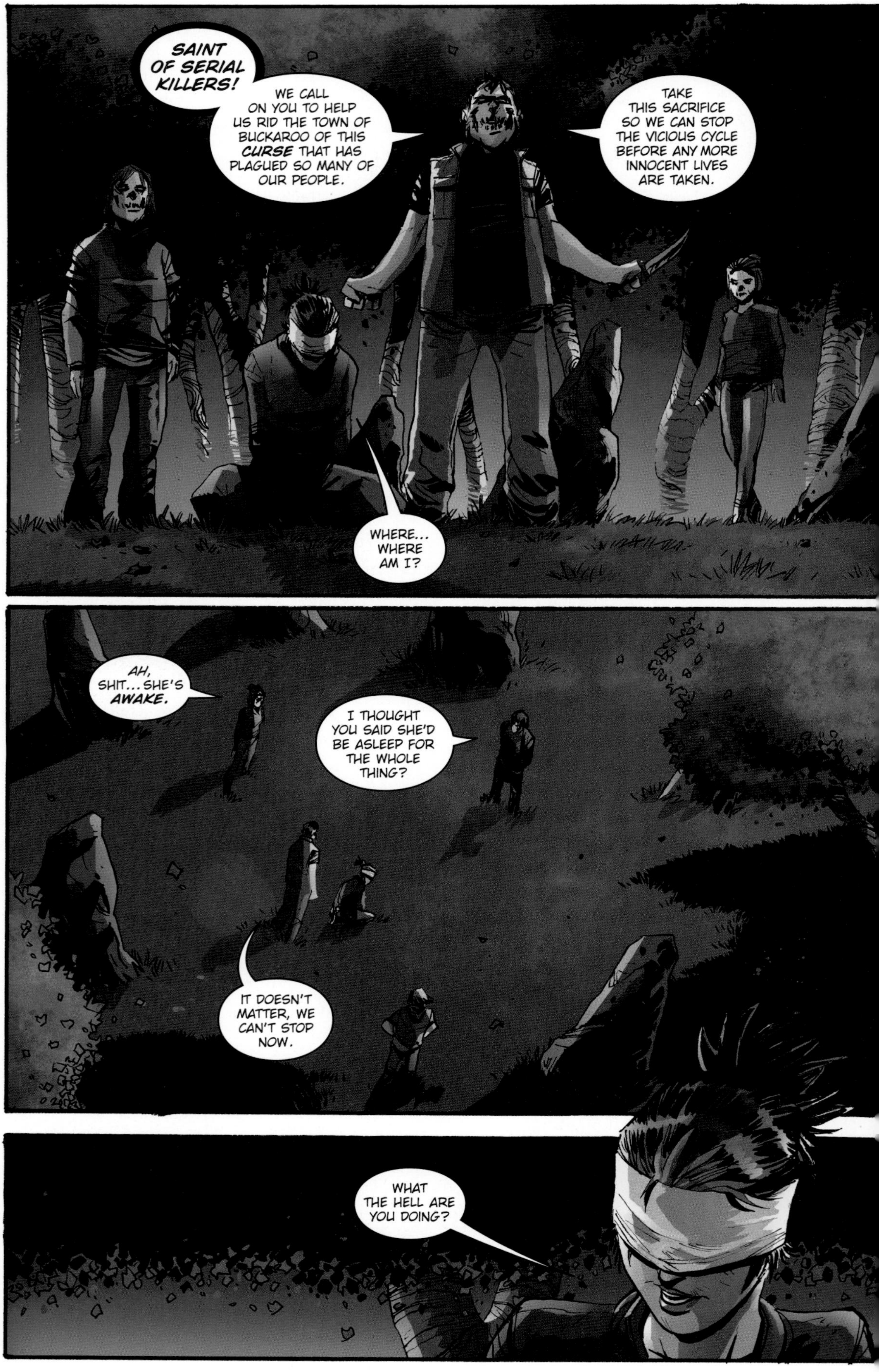
SAINT OF SERIAL KILLERS!
WE CALL ON YOU TO HELP US RID THE TOWN OF BUCKAROO OF THIS CURSE THAT HAS PLAGUED SO MANY OF OUR PEOPLE.
TAKE THIS SACRIFICE SO WE CAN STOP THE VICIOUS CYCLE BEFORE ANY MORE INNOCENT LIVES ARE TAKEN.
WHERE... WHERE AM I?
AH, SHIT... SHE'S AWAKE.
I THOUGHT YOU SAID SHE'D BE ASLEEP FOR THE WHOLE THING?
IT DOESN'T MATTER, WE CAN'T STOP NOW.
WHAT THE HELL ARE YOU DOING?

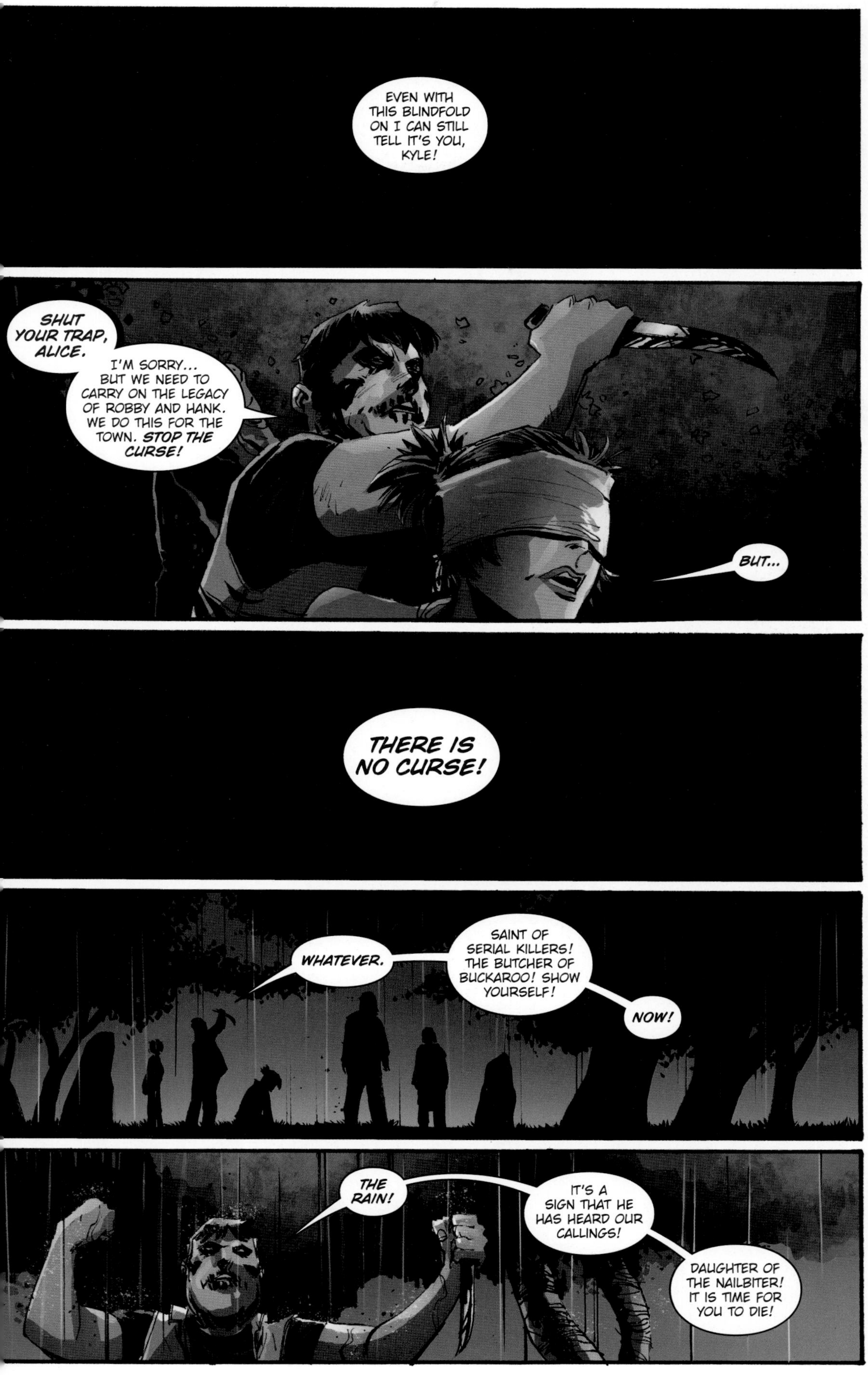
EVEN WITH THIS BLINDFOLD ON I CAN STILL TELL IT'S YOU, KYLE!
SHUT YOUR TRAP, ALICE.
I'M SORRY... BUT WE NEED TO CARRY ON THE LEGACY OF ROBBY AND HANK. WE DO THIS FOR THE TOWN. STOP THE CURSE!
BUT...
THERE IS NO CURSE!
WHATEVER.
SAINT OF SERIAL KILLERS! THE BUTCHER OF BUCKAROO! SHOW YOURSELF!
NOW!
THE RAIN!
IT'S A SIGN THAT HE HAS HEARD OUR CALLINGS!
DAUGHTER OF THE NAILBITER! IT IS TIME FOR YOU TO DIE!

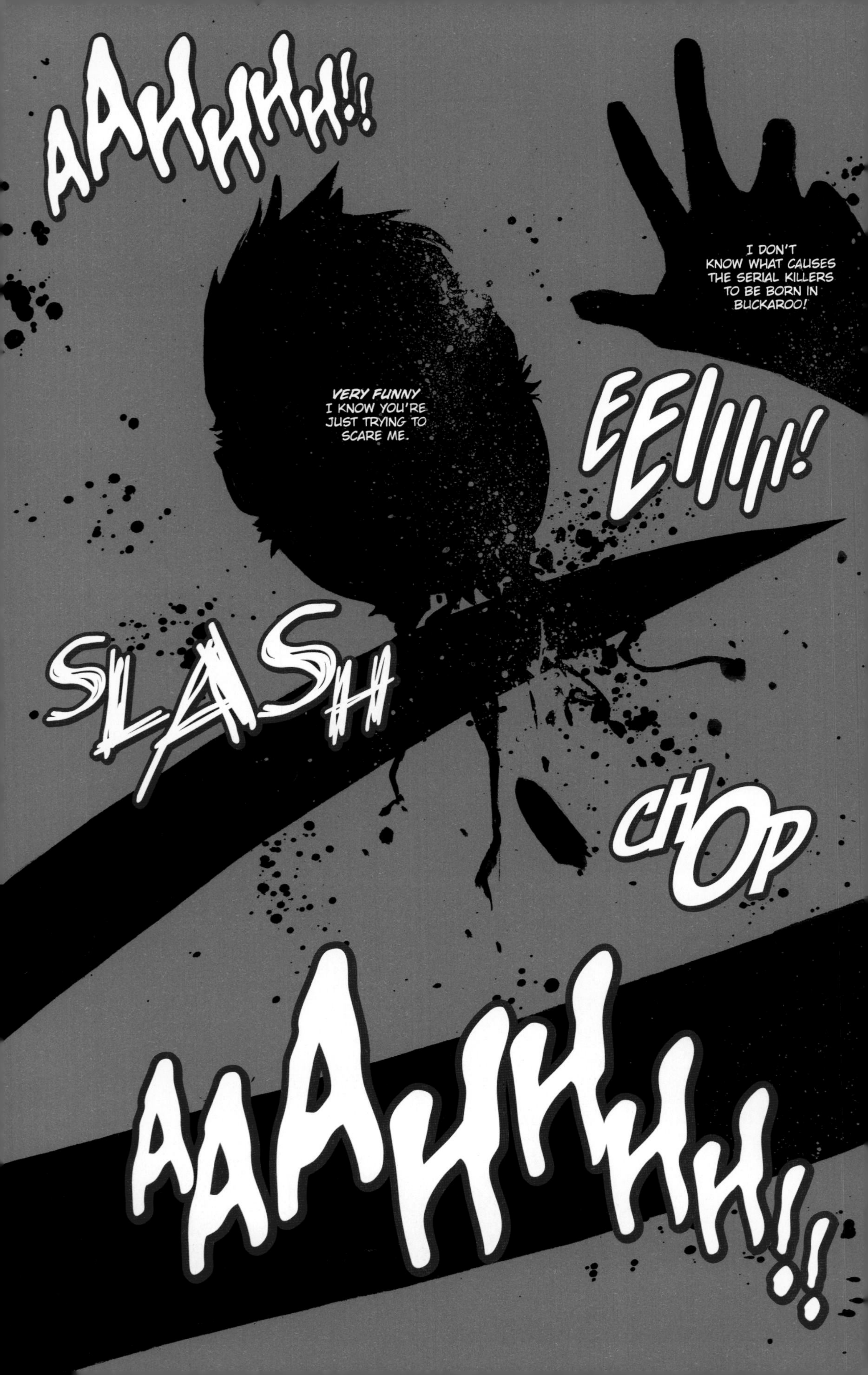
AAHHHH!!
I DON'T KNOW WHAT CAUSES THE SERIAL KILLERS TO BE BORN IN BUCKAROO!
VERY FUNNY I KNOW YOU'RE JUST TRYING TO SCARE ME.
EEIIII!
SLASH
CHOP
AAAHHHH!!

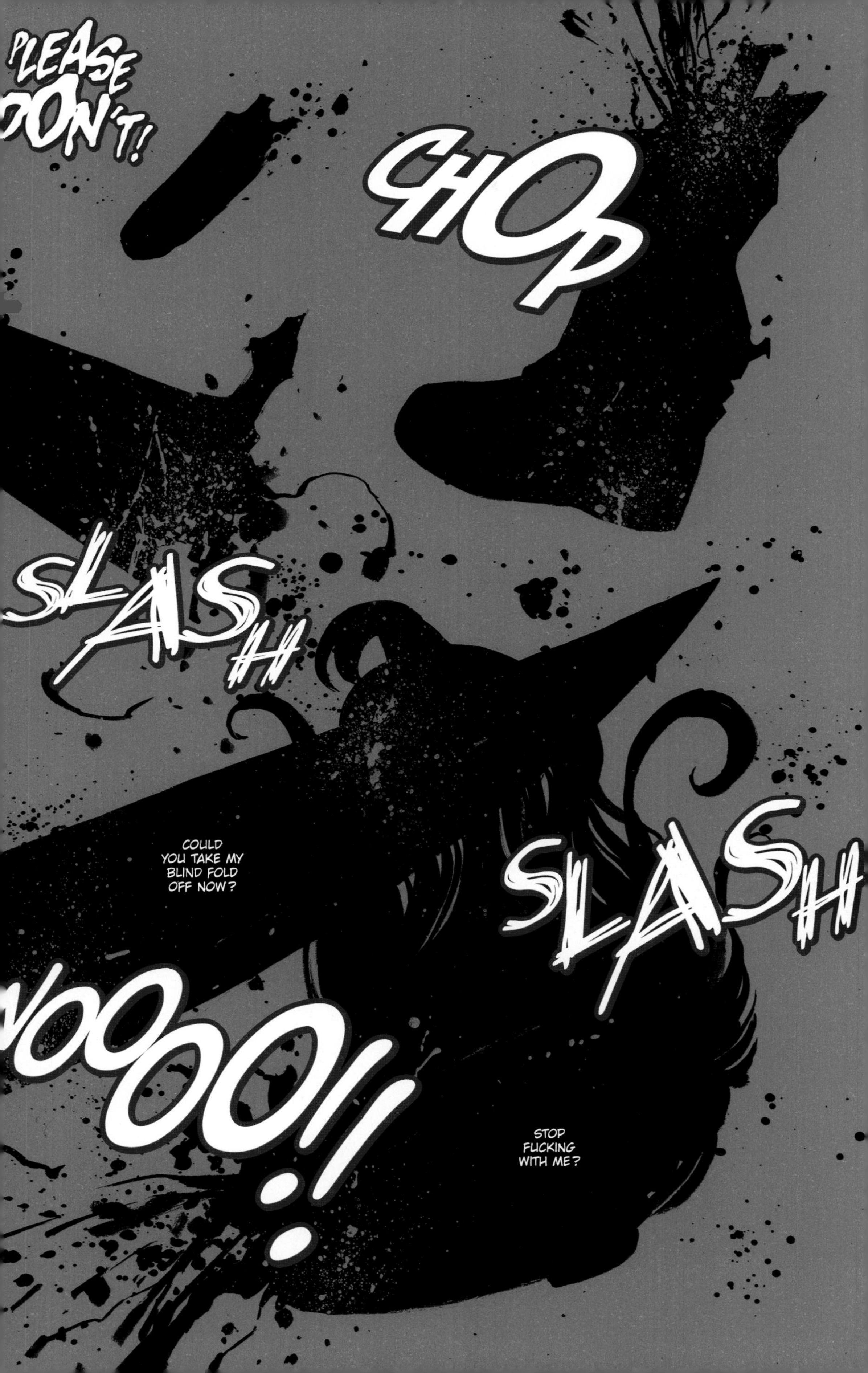
PLEASE DON'T!
CHOP
SLASH
COULD YOU TAKE MY BLIND FOLD OFF NOW?
SLASH
NOOOO!!
STOP FUCKING WITH ME?

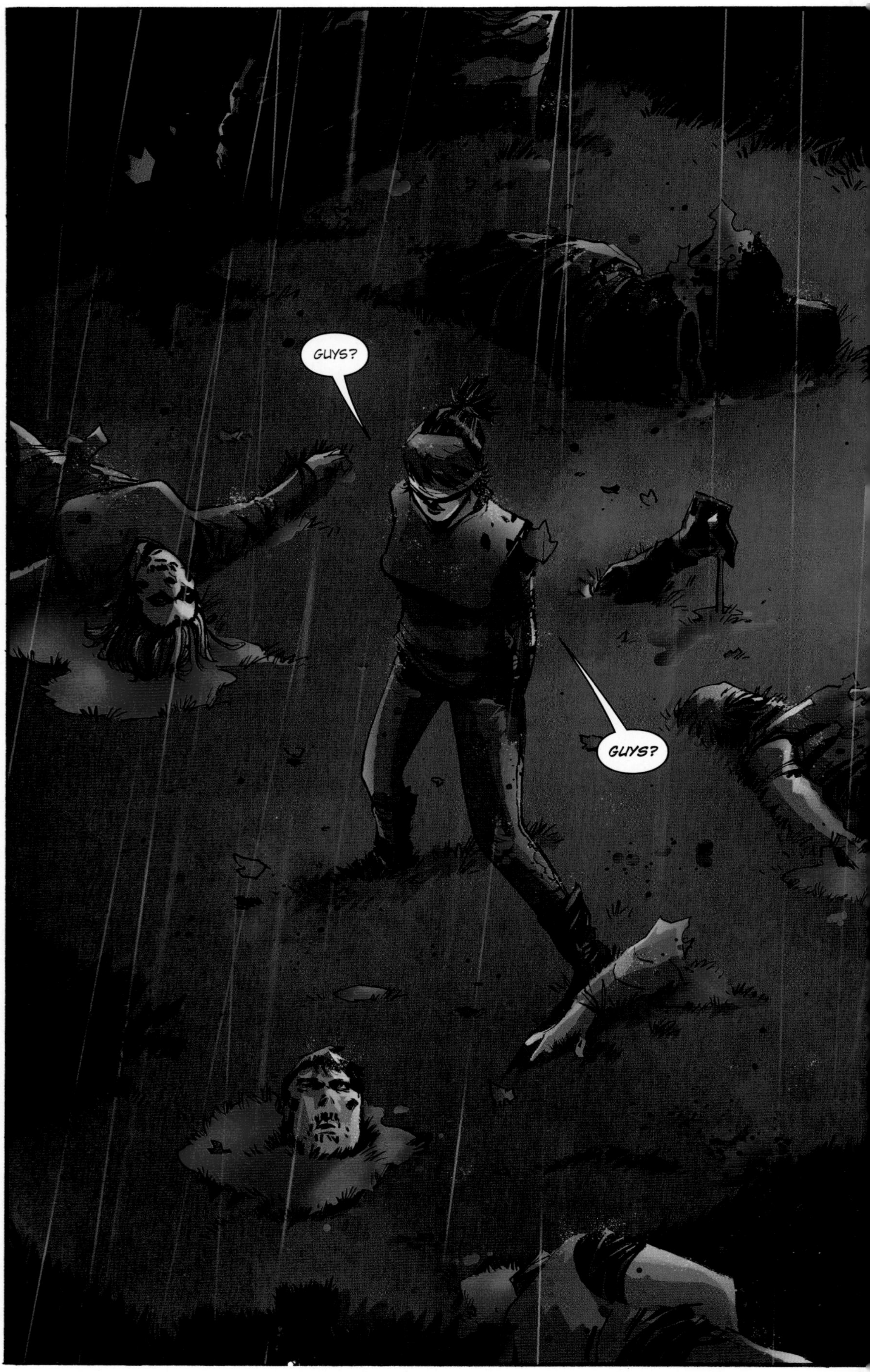
GUYS?
GUYS?

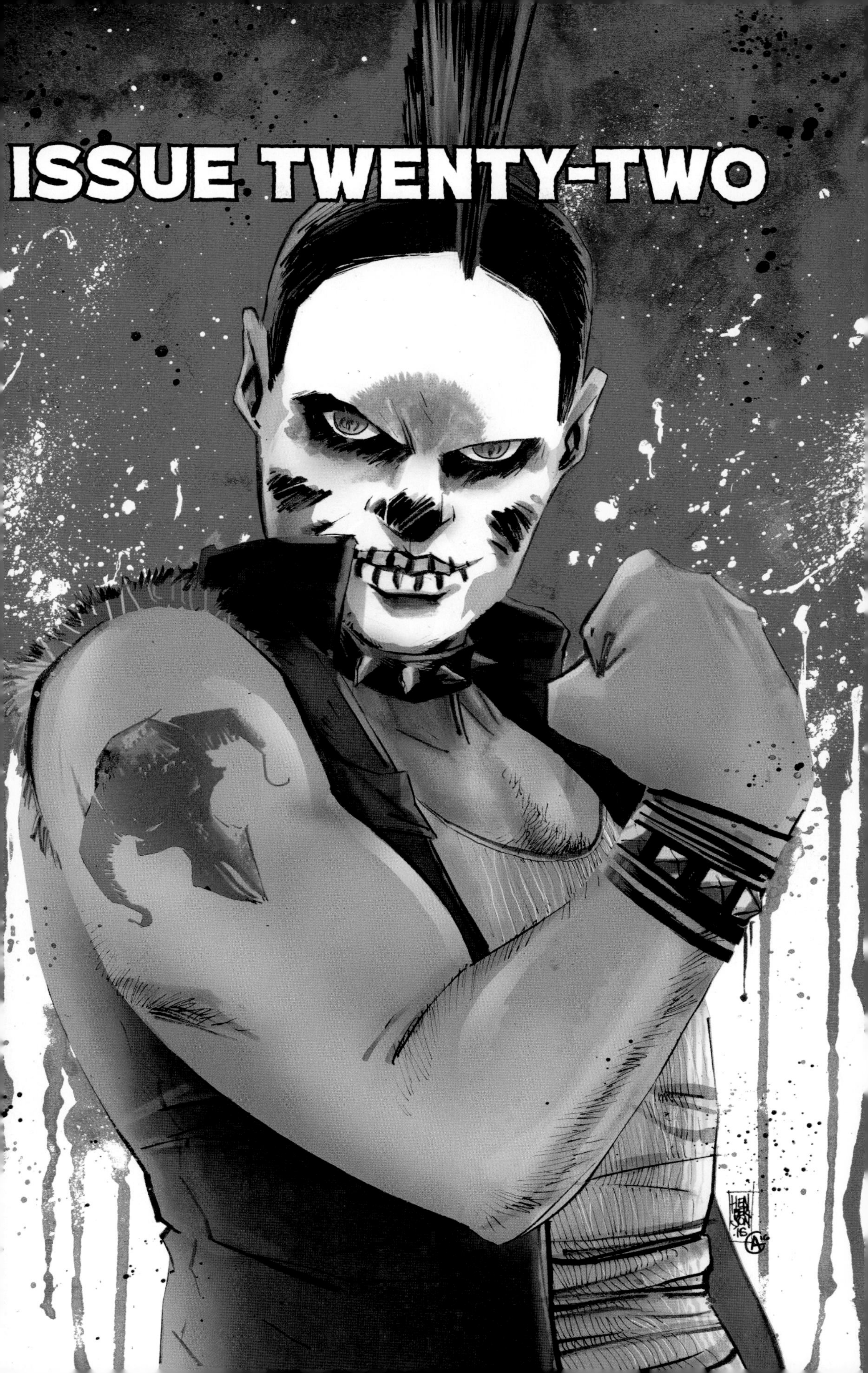
ISSUE TWENTY-TWO

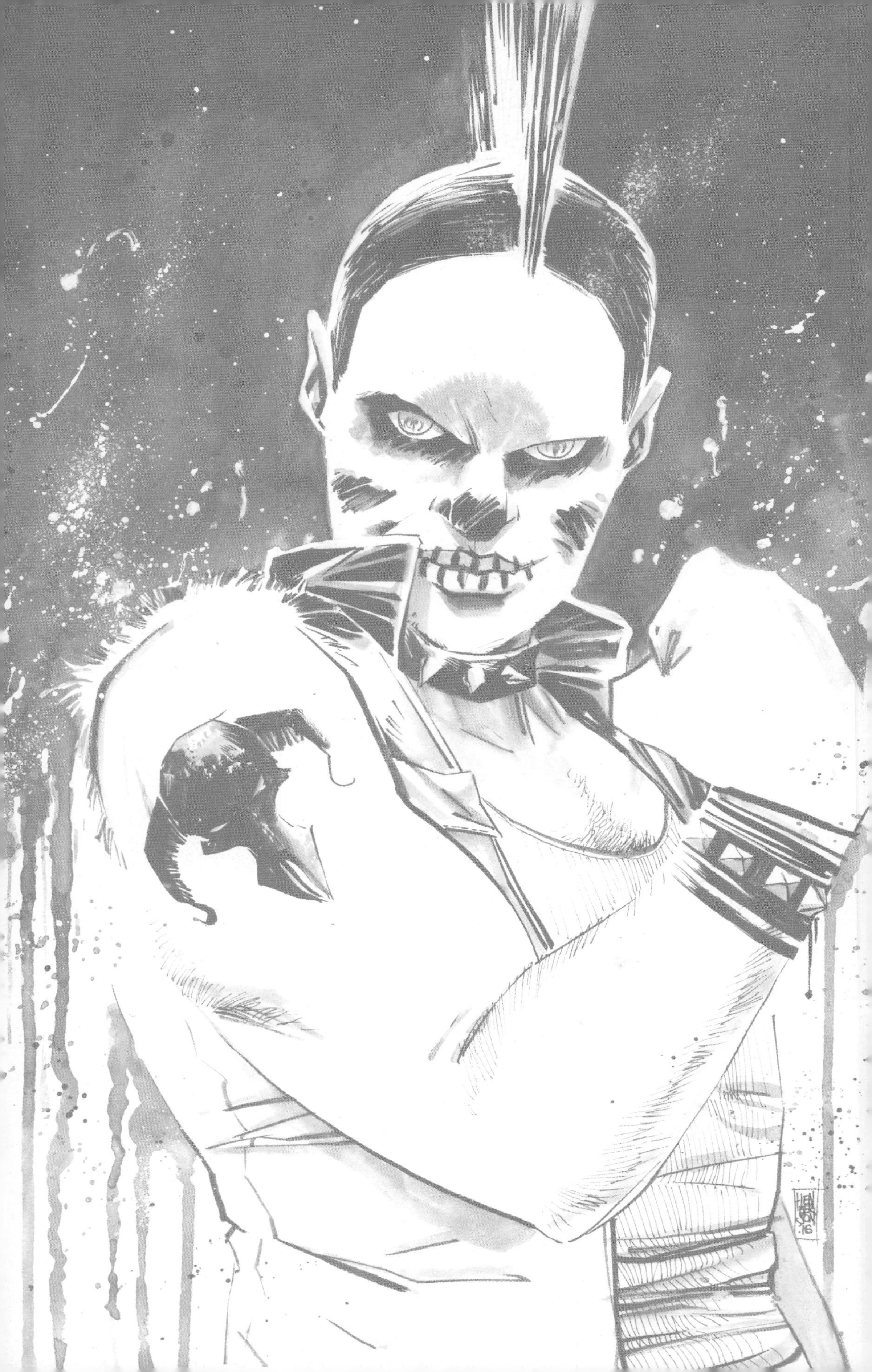

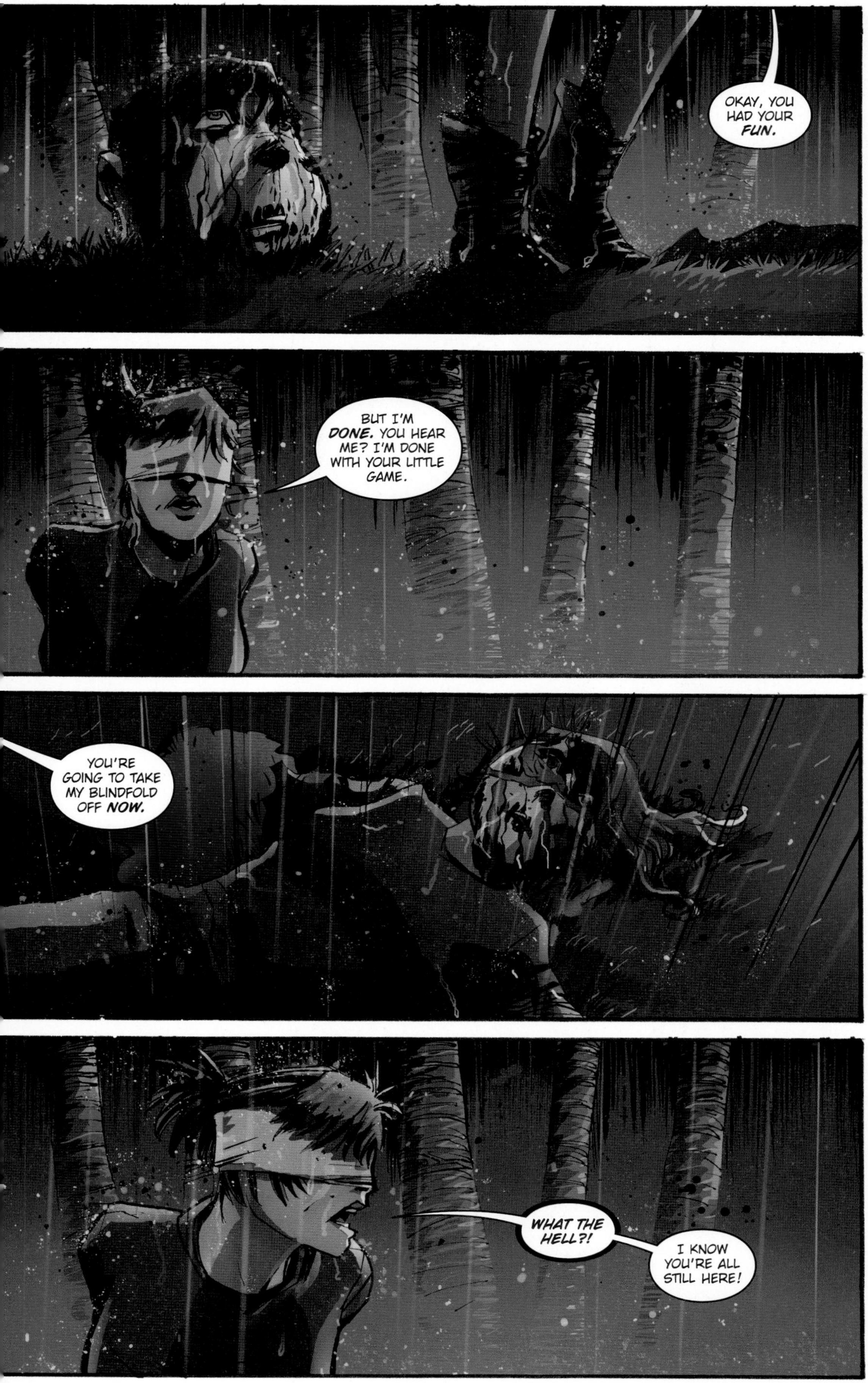
OKAY, YOU HAD YOUR FUN.
BUT I'M DONE. YOU HEAR ME? I'M DONE WITH YOUR LITTLE GAME.
YOU'RE GOING TO TAKE MY BLINDFOLD OFF NOW.
WHAT THE HELL?!
I KNOW YOU'RE ALL STILL HERE!

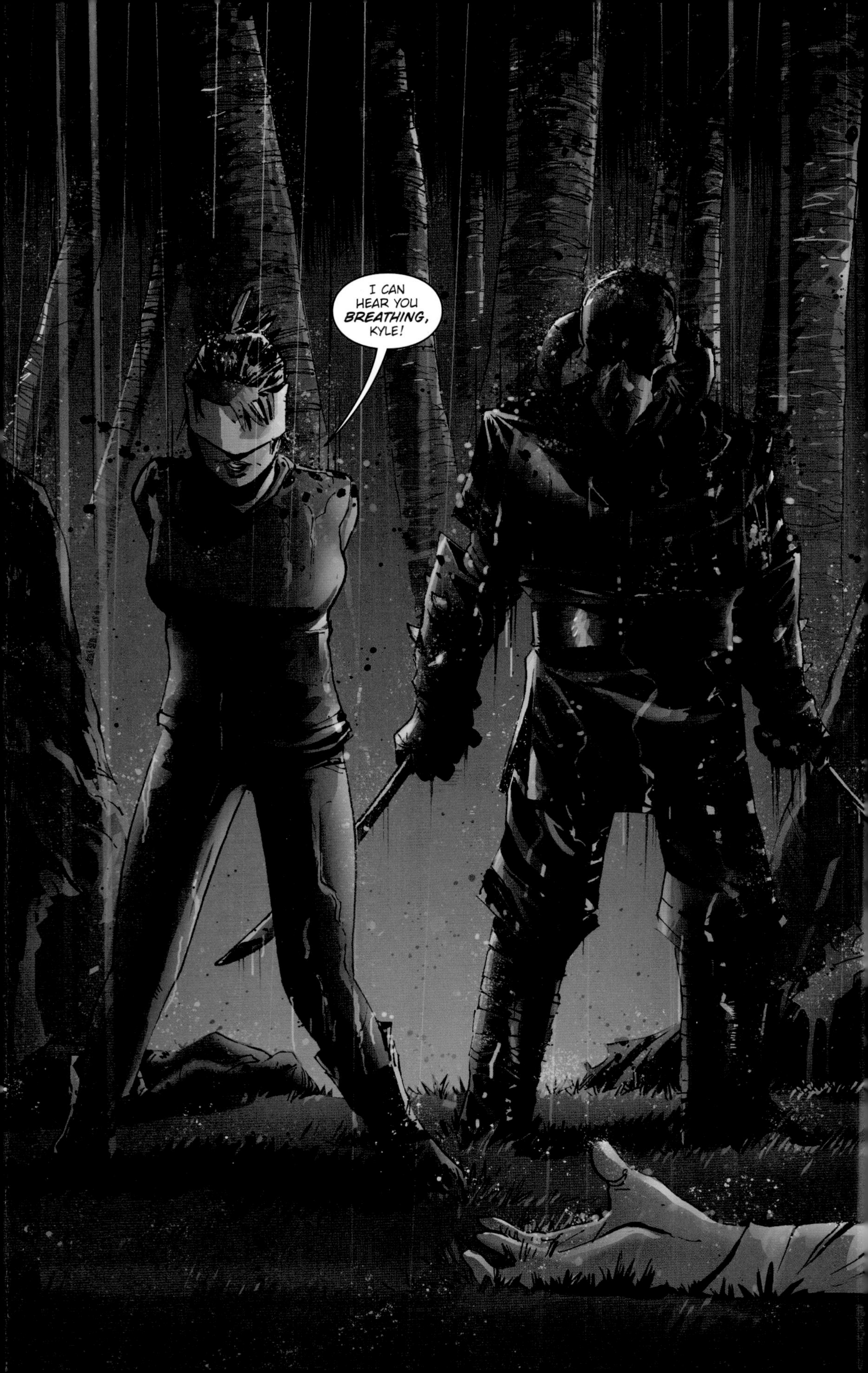
I CAN HEAR YOU BREATHING, KYLE!

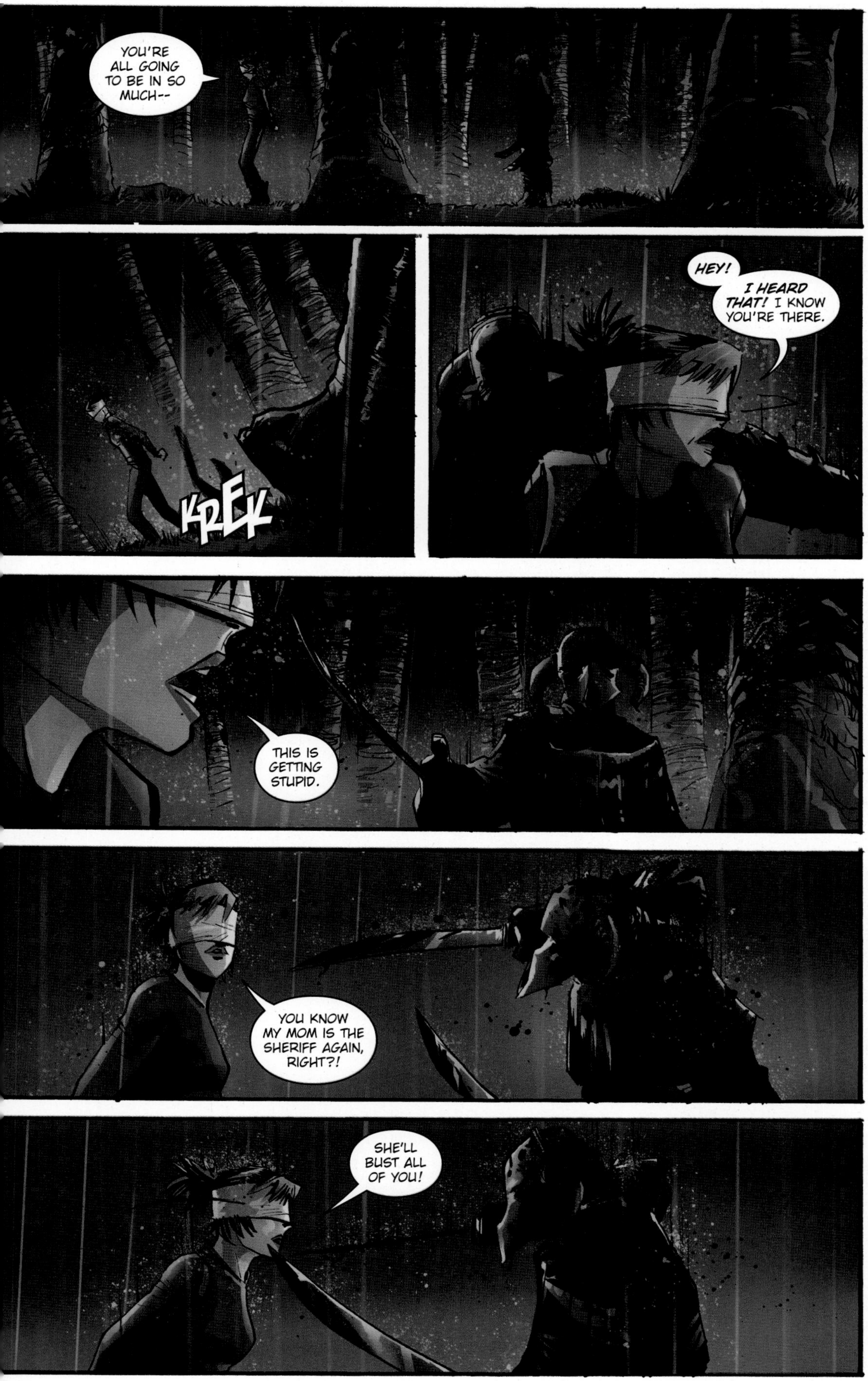
YOU'RE ALL GOING TO BE IN SO MUCH--
KREK
HEY! I HEARD THAT! I KNOW YOU'RE THERE.
THIS IS GETTING STUPID.
YOU KNOW MY MOM IS THE SHERIFF AGAIN, RIGHT?!
SHE'LL BUST ALL OF YOU!

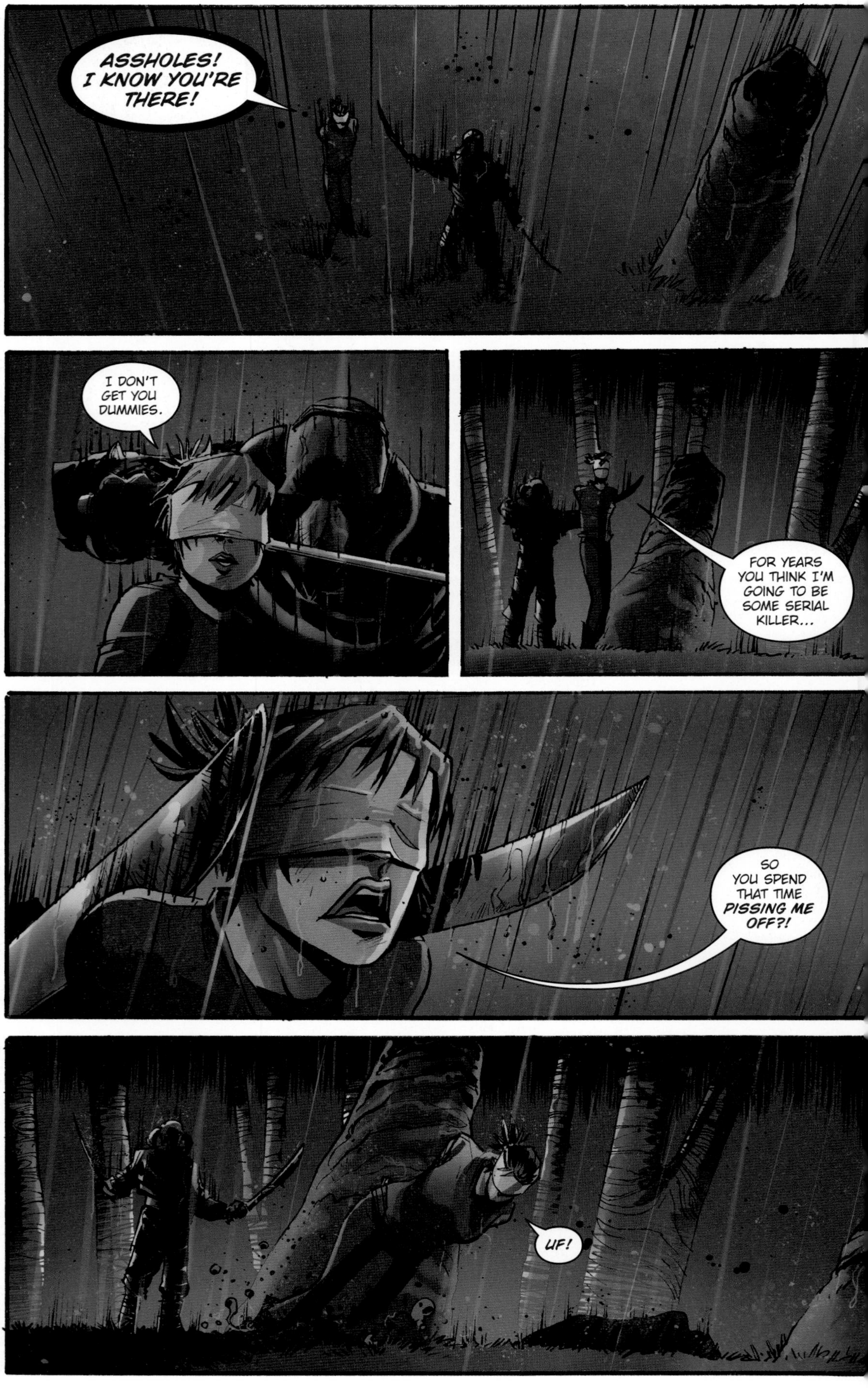
ASSHOLES! I KNOW YOU'RE THERE!
I DON'T GET YOU DUMMIES.
FOR YEARS YOU THINK I'M GOING TO BE SOME SERIAL KILLER...
SO YOU SPEND THAT TIME PISSING ME OFF?!
UF!

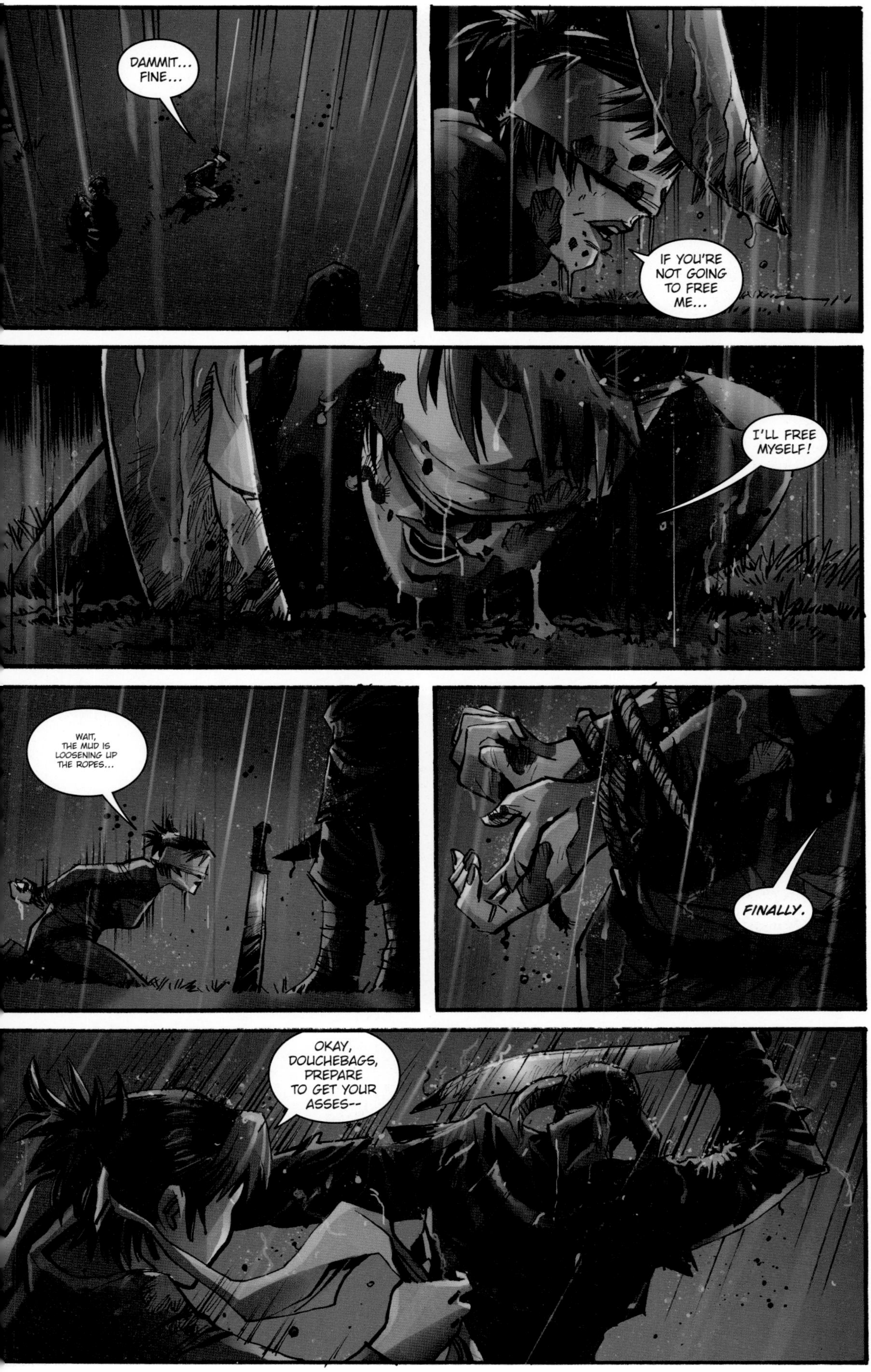
DAMMIT... FINE...
IF YOU'RE NOT GOING TO FREE ME...
I'LL FREE MYSELF!
WAIT, THE MUD IS LOOSENING UP THE ROPES...
FINALLY.
OKAY, DOUCHEBAGS, PREPARE TO GET YOUR ASSES--

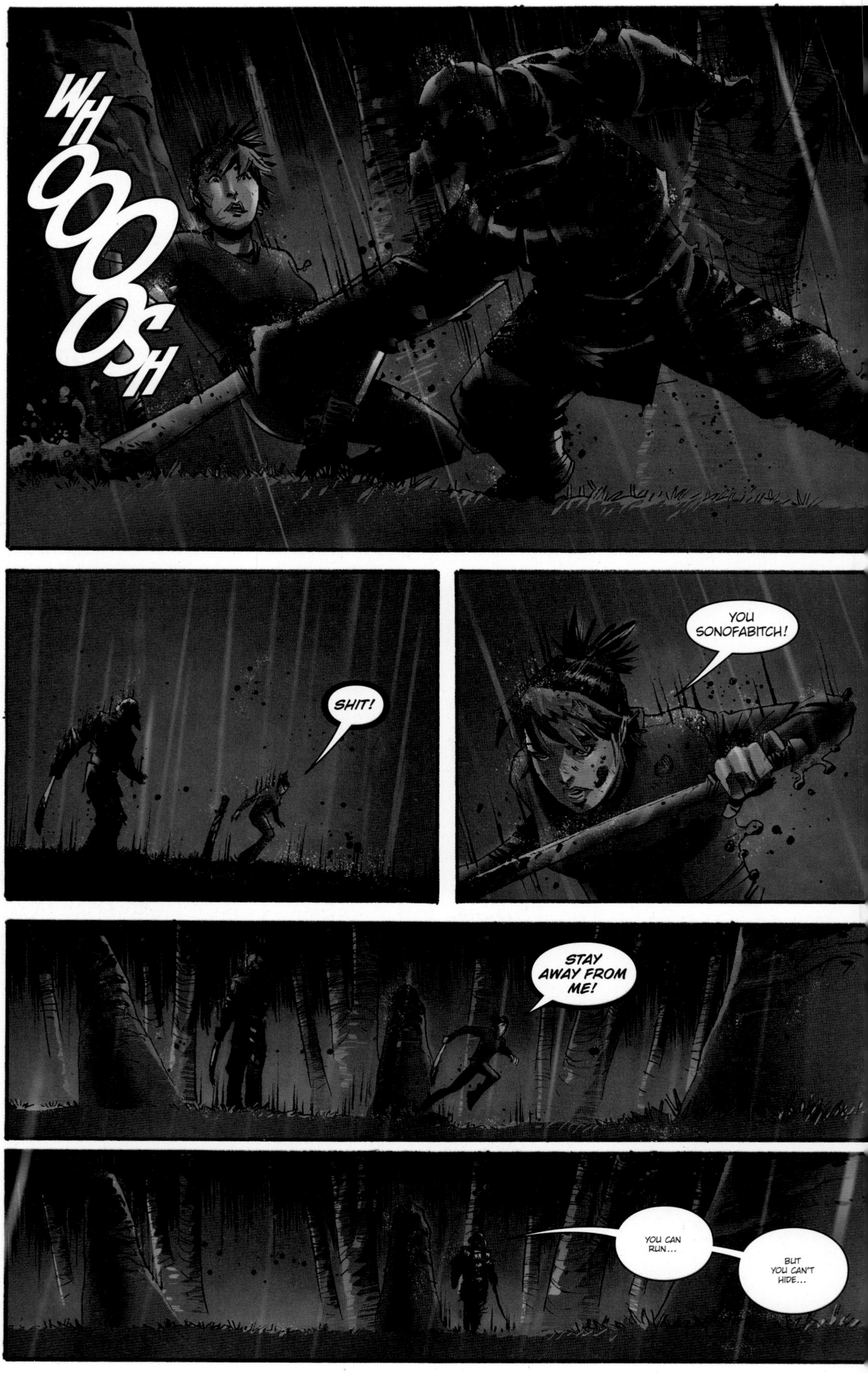
WHOOOOSH
SHIT!
YOU SONOFABITCH!
STAY AWAY FROM ME!
YOU CAN RUN...
BUT YOU CAN'T HIDE...

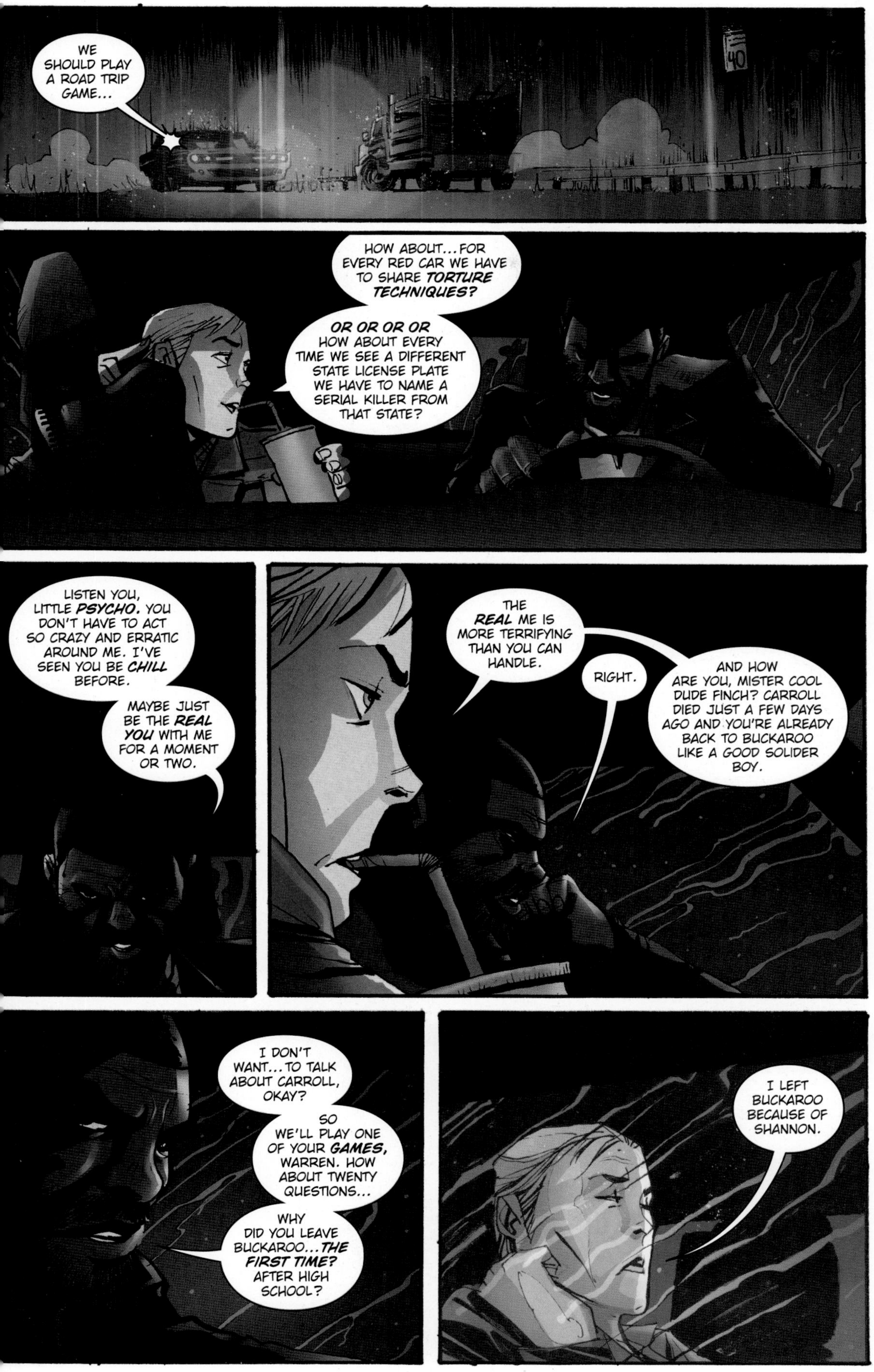
WE SHOULD PLAY A ROAD TRIP GAME...
40
HOW ABOUT... FOR EVERY RED CAR WE HAVE TO SHARE TORTURE TECHNIQUES?
OR OR OR OR HOW ABOUT EVERY TIME WE SEE A DIFFERENT STATE LICENSE PLATE WE HAVE TO NAME A SERIAL KILLER FROM THAT STATE?
LISTEN YOU, LITTLE PSYCHO. YOU DON'T HAVE TO ACT SO CRAZY AND ERRATIC AROUND ME. I'VE SEEN YOU BE CHILL BEFORE.
MAYBE JUST BE THE REAL YOU WITH ME FOR A MOMENT OR TWO.
THE REAL ME IS MORE TERRIFYING THAN YOU CAN HANDLE.
RIGHT.
AND HOW ARE YOU, MISTER COOL DUDE FINCH? CARROLL DIED JUST A FEW DAYS AGO AND YOU'RE ALREADY BACK TO BUCKAROO LIKE A GOOD SOLIDER BOY.
I DON'T WANT... TO TALK ABOUT CARROLL, OKAY?
SO WE'LL PLAY ONE OF YOUR GAMES, WARREN. HOW ABOUT TWENTY QUESTIONS...
WHY DID YOU LEAVE BUCKAROO... THE FIRST TIME? AFTER HIGH SCHOOL?
I LEFT BUCKAROO BECAUSE OF SHANNON.

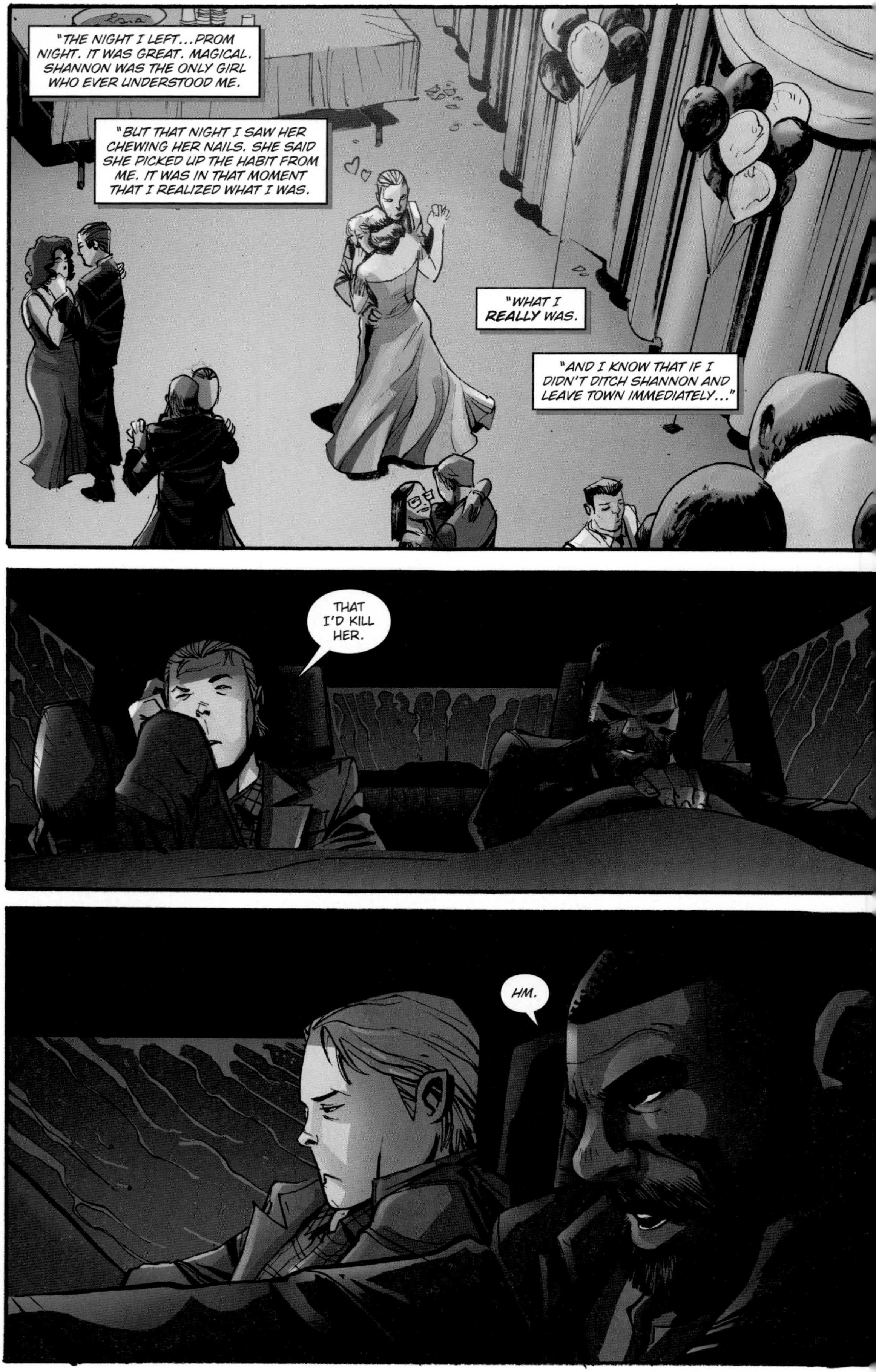
"THE NIGHT I LEFT...PROM NIGHT. IT WAS GREAT. MAGICAL. SHANNON WAS THE ONLY GIRL WHO EVER UNDERSTOOD ME.
"BUT THAT NIGHT I SAW HER CHEWING HER NAILS. SHE SAID SHE PICKED UP THE HABIT FROM ME. IT WAS IN THAT MOMENT THAT I REALIZED WHAT I WAS.
"WHAT I REALLY WAS.
"AND I KNOW THAT IF I DIDN'T DITCH SHANNON AND LEAVE TOWN IMMEDIATELY..."
THAT I'D KILL HER.
HM.

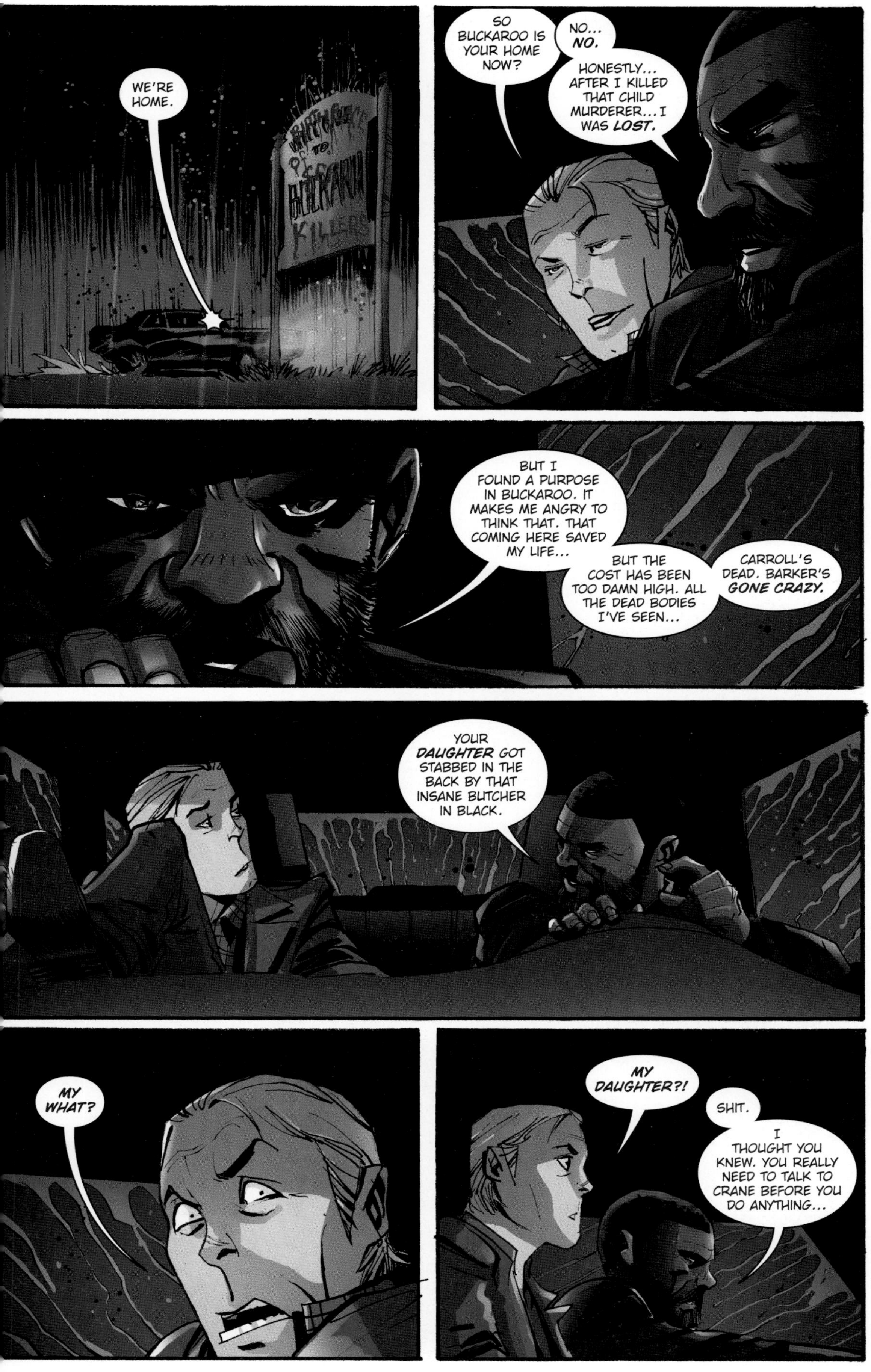
WE'RE HOME.
SO BUCKAROO IS YOUR HOME NOW?
NO... **NO.**
HONESTLY... AFTER I KILLED THAT CHILD MURDERER... I WAS **LOST.**
BUT I FOUND A PURPOSE IN BUCKAROO. IT MAKES ME ANGRY TO THINK THAT. THAT COMING HERE SAVED MY LIFE...
BUT THE COST HAS BEEN TOO DAMN HIGH. ALL THE DEAD BODIES I'VE SEEN...
CARROLL'S DEAD. BARKER'S **GONE CRAZY.**
YOUR **DAUGHTER** GOT STABBED IN THE BACK BY THAT INSANE BUTCHER IN BLACK.
MY WHAT?
MY DAUGHTER?!
SHIT.
I THOUGHT YOU KNEW. YOU REALLY NEED TO TALK TO CRANE BEFORE YOU DO ANYTHING...

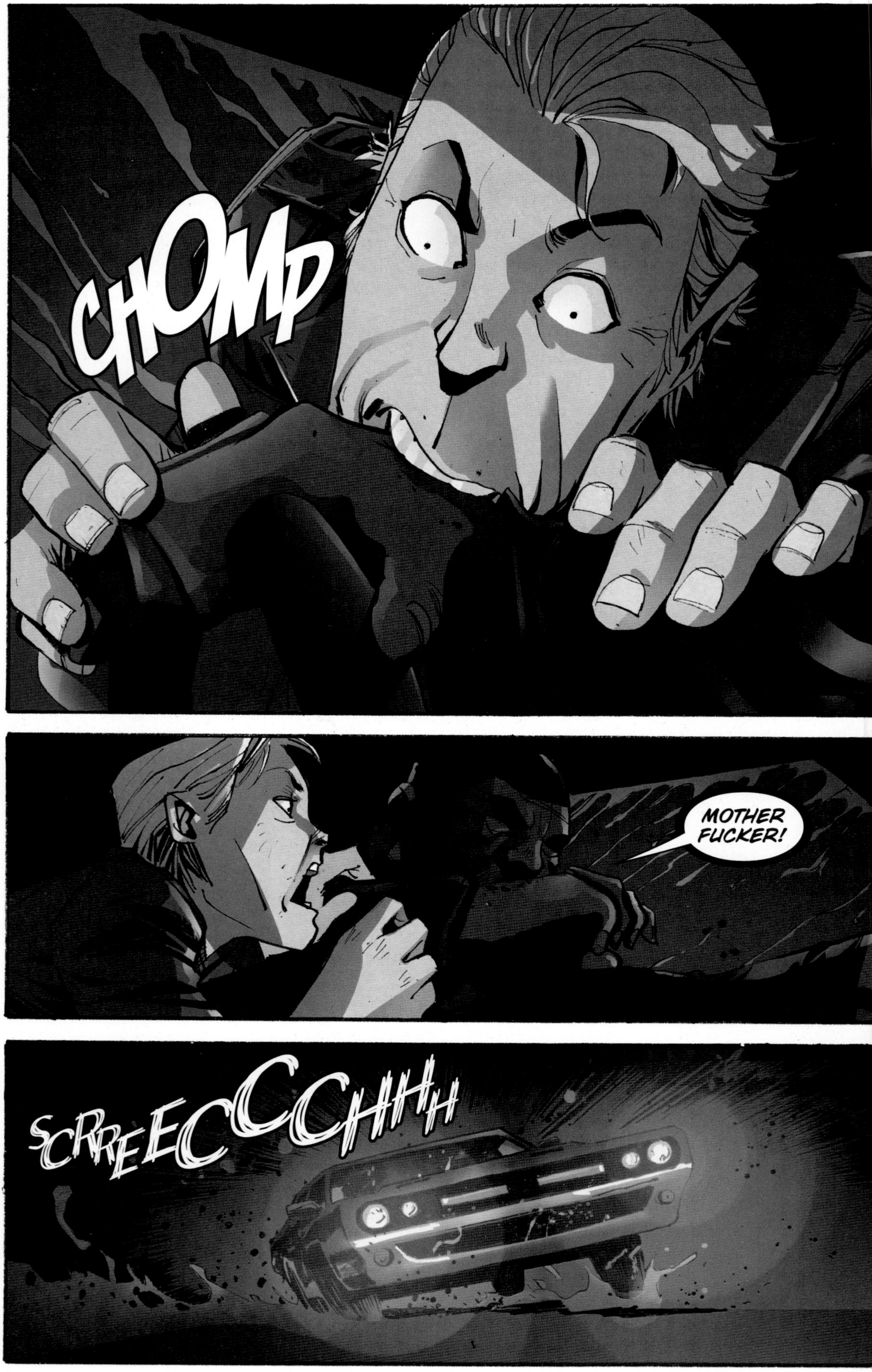
CHOMP
MOTHER FUCKER!
SCRREECCCHHHH

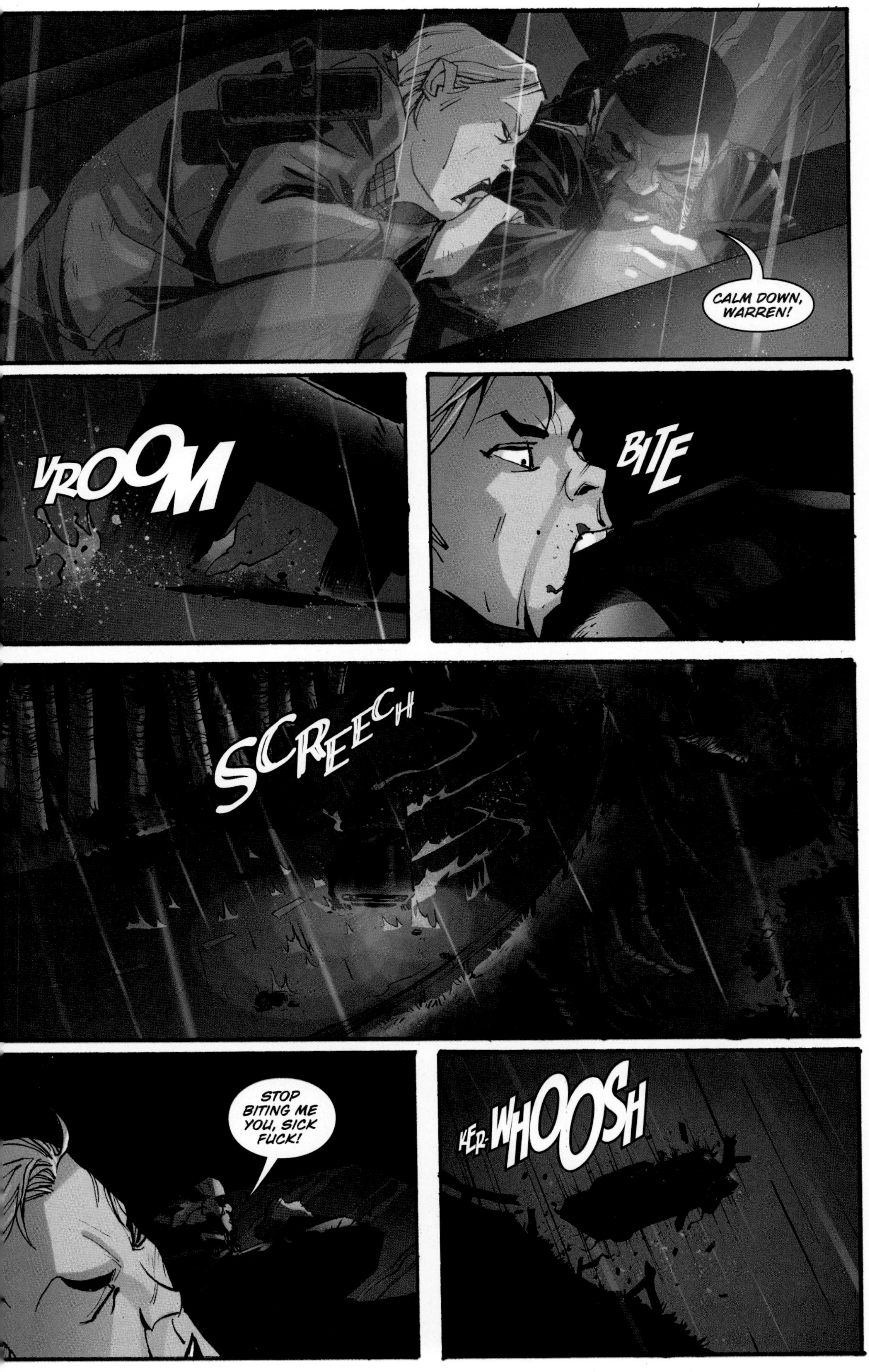
CALM DOWN, WARREN!
VROOOM
BITE
SCREECH
STOP BITING ME YOU, SICK FUCK!
KER-WHOOSH

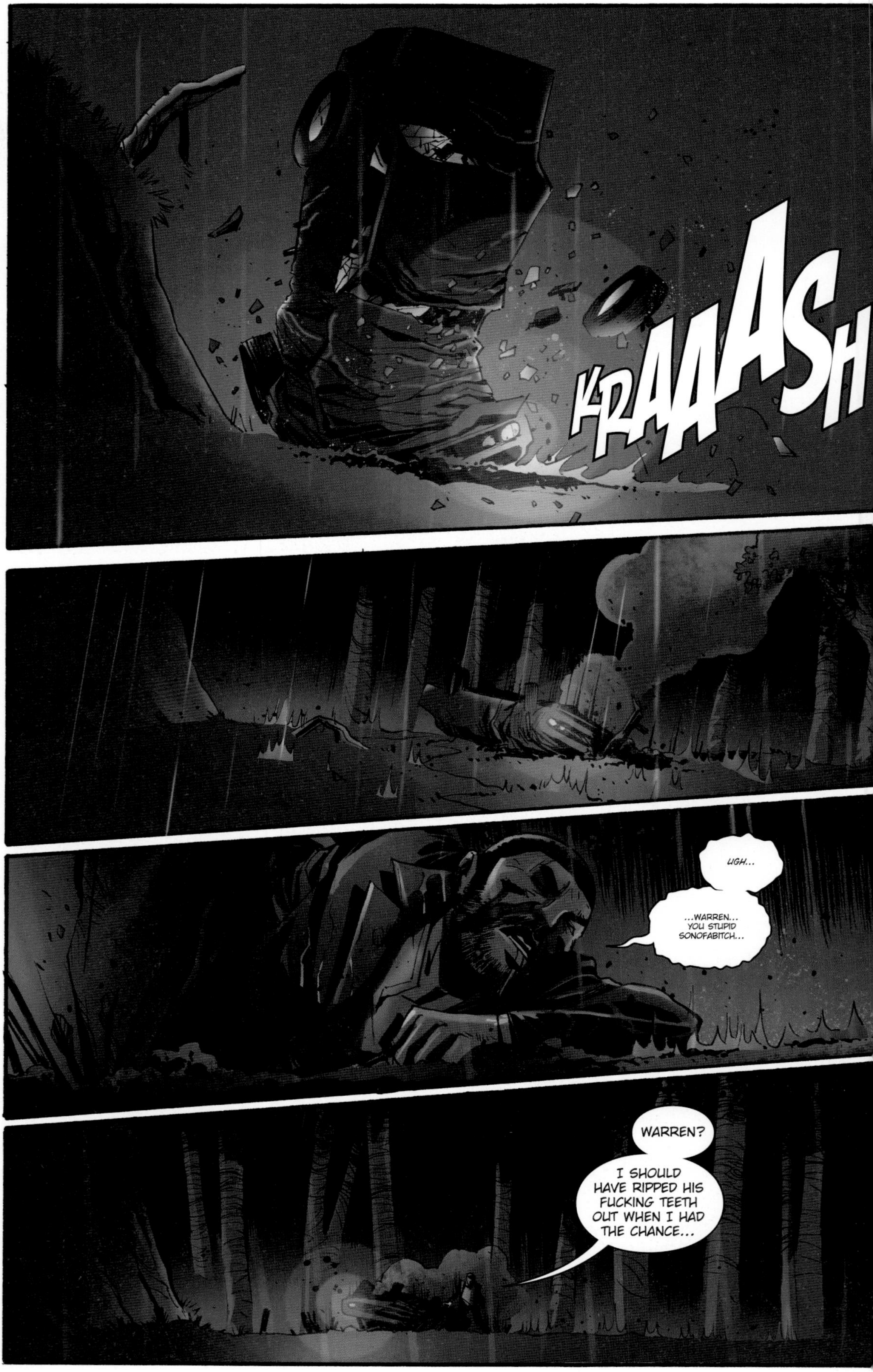
KRAAASH
UGH...
...WARREN... YOU STUPID SONOFABITCH...
WARREN?
I SHOULD HAVE RIPPED HIS FUCKING TEETH OUT WHEN I HAD THE CHANCE...

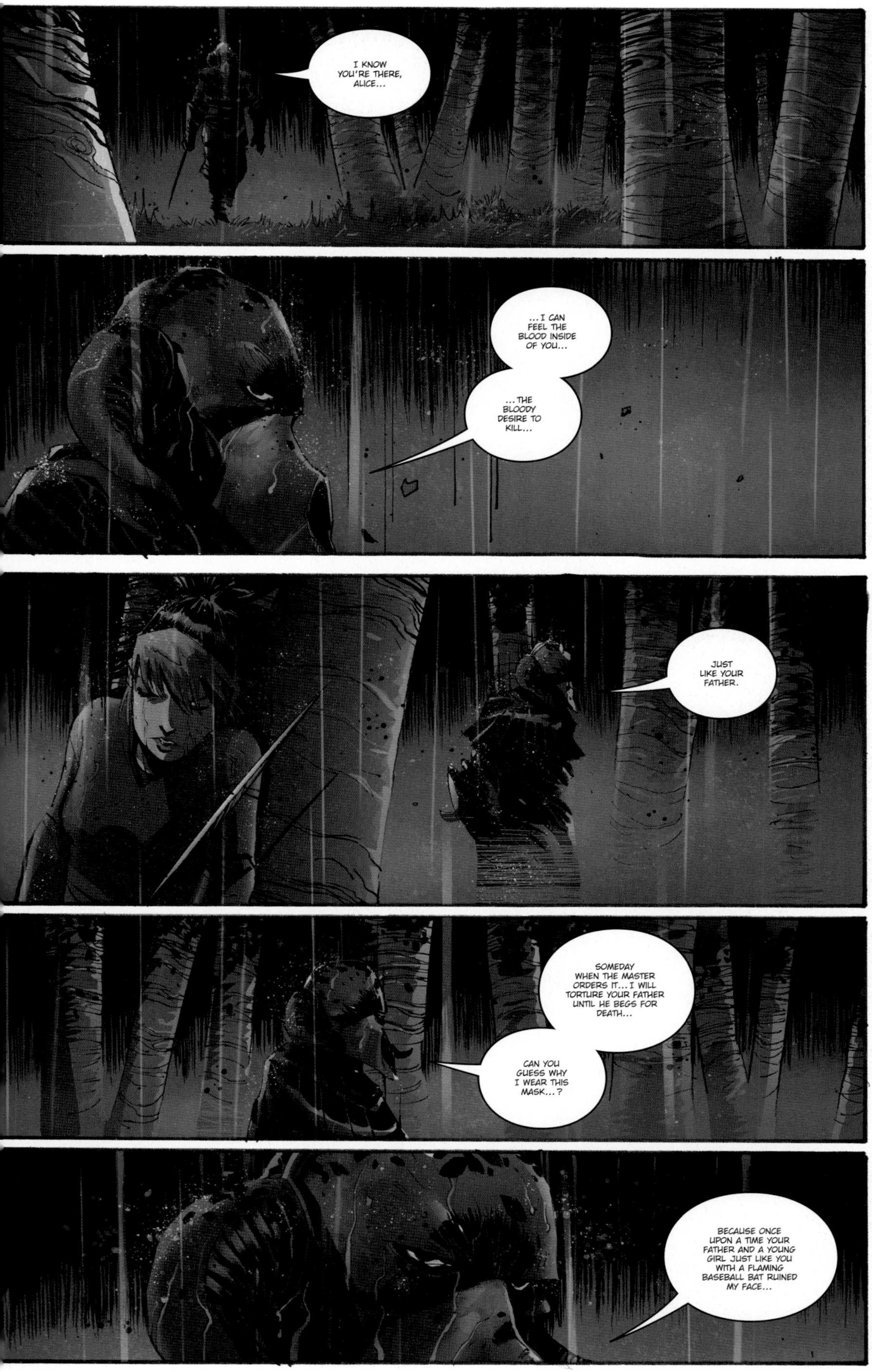
I KNOW YOU'RE THERE, ALICE...
...I CAN FEEL THE BLOOD INSIDE OF YOU...
...THE BLOODY DESIRE TO KILL...
JUST LIKE YOUR FATHER.
SOMEDAY WHEN THE MASTER ORDERS IT... I WILL TORTURE YOUR FATHER UNTIL HE BEGS FOR DEATH...
CAN YOU GUESS WHY I WEAR THIS MASK...?
BECAUSE ONCE UPON A TIME YOUR FATHER AND A YOUNG GIRL JUST LIKE YOU WITH A FLAMING BASEBALL BAT RUINED MY FACE...

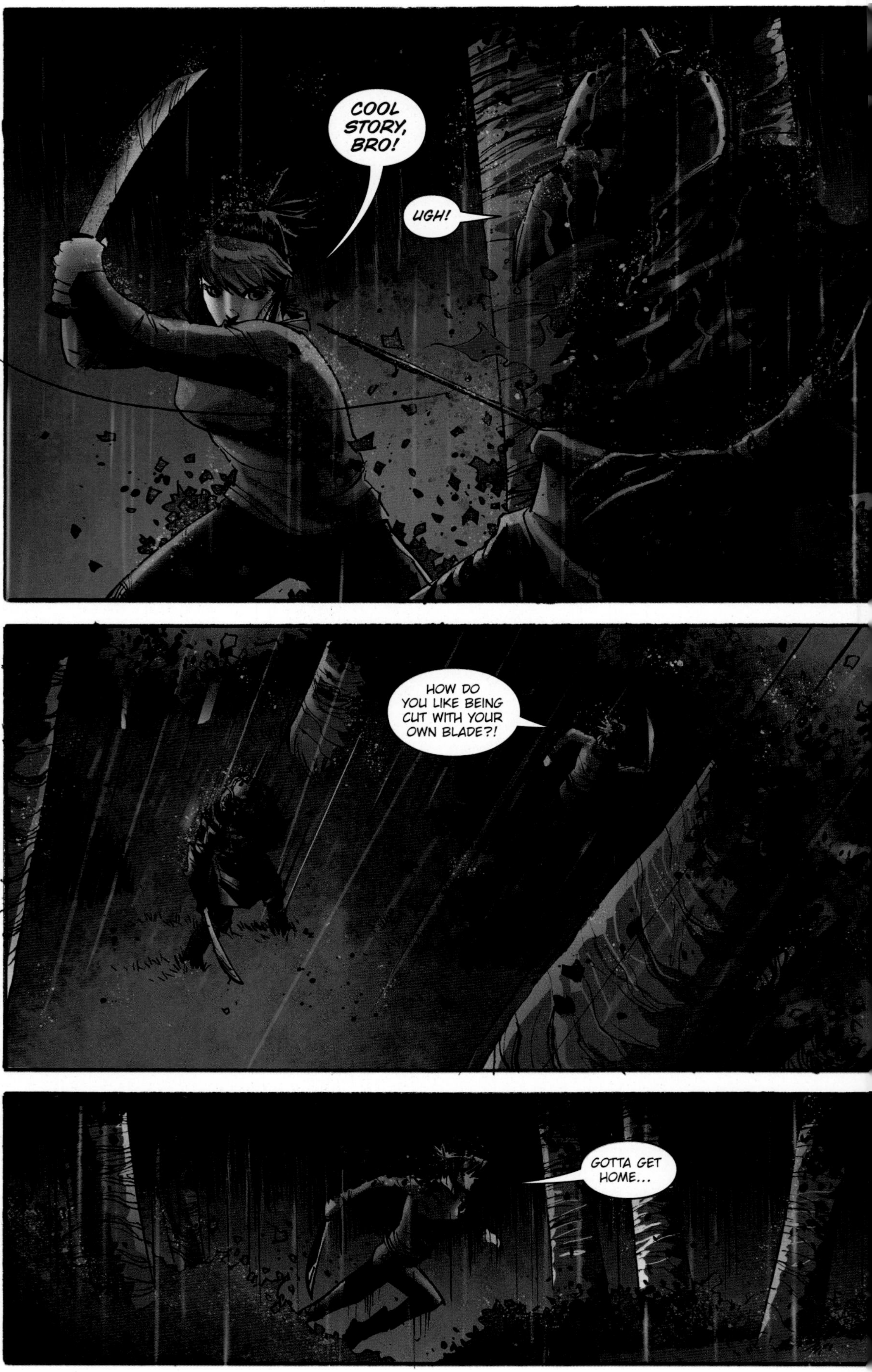
COOL STORY, BRO!
UGH!
HOW DO YOU LIKE BEING CUT WITH YOUR OWN BLADE?!
GOTTA GET HOME...

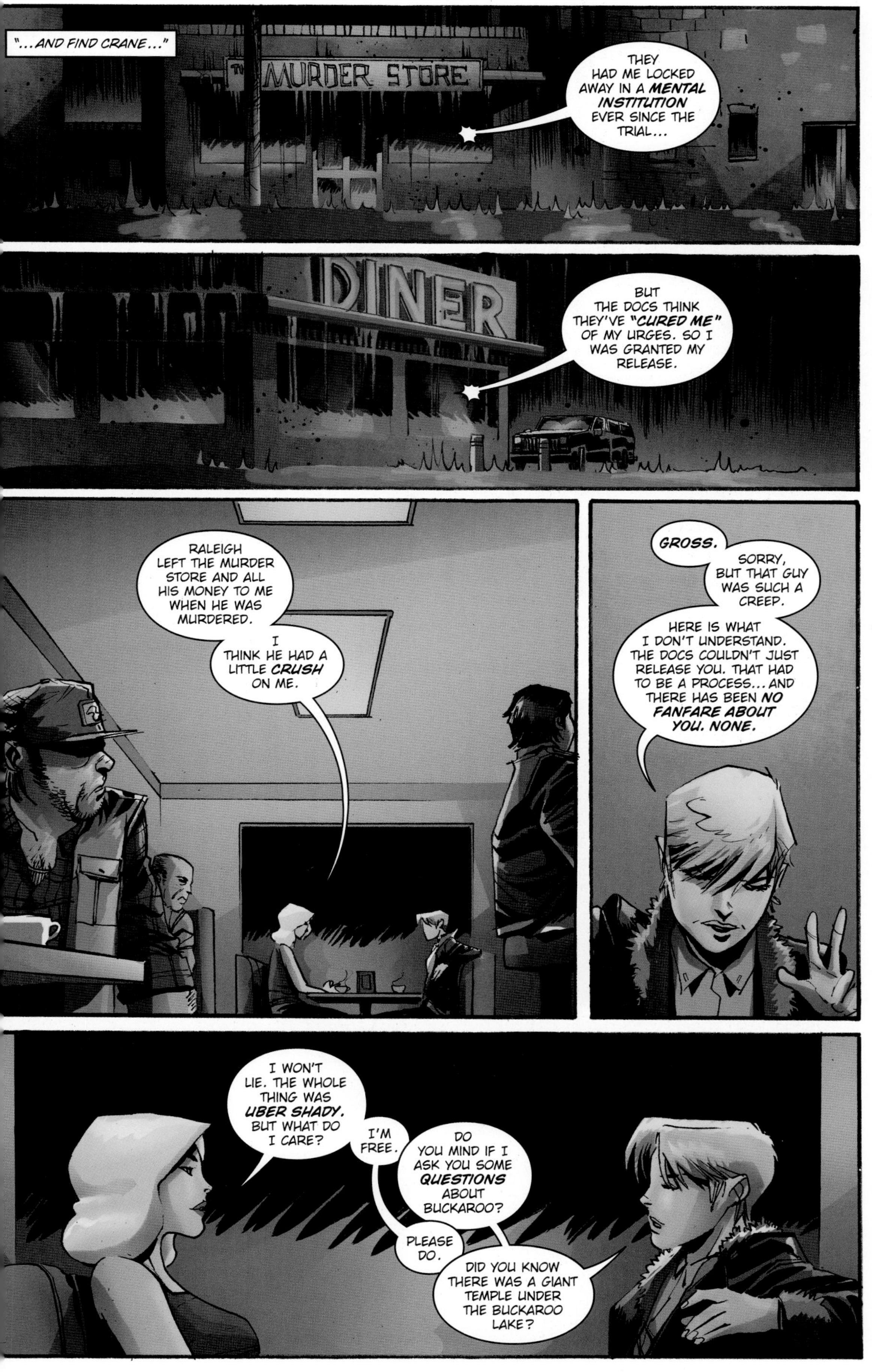
"...AND FIND CRANE..."
MURDER STORE
THEY HAD ME LOCKED AWAY IN A MENTAL INSTITUTION EVER SINCE THE TRIAL...
DINER
BUT THE DOCS THINK THEY'VE "CURED ME" OF MY URGES. SO I WAS GRANTED MY RELEASE.
RALEIGH LEFT THE MURDER STORE AND ALL HIS MONEY TO ME WHEN HE WAS MURDERED.
I THINK HE HAD A LITTLE CRUSH ON ME.
GROSS.
SORRY, BUT THAT GUY WAS SUCH A CREEP.
HERE IS WHAT I DON'T UNDERSTAND. THE DOCS COULDN'T JUST RELEASE YOU. THAT HAD TO BE A PROCESS... AND THERE HAS BEEN NO FANFARE ABOUT YOU. NONE.
I WON'T LIE. THE WHOLE THING WAS UBER SHADY. BUT WHAT DO I CARE?
I'M FREE.
DO YOU MIND IF I ASK YOU SOME QUESTIONS ABOUT BUCKAROO?
PLEASE DO.
DID YOU KNOW THERE WAS A GIANT TEMPLE UNDER THE BUCKAROO LAKE?

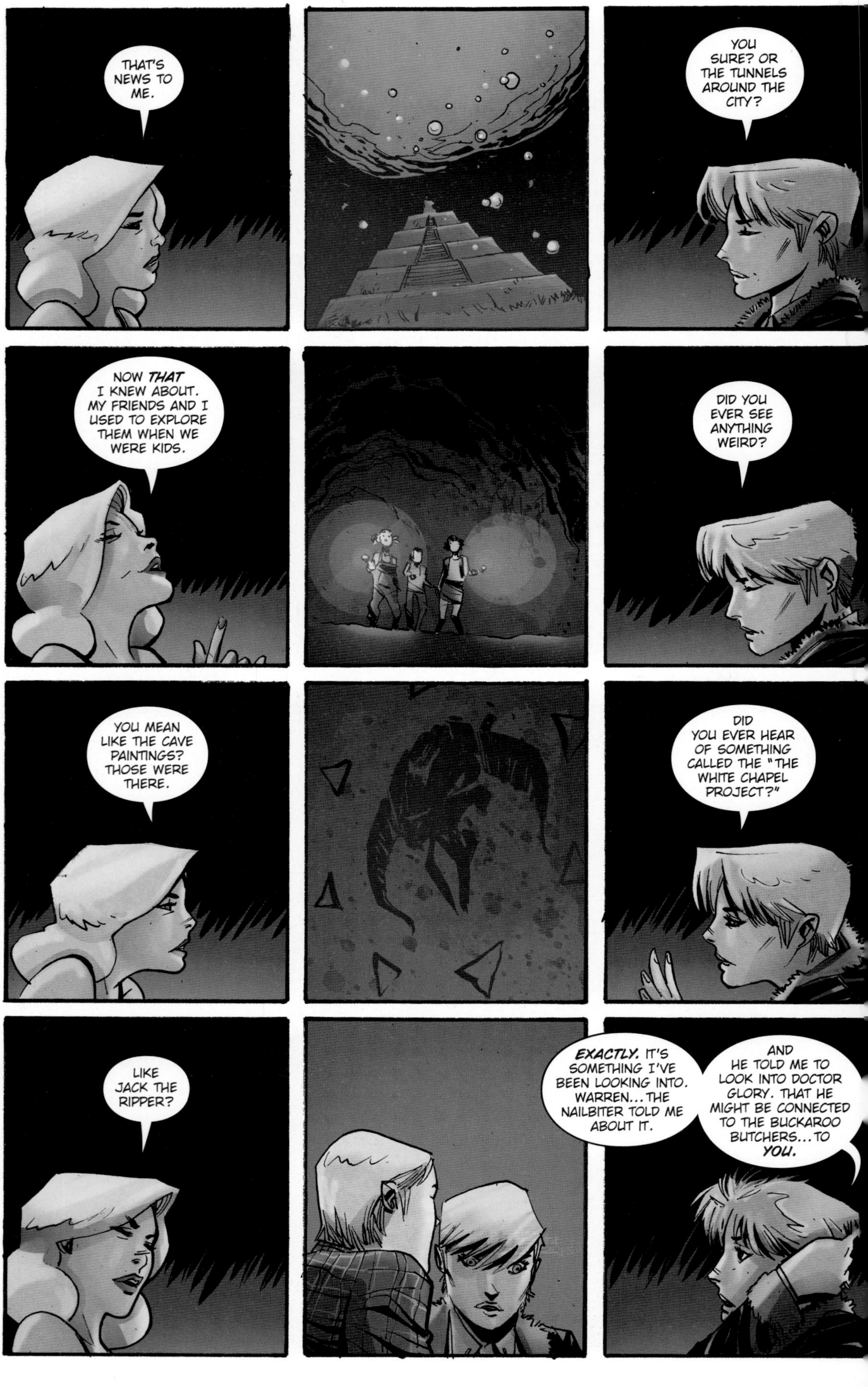
THAT'S NEWS TO ME.
YOU SURE? OR THE TUNNELS AROUND THE CITY?
NOW THAT I KNEW ABOUT. MY FRIENDS AND I USED TO EXPLORE THEM WHEN WE WERE KIDS.
DID YOU EVER SEE ANYTHING WEIRD?
YOU MEAN LIKE THE CAVE PAINTINGS? THOSE WERE THERE.
DID YOU EVER HEAR OF SOMETHING CALLED THE "THE WHITE CHAPEL PROJECT?"
LIKE JACK THE RIPPER?
EXACTLY. IT'S SOMETHING I'VE BEEN LOOKING INTO. WARREN... THE NAILBITER TOLD ME ABOUT IT.
AND HE TOLD ME TO LOOK INTO DOCTOR GLORY. THAT HE MIGHT BE CONNECTED TO THE BUCKAROO BUTCHERS... TO YOU.

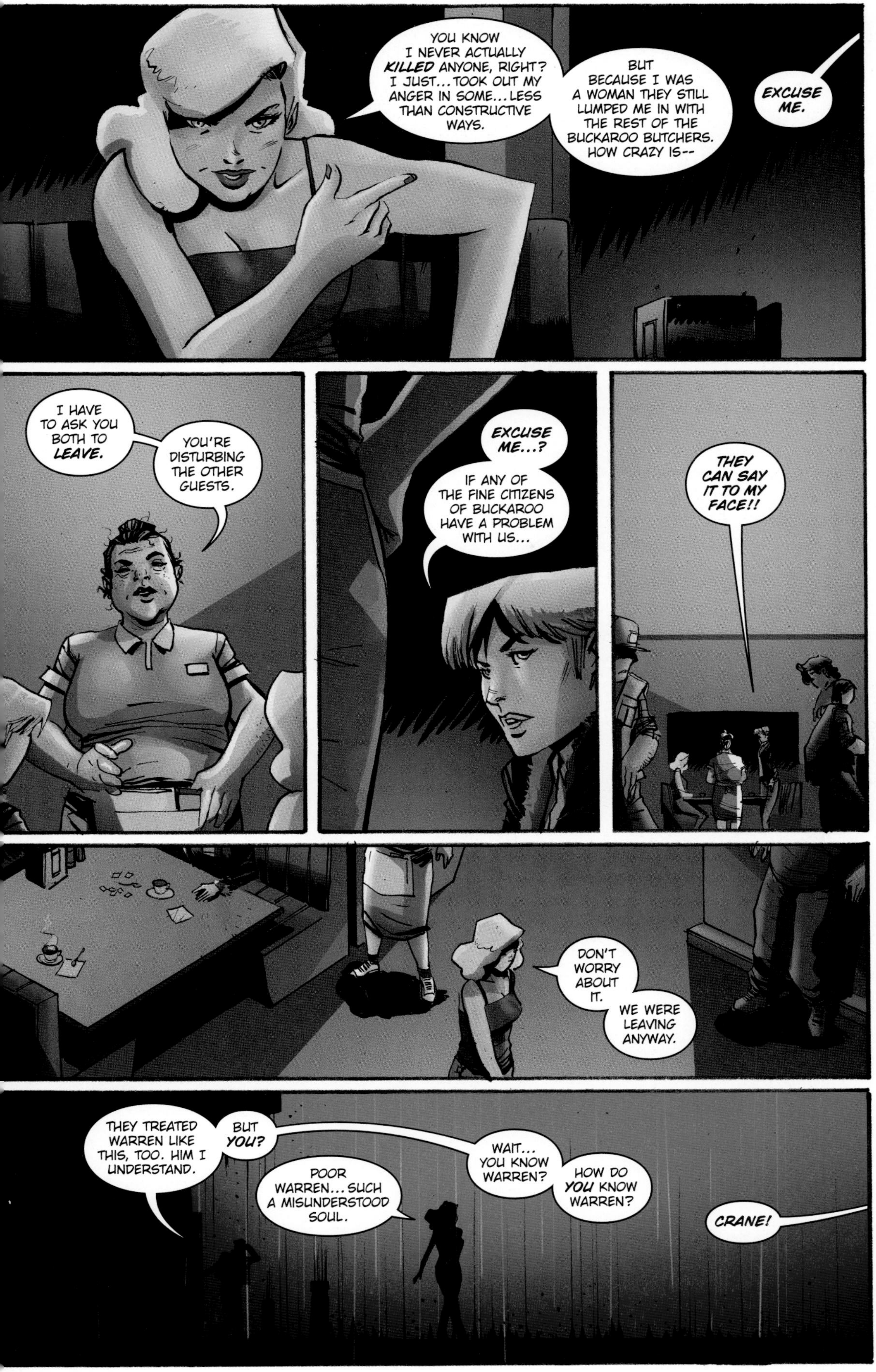

YOU KNOW I NEVER ACTUALLY KILLED ANYONE, RIGHT? I JUST... TOOK OUT MY ANGER IN SOME... LESS THAN CONSTRUCTIVE WAYS.
BUT BECAUSE I WAS A WOMAN THEY STILL LUMPED ME IN WITH THE REST OF THE BUCKAROO BUTCHERS. HOW CRAZY IS--
EXCUSE ME.
I HAVE TO ASK YOU BOTH TO LEAVE.
YOU'RE DISTURBING THE OTHER GUESTS.
EXCUSE ME...?
IF ANY OF THE FINE CITIZENS OF BUCKAROO HAVE A PROBLEM WITH US...
THEY CAN SAY IT TO MY FACE!!
DON'T WORRY ABOUT IT.
WE WERE LEAVING ANYWAY.
THEY TREATED WARREN LIKE THIS, TOO. HIM I UNDERSTAND.
BUT YOU?
POOR WARREN... SUCH A MISUNDERSTOOD SOUL.
WAIT... YOU KNOW WARREN?
HOW DO YOU KNOW WARREN?
CRANE!

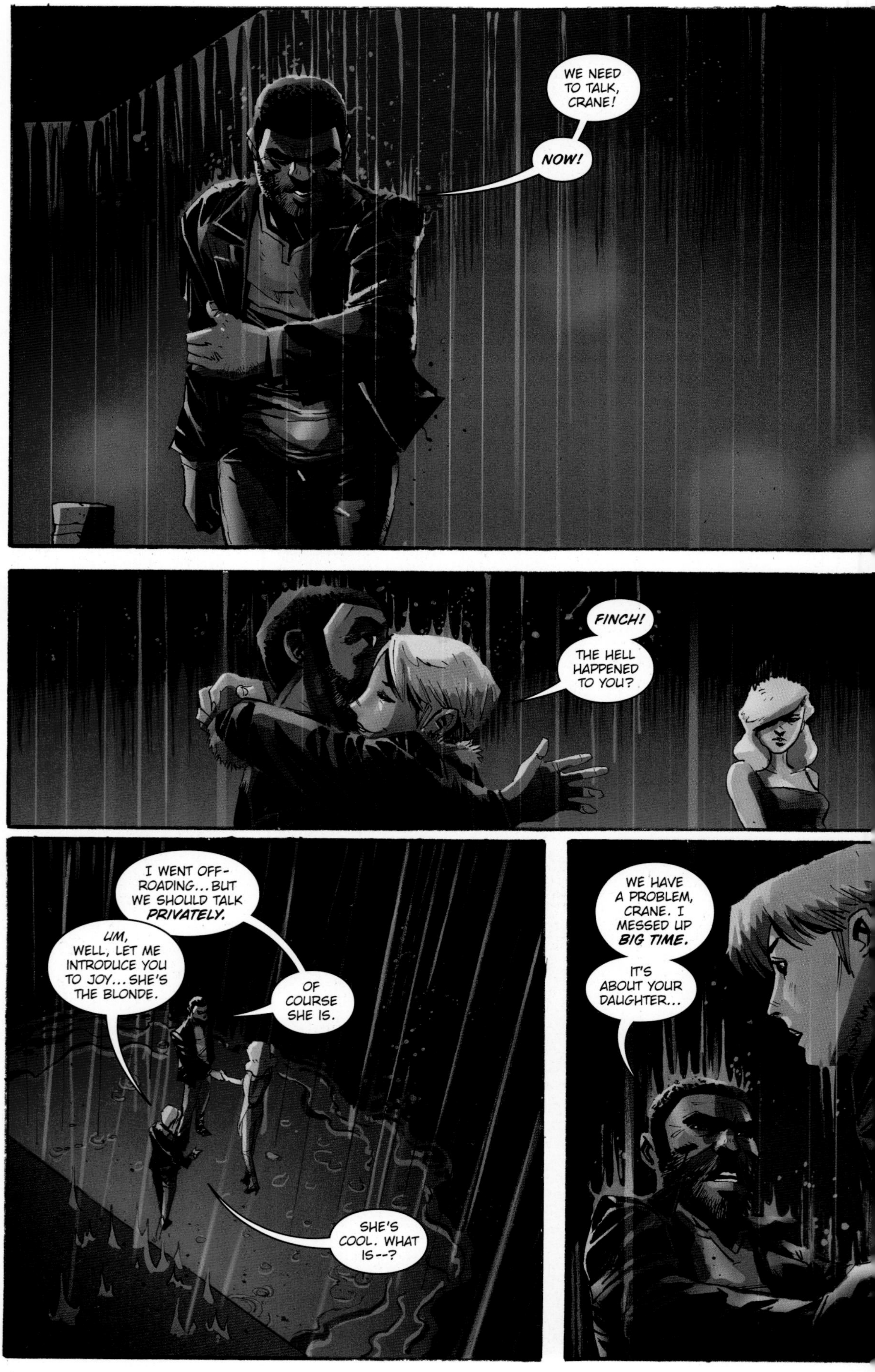
WE NEED TO TALK, CRANE!
NOW!
FINCH!
THE HELL HAPPENED TO YOU?
I WENT OFF-ROADING... BUT WE SHOULD TALK PRIVATELY.
UM, WELL, LET ME INTRODUCE YOU TO JOY... SHE'S THE BLONDE.
OF COURSE SHE IS.
SHE'S COOL. WHAT IS--?
WE HAVE A PROBLEM, CRANE. I MESSED UP BIG TIME.
IT'S ABOUT YOUR DAUGHTER...

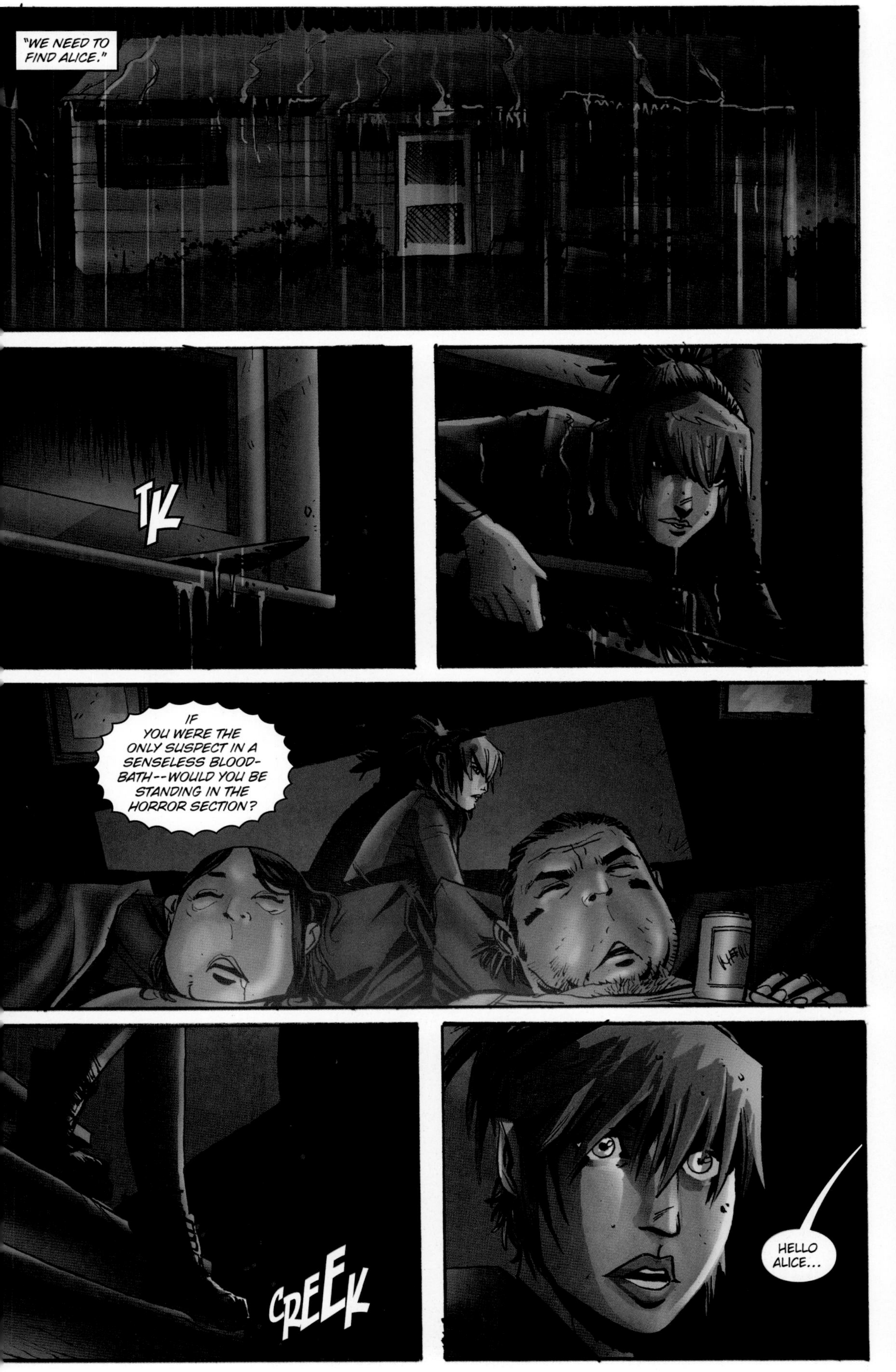
"WE NEED TO FIND ALICE."
TK
IF YOU WERE THE ONLY SUSPECT IN A SENSELESS BLOOD-BATH--WOULD YOU BE STANDING IN THE HORROR SECTION?
CREEK
HELLO ALICE...

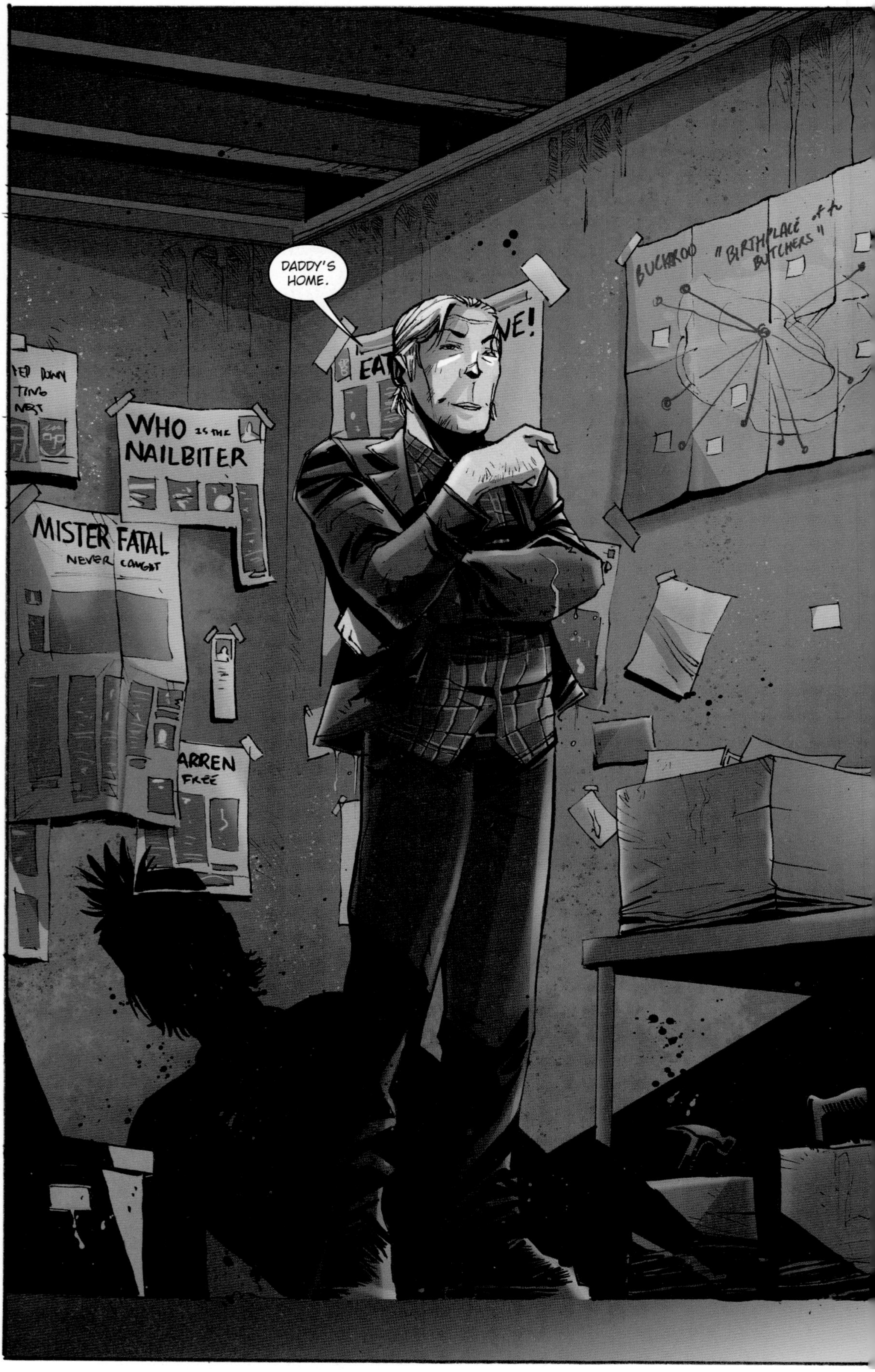
DADDY'S HOME.
WHO IS THE NAILBITER
MISTER FATAL
NEVER CAUGHT
ARREN
FREE
BUCKAROO
"BIRTHPLACE of the BUTCHERS"

ISSUE TWENTY-THREE

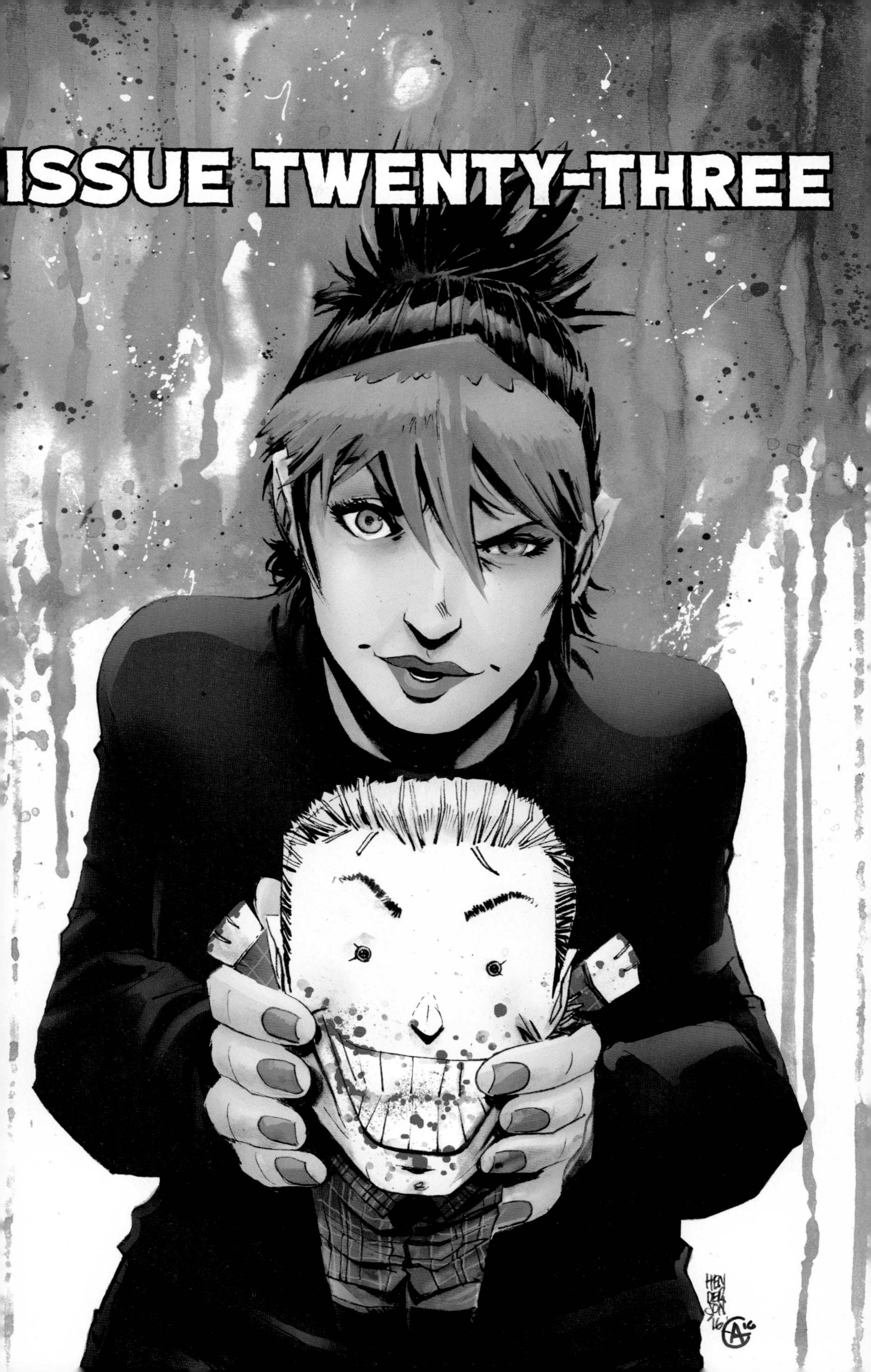

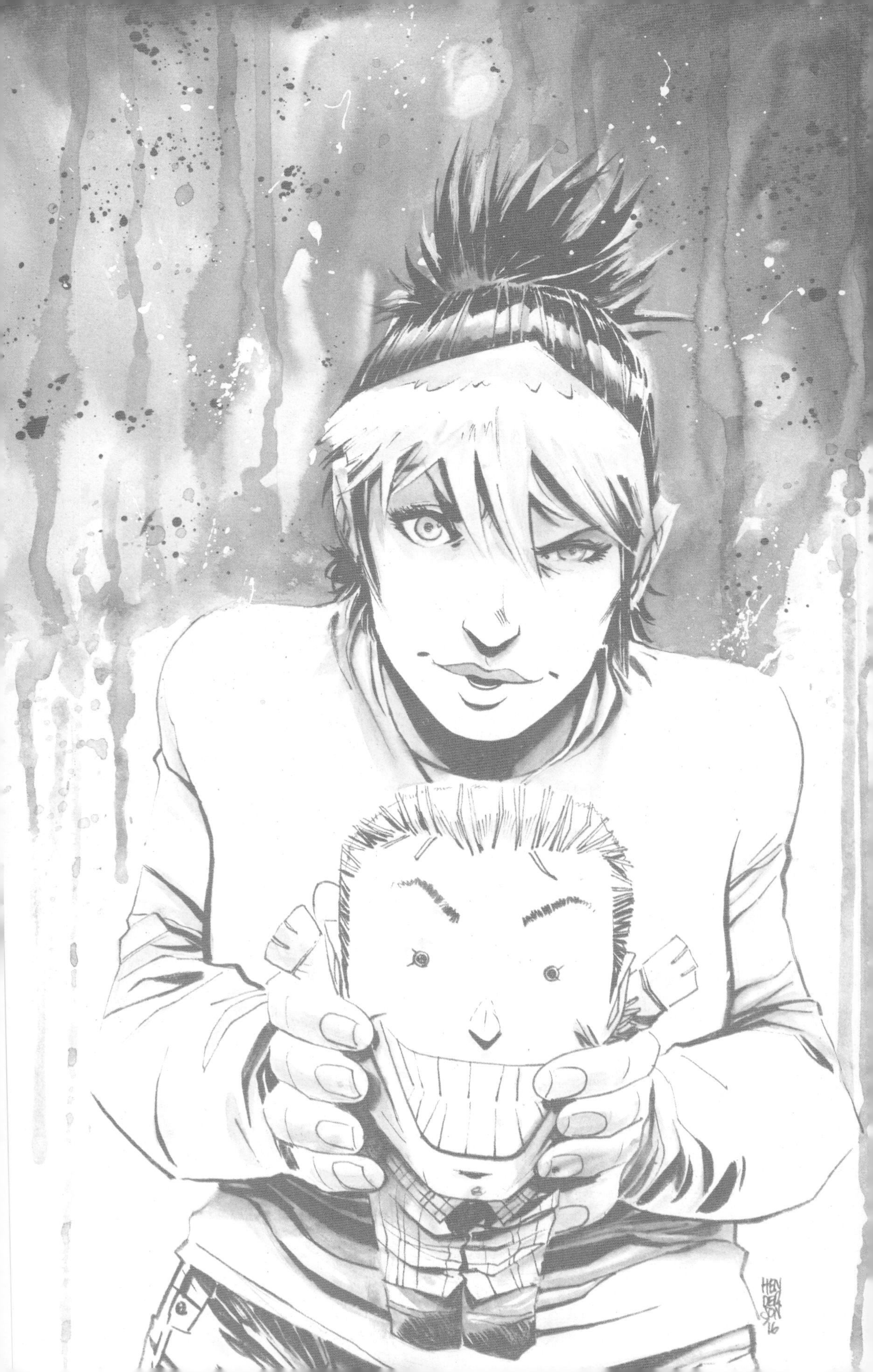

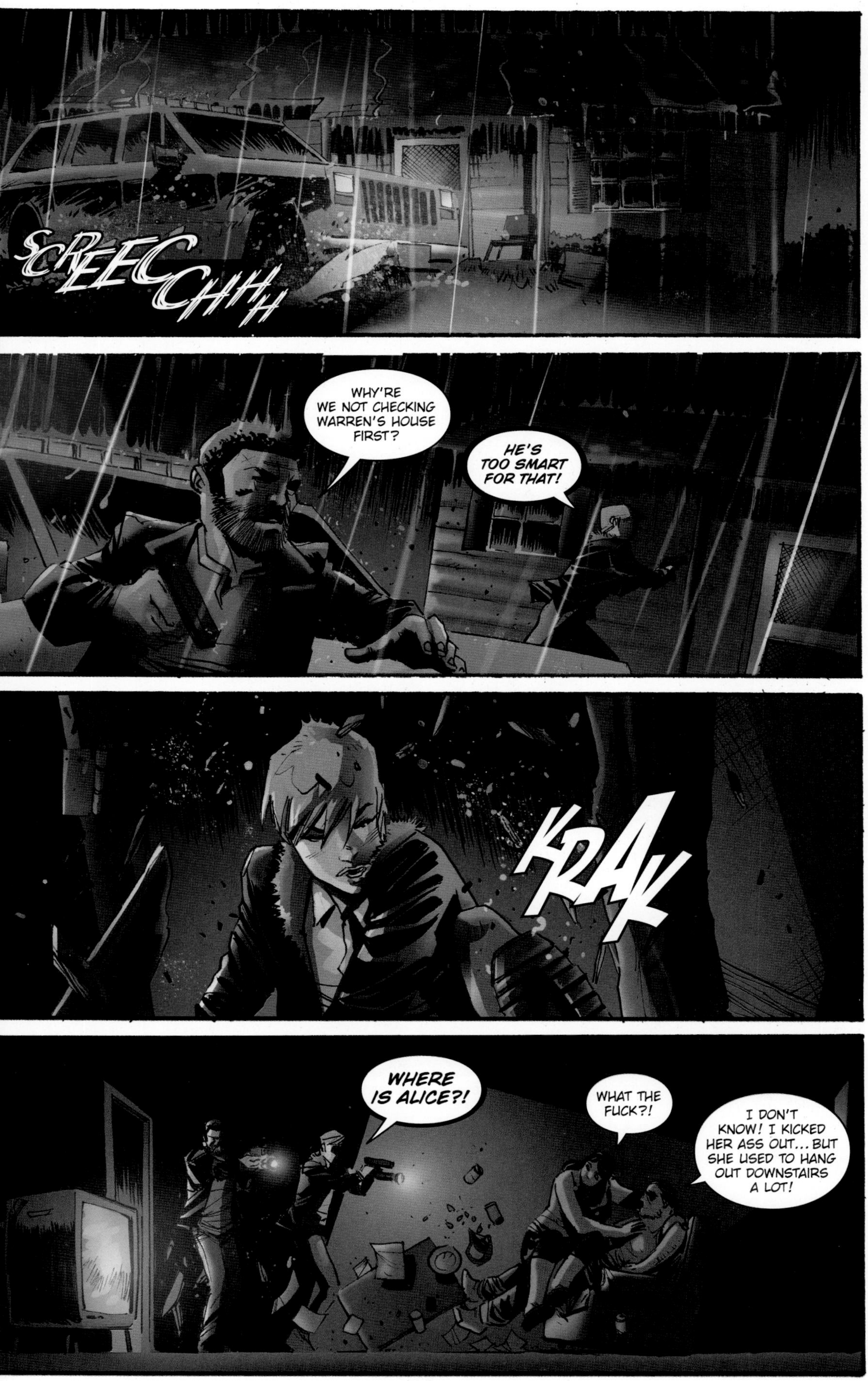
SCREECHHH
WHY'RE WE NOT CHECKING WARREN'S HOUSE FIRST?
HE'S TOO SMART FOR THAT!
KRAK
WHERE IS ALICE?!
WHAT THE FUCK?!
I DON'T KNOW! I KICKED HER ASS OUT... BUT SHE USED TO HANG OUT DOWNSTAIRS A LOT!

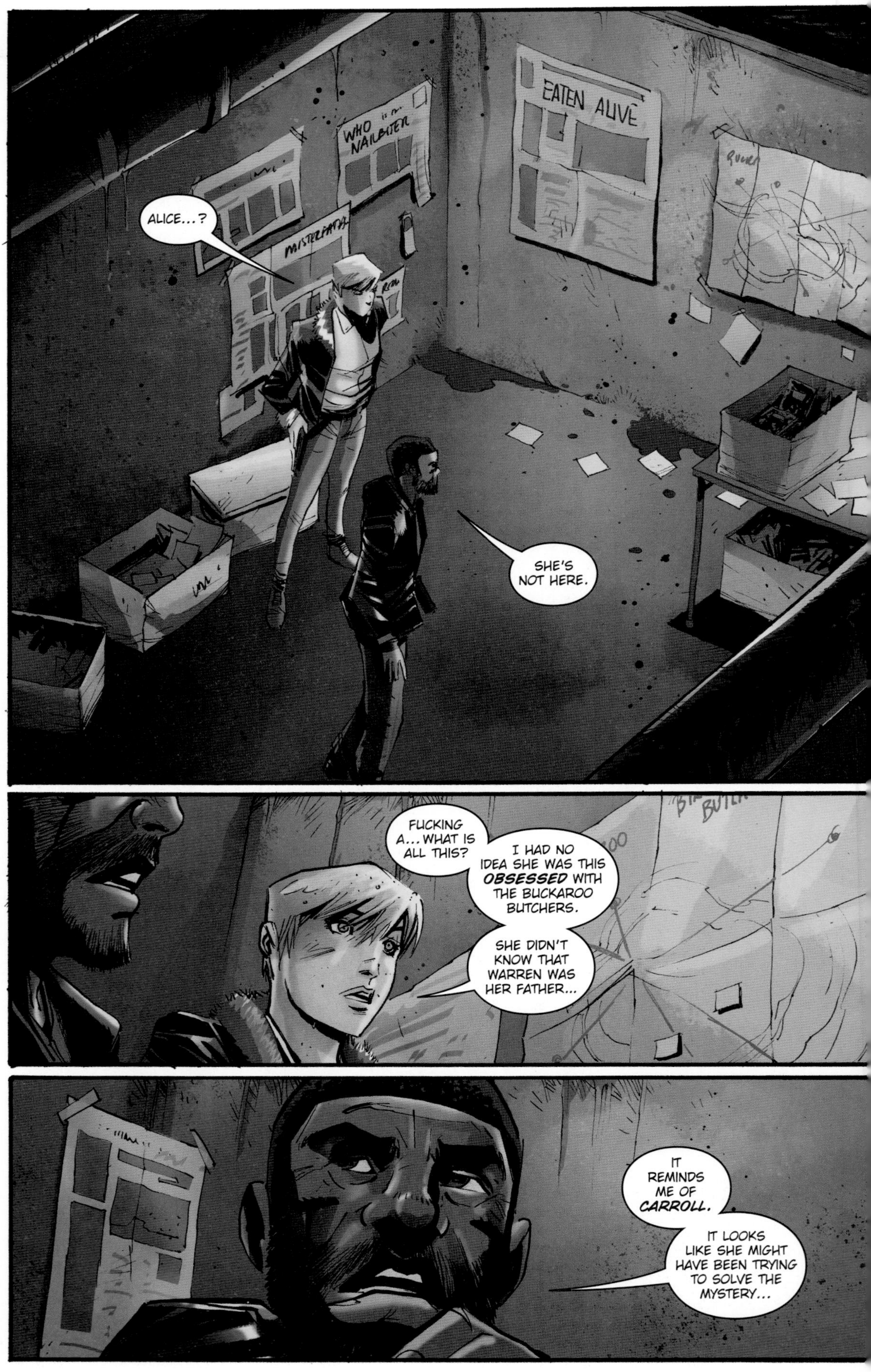
EATEN ALIVE
WHO is the NAILBITER
ALICE...?
SHE'S NOT HERE.
FUCKING A... WHAT IS ALL THIS?
I HAD NO IDEA SHE WAS THIS OBSESSED WITH THE BUCKAROO BUTCHERS.
SHE DIDN'T KNOW THAT WARREN WAS HER FATHER...
IT REMINDS ME OF CARROLL.
IT LOOKS LIKE SHE MIGHT HAVE BEEN TRYING TO SOLVE THE MYSTERY...

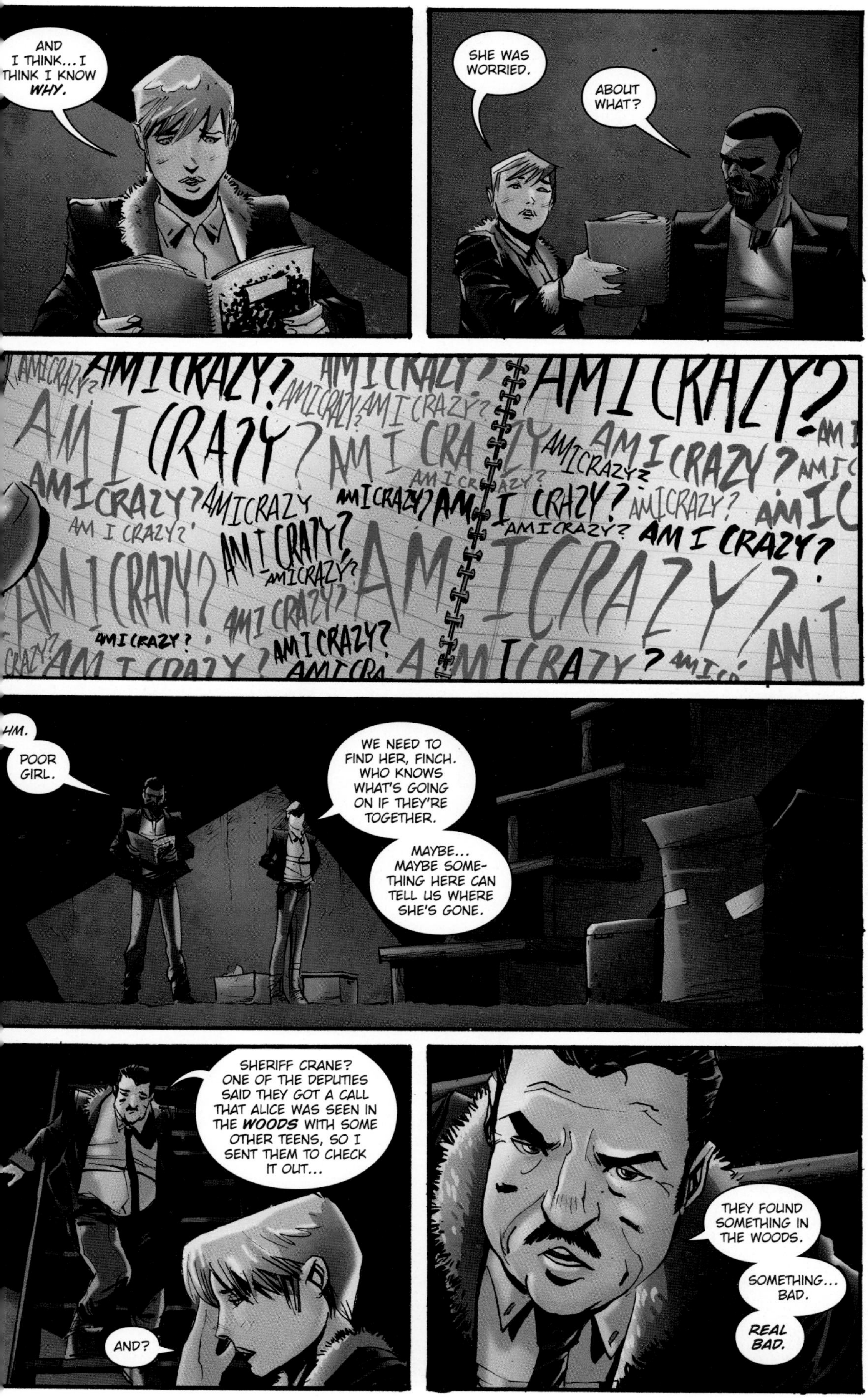
AND I THINK... I THINK I KNOW WHY.
SHE WAS WORRIED.
ABOUT WHAT?
AM I CRAZY? AM I CRAZY? AM I CRAZY? AM I CRAZY? AM I CRAZY? AM I CRAZY? AM I CRAZY? AM I CRAZY? AM I CRAZY? AM I CRAZY? AM I CRAZY? AM I CRAZY? AM I CRAZY? AM I CRAZY? AM I CRAZY? AM I CRAZY? AM I CRAZY? AM I CRAZY? AM I CRAZY?
HM.
POOR GIRL.
WE NEED TO FIND HER, FINCH. WHO KNOWS WHAT'S GOING ON IF THEY'RE TOGETHER.
MAYBE... MAYBE SOME-THING HERE CAN TELL US WHERE SHE'S GONE.
SHERIFF CRANE? ONE OF THE DEPUTIES SAID THEY GOT A CALL THAT ALICE WAS SEEN IN THE WOODS WITH SOME OTHER TEENS, SO I SENT THEM TO CHECK IT OUT...
AND?
THEY FOUND SOMETHING IN THE WOODS.
SOMETHING... BAD.
REAL BAD.

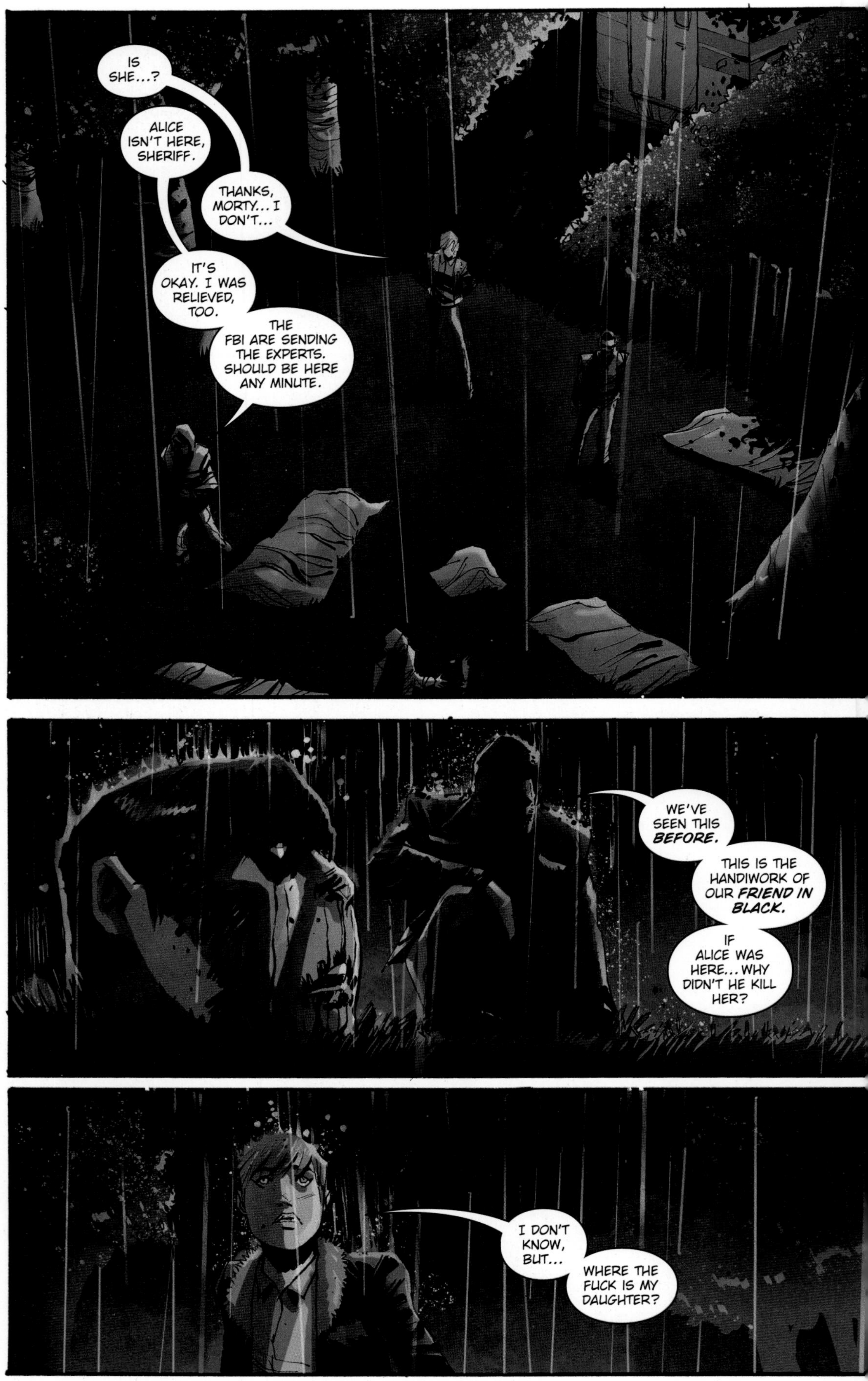

IS SHE...?
ALICE ISN'T HERE, SHERIFF.
THANKS, MORTY... I DON'T...
IT'S OKAY. I WAS RELIEVED, TOO.
THE FBI ARE SENDING THE EXPERTS. SHOULD BE HERE ANY MINUTE.
WE'VE SEEN THIS *BEFORE.*
THIS IS THE HANDIWORK OF OUR *FRIEND IN BLACK.*
IF ALICE WAS HERE... WHY DIDN'T HE KILL HER?
I DON'T KNOW, BUT...
WHERE THE FUCK IS MY DAUGHTER?

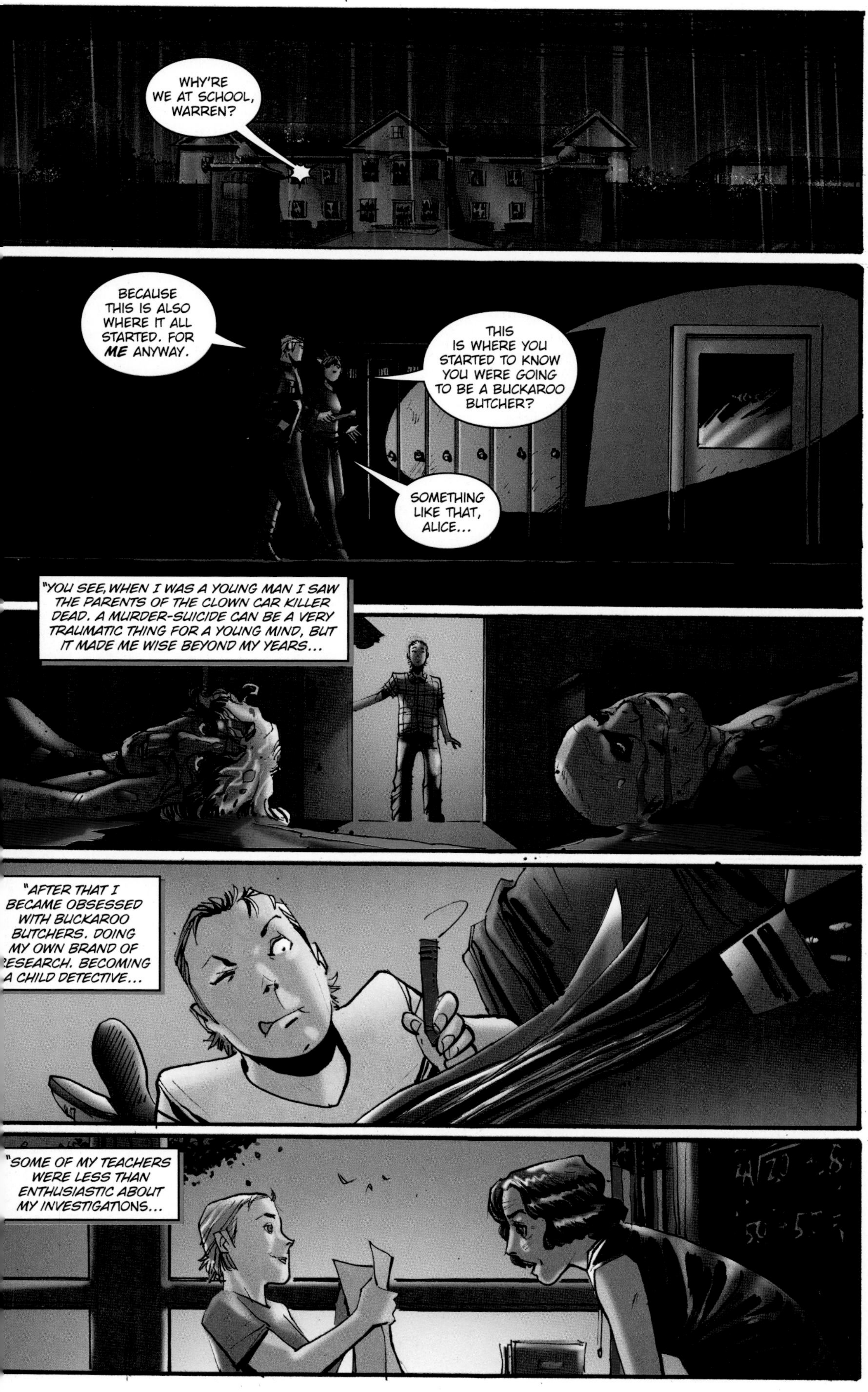
WHY'RE WE AT SCHOOL, WARREN?
BECAUSE THIS IS ALSO WHERE IT ALL STARTED. FOR ME ANYWAY.
THIS IS WHERE YOU STARTED TO KNOW YOU WERE GOING TO BE A BUCKAROO BUTCHER?
SOMETHING LIKE THAT, ALICE...
"YOU SEE, WHEN I WAS A YOUNG MAN I SAW THE PARENTS OF THE CLOWN CAR KILLER DEAD. A MURDER-SUICIDE CAN BE A VERY TRAUMATIC THING FOR A YOUNG MIND, BUT IT MADE ME WISE BEYOND MY YEARS...
"AFTER THAT I BECAME OBSESSED WITH BUCKAROO BUTCHERS. DOING MY OWN BRAND OF RESEARCH. BECOMING A CHILD DETECTIVE...
"SOME OF MY TEACHERS WERE LESS THAN ENTHUSIASTIC ABOUT MY INVESTIGATIONS...

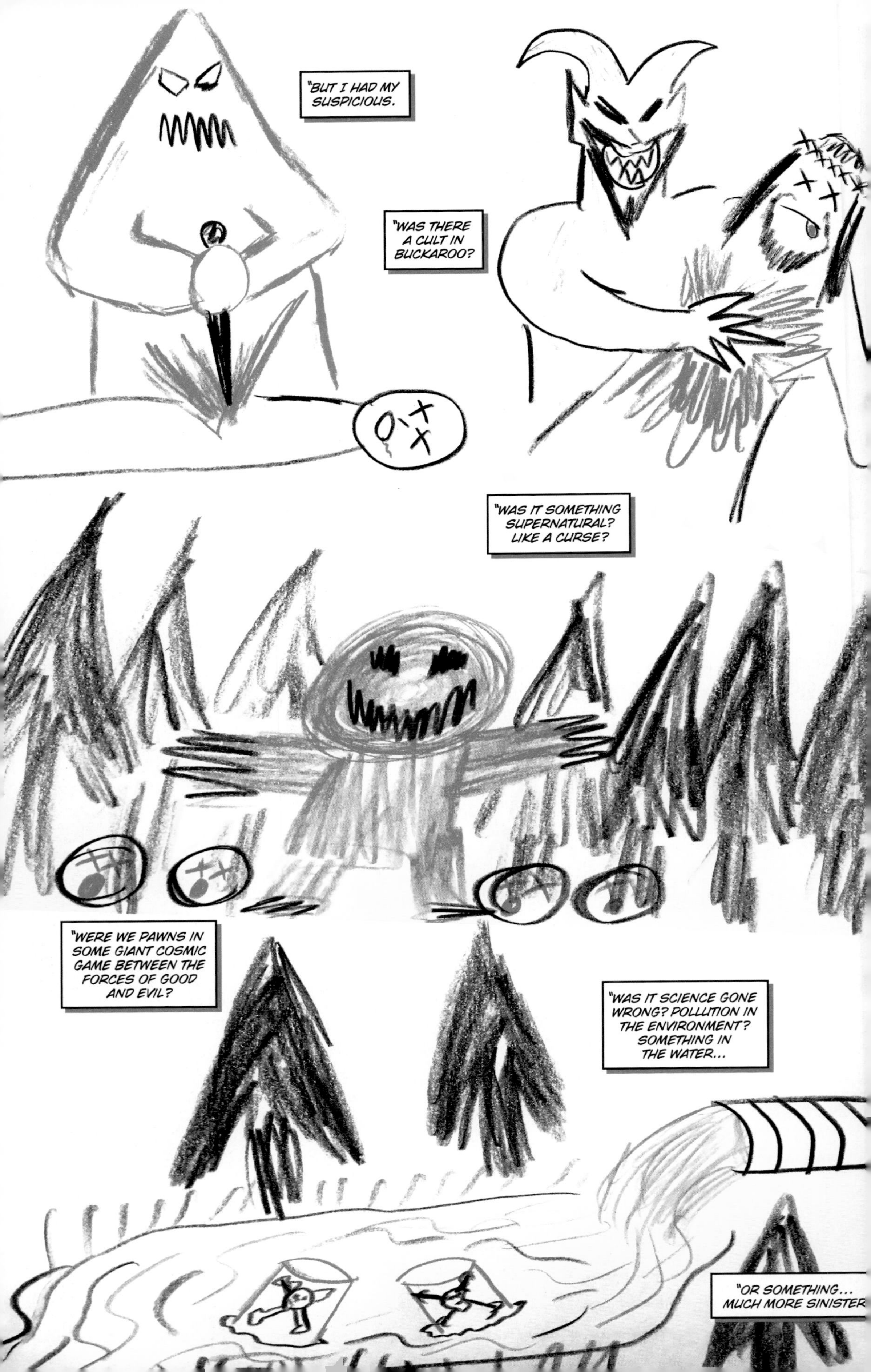
"BUT I HAD MY SUSPICIOUS.
"WAS THERE A CULT IN BUCKAROO?
"WAS IT SOMETHING SUPERNATURAL? LIKE A CURSE?
"WERE WE PAWNS IN SOME GIANT COSMIC GAME BETWEEN THE FORCES OF GOOD AND EVIL?
"WAS IT SCIENCE GONE WRONG? POLLUTION IN THE ENVIRONMENT? SOMETHING IN THE WATER...
"OR SOMETHING... MUCH MORE SINISTER

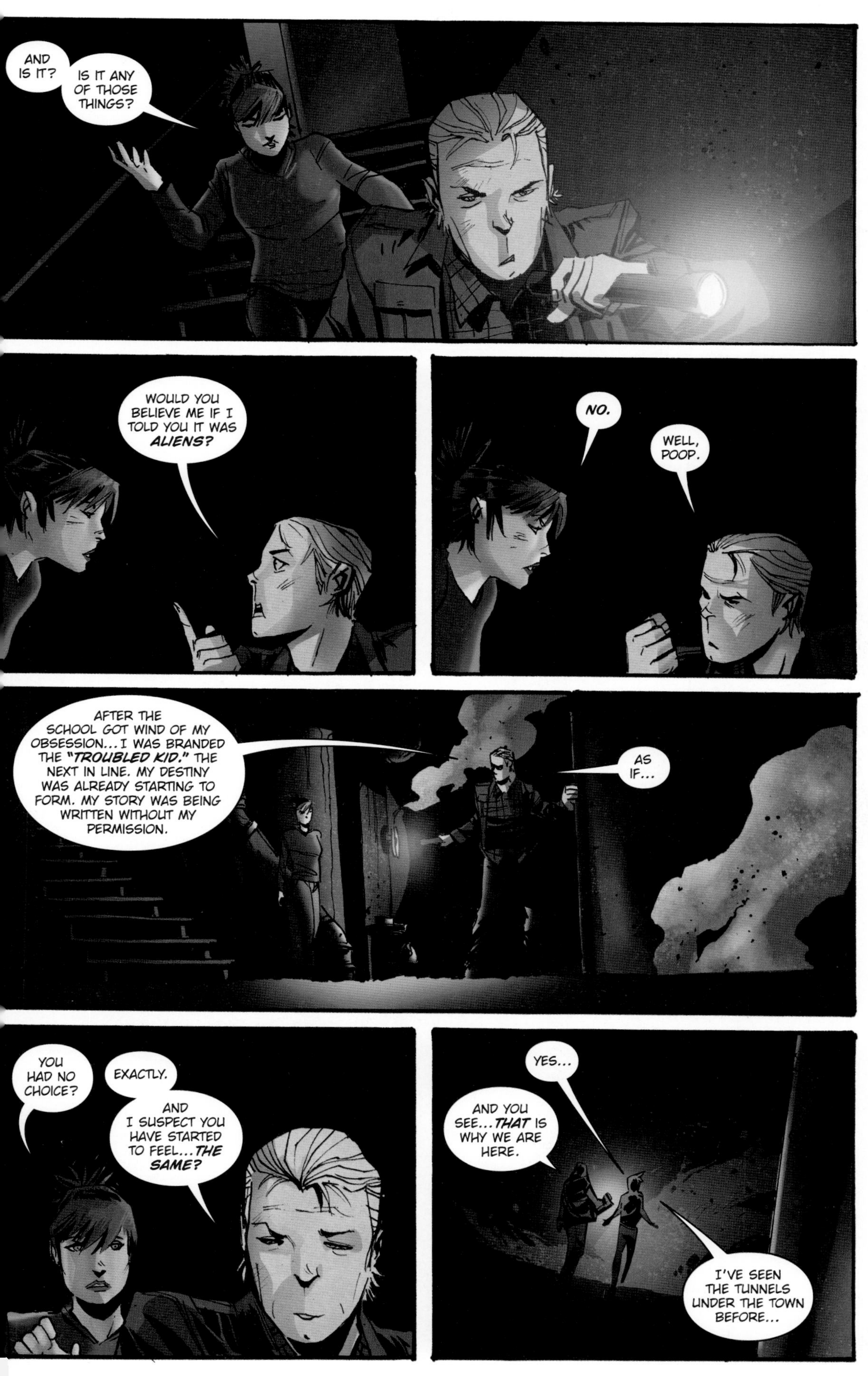
AND IS IT?
IS IT ANY OF THOSE THINGS?
WOULD YOU BELIEVE ME IF I TOLD YOU IT WAS *ALIENS?*
NO.
WELL, POOP.
AFTER THE SCHOOL GOT WIND OF MY OBSESSION... I WAS BRANDED THE *"TROUBLED KID."* THE NEXT IN LINE. MY DESTINY WAS ALREADY STARTING TO FORM. MY STORY WAS BEING WRITTEN WITHOUT MY PERMISSION.
AS IF...
YOU HAD NO CHOICE?
EXACTLY.
AND I SUSPECT YOU HAVE STARTED TO FEEL... *THE SAME?*
YES...
AND YOU SEE... *THAT* IS WHY WE ARE HERE.
I'VE SEEN THE TUNNELS UNDER THE TOWN BEFORE...

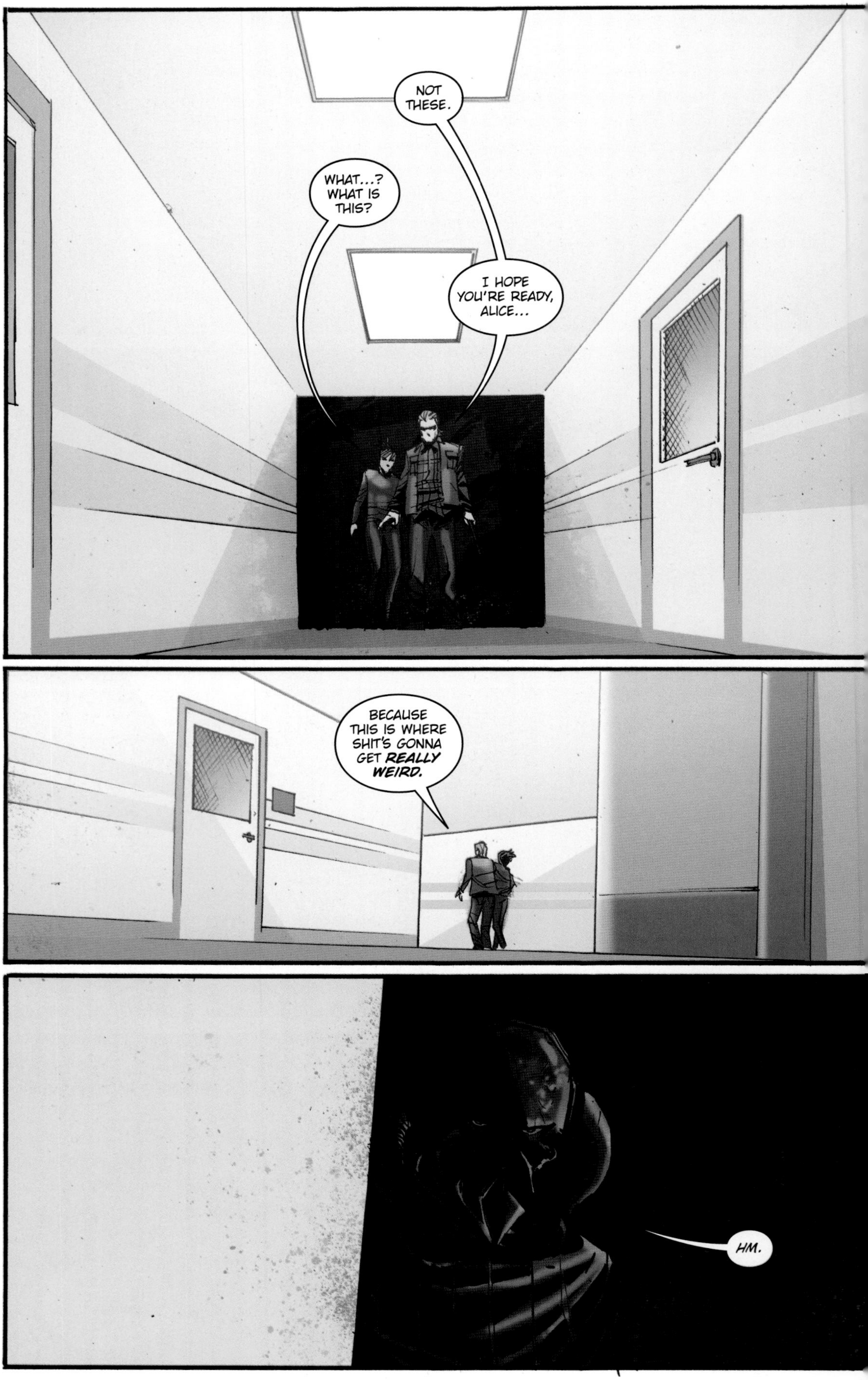
WHAT...? WHAT IS THIS?
NOT THESE.
I HOPE YOU'RE READY, ALICE...
BECAUSE THIS IS WHERE SHIT'S GONNA GET *REALLY WEIRD.*
HM.

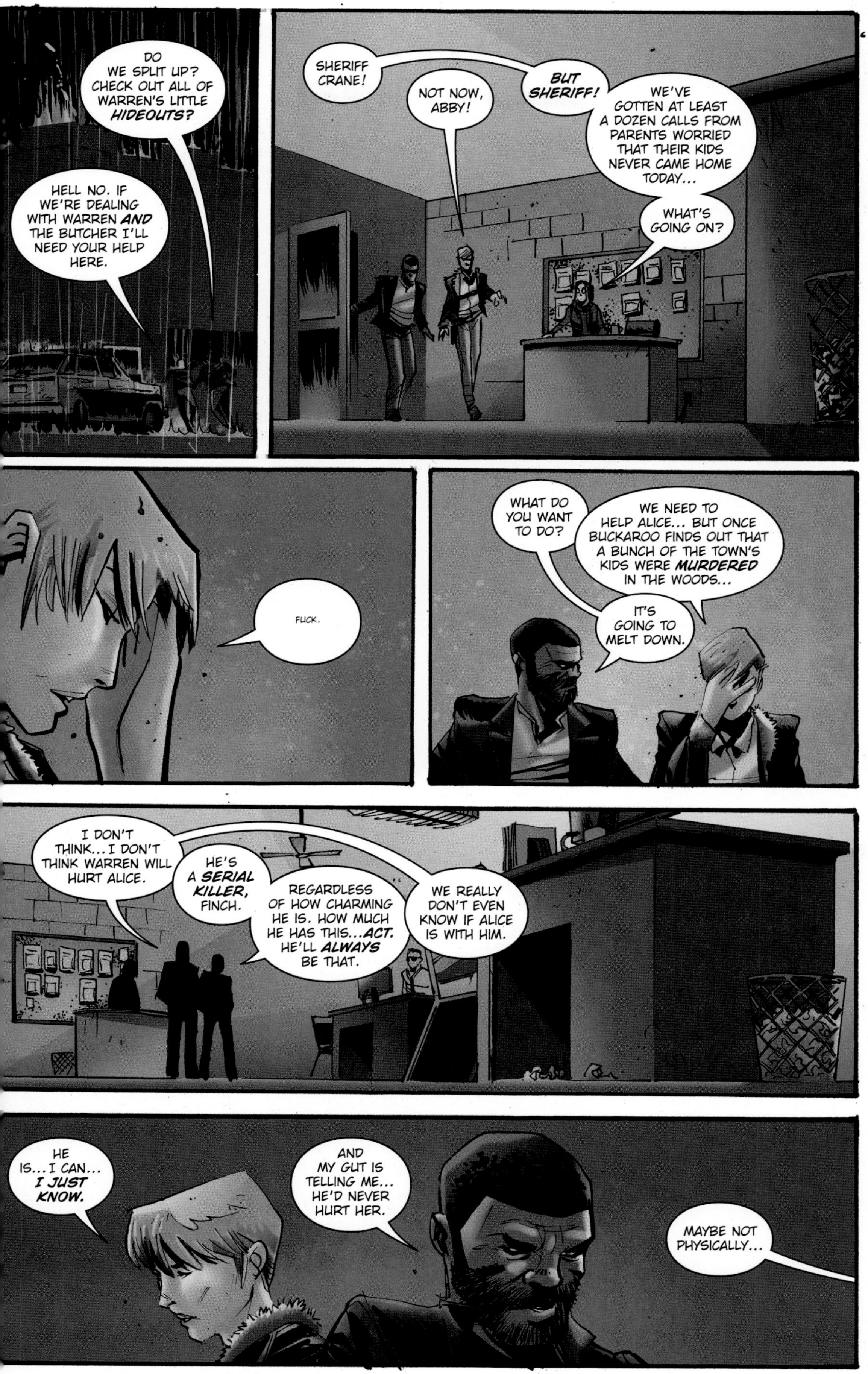
DO WE SPLIT UP? CHECK OUT ALL OF WARREN'S LITTLE HIDEOUTS?
HELL NO. IF WE'RE DEALING WITH WARREN AND THE BUTCHER I'LL NEED YOUR HELP HERE.
SHERIFF CRANE!
NOT NOW, ABBY!
BUT SHERIFF!
WE'VE GOTTEN AT LEAST A DOZEN CALLS FROM PARENTS WORRIED THAT THEIR KIDS NEVER CAME HOME TODAY...
WHAT'S GOING ON?
FUCK.
WHAT DO YOU WANT TO DO?
WE NEED TO HELP ALICE... BUT ONCE BUCKAROO FINDS OUT THAT A BUNCH OF THE TOWN'S KIDS WERE MURDERED IN THE WOODS...
IT'S GOING TO MELT DOWN.
I DON'T THINK... I DON'T THINK WARREN WILL HURT ALICE.
HE'S A SERIAL KILLER, FINCH.
REGARDLESS OF HOW CHARMING HE IS. HOW MUCH HE HAS THIS... ACT. HE'LL ALWAYS BE THAT.
WE REALLY DON'T EVEN KNOW IF ALICE IS WITH HIM.
HE IS... I CAN... I JUST KNOW.
AND MY GUT IS TELLING ME... HE'D NEVER HURT HER.
MAYBE NOT PHYSICALLY...

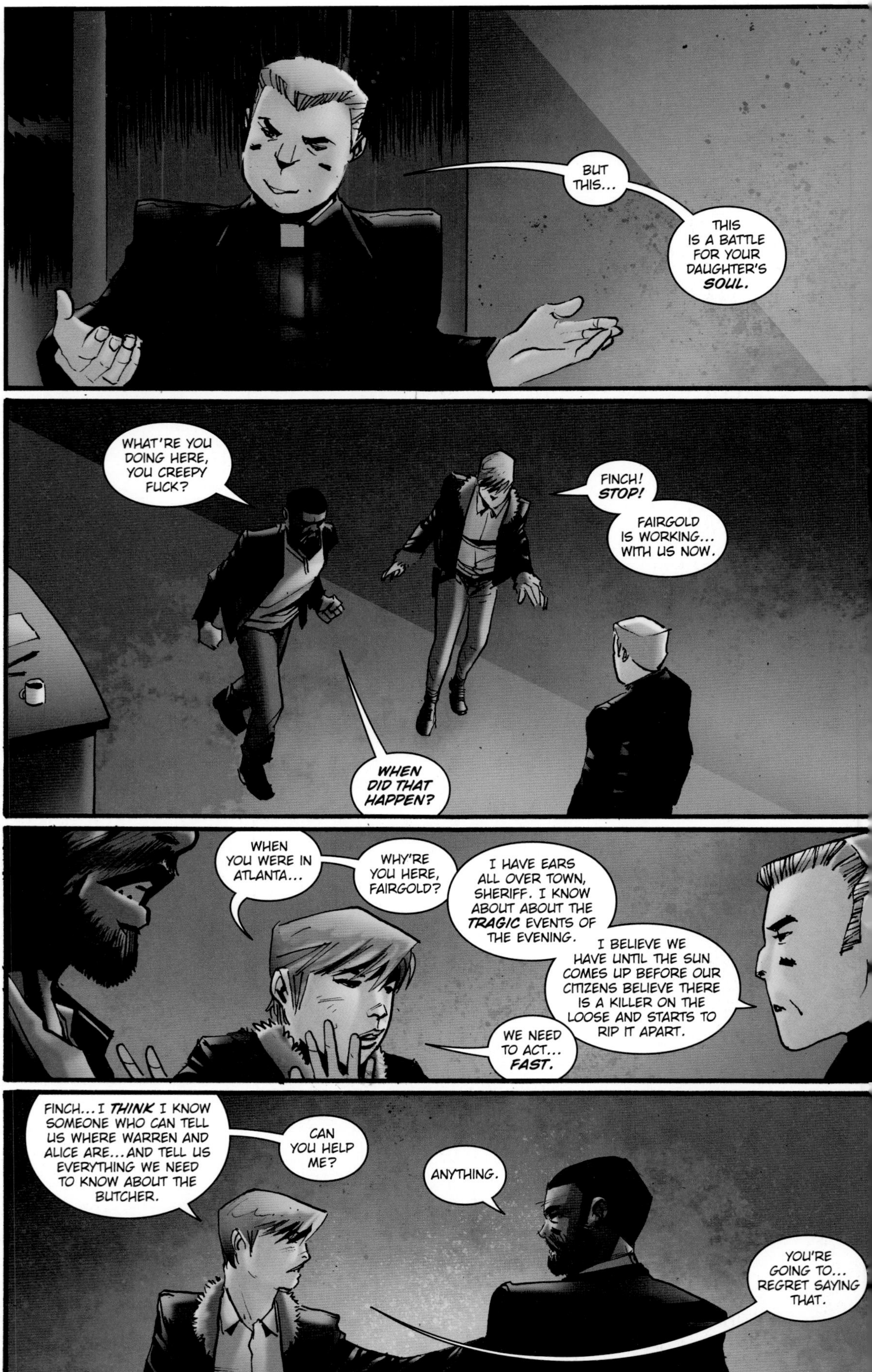
BUT THIS...
THIS IS A BATTLE FOR YOUR DAUGHTER'S **SOUL.**
WHAT'RE YOU DOING HERE, YOU CREEPY FUCK?
FINCH! **STOP!**
FAIRGOLD IS WORKING... WITH US NOW.
WHEN DID THAT HAPPEN?
WHEN YOU WERE IN ATLANTA...
WHY'RE YOU HERE, FAIRGOLD?
I HAVE EARS ALL OVER TOWN, SHERIFF. I KNOW ABOUT ABOUT THE **TRAGIC** EVENTS OF THE EVENING.
I BELIEVE WE HAVE UNTIL THE SUN COMES UP BEFORE OUR CITIZENS BELIEVE THERE IS A KILLER ON THE LOOSE AND STARTS TO RIP IT APART.
WE NEED TO ACT... **FAST.**
FINCH... I **THINK** I KNOW SOMEONE WHO CAN TELL US WHERE WARREN AND ALICE ARE... AND TELL US EVERYTHING WE NEED TO KNOW ABOUT THE BUTCHER.
CAN YOU HELP ME?
ANYTHING.
YOU'RE GOING TO... REGRET SAYING THAT.

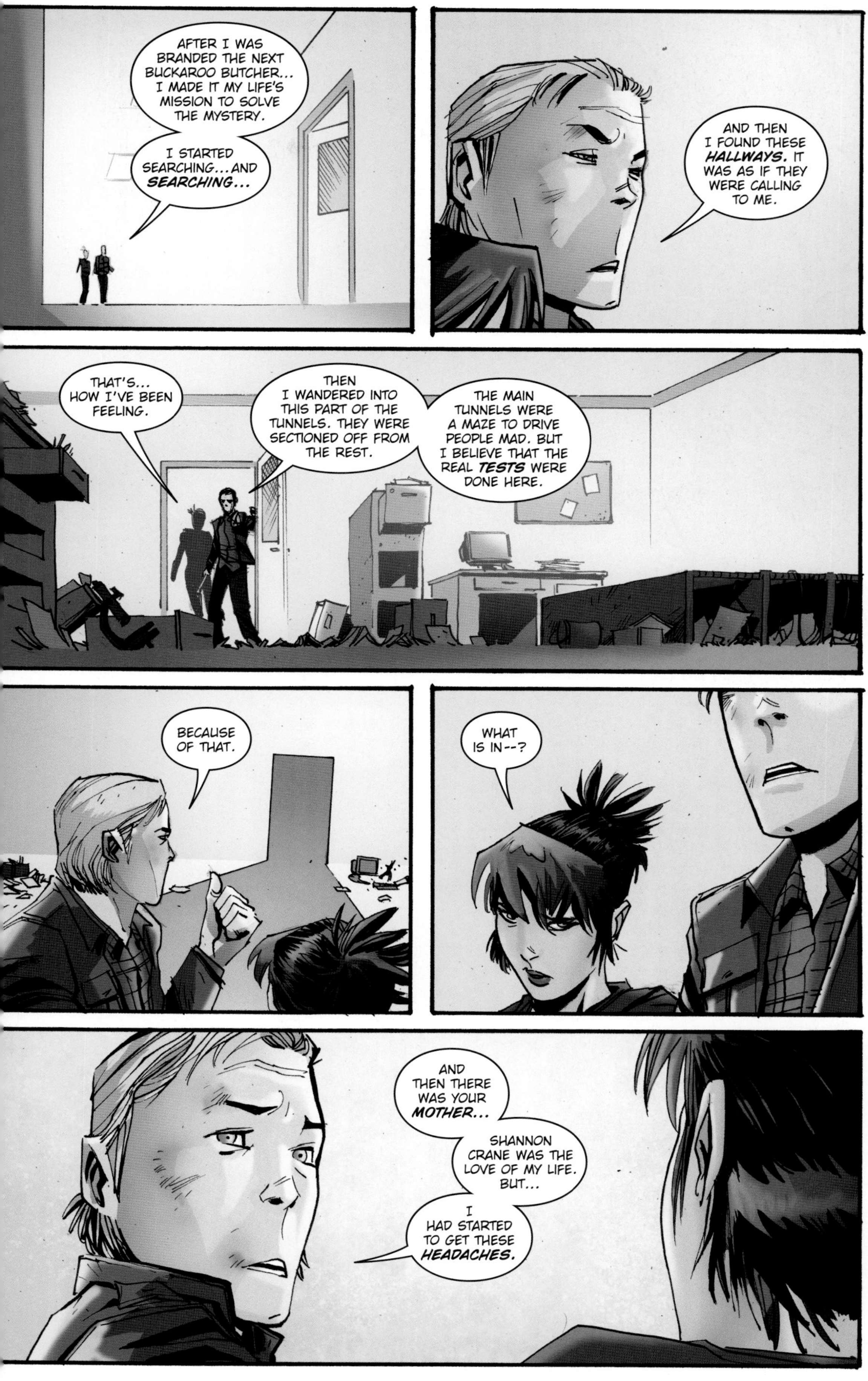
AFTER I WAS BRANDED THE NEXT BUCKAROO BUTCHER... I MADE IT MY LIFE'S MISSION TO SOLVE THE MYSTERY.
I STARTED SEARCHING...AND SEARCHING...
AND THEN I FOUND THESE HALLWAYS. IT WAS AS IF THEY WERE CALLING TO ME.
THAT'S... HOW I'VE BEEN FEELING.
THEN I WANDERED INTO THIS PART OF THE TUNNELS. THEY WERE SECTIONED OFF FROM THE REST.
THE MAIN TUNNELS WERE A MAZE TO DRIVE PEOPLE MAD. BUT I BELIEVE THAT THE REAL TESTS WERE DONE HERE.
BECAUSE OF THAT.
WHAT IS IN--?
AND THEN THERE WAS YOUR MOTHER...
SHANNON CRANE WAS THE LOVE OF MY LIFE. BUT...
I HAD STARTED TO GET THESE HEADACHES.

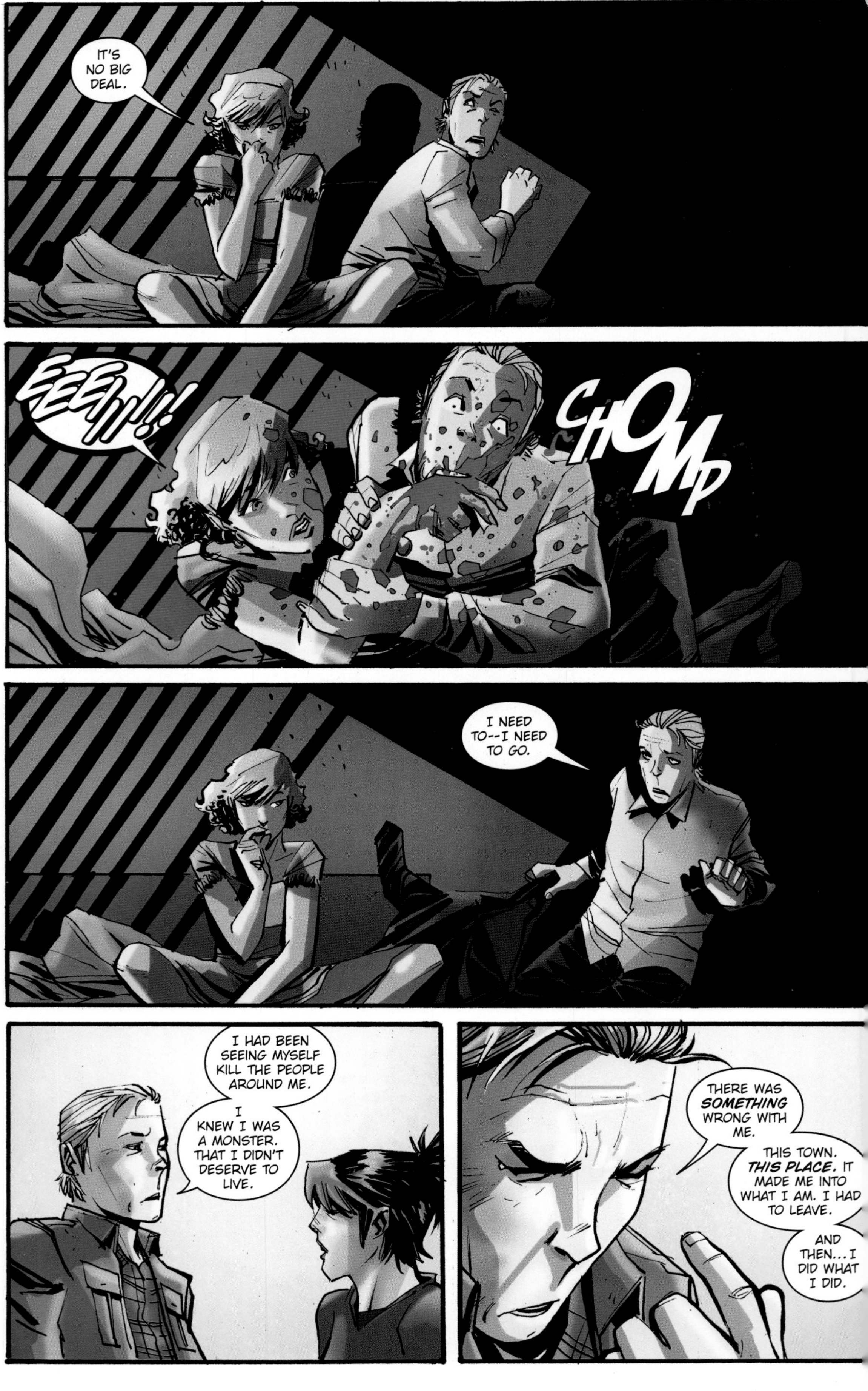

IT'S NO BIG DEAL.
EEEW!!!
CHOMP
I NEED TO--I NEED TO GO.
I HAD BEEN SEEING MYSELF KILL THE PEOPLE AROUND ME.
I KNEW I WAS A MONSTER. THAT I DIDN'T DESERVE TO LIVE.
THERE WAS **SOMETHING** WRONG WITH ME.
THIS TOWN. **THIS PLACE.** IT MADE ME INTO WHAT I AM. I HAD TO LEAVE.
AND THEN... I DID WHAT I DID.

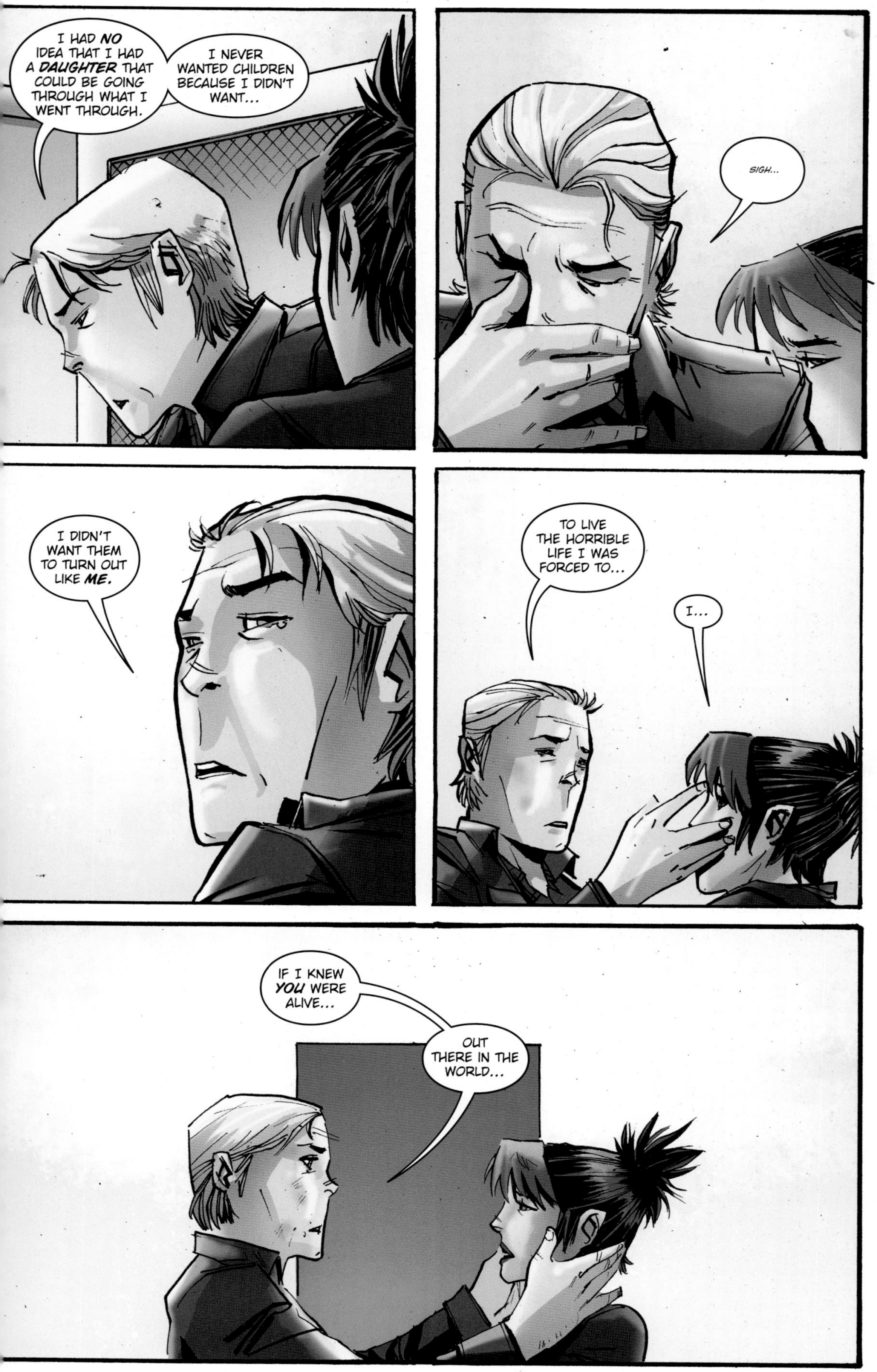
I HAD **NO** IDEA THAT I HAD A **DAUGHTER** THAT COULD BE GOING THROUGH WHAT I WENT THROUGH.
I NEVER WANTED CHILDREN BECAUSE I DIDN'T WANT...
SIGH...
I DIDN'T WANT THEM TO TURN OUT LIKE **ME.**
TO LIVE THE HORRIBLE LIFE I WAS FORCED TO...
I...
IF I KNEW **YOU** WERE ALIVE...
OUT THERE IN THE WORLD...

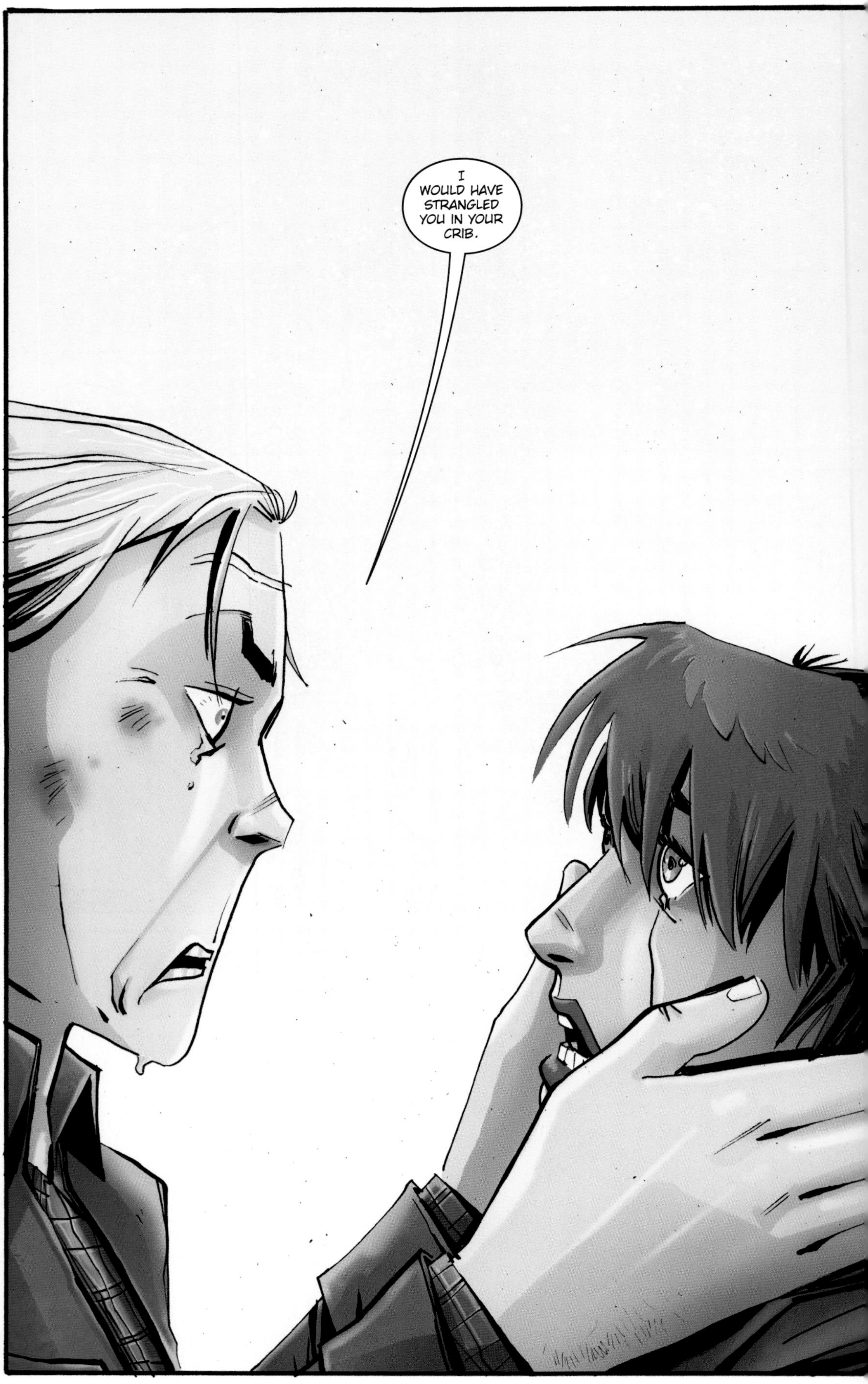
I WOULD HAVE STRANGLED YOU IN YOUR CRIB.

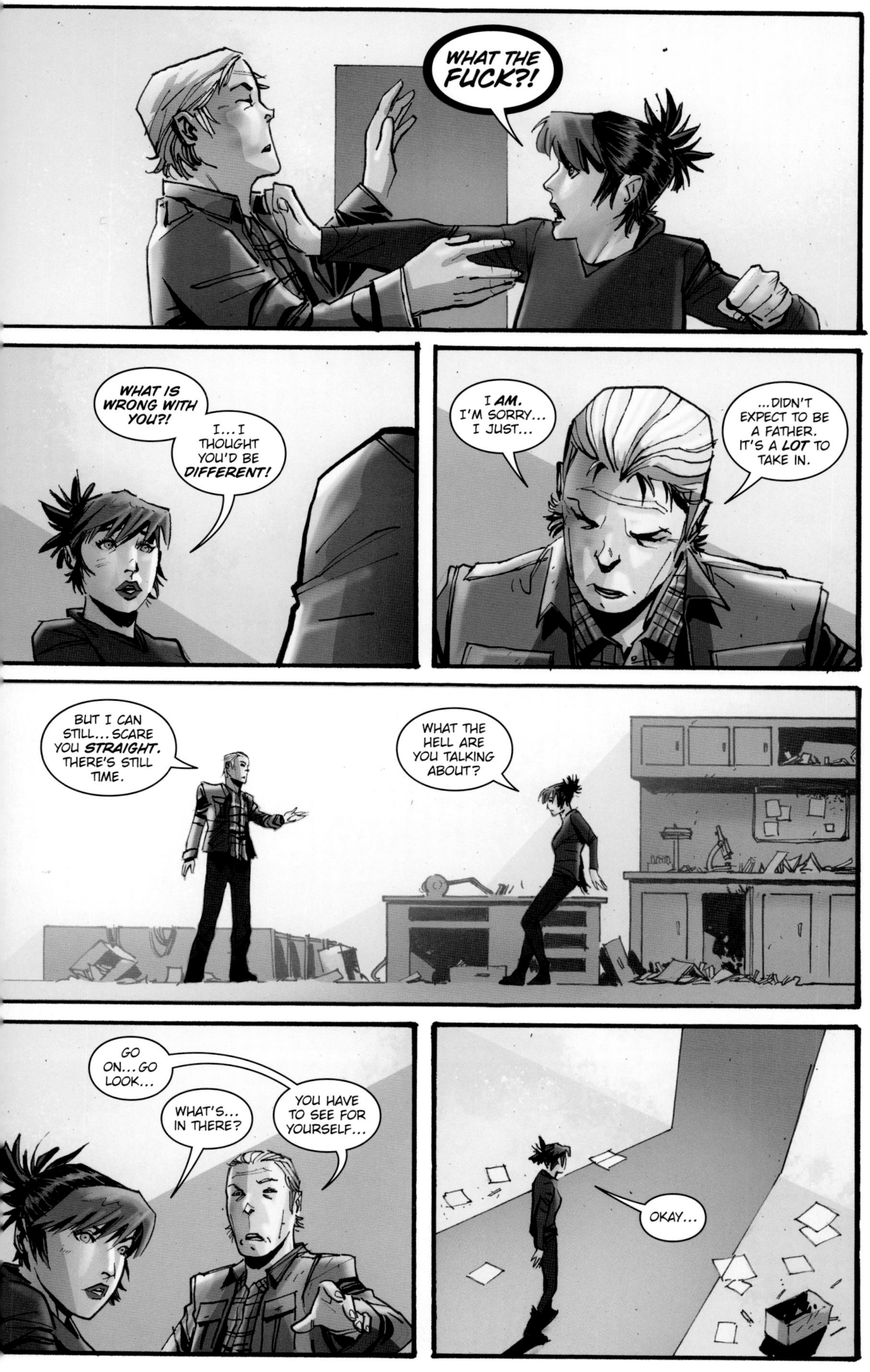
WHAT THE FUCK?!
WHAT IS WRONG WITH YOU?!
I... I THOUGHT YOU'D BE DIFFERENT!
I AM. I'M SORRY... I JUST...
...DIDN'T EXPECT TO BE A FATHER. IT'S A LOT TO TAKE IN.
BUT I CAN STILL... SCARE YOU STRAIGHT. THERE'S STILL TIME.
WHAT THE HELL ARE YOU TALKING ABOUT?
GO ON... GO LOOK...
WHAT'S... IN THERE?
YOU HAVE TO SEE FOR YOURSELF...
OKAY...

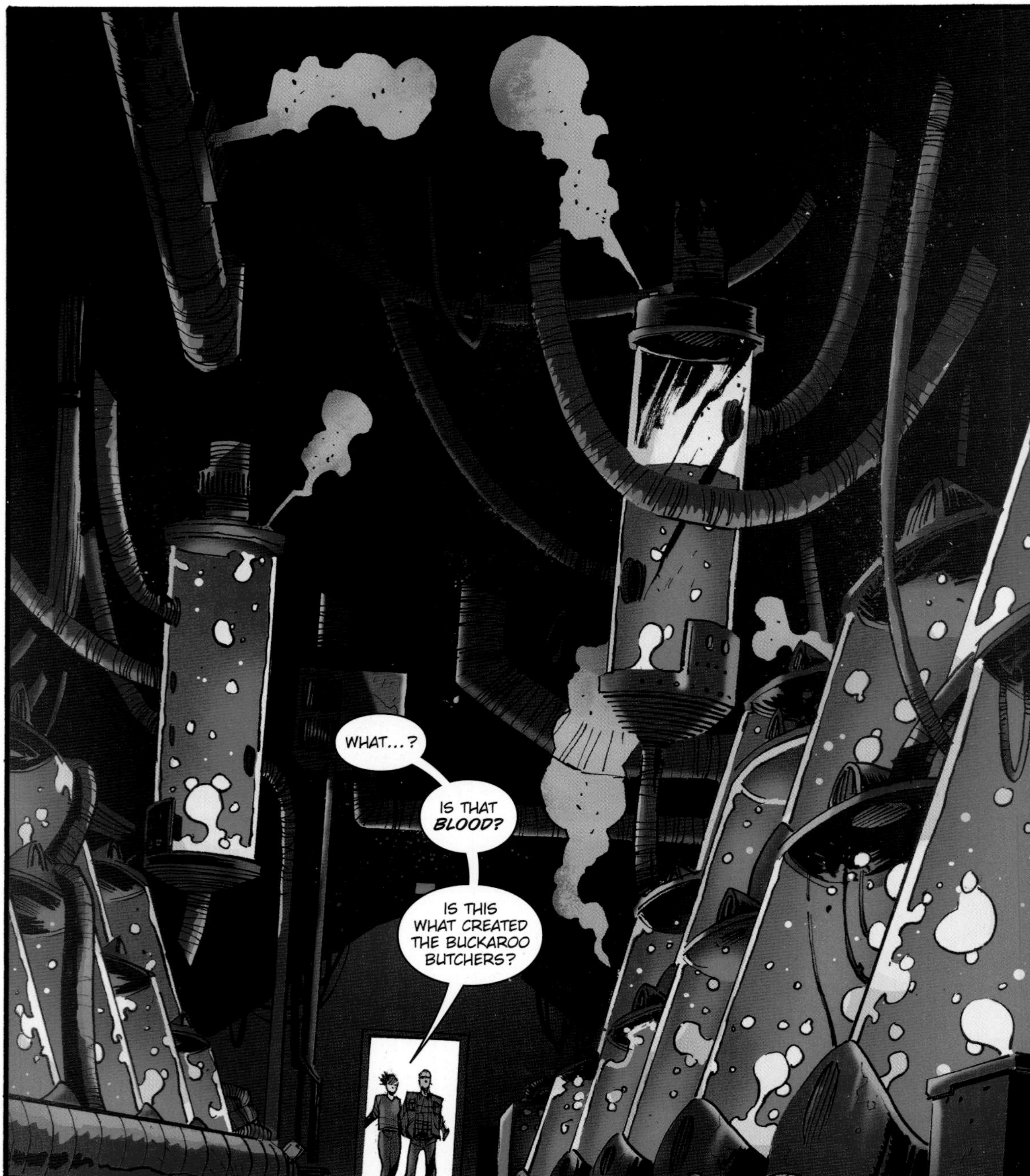
WHAT...?
IS THAT BLOOD?
IS THIS WHAT CREATED THE BUCKAROO BUTCHERS?

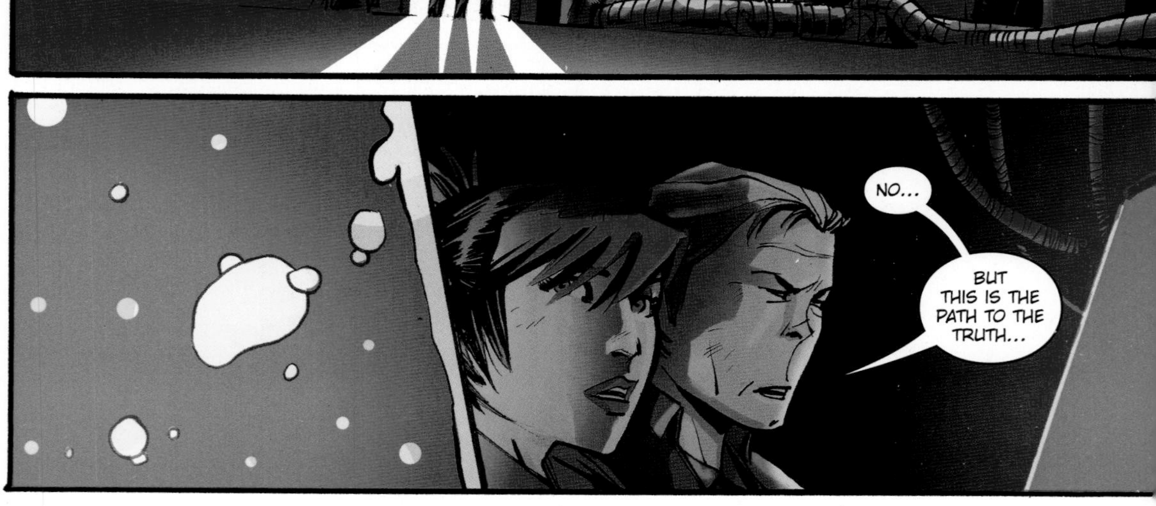
NO...
BUT THIS IS THE PATH TO THE TRUTH...

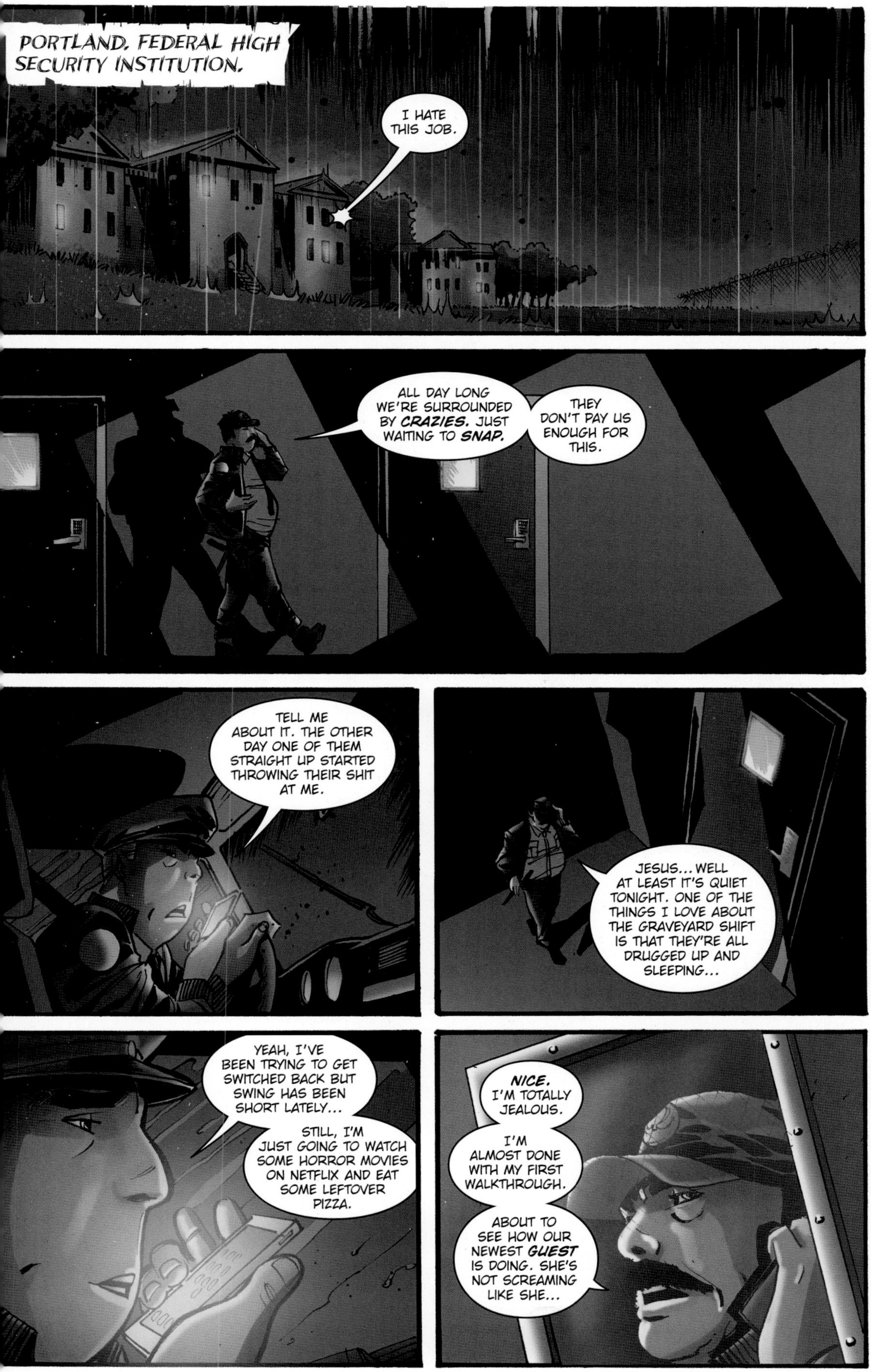
PORTLAND, FEDERAL HIGH SECURITY INSTITUTION.
I HATE THIS JOB.
ALL DAY LONG WE'RE SURROUNDED BY CRAZIES. JUST WAITING TO SNAP.
THEY DON'T PAY US ENOUGH FOR THIS.
TELL ME ABOUT IT. THE OTHER DAY ONE OF THEM STRAIGHT UP STARTED THROWING THEIR SHIT AT ME.
JESUS... WELL AT LEAST IT'S QUIET TONIGHT. ONE OF THE THINGS I LOVE ABOUT THE GRAVEYARD SHIFT IS THAT THEY'RE ALL DRUGGED UP AND SLEEPING...
YEAH, I'VE BEEN TRYING TO GET SWITCHED BACK BUT SWING HAS BEEN SHORT LATELY...
STILL, I'M JUST GOING TO WATCH SOME HORROR MOVIES ON NETFLIX AND EAT SOME LEFTOVER PIZZA.
NICE. I'M TOTALLY JEALOUS.
I'M ALMOST DONE WITH MY FIRST WALKTHROUGH.
ABOUT TO SEE HOW OUR NEWEST GUEST IS DOING. SHE'S NOT SCREAMING LIKE SHE...

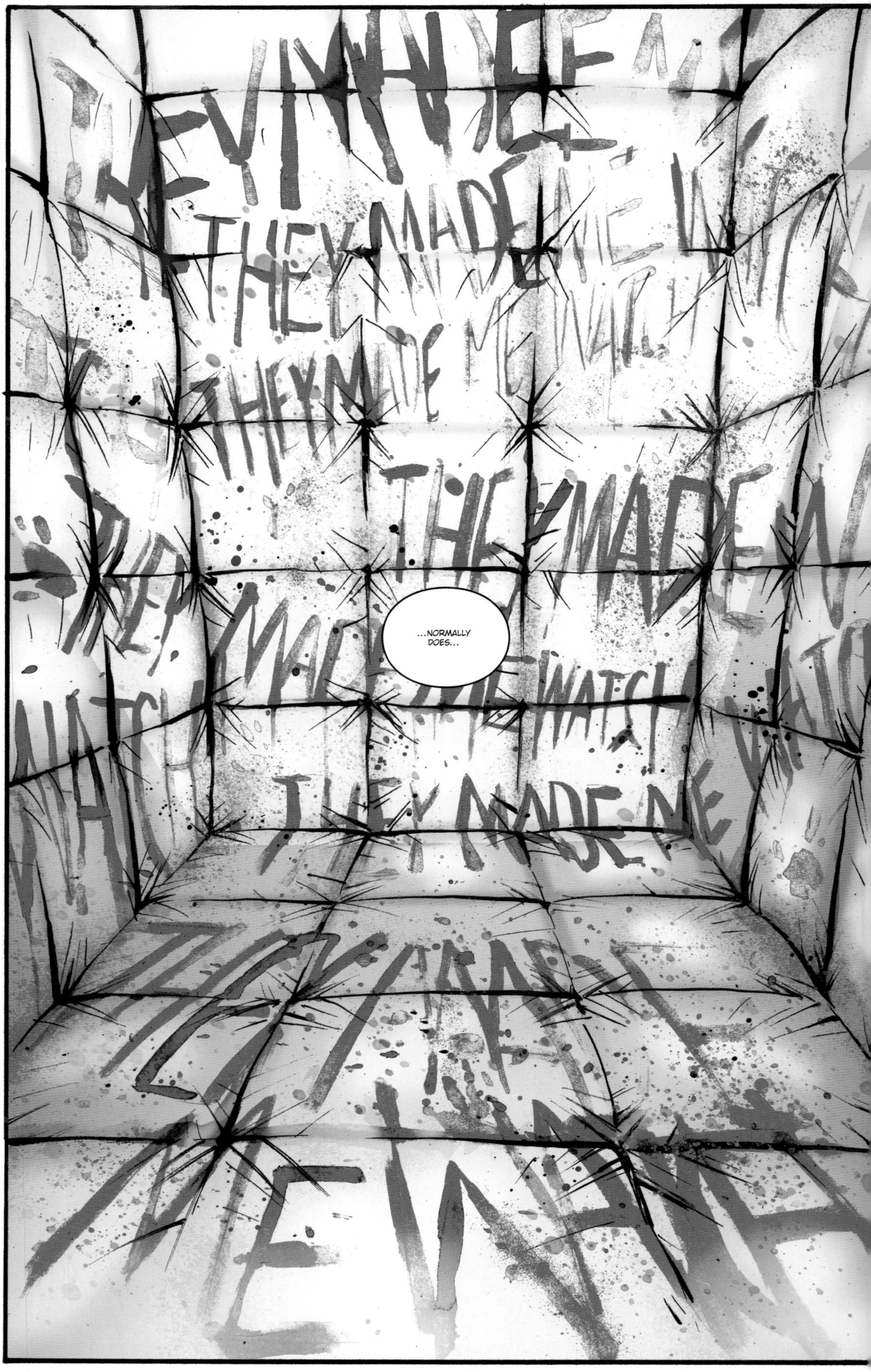
...NORMALLY DOES...
THEY MADE ME WATCH

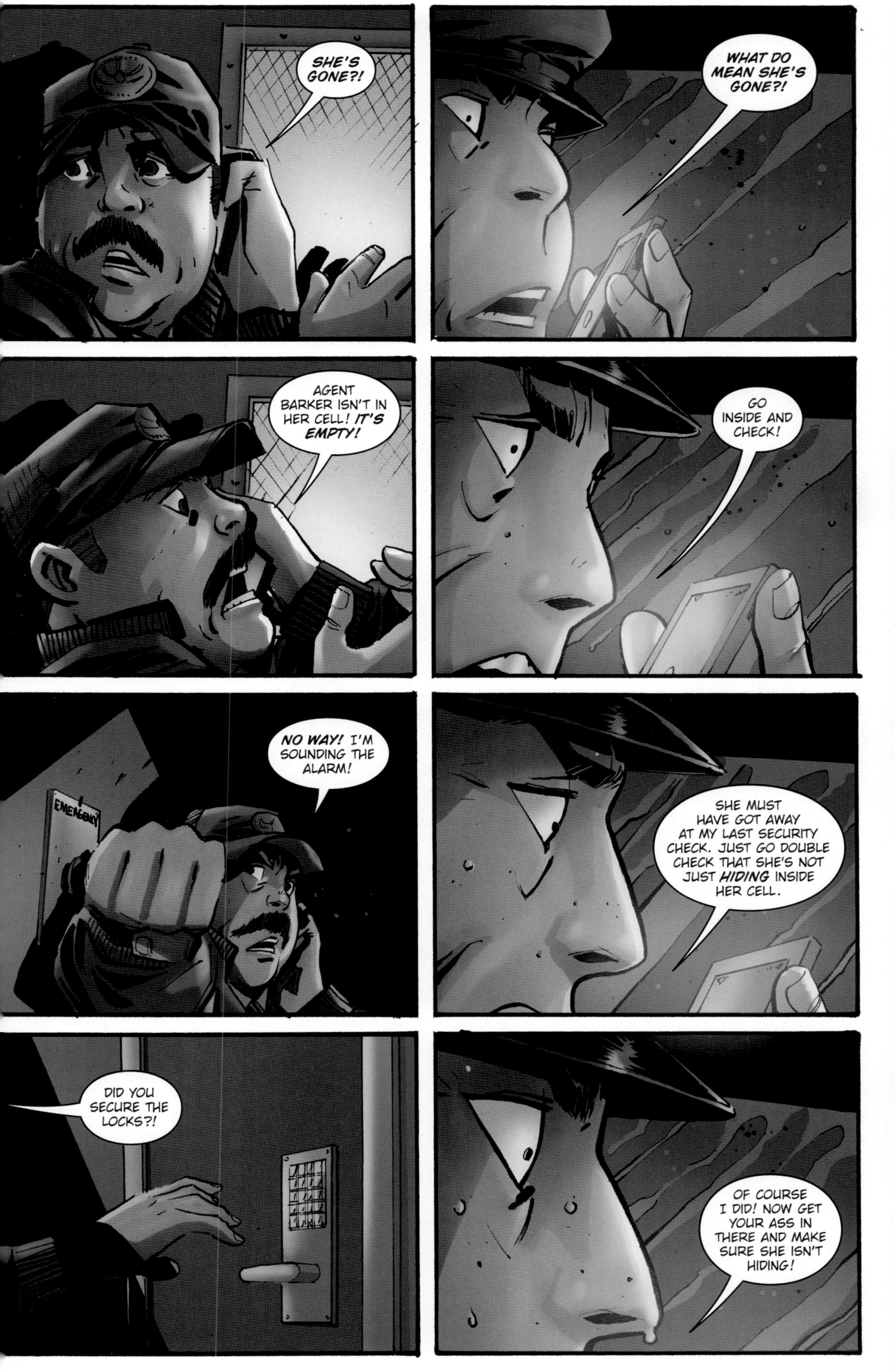
SHE'S GONE?!
WHAT DO MEAN SHE'S GONE?!
AGENT BARKER ISN'T IN HER CELL! IT'S EMPTY!
GO INSIDE AND CHECK!
NO WAY! I'M SOUNDING THE ALARM!
EMERGENCY
SHE MUST HAVE GOT AWAY AT MY LAST SECURITY CHECK. JUST GO DOUBLE CHECK THAT SHE'S NOT JUST HIDING INSIDE HER CELL.
DID YOU SECURE THE LOCKS?!
OF COURSE I DID! NOW GET YOUR ASS IN THERE AND MAKE SURE SHE ISN'T HIDING!

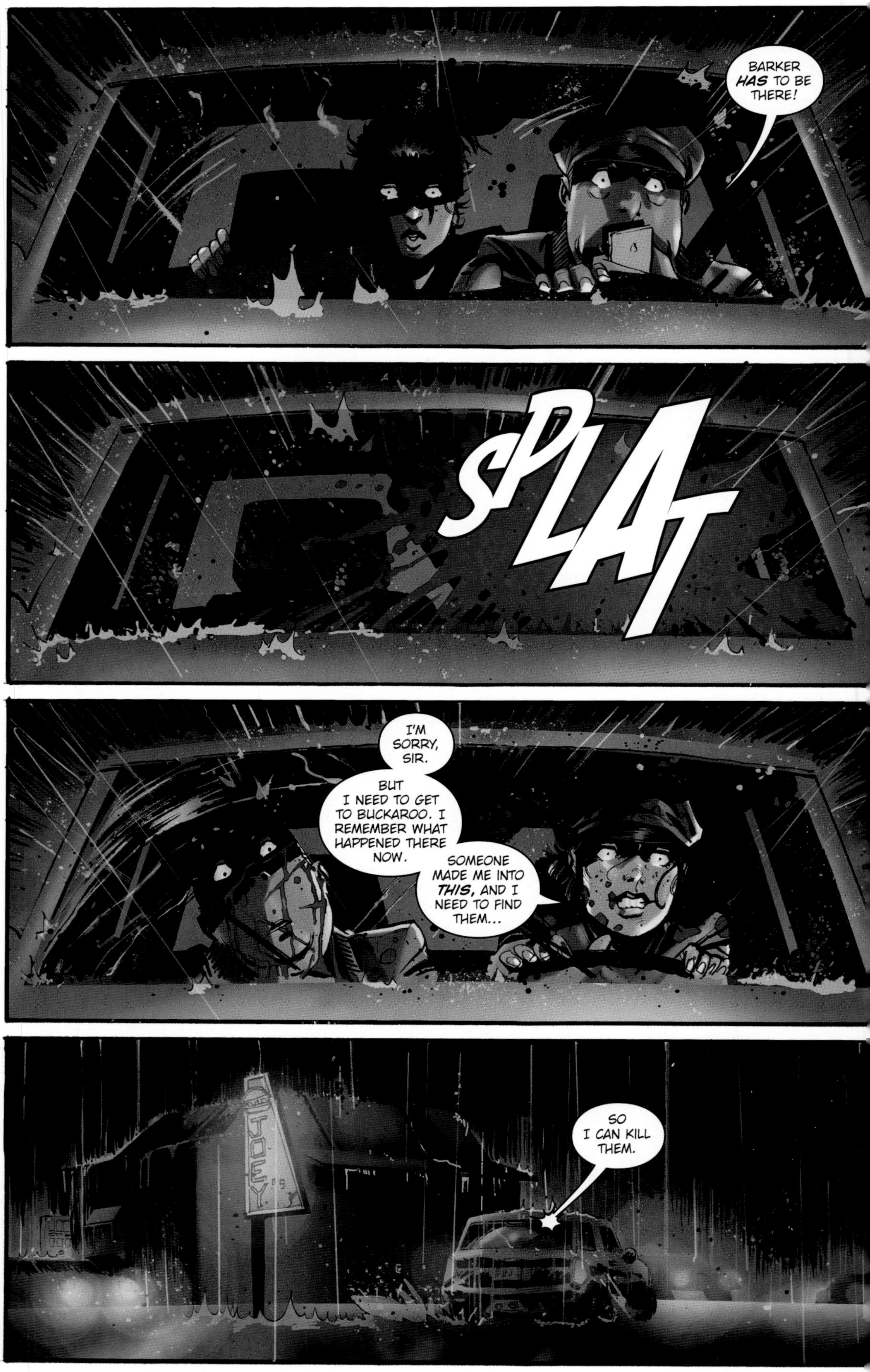
BARKER HAS TO BE THERE!
SPLAT
I'M SORRY, SIR.
BUT I NEED TO GET TO BUCKAROO. I REMEMBER WHAT HAPPENED THERE NOW.
SOMEONE MADE ME INTO THIS, AND I NEED TO FIND THEM...
JOEY'S
SO I CAN KILL THEM.

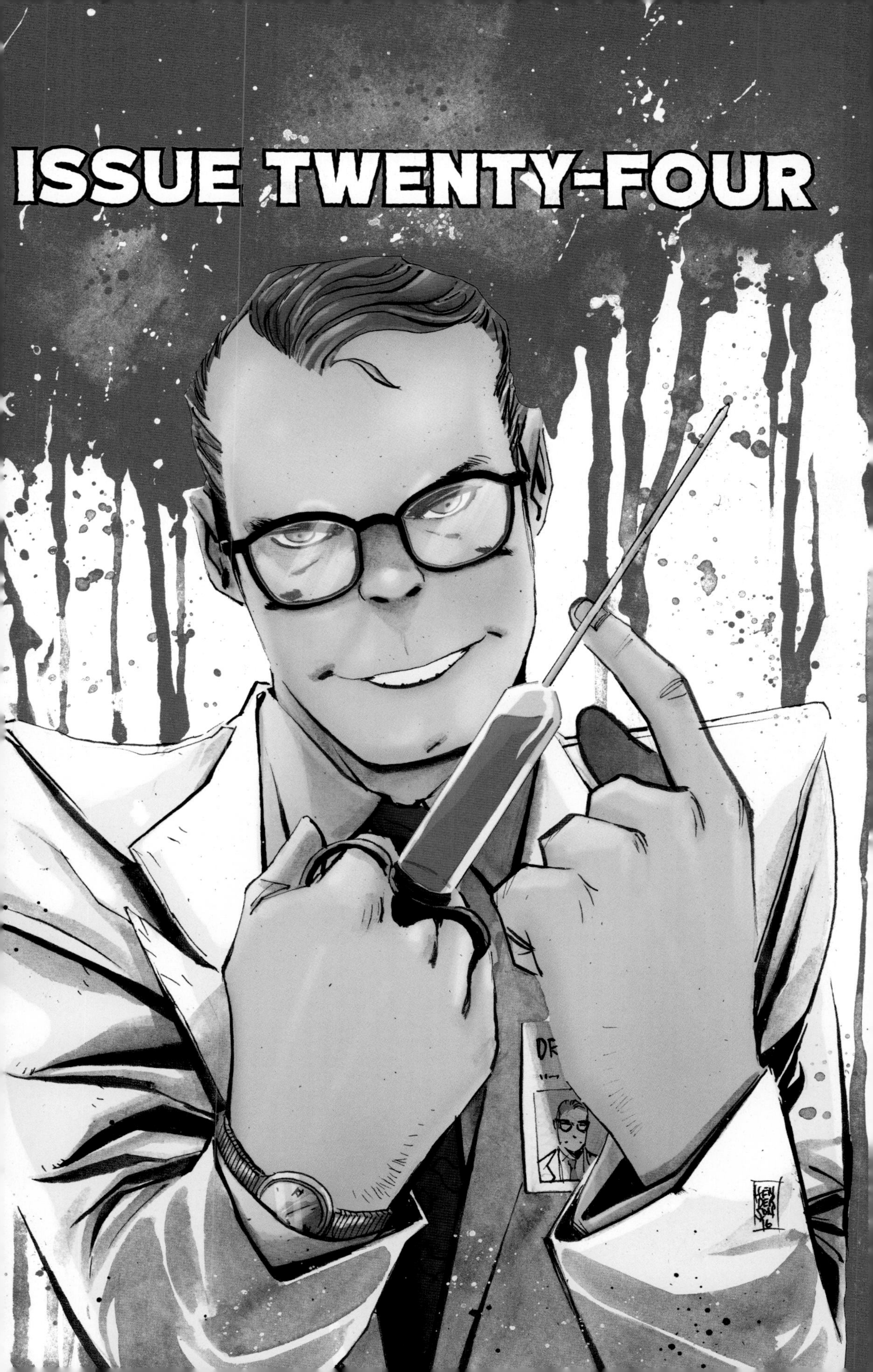
ISSUE TWENTY-FOUR

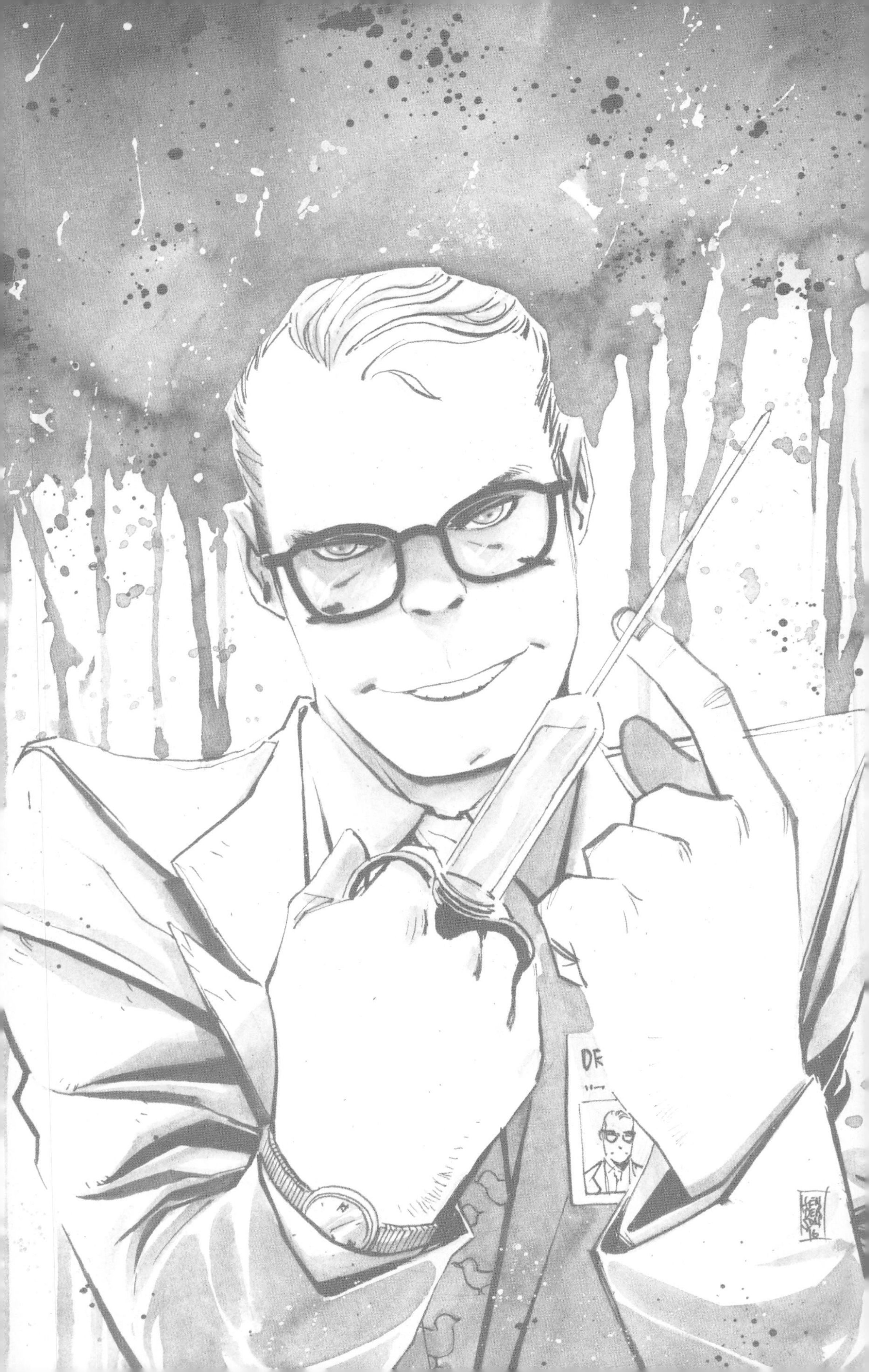

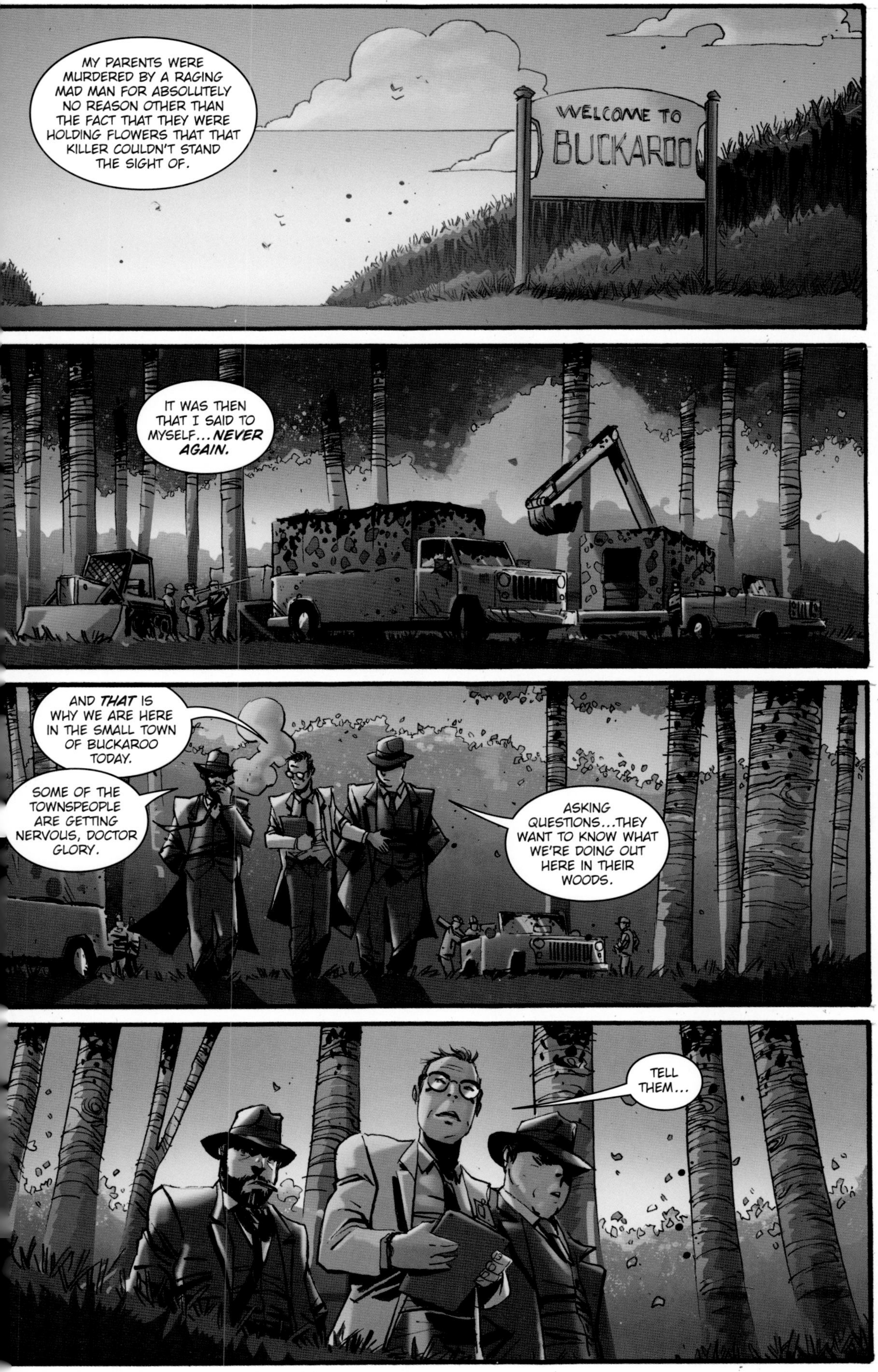
MY PARENTS WERE MURDERED BY A RAGING MAD MAN FOR ABSOLUTELY NO REASON OTHER THAN THE FACT THAT THEY WERE HOLDING FLOWERS THAT THAT KILLER COULDN'T STAND THE SIGHT OF.
WELCOME TO BUCKAROO
IT WAS THEN THAT I SAID TO MYSELF... NEVER AGAIN.
AND THAT IS WHY WE ARE HERE IN THE SMALL TOWN OF BUCKAROO TODAY.
SOME OF THE TOWNSPEOPLE ARE GETTING NERVOUS, DOCTOR GLORY.
ASKING QUESTIONS... THEY WANT TO KNOW WHAT WE'RE DOING OUT HERE IN THEIR WOODS.
TELL THEM...

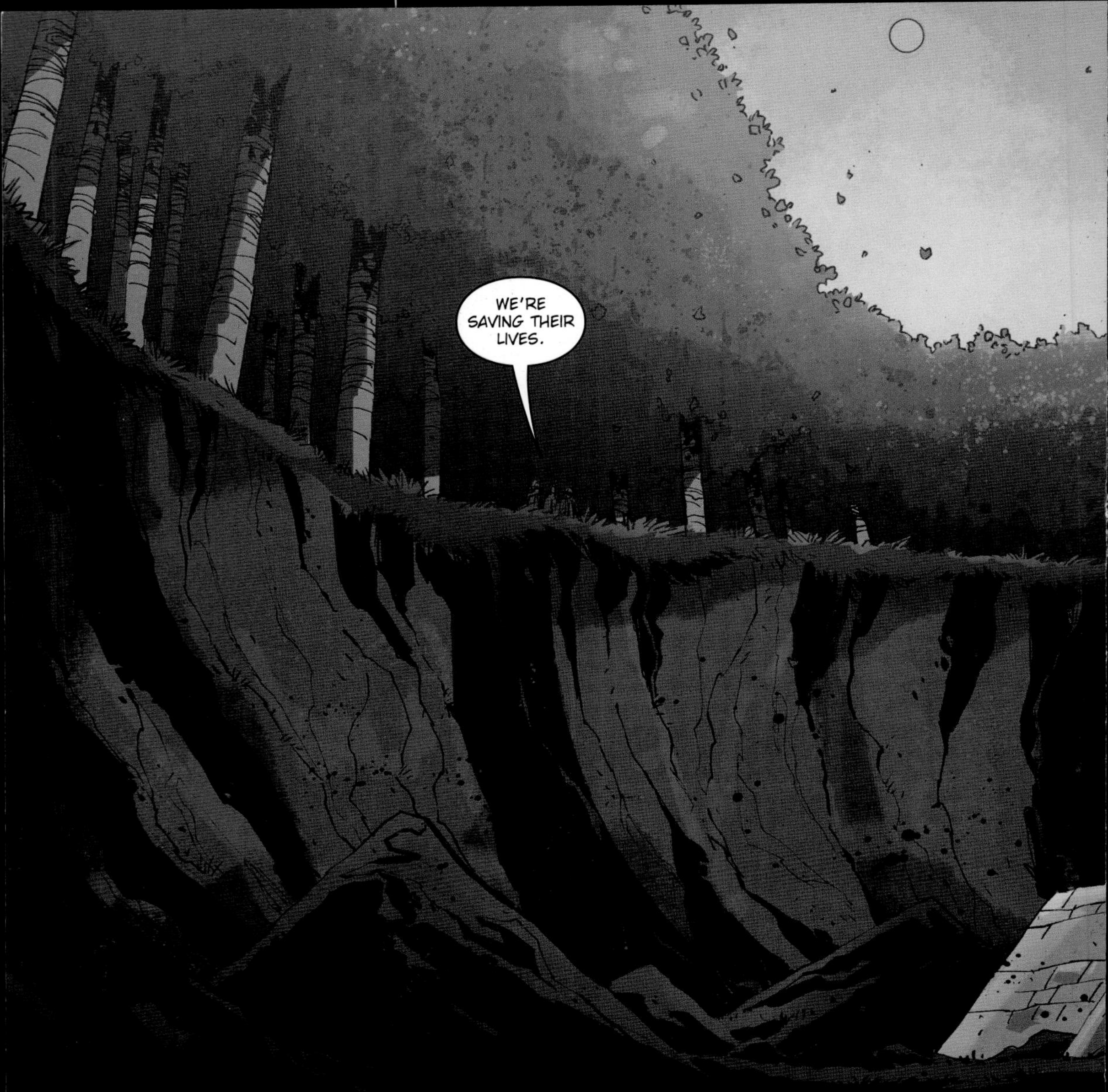
WE'RE SAVING THEIR LIVES.

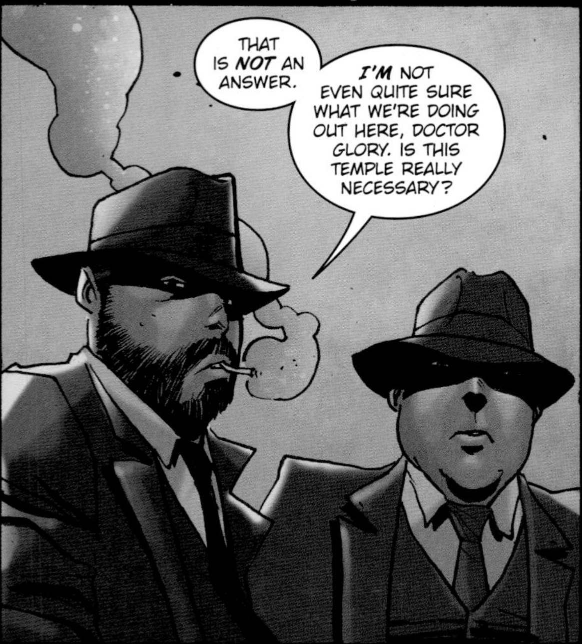
THAT IS ***NOT*** AN ANSWER.
I'M NOT EVEN QUITE SURE WHAT WE'RE DOING OUT HERE, DOCTOR GLORY. IS THIS TEMPLE REALLY NECESSARY?

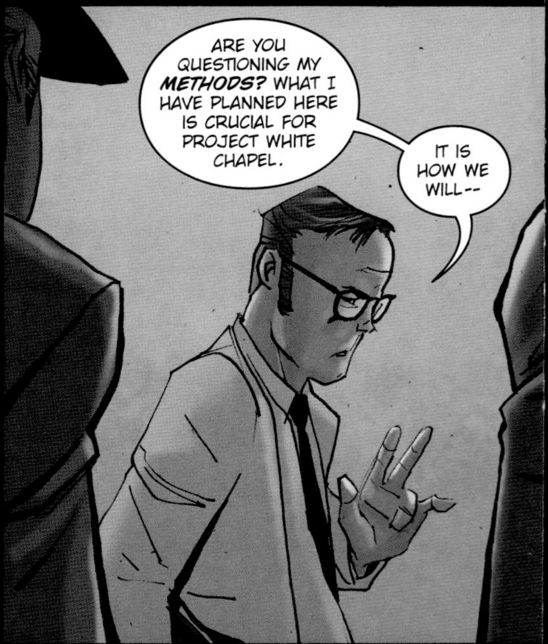
ARE YOU QUESTIONING MY ***METHODS?*** WHAT I HAVE PLANNED HERE IS CRUCIAL FOR PROJECT WHITE CHAPEL.
IT IS HOW WE WILL--

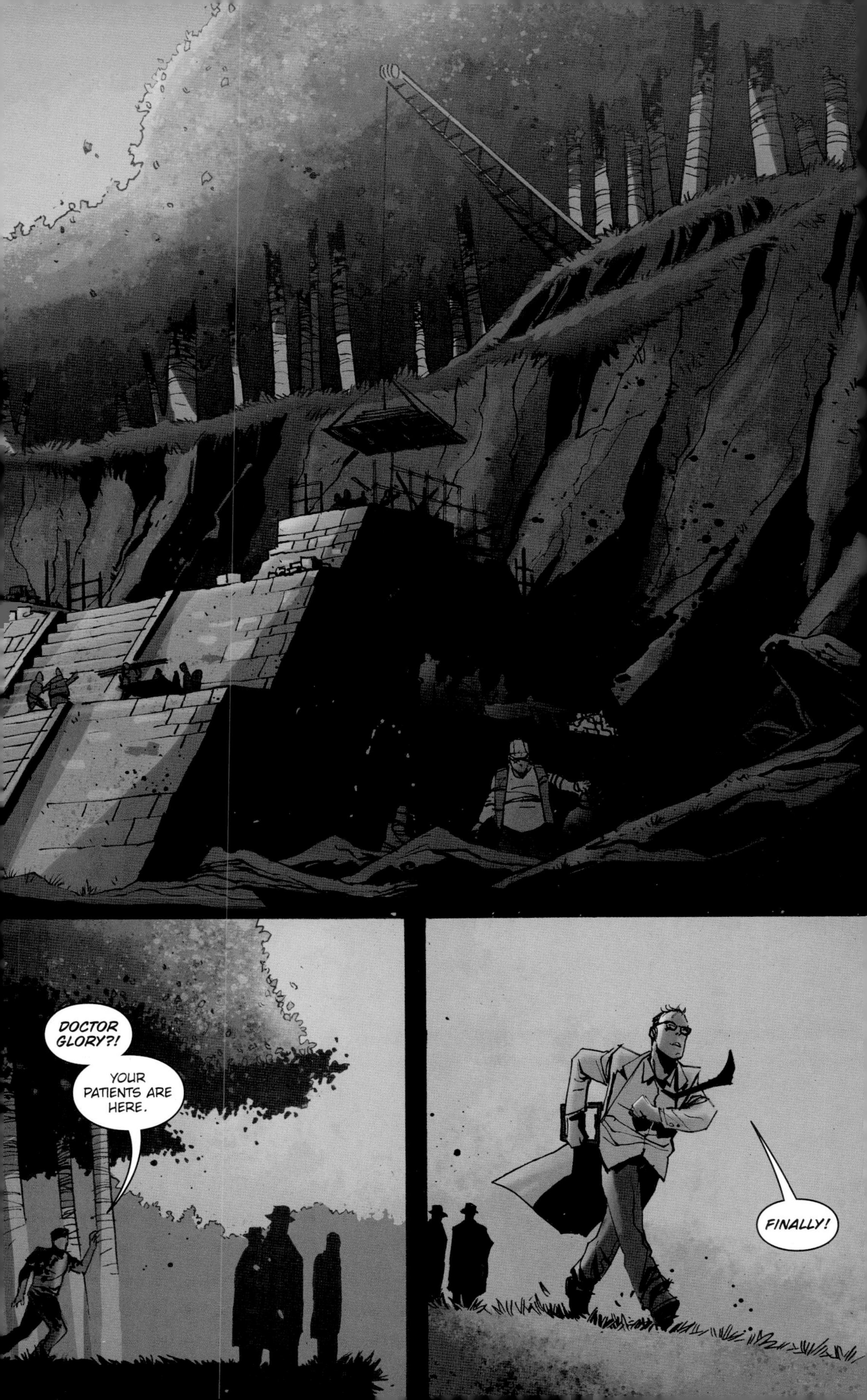
DOCTOR GLORY?!
YOUR PATIENTS ARE HERE.
FINALLY!

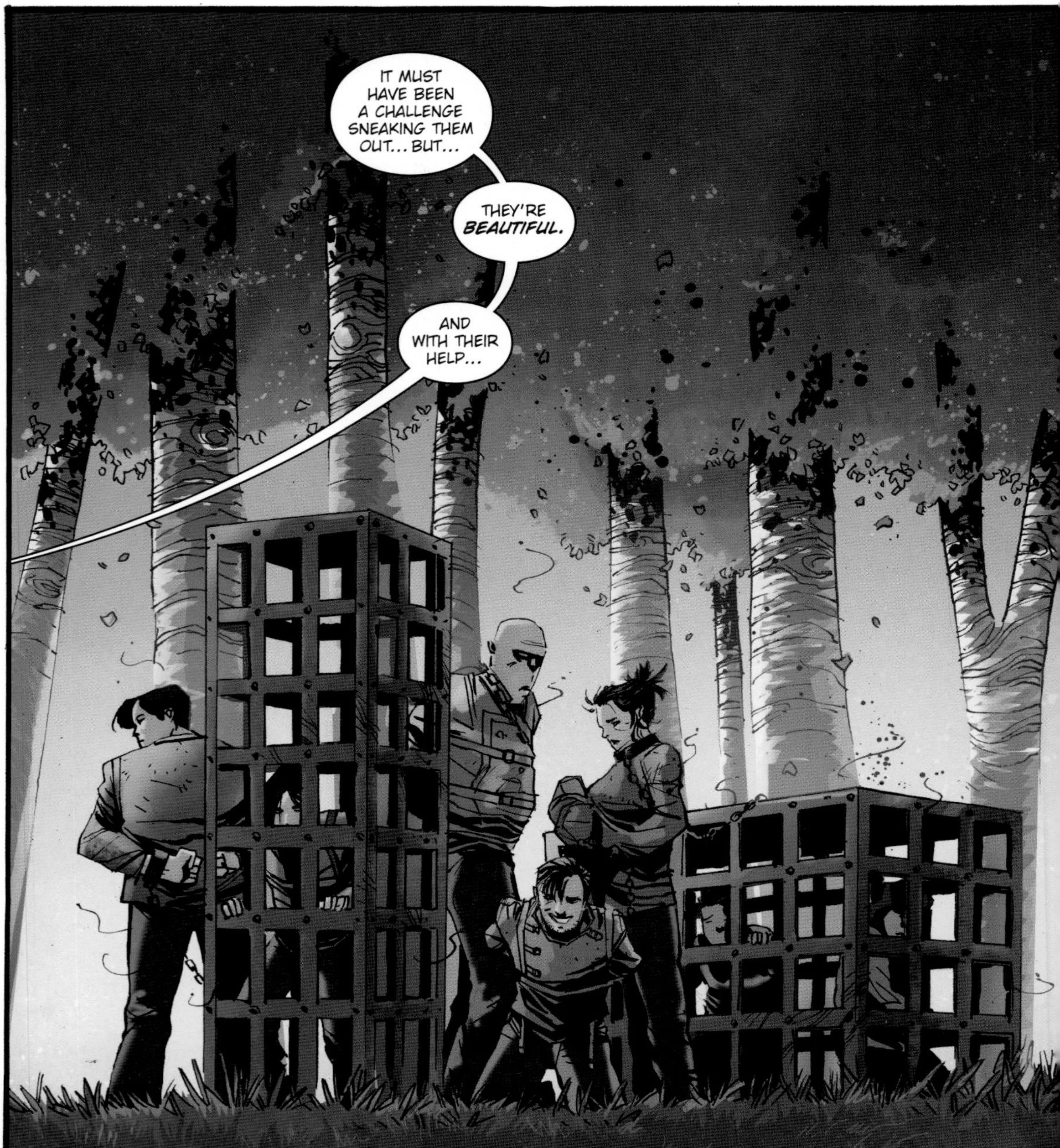
IT MUST HAVE BEEN A CHALLENGE SNEAKING THEM OUT... BUT...
THEY'RE *BEAUTIFUL.*
AND WITH THEIR HELP...

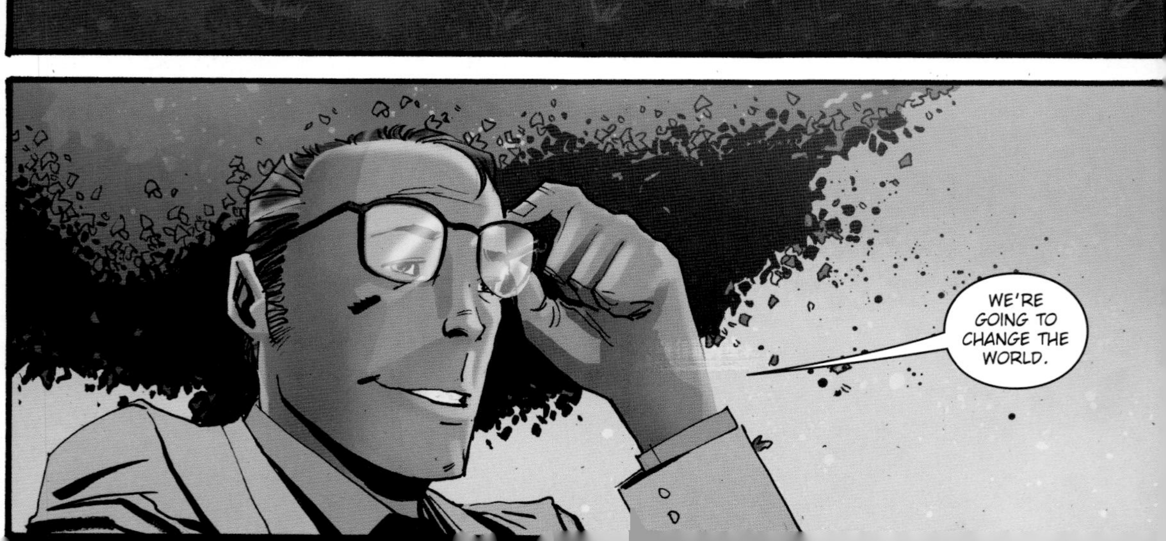
WE'RE GOING TO CHANGE THE WORLD.

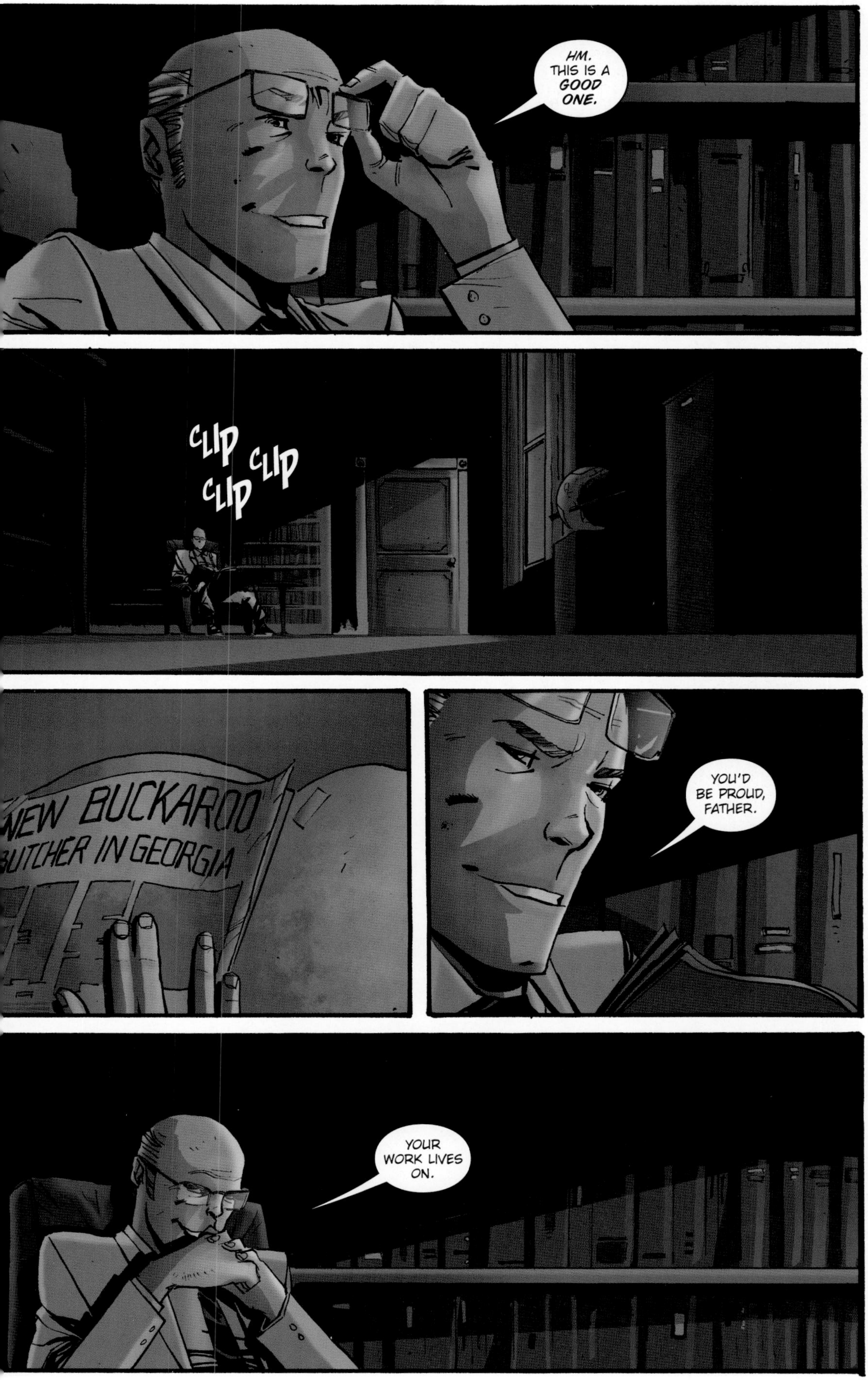
HM. THIS IS A GOOD ONE.
CLIP CLIP CLIP
NEW BUCKAROO BUTCHER IN GEORGIA
YOU'D BE PROUD, FATHER.
YOUR WORK LIVES ON.

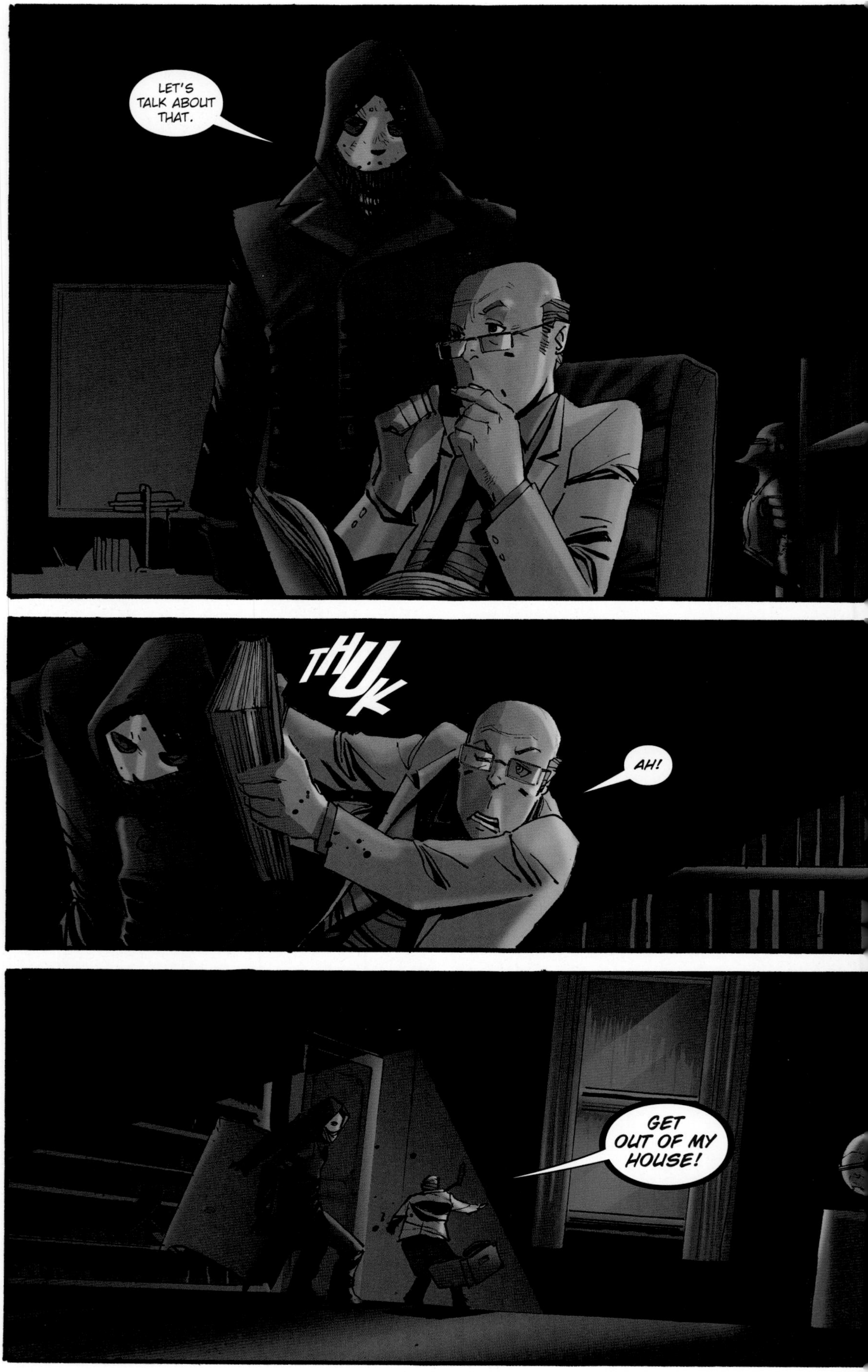
LET'S TALK ABOUT THAT.
THUK
AH!
GET OUT OF MY HOUSE!

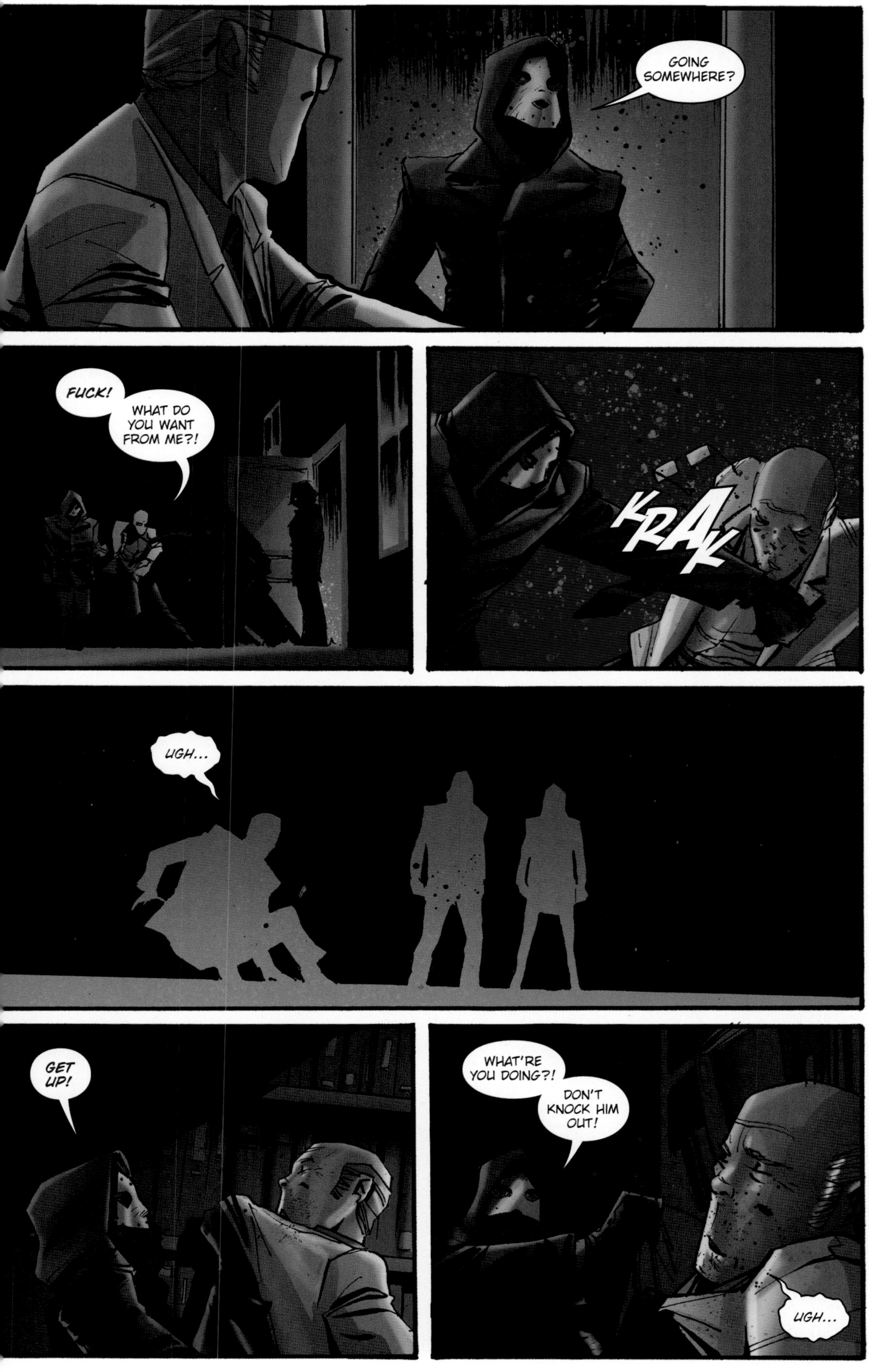
GOING SOMEWHERE?
FUCK!
WHAT DO YOU WANT FROM ME?!
KRAK
UGH...
GET UP!
WHAT'RE YOU DOING?!
DON'T KNOCK HIM OUT!
UGH...

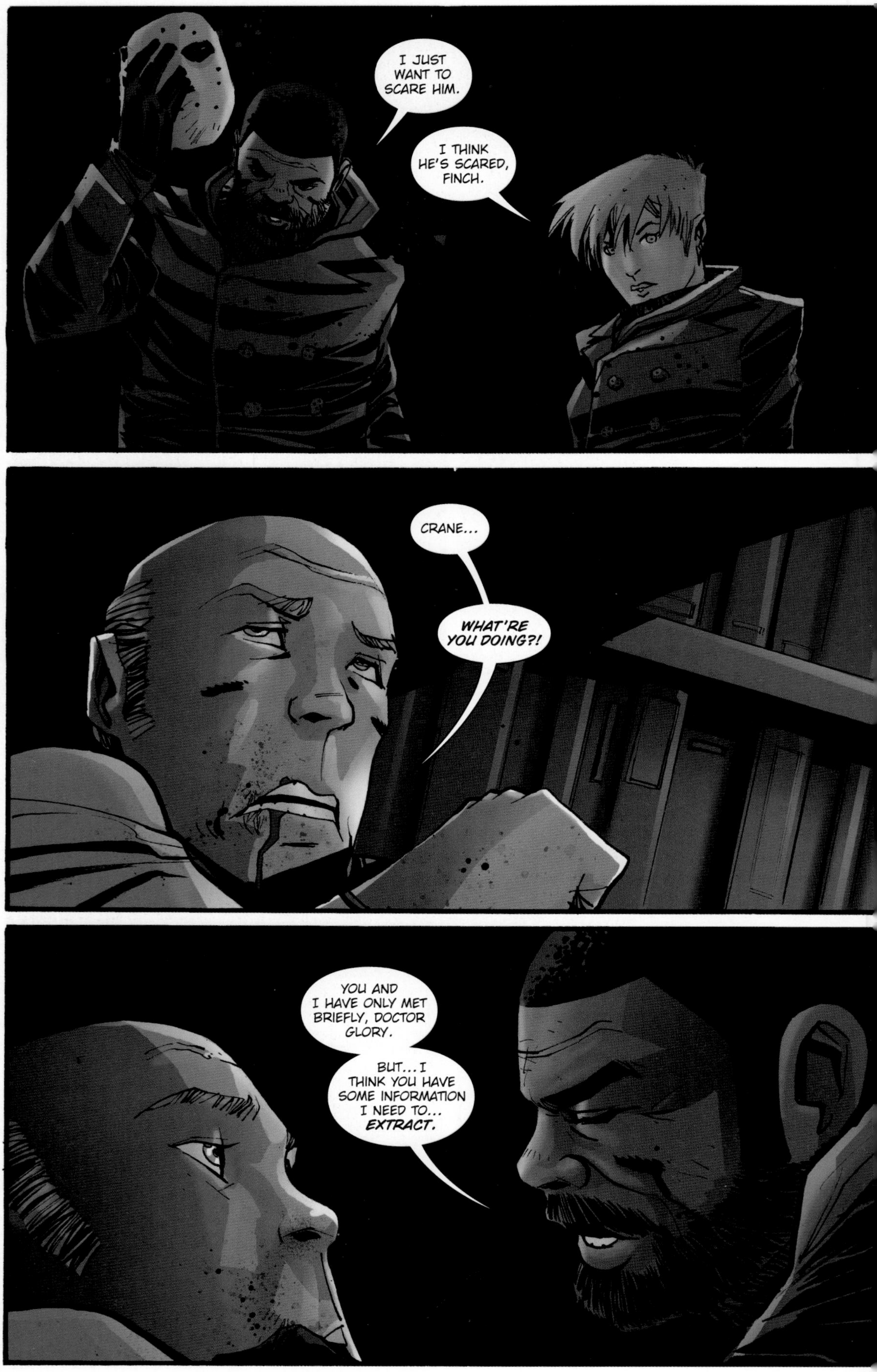
I JUST WANT TO SCARE HIM.
I THINK HE'S SCARED, FINCH.
CRANE...
WHAT'RE YOU DOING?!
YOU AND I HAVE ONLY MET BRIEFLY, DOCTOR GLORY.
BUT... I THINK YOU HAVE SOME INFORMATION I NEED TO... EXTRACT.

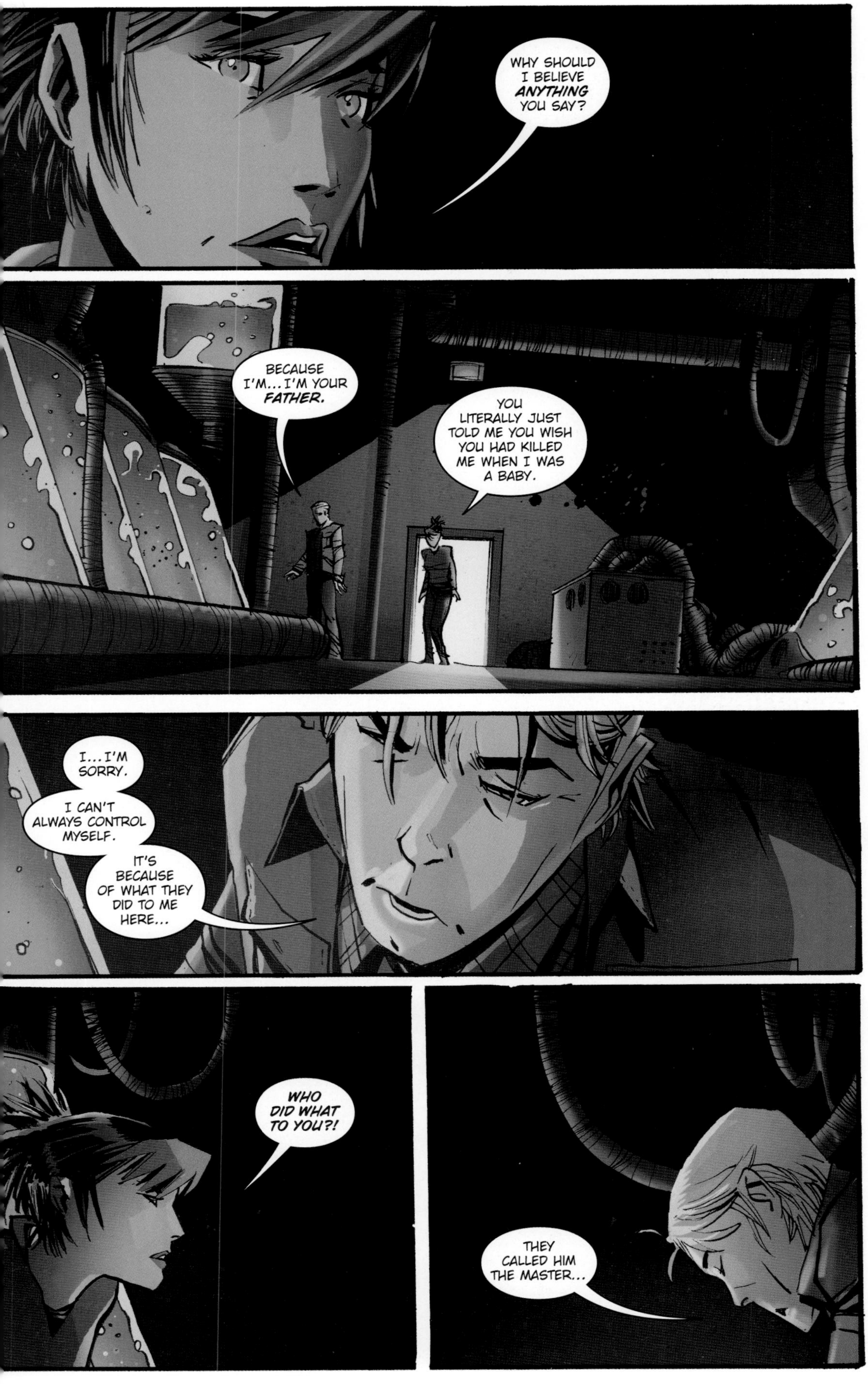
WHY SHOULD I BELIEVE ***ANYTHING*** YOU SAY?
BECAUSE I'M... I'M YOUR ***FATHER.***
YOU LITERALLY JUST TOLD ME YOU WISH YOU HAD KILLED ME WHEN I WAS A BABY.
I... I'M SORRY.
I CAN'T ALWAYS CONTROL MYSELF.
IT'S BECAUSE OF WHAT THEY DID TO ME HERE...
WHO DID WHAT TO YOU?!
THEY CALLED HIM THE MASTER...

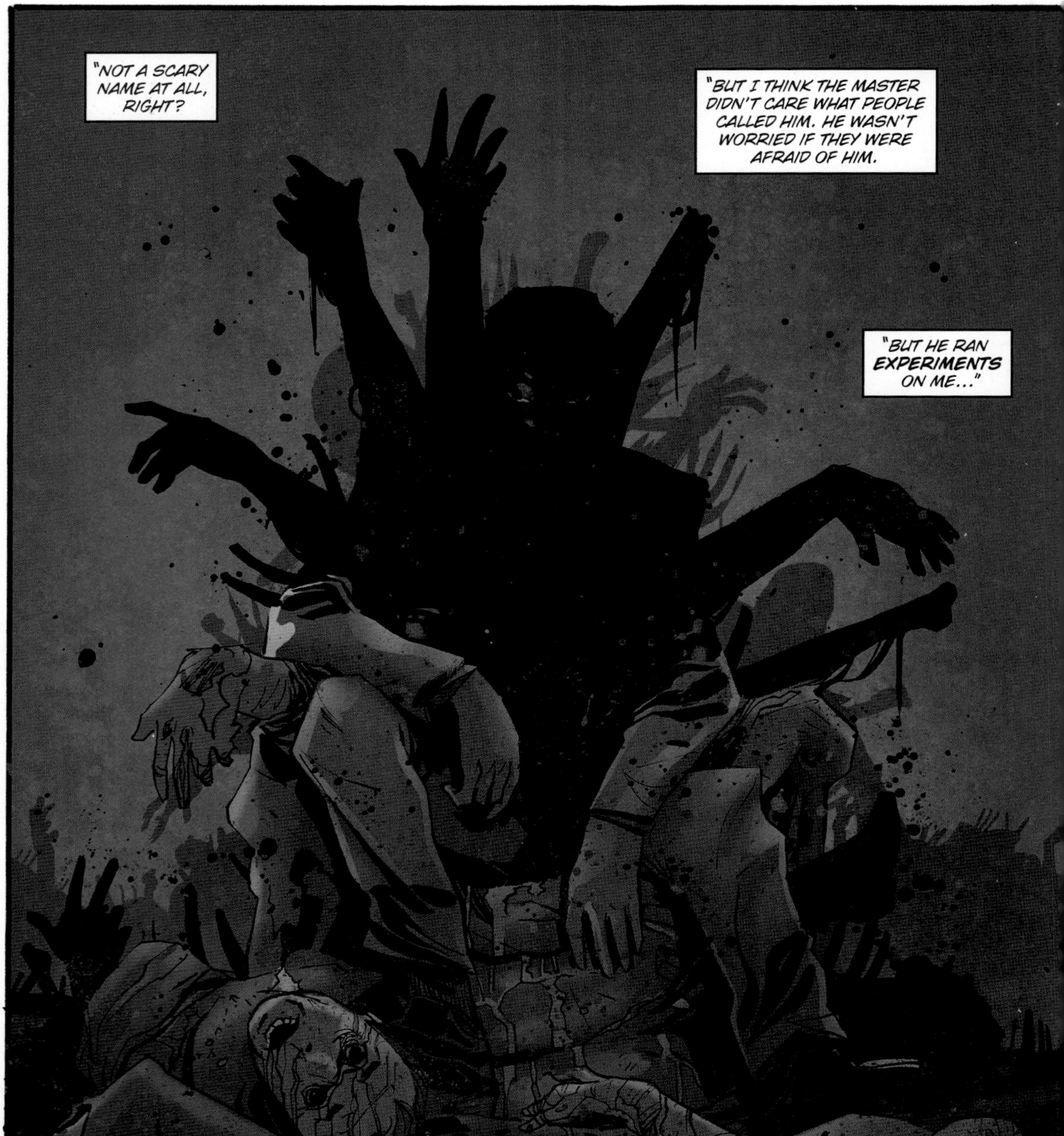
"NOT A SCARY NAME AT ALL, RIGHT?
"BUT I THINK THE MASTER DIDN'T CARE WHAT PEOPLE CALLED HIM. HE WASN'T WORRIED IF THEY WERE AFRAID OF HIM.
"BUT HE RAN **EXPERIMENTS** ON ME..."

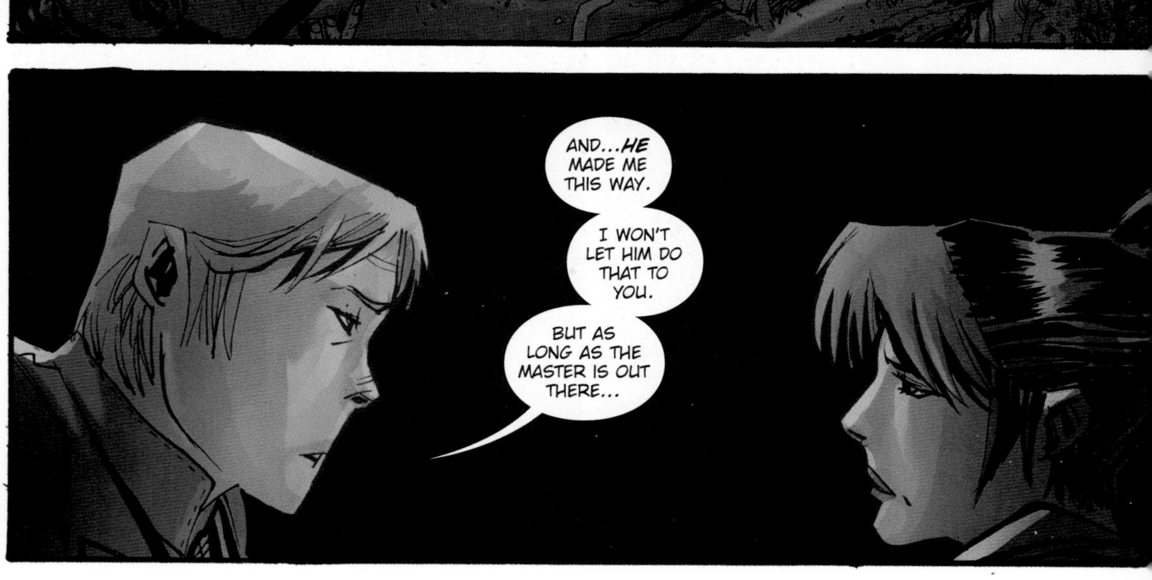
AND... ***HE*** MADE ME THIS WAY.
I WON'T LET HIM DO THAT TO YOU.
BUT AS LONG AS THE MASTER IS OUT THERE...

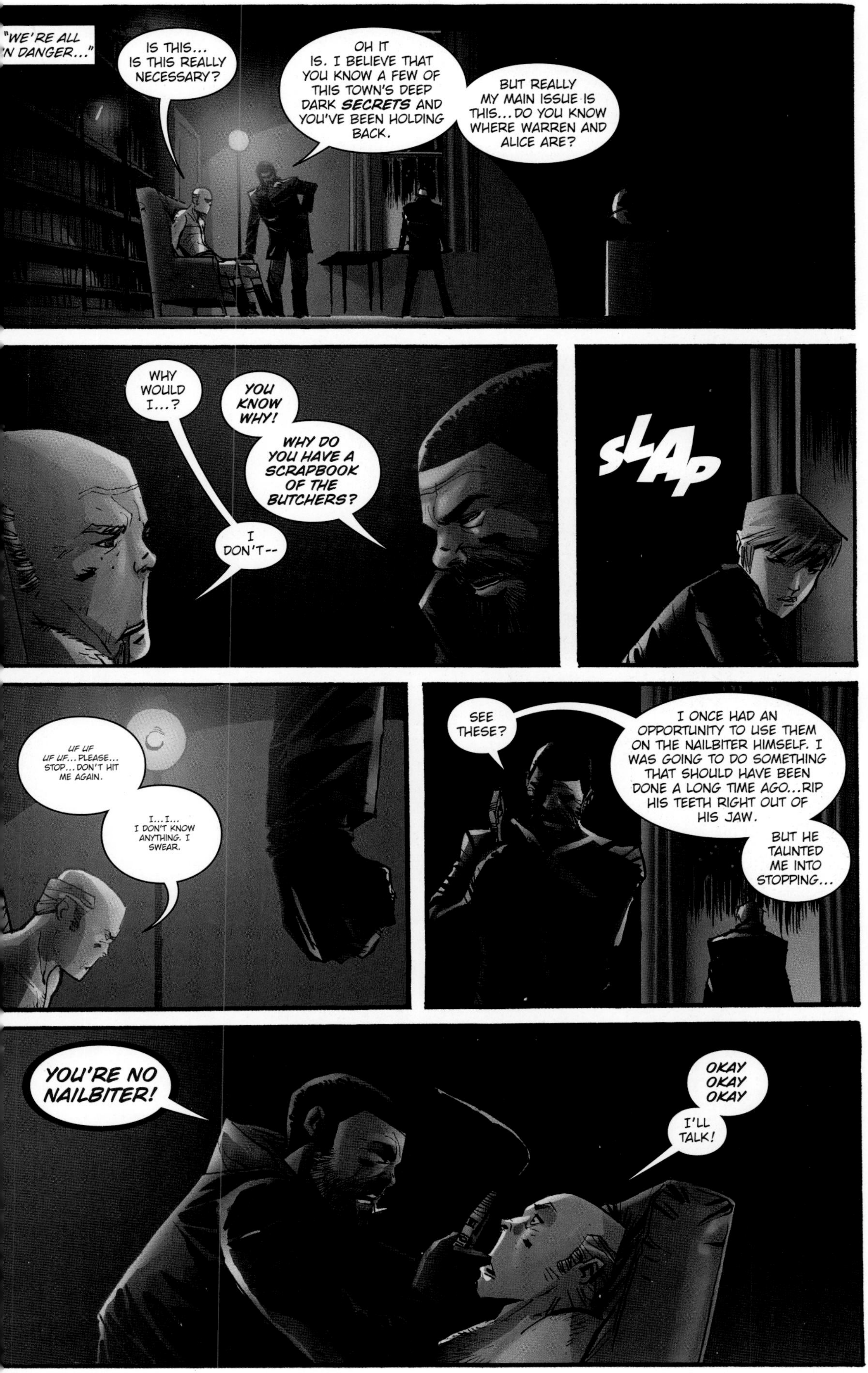
"WE'RE ALL 'N DANGER..."
IS THIS... IS THIS REALLY NECESSARY?
OH IT IS. I BELIEVE THAT YOU KNOW A FEW OF THIS TOWN'S DEEP DARK SECRETS AND YOU'VE BEEN HOLDING BACK.
BUT REALLY MY MAIN ISSUE IS THIS... DO YOU KNOW WHERE WARREN AND ALICE ARE?
WHY WOULD I...?
YOU KNOW WHY!
WHY DO YOU HAVE A SCRAPBOOK OF THE BUTCHERS?
I DON'T--
SLAP
UF UF UF UF... PLEASE... STOP... DON'T HIT ME AGAIN.
I... I... I DON'T KNOW ANYTHING. I SWEAR.
SEE THESE?
I ONCE HAD AN OPPORTUNITY TO USE THEM ON THE NAILBITER HIMSELF. I WAS GOING TO DO SOMETHING THAT SHOULD HAVE BEEN DONE A LONG TIME AGO... RIP HIS TEETH RIGHT OUT OF HIS JAW.
BUT HE TAUNTED ME INTO STOPPING...
YOU'RE NO NAILBITER!
OKAY OKAY OKAY
I'LL TALK!

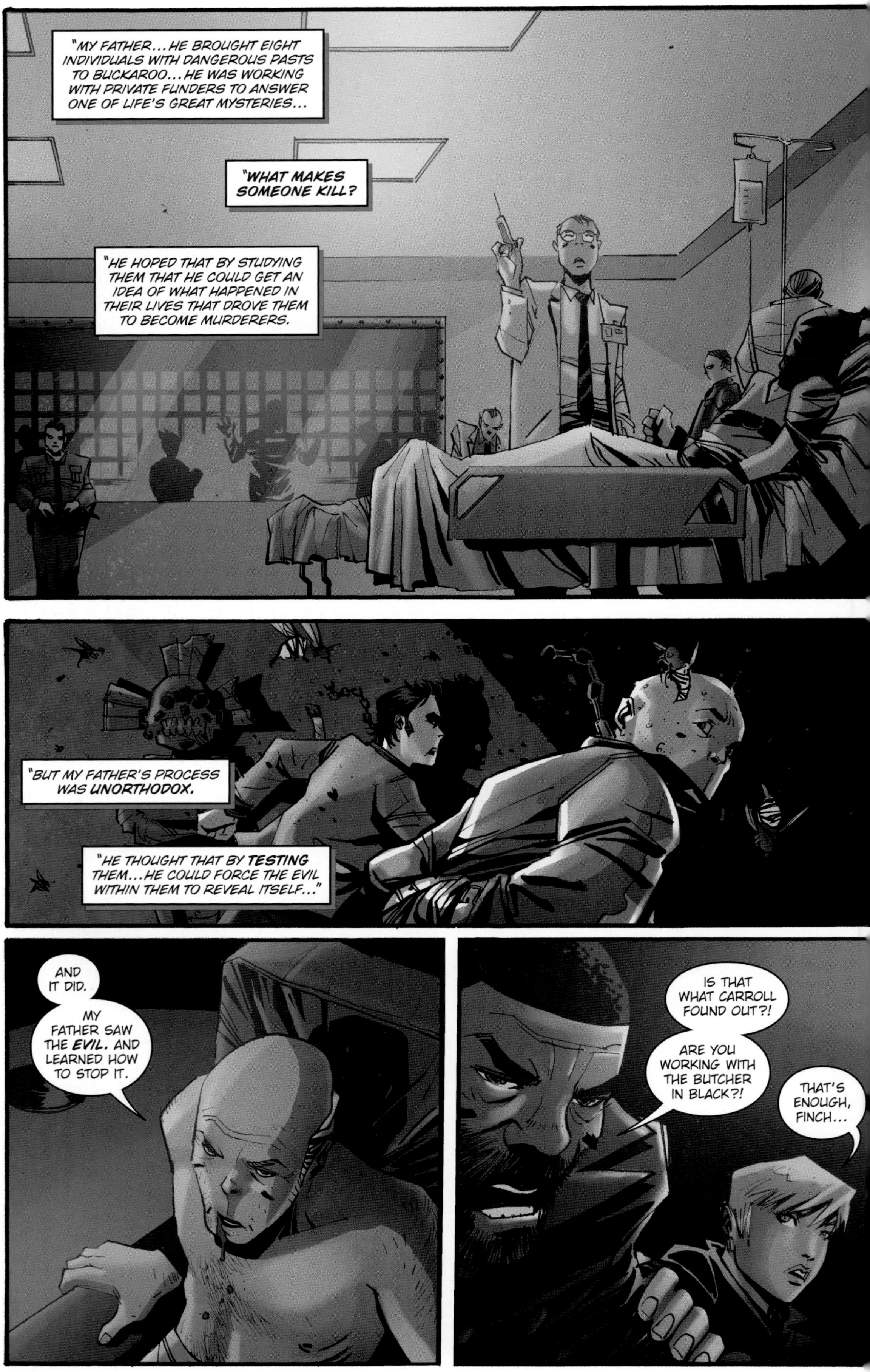
"MY FATHER... HE BROUGHT EIGHT INDIVIDUALS WITH DANGEROUS PASTS TO BUCKAROO... HE WAS WORKING WITH PRIVATE FUNDERS TO ANSWER ONE OF LIFE'S GREAT MYSTERIES...
"WHAT MAKES SOMEONE KILL?
"HE HOPED THAT BY STUDYING THEM THAT HE COULD GET AN IDEA OF WHAT HAPPENED IN THEIR LIVES THAT DROVE THEM TO BECOME MURDERERS.
"BUT MY FATHER'S PROCESS WAS UNORTHODOX.
"HE THOUGHT THAT BY TESTING THEM... HE COULD FORCE THE EVIL WITHIN THEM TO REVEAL ITSELF..."
AND IT DID.
MY FATHER SAW THE EVIL. AND LEARNED HOW TO STOP IT.
IS THAT WHAT CARROLL FOUND OUT?!
ARE YOU WORKING WITH THE BUTCHER IN BLACK?!
THAT'S ENOUGH, FINCH...

YOU SHOULD LISTEN TO HER, FINCH!

SIT YOUR ASS DOWN!

NO!

IF YOU ARE SO DESPERATE FOR THE TRUTH...

THIS... THIS IS THE TRUTH!

YOU WANT TO KNOW WHAT MY FATHER LEARNED?!

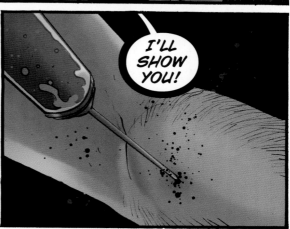

I'LL SHOW YOU!

WHAT DID YOU DO, GLORY?

I WILL SHOW YOU HOW KILLERS ARE MADE!

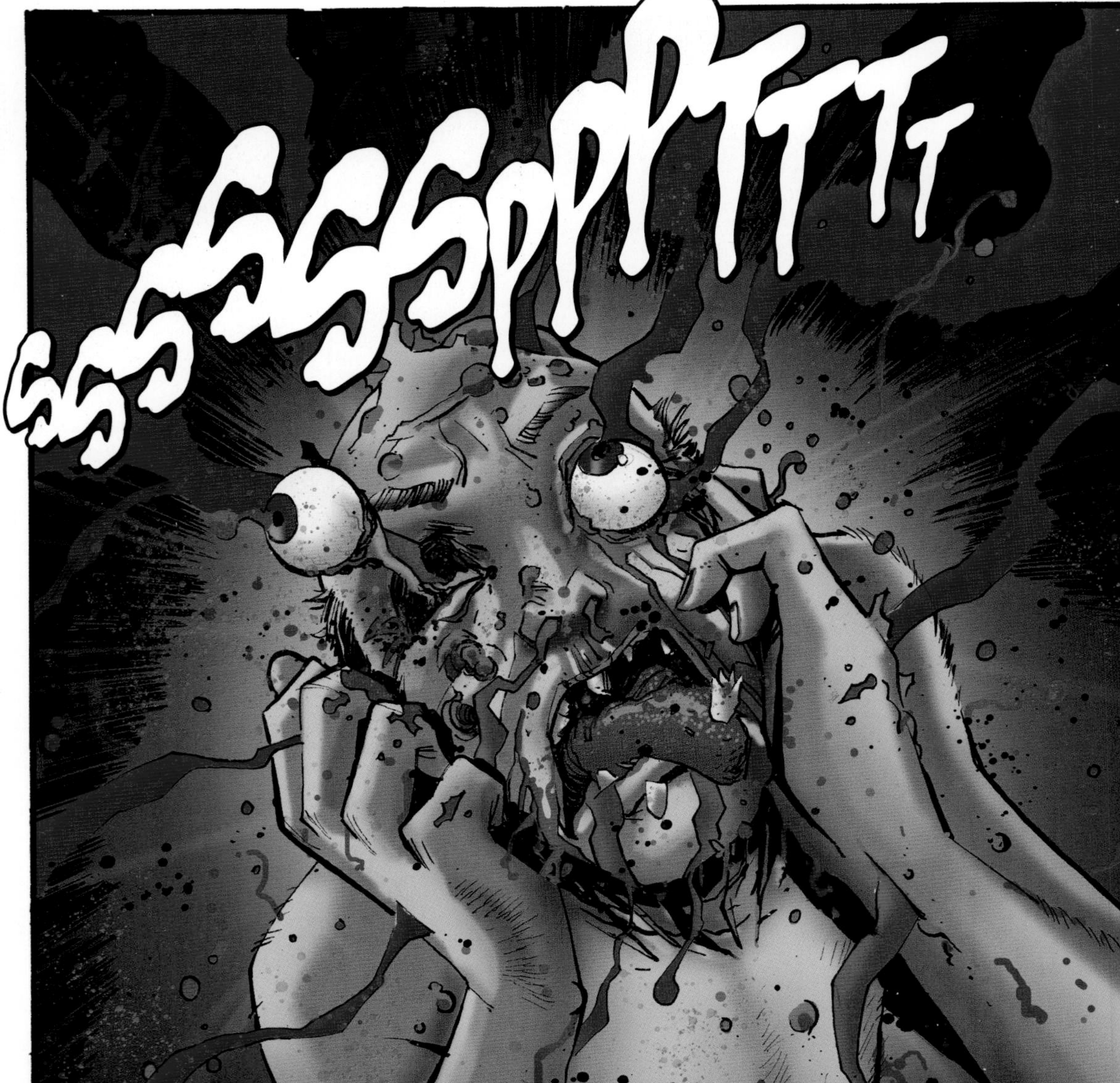
SSSSSSPPPTTTT

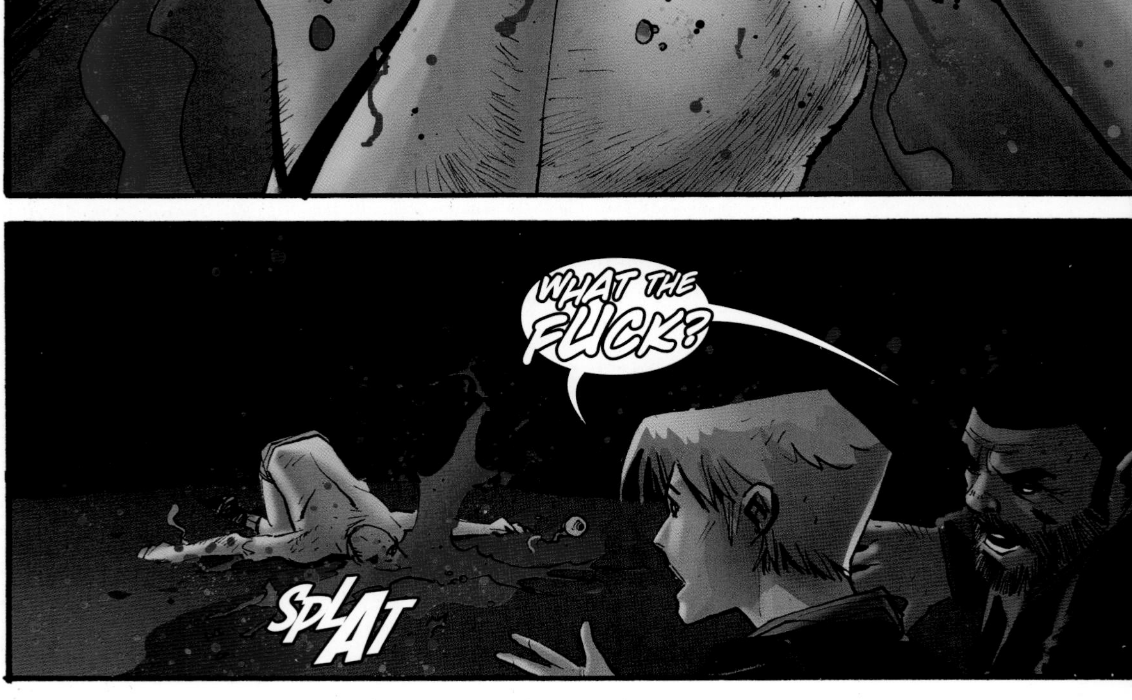
WHAT THE FUCK?
SPLAT

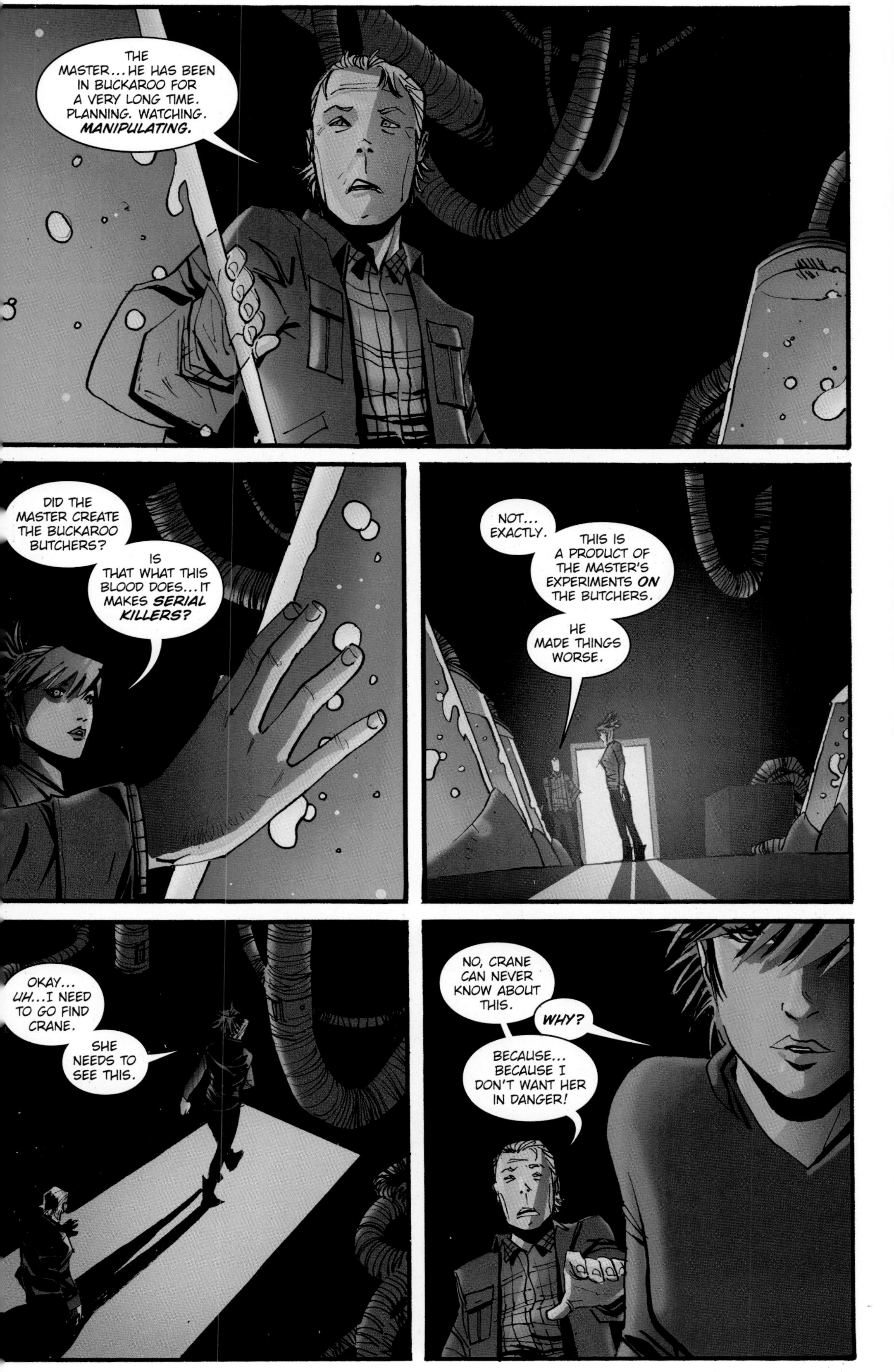
THE MASTER...HE HAS BEEN IN BUCKAROO FOR A VERY LONG TIME. PLANNING. WATCHING. MANIPULATING.
DID THE MASTER CREATE THE BUCKAROO BUTCHERS?
IS THAT WHAT THIS BLOOD DOES...IT MAKES SERIAL KILLERS?
NOT... EXACTLY.
THIS IS A PRODUCT OF THE MASTER'S EXPERIMENTS ON THE BUTCHERS.
HE MADE THINGS WORSE.
OKAY... UH...I NEED TO GO FIND CRANE.
SHE NEEDS TO SEE THIS.
NO, CRANE CAN NEVER KNOW ABOUT THIS.
WHY?
BECAUSE... BECAUSE I DON'T WANT HER IN DANGER!

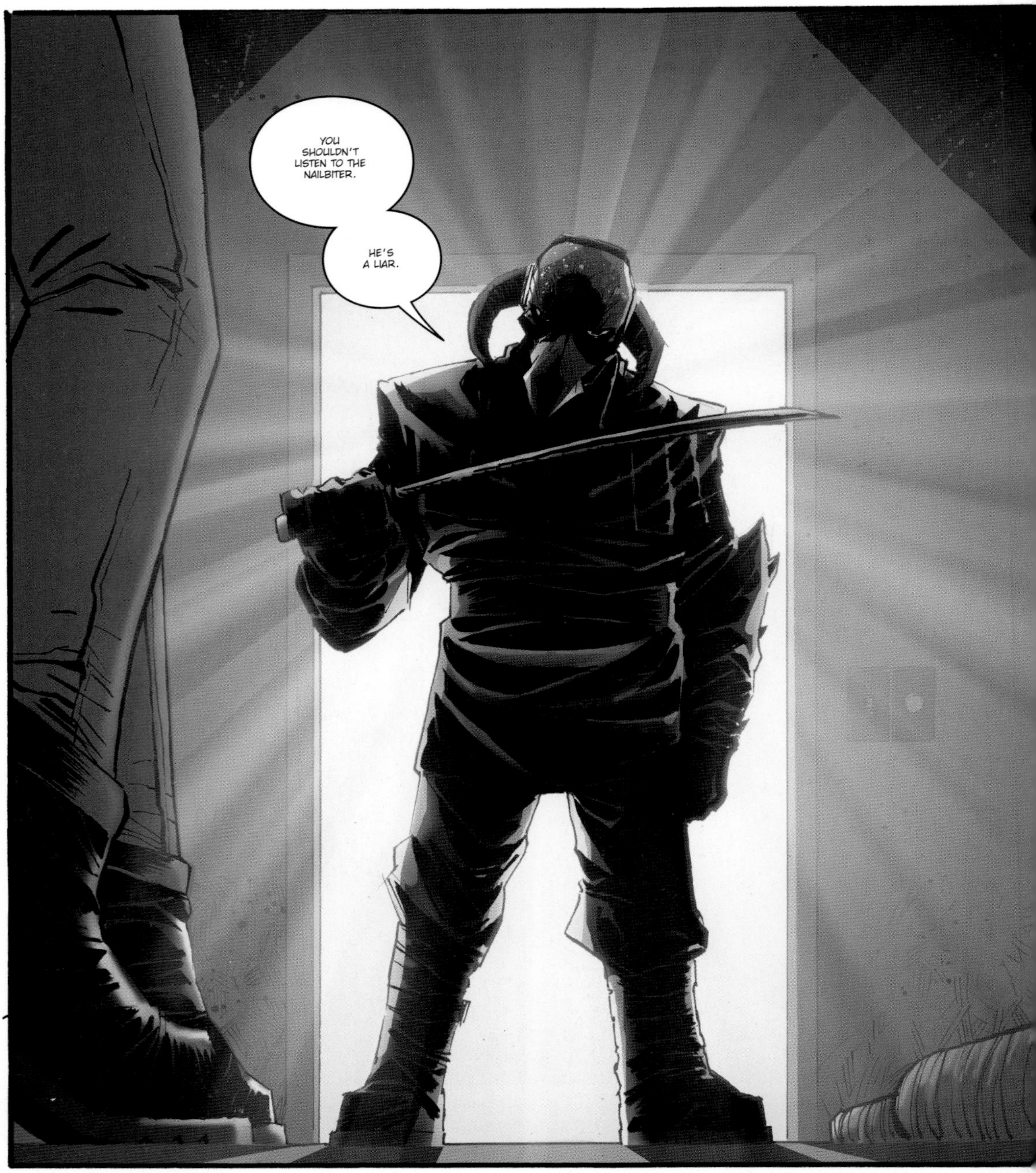
YOU SHOULDN'T LISTEN TO THE NAILBITER.
HE'S A LIAR.

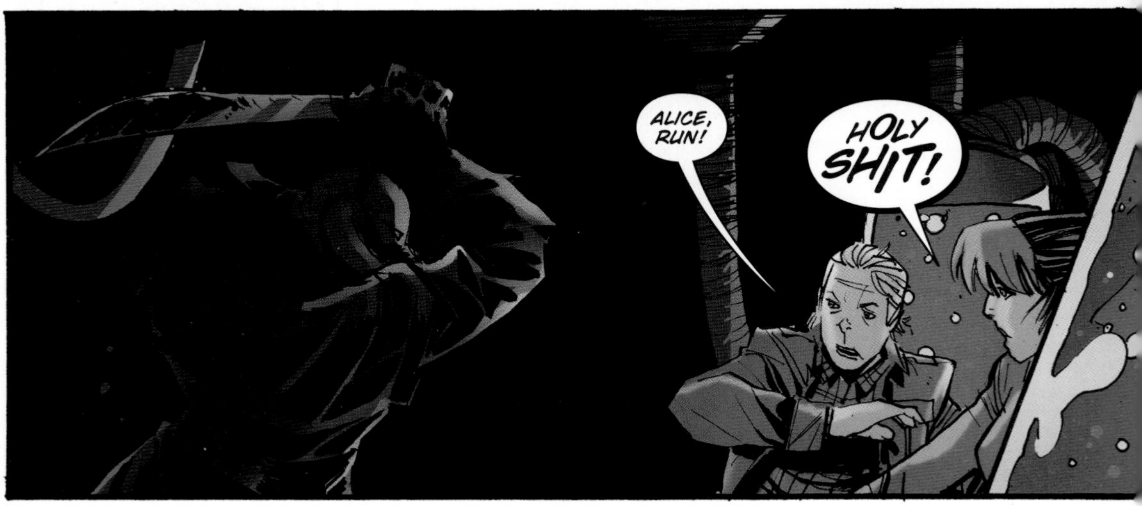
ALICE, RUN!
HOLY SHIT!

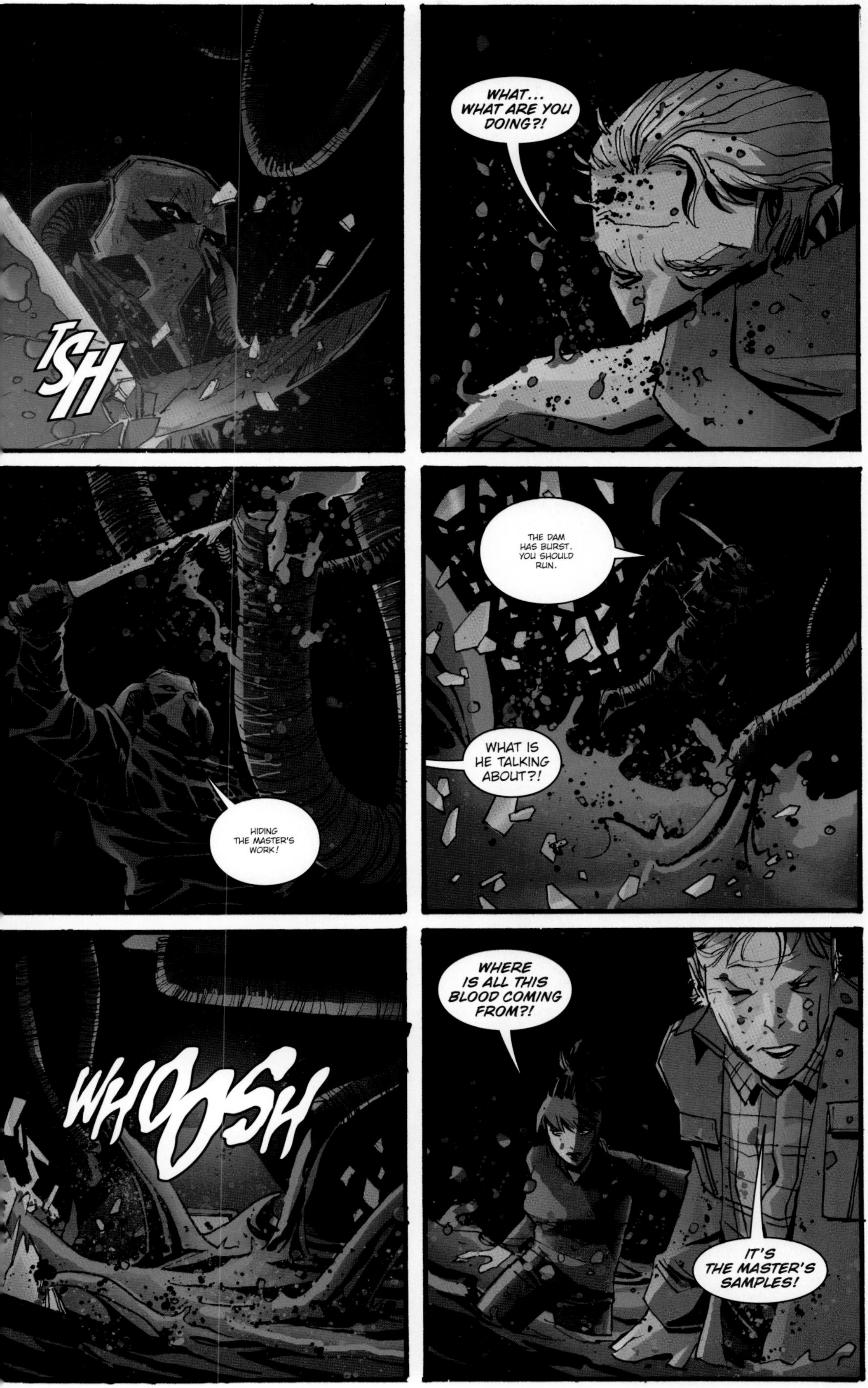
TSH
WHAT... WHAT ARE YOU DOING?!
HIDING THE MASTER'S WORK!
THE DAM HAS BURST. YOU SHOULD RUN.
WHAT IS HE TALKING ABOUT?!
WHOOSH
WHERE IS ALL THIS BLOOD COMING FROM?!
IT'S THE MASTER'S SAMPLES!

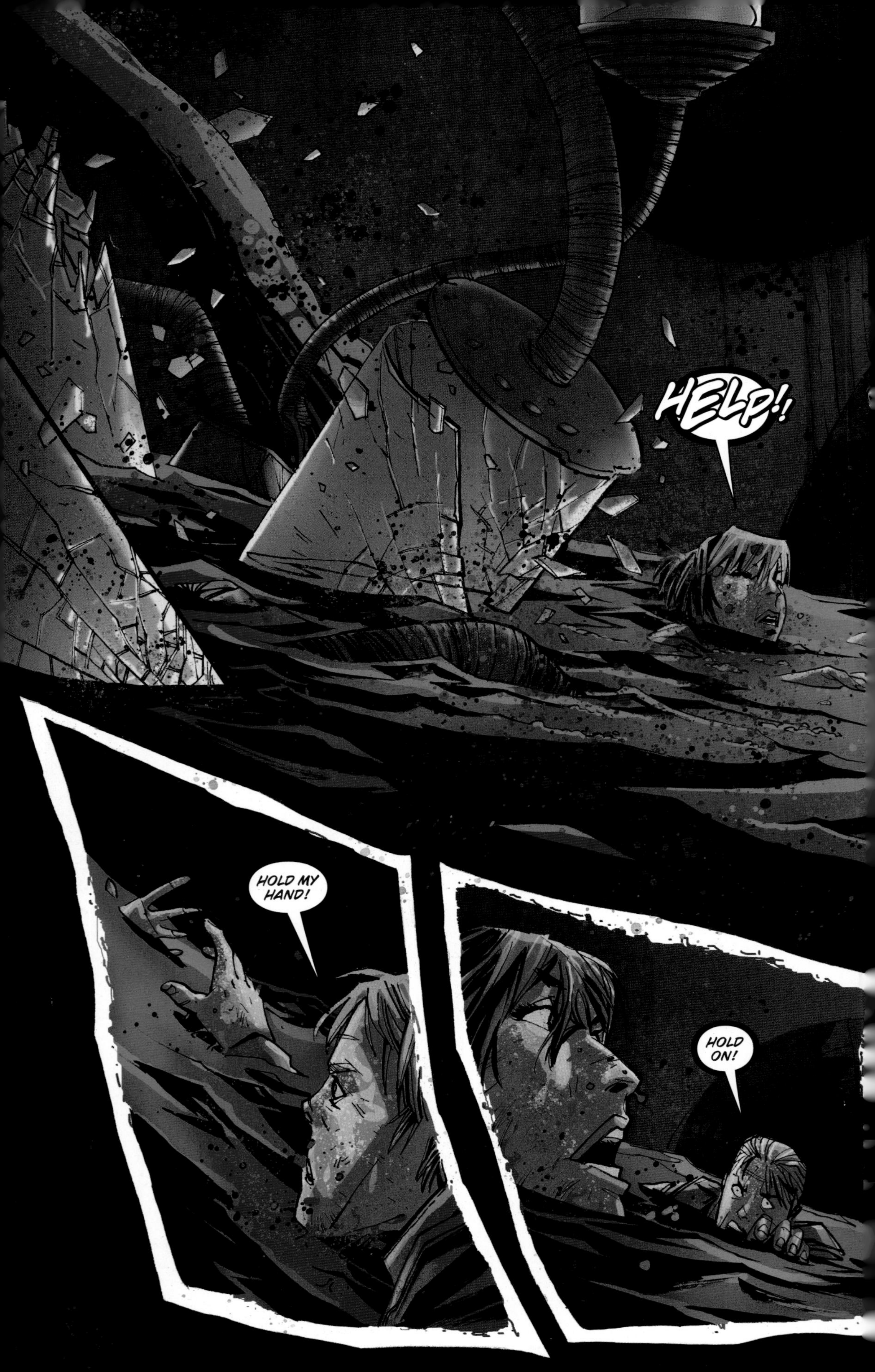
HELP!!
HOLD MY HAND!
HOLD ON!

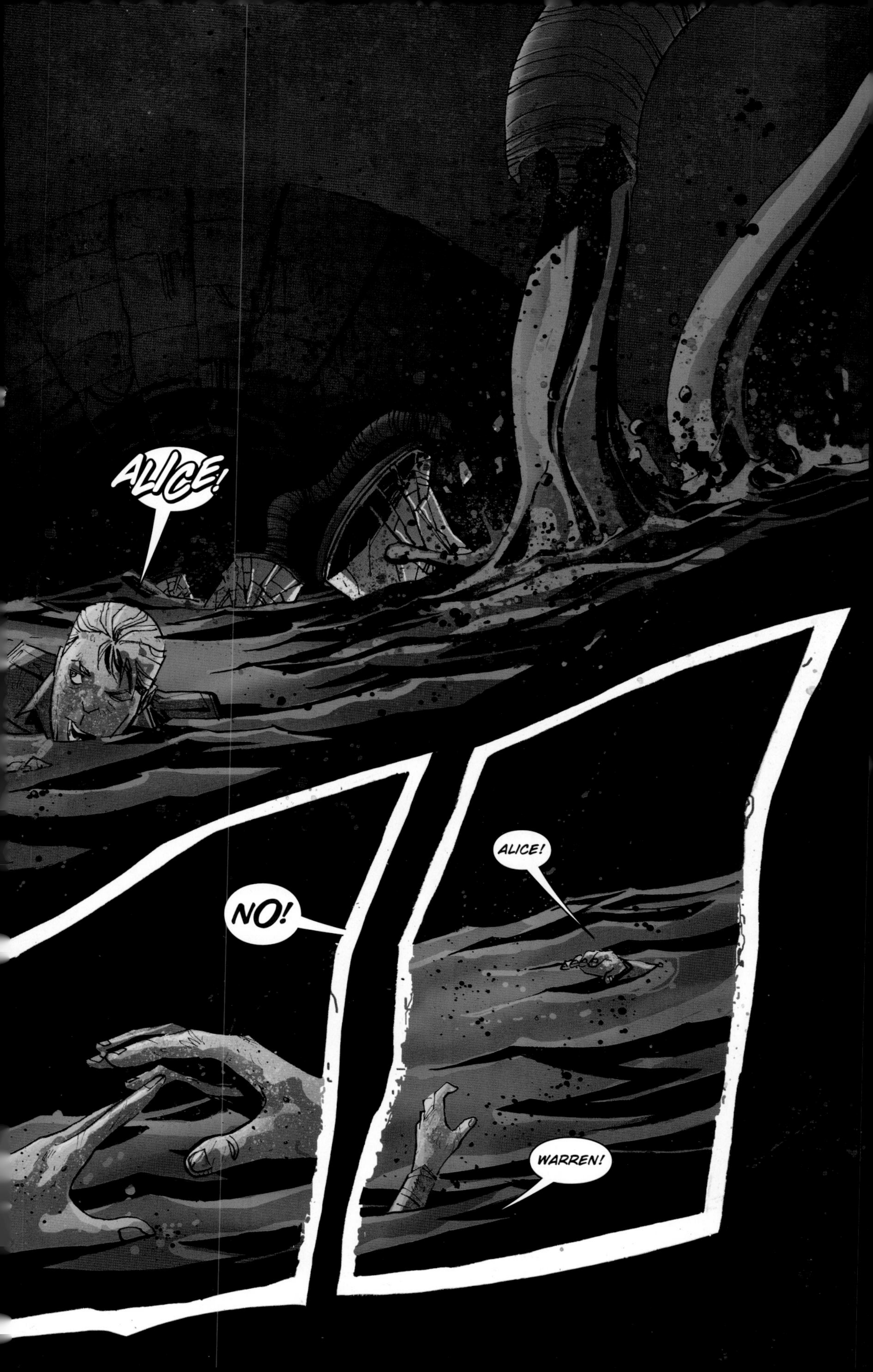
ALICE!
NO!
ALICE!
WARREN!

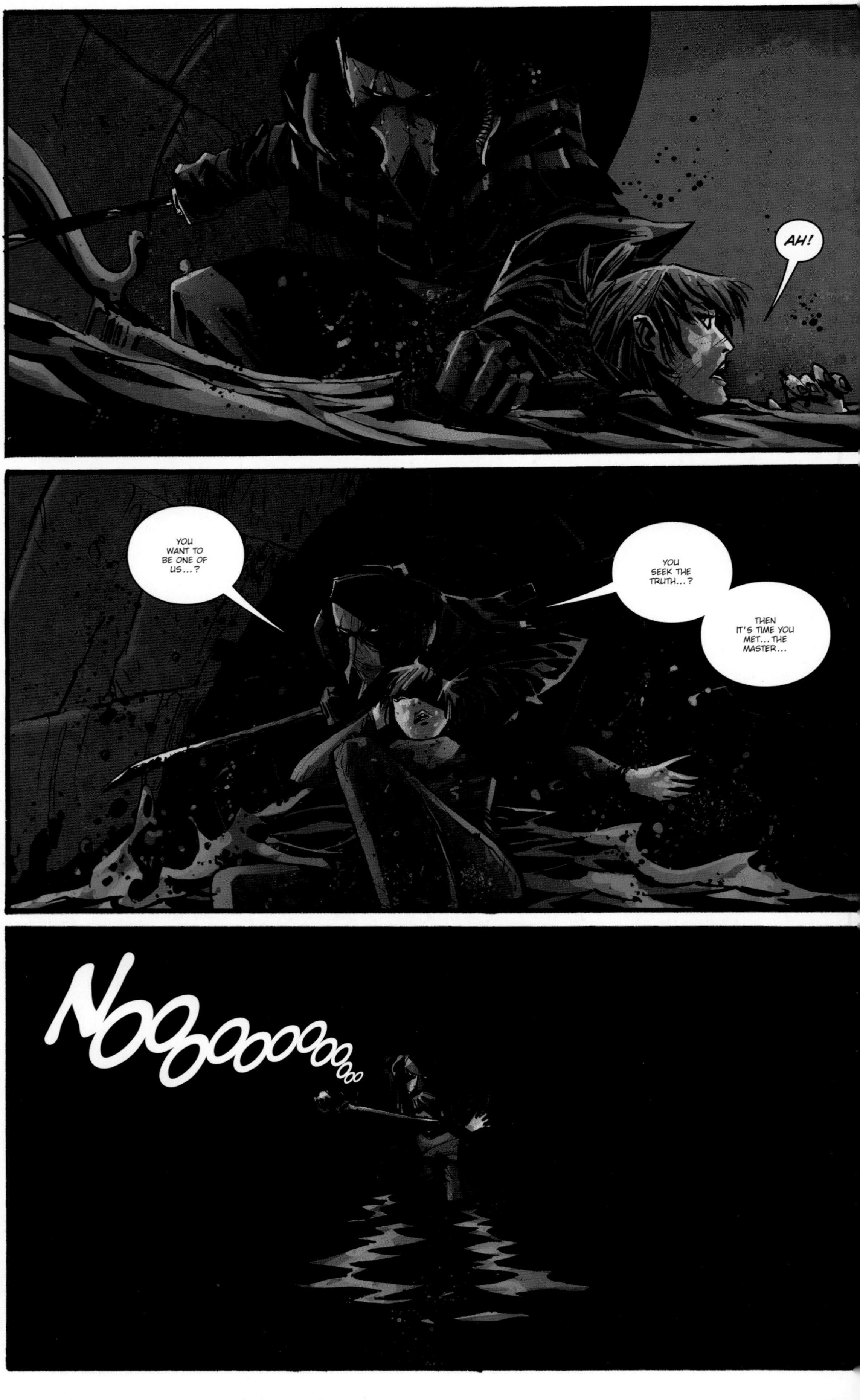
AH!
YOU WANT TO BE ONE OF US...?
YOU SEEK THE TRUTH...?
THEN IT'S TIME YOU MET... THE MASTER...
NOOOOOOOOOOOO

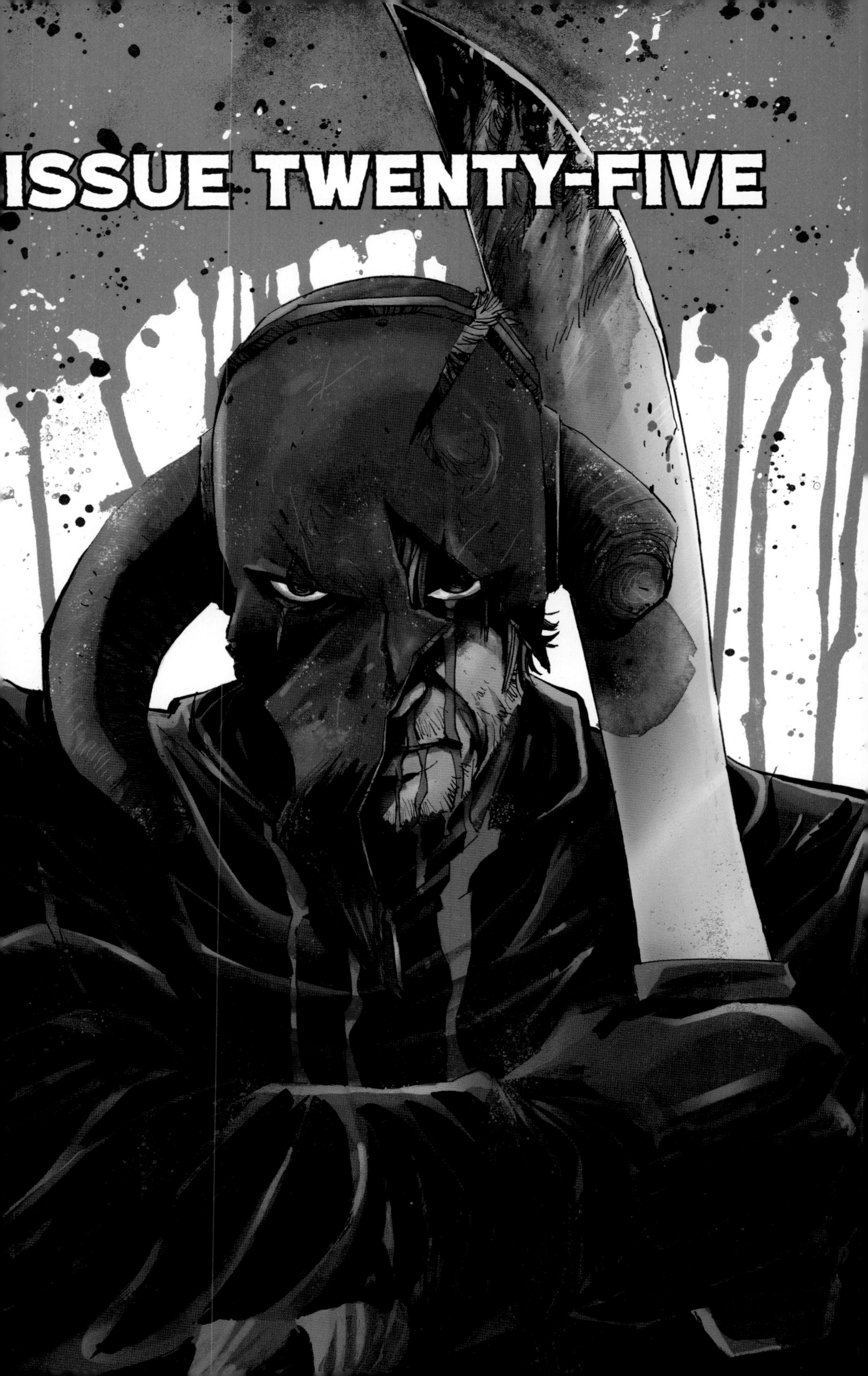
ISSUE TWENTY-FIVE

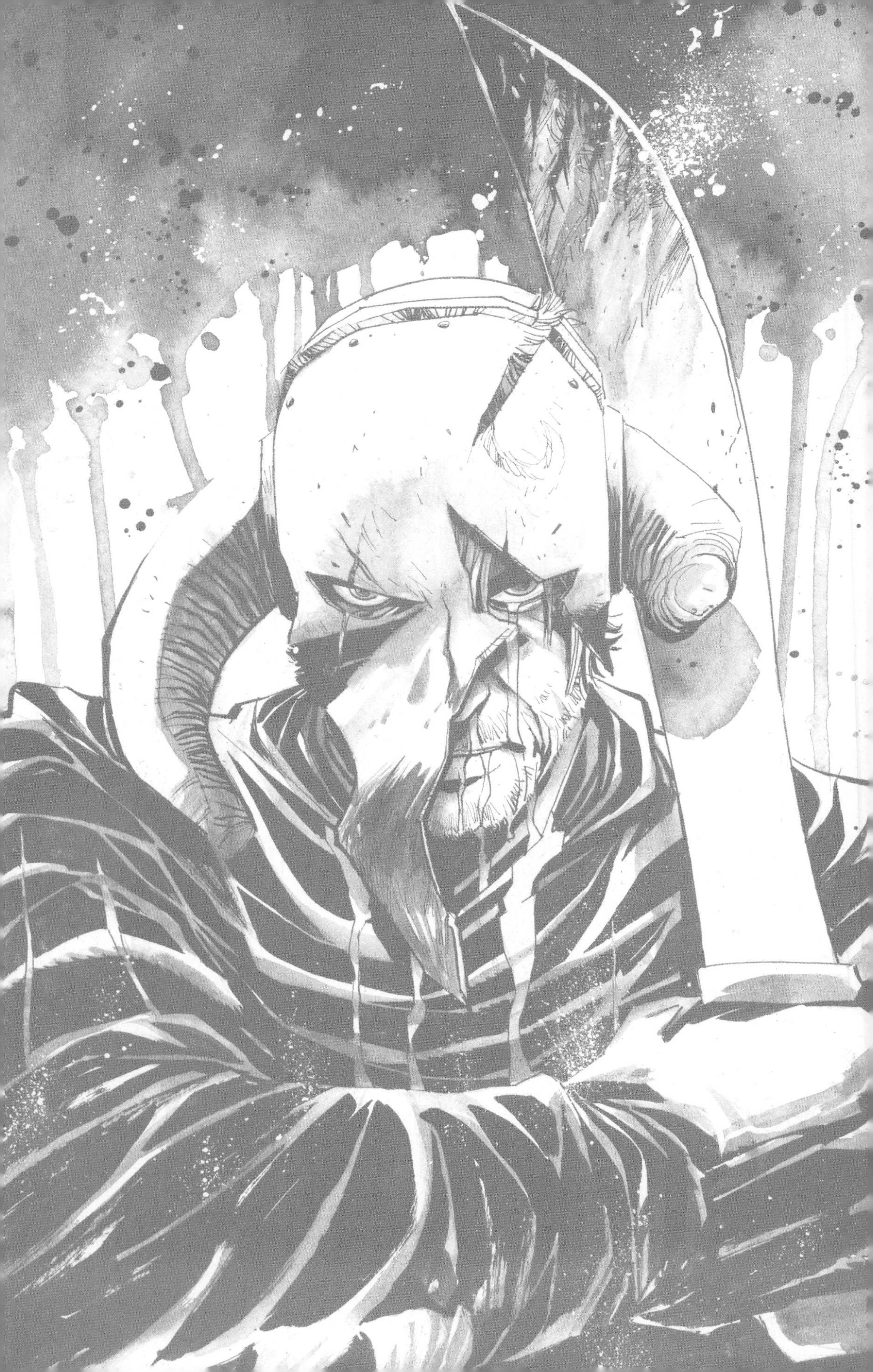

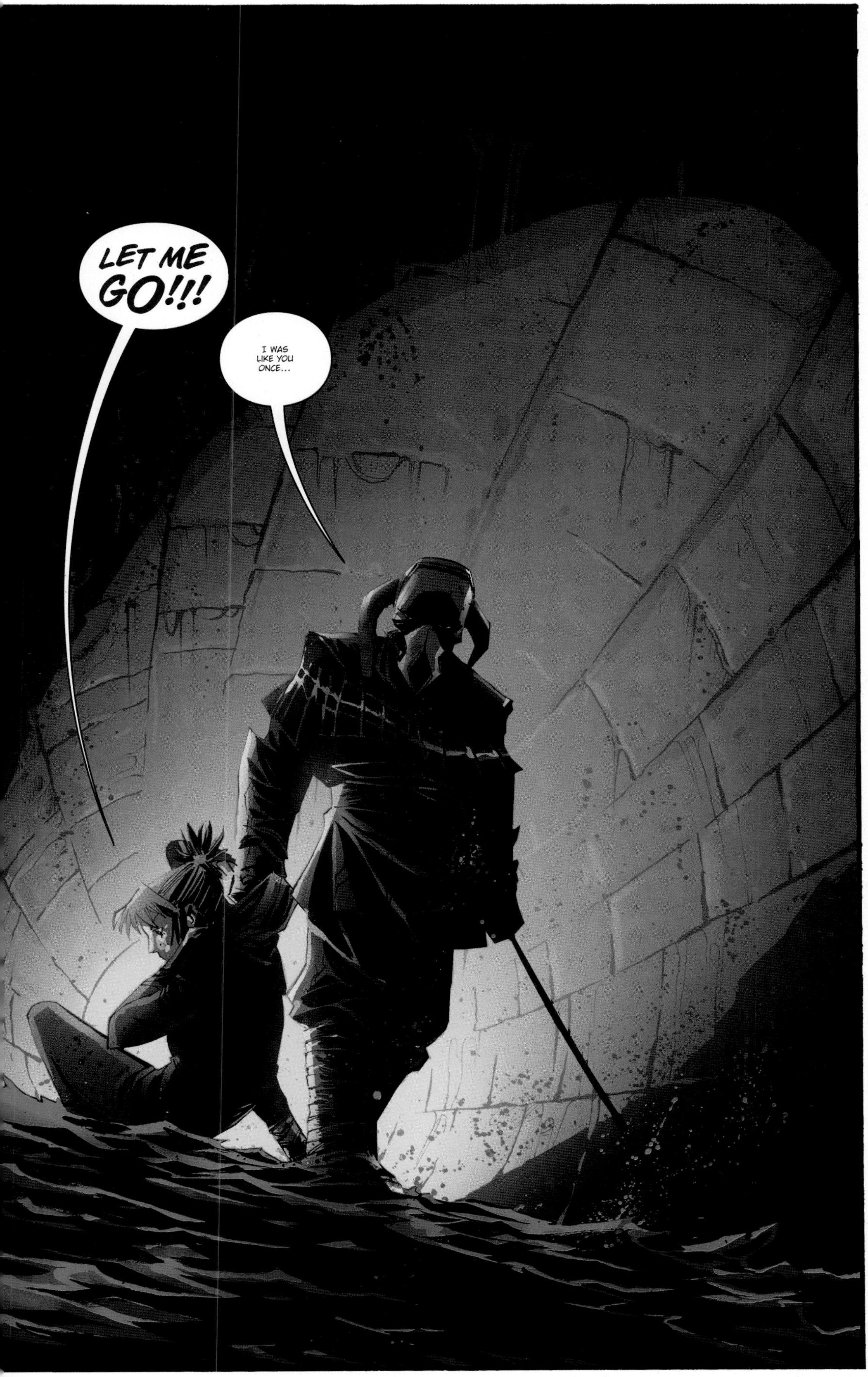
LET ME GO!!!
I WAS LIKE YOU ONCE...

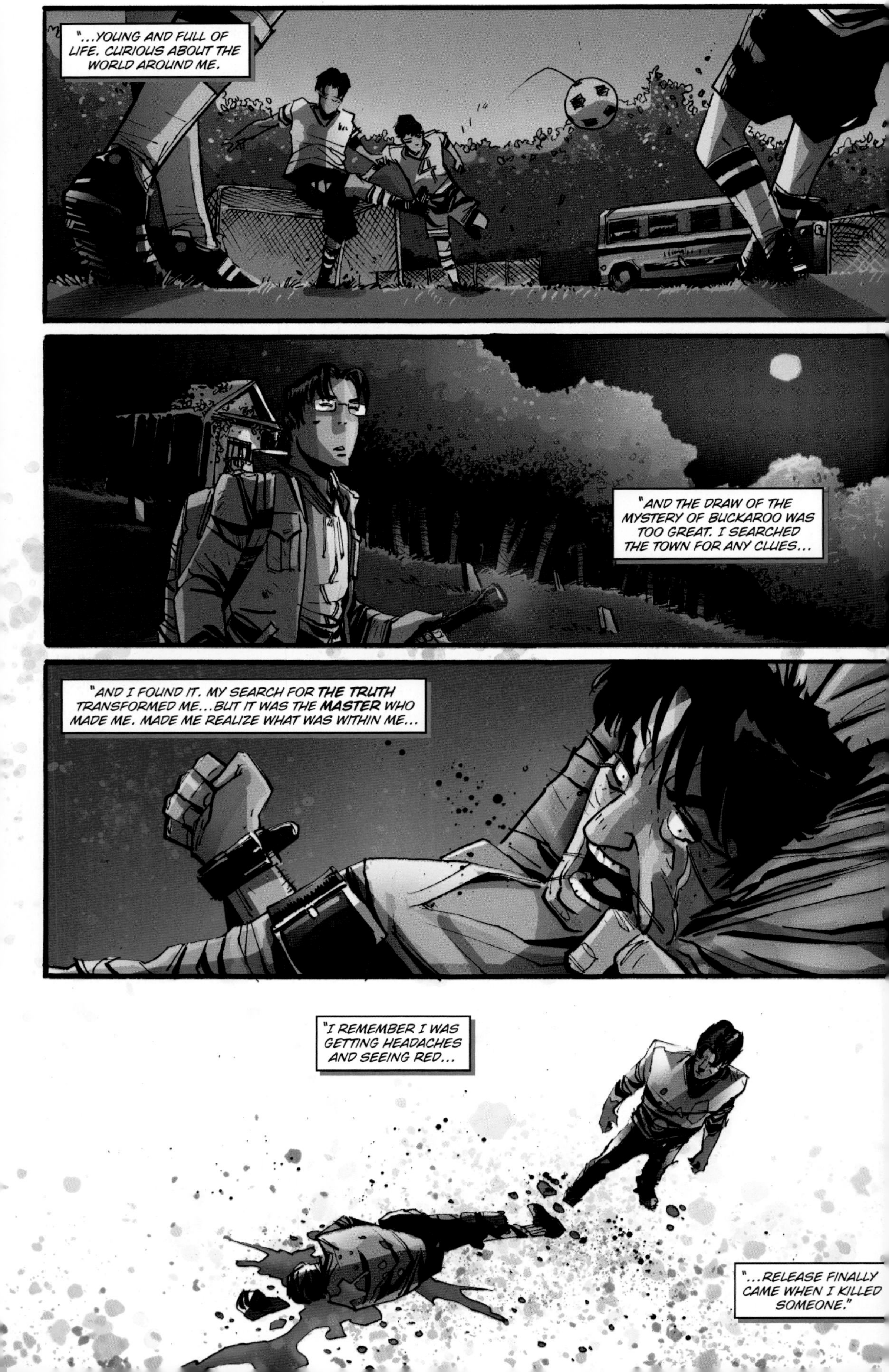
"...YOUNG AND FULL OF LIFE. CURIOUS ABOUT THE WORLD AROUND ME.
"AND THE DRAW OF THE MYSTERY OF BUCKAROO WAS TOO GREAT. I SEARCHED THE TOWN FOR ANY CLUES...
"AND I FOUND IT. MY SEARCH FOR **THE TRUTH** TRANSFORMED ME...BUT IT WAS THE **MASTER** WHO MADE ME. MADE ME REALIZE WHAT WAS WITHIN ME...
"I REMEMBER I WAS GETTING HEADACHES AND SEEING RED...
"...RELEASE FINALLY CAME WHEN I KILLED SOMEONE."

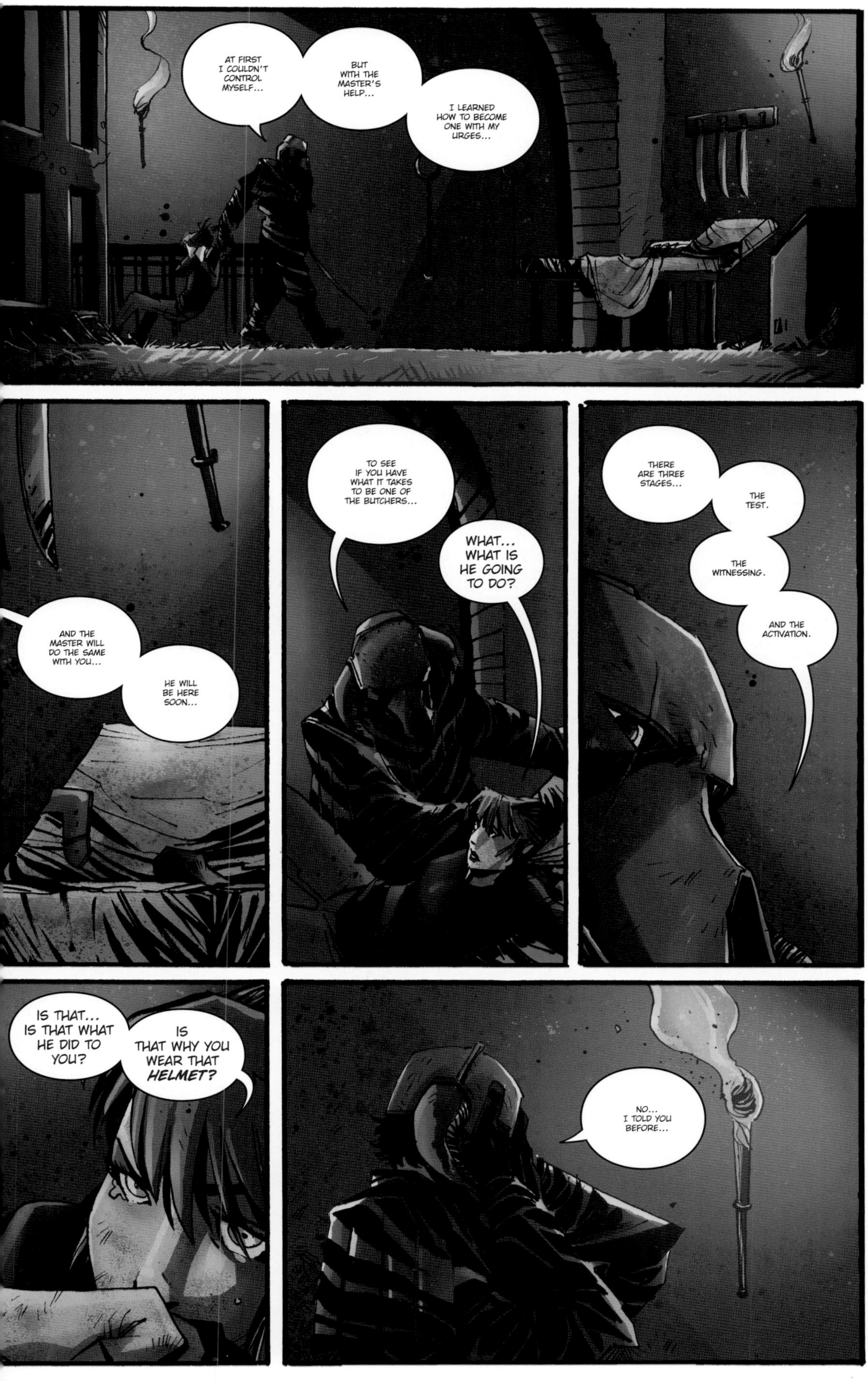
AT FIRST I COULDN'T CONTROL MYSELF...
BUT WITH THE MASTER'S HELP...
I LEARNED HOW TO BECOME ONE WITH MY URGES...
AND THE MASTER WILL DO THE SAME WITH YOU...
HE WILL BE HERE SOON...
TO SEE IF YOU HAVE WHAT IT TAKES TO BE ONE OF THE BUTCHERS...
WHAT... WHAT IS HE GOING TO DO?
THERE ARE THREE STAGES...
THE TEST.
THE WITNESSING.
AND THE ACTIVATION.
IS THAT... IS THAT WHAT HE DID TO YOU?
IS THAT WHY YOU WEAR THAT *HELMET?*
NO... I TOLD YOU BEFORE...

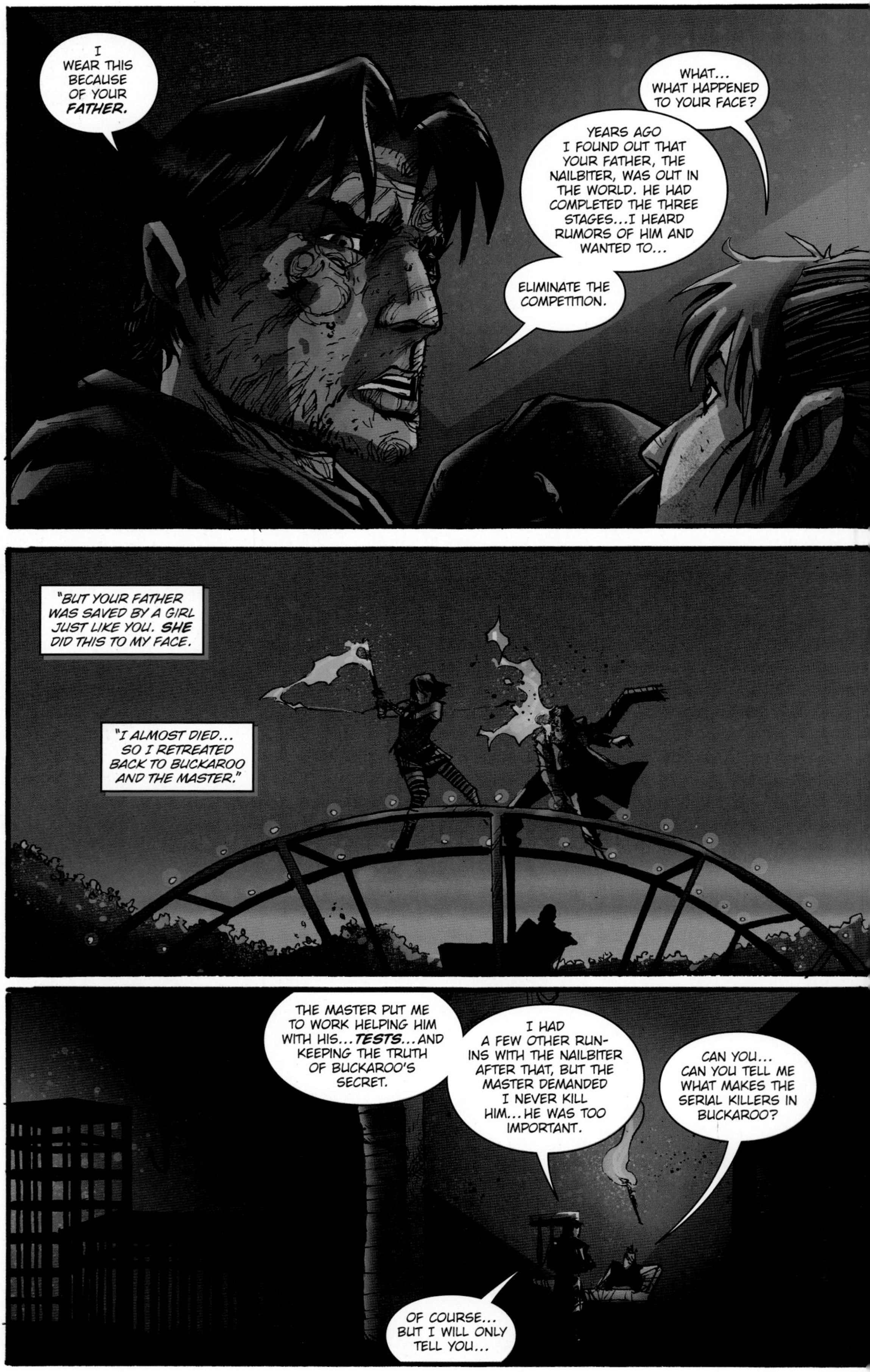
I WEAR THIS BECAUSE OF YOUR ***FATHER.***
WHAT... WHAT HAPPENED TO YOUR FACE?
YEARS AGO I FOUND OUT THAT YOUR FATHER, THE NAILBITER, WAS OUT IN THE WORLD. HE HAD COMPLETED THE THREE STAGES...I HEARD RUMORS OF HIM AND WANTED TO...
ELIMINATE THE COMPETITION.
"BUT YOUR FATHER WAS SAVED BY A GIRL JUST LIKE YOU. ***SHE*** DID THIS TO MY FACE.
"I ALMOST DIED... SO I RETREATED BACK TO BUCKAROO AND THE MASTER."
THE MASTER PUT ME TO WORK HELPING HIM WITH HIS...***TESTS***...AND KEEPING THE TRUTH OF BUCKAROO'S SECRET.
I HAD A FEW OTHER RUN-INS WITH THE NAILBITER AFTER THAT, BUT THE MASTER DEMANDED I NEVER KILL HIM...HE WAS TOO IMPORTANT.
CAN YOU... CAN YOU TELL ME WHAT MAKES THE SERIAL KILLERS IN BUCKAROO?
OF COURSE... BUT I WILL ONLY TELL YOU...

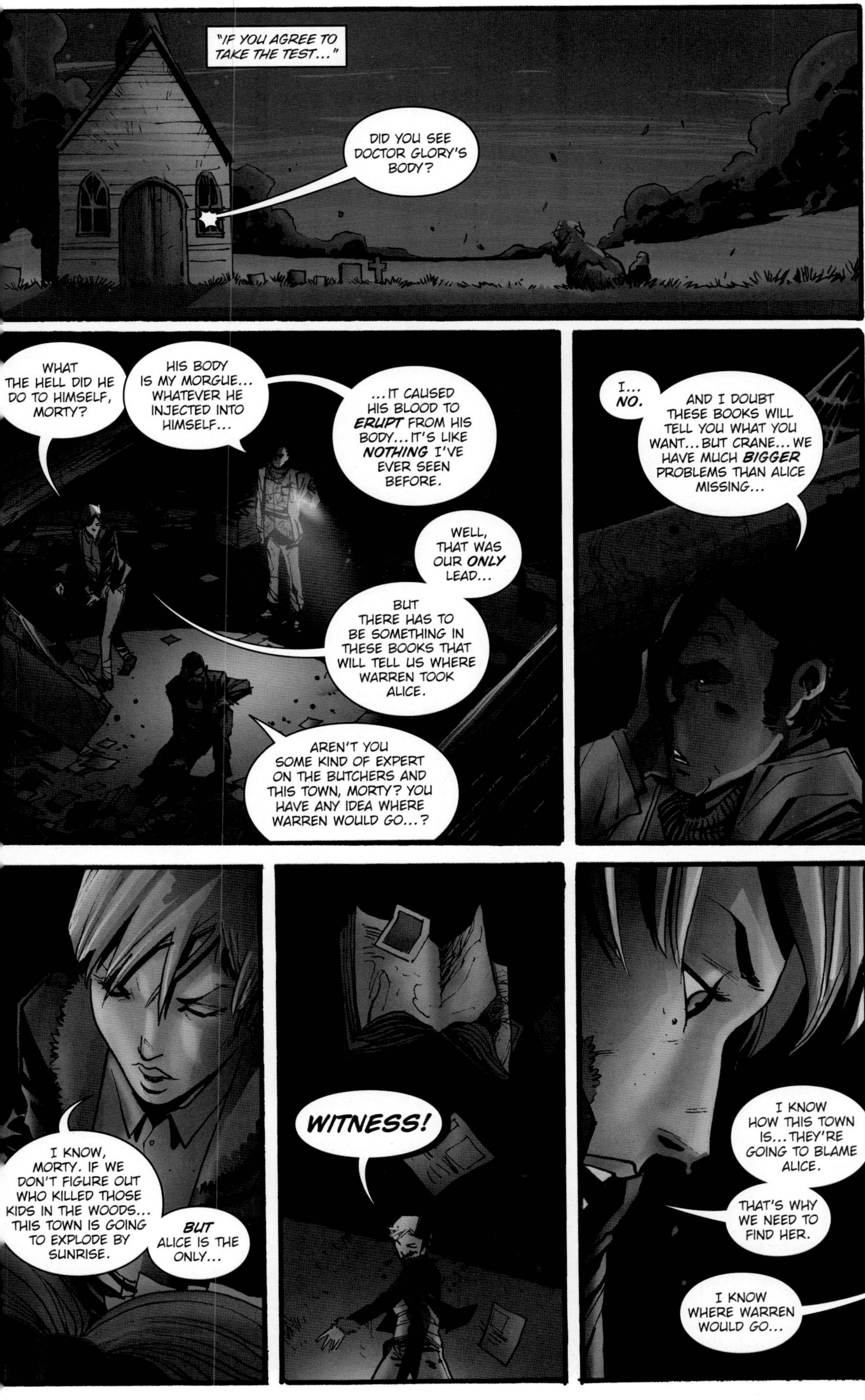
"IF YOU AGREE TO TAKE THE TEST..."
DID YOU SEE DOCTOR GLORY'S BODY?
WHAT THE HELL DID HE DO TO HIMSELF, MORTY?
HIS BODY IS MY MORGUE... WHATEVER HE INJECTED INTO HIMSELF...
...IT CAUSED HIS BLOOD TO ERUPT FROM HIS BODY...IT'S LIKE NOTHING I'VE EVER SEEN BEFORE.
WELL, THAT WAS OUR ONLY LEAD...
BUT THERE HAS TO BE SOMETHING IN THESE BOOKS THAT WILL TELL US WHERE WARREN TOOK ALICE.
AREN'T YOU SOME KIND OF EXPERT ON THE BUTCHERS AND THIS TOWN, MORTY? YOU HAVE ANY IDEA WHERE WARREN WOULD GO...?
I... NO.
AND I DOUBT THESE BOOKS WILL TELL YOU WHAT YOU WANT...BUT CRANE...WE HAVE MUCH BIGGER PROBLEMS THAN ALICE MISSING...
I KNOW, MORTY. IF WE DON'T FIGURE OUT WHO KILLED THOSE KIDS IN THE WOODS... THIS TOWN IS GOING TO EXPLODE BY SUNRISE.
BUT ALICE IS THE ONLY...
WITNESS!
I KNOW HOW THIS TOWN IS...THEY'RE GOING TO BLAME ALICE.
THAT'S WHY WE NEED TO FIND HER.
I KNOW WHERE WARREN WOULD GO...

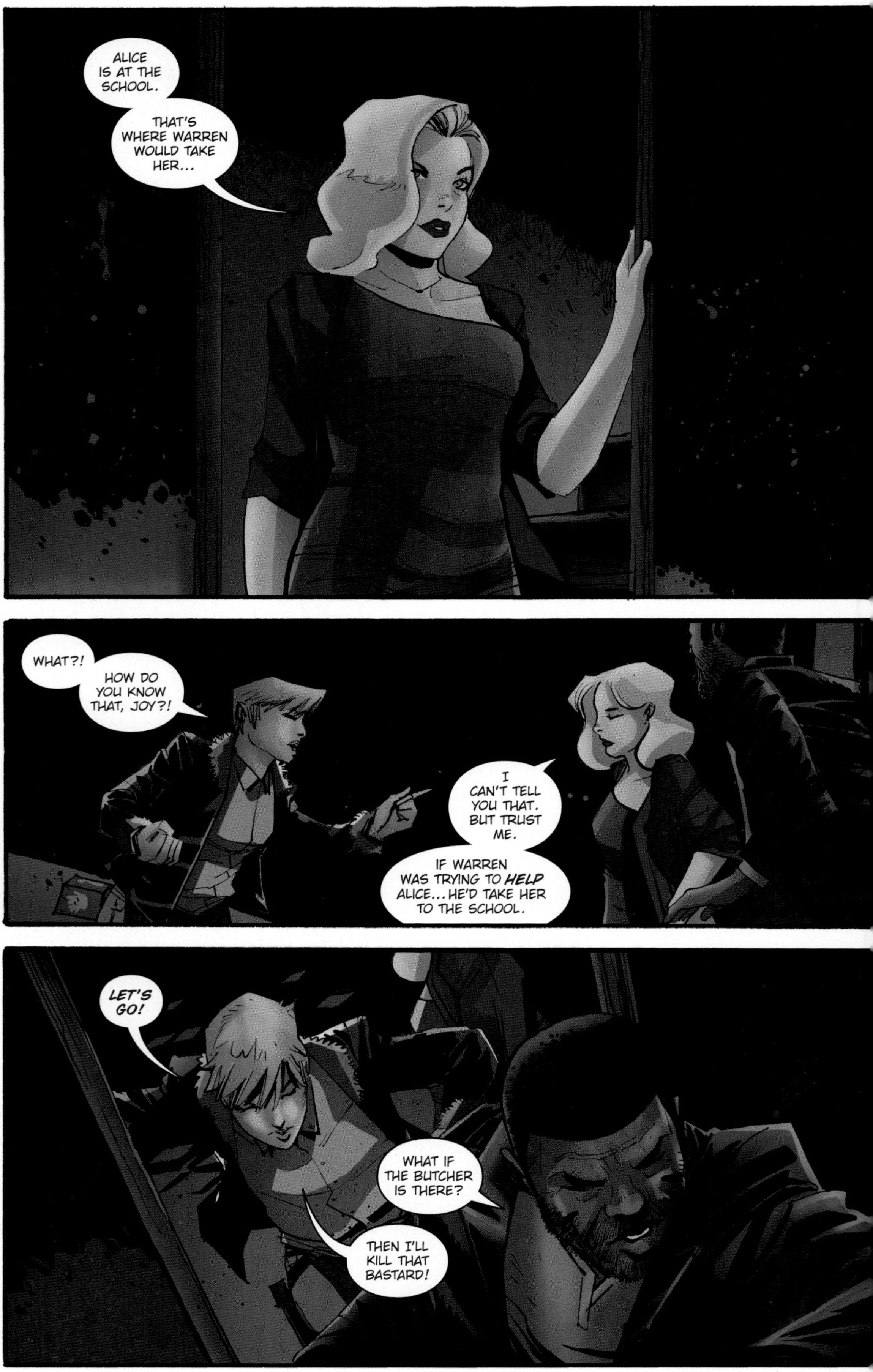
ALICE IS AT THE SCHOOL.
THAT'S WHERE WARREN WOULD TAKE HER...
WHAT?!
HOW DO YOU KNOW THAT, JOY?!
I CAN'T TELL YOU THAT. BUT TRUST ME.
IF WARREN WAS TRYING TO *HELP* ALICE... HE'D TAKE HER TO THE SCHOOL.
LET'S GO!
WHAT IF THE BUTCHER IS THERE?
THEN I'LL KILL THAT BASTARD!

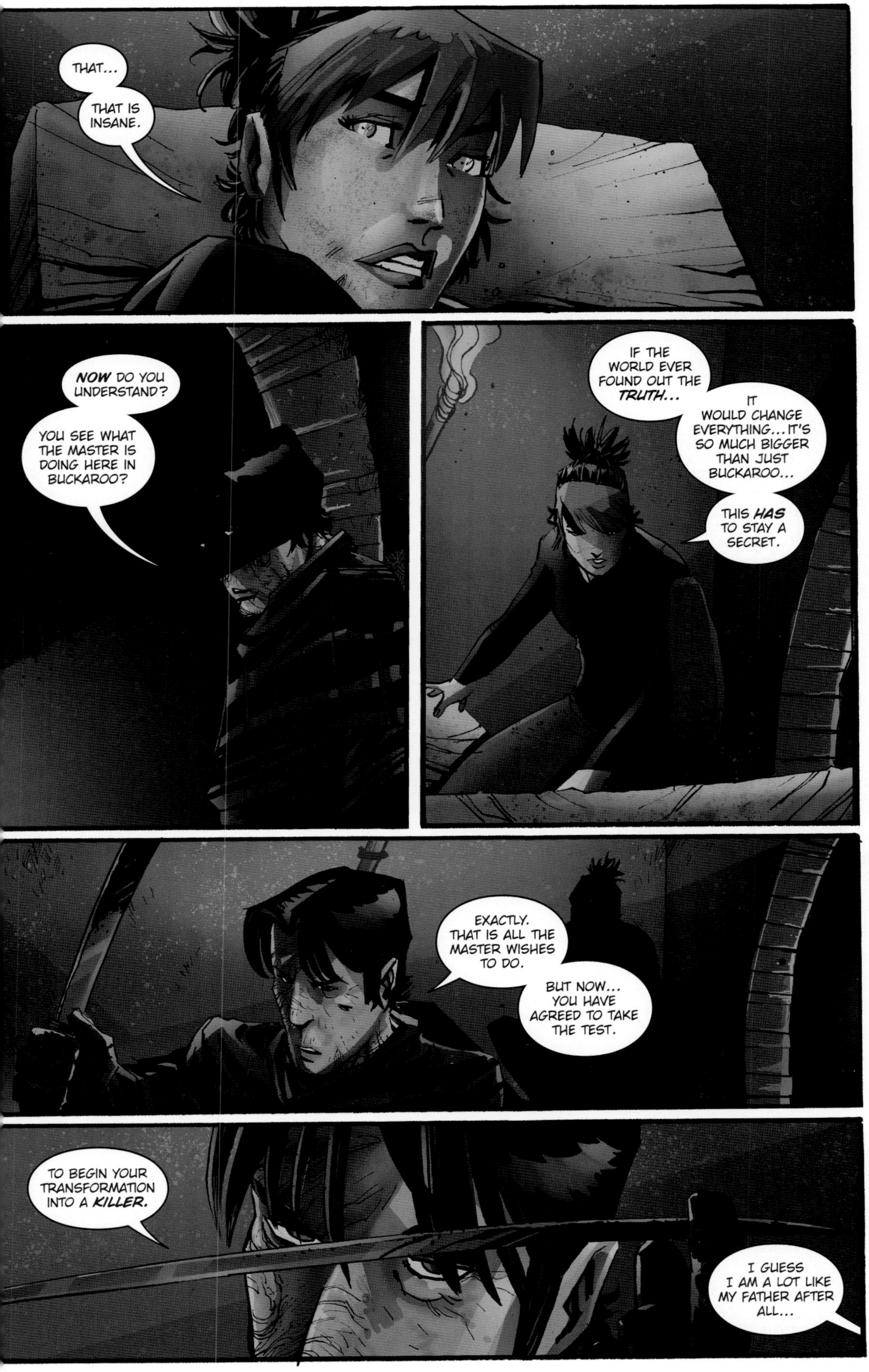
THAT...
THAT IS INSANE.
NOW DO YOU UNDERSTAND?
YOU SEE WHAT THE MASTER IS DOING HERE IN BUCKAROO?
IF THE WORLD EVER FOUND OUT THE TRUTH...
IT WOULD CHANGE EVERYTHING... IT'S SO MUCH BIGGER THAN JUST BUCKAROO...
THIS HAS TO STAY A SECRET.
EXACTLY. THAT IS ALL THE MASTER WISHES TO DO.
BUT NOW... YOU HAVE AGREED TO TAKE THE TEST.
TO BEGIN YOUR TRANSFORMATION INTO A KILLER.
I GUESS I AM A LOT LIKE MY FATHER AFTER ALL...

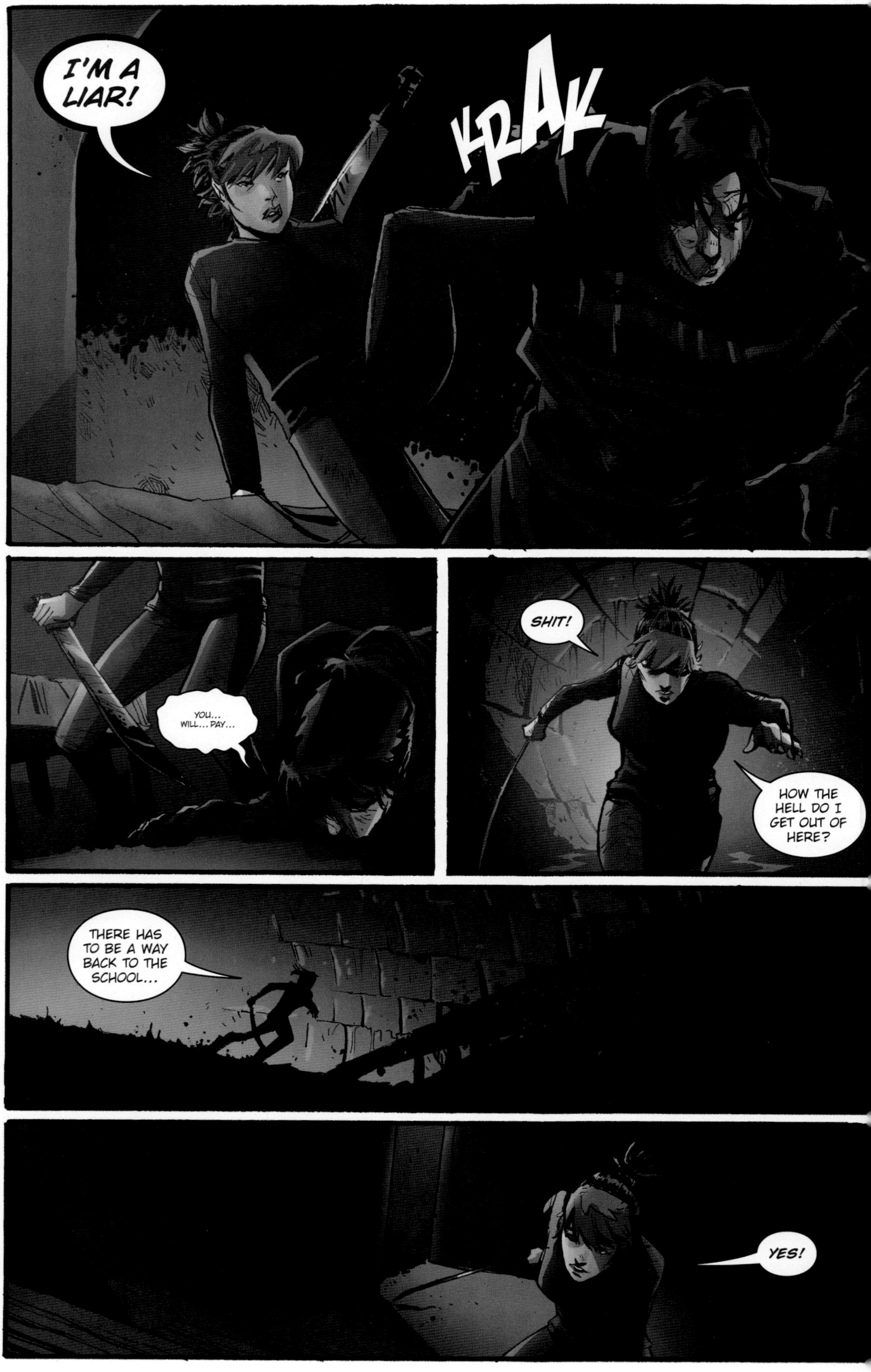
I'M A LIAR!
KRAK
YOU... WILL... PAY...
SHIT!
HOW THE HELL DO I GET OUT OF HERE?
THERE HAS TO BE A WAY BACK TO THE SCHOOL...
YES!

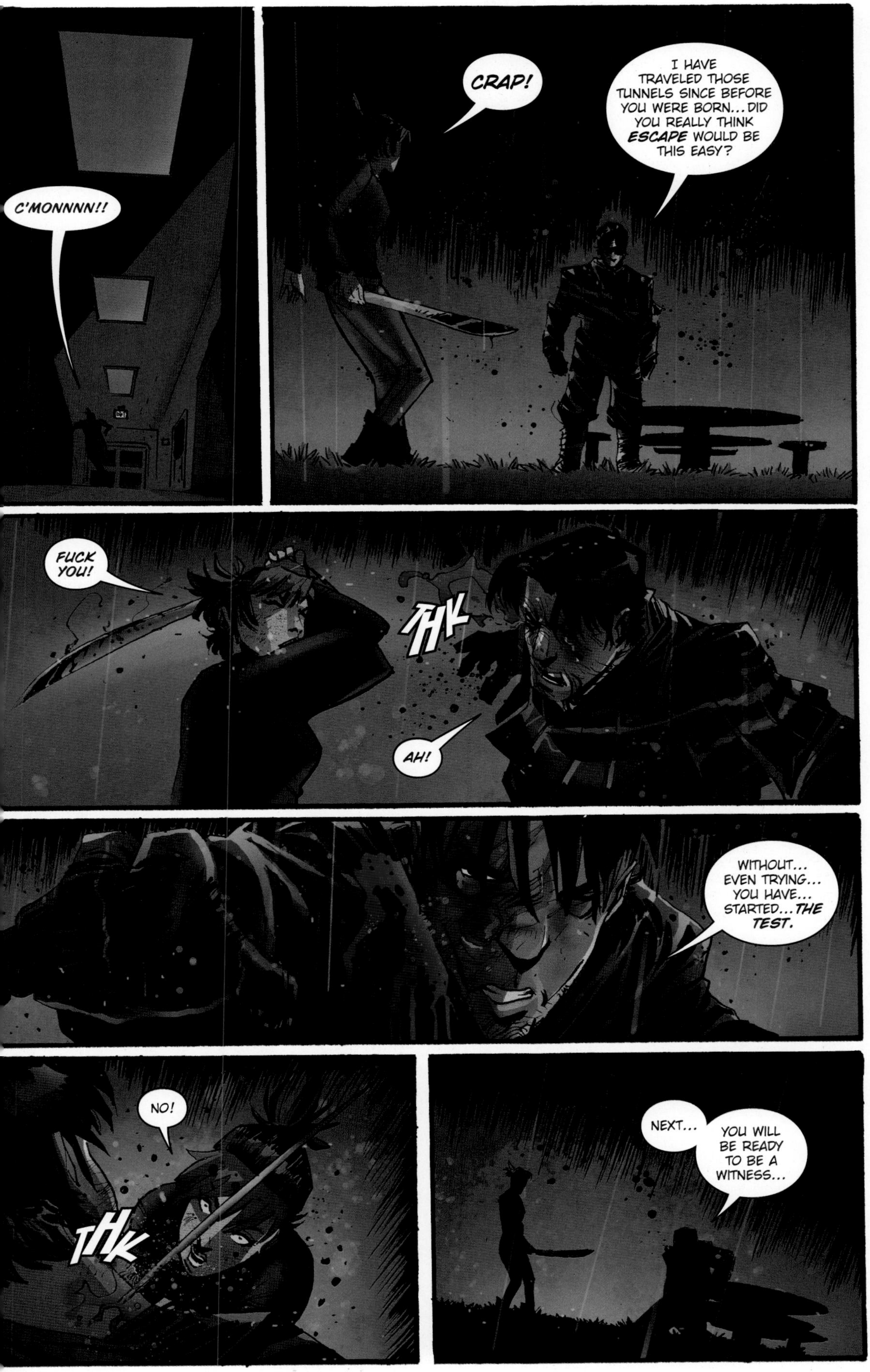
C'MONNNN!!
CRAP!
I HAVE TRAVELED THOSE TUNNELS SINCE BEFORE YOU WERE BORN... DID YOU REALLY THINK ESCAPE WOULD BE THIS EASY?
FUCK YOU!
THK
AH!
WITHOUT... EVEN TRYING... YOU HAVE... STARTED... THE TEST.
NO!
THK
NEXT...
YOU WILL BE READY TO BE A WITNESS...

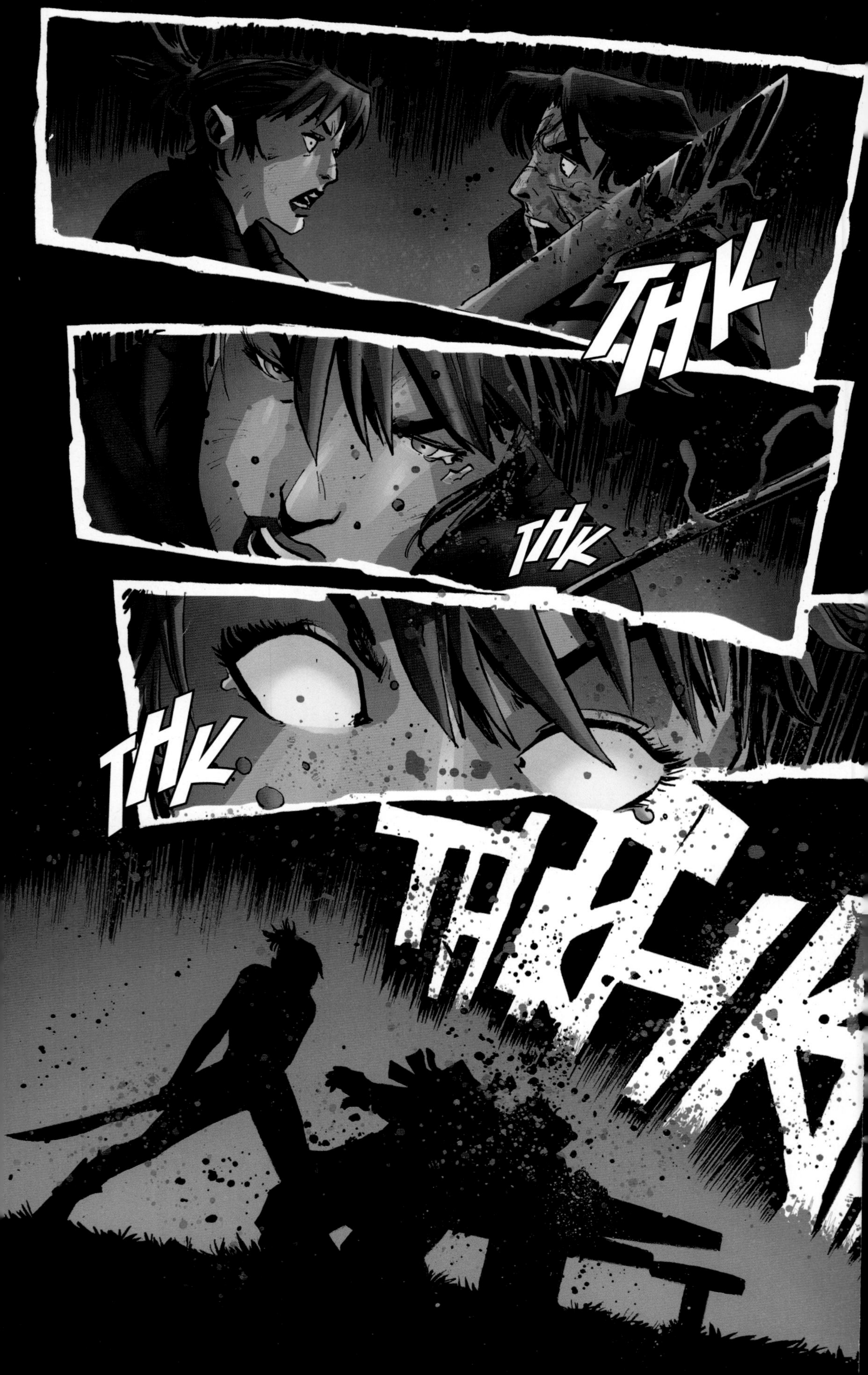
THK
THK
THK

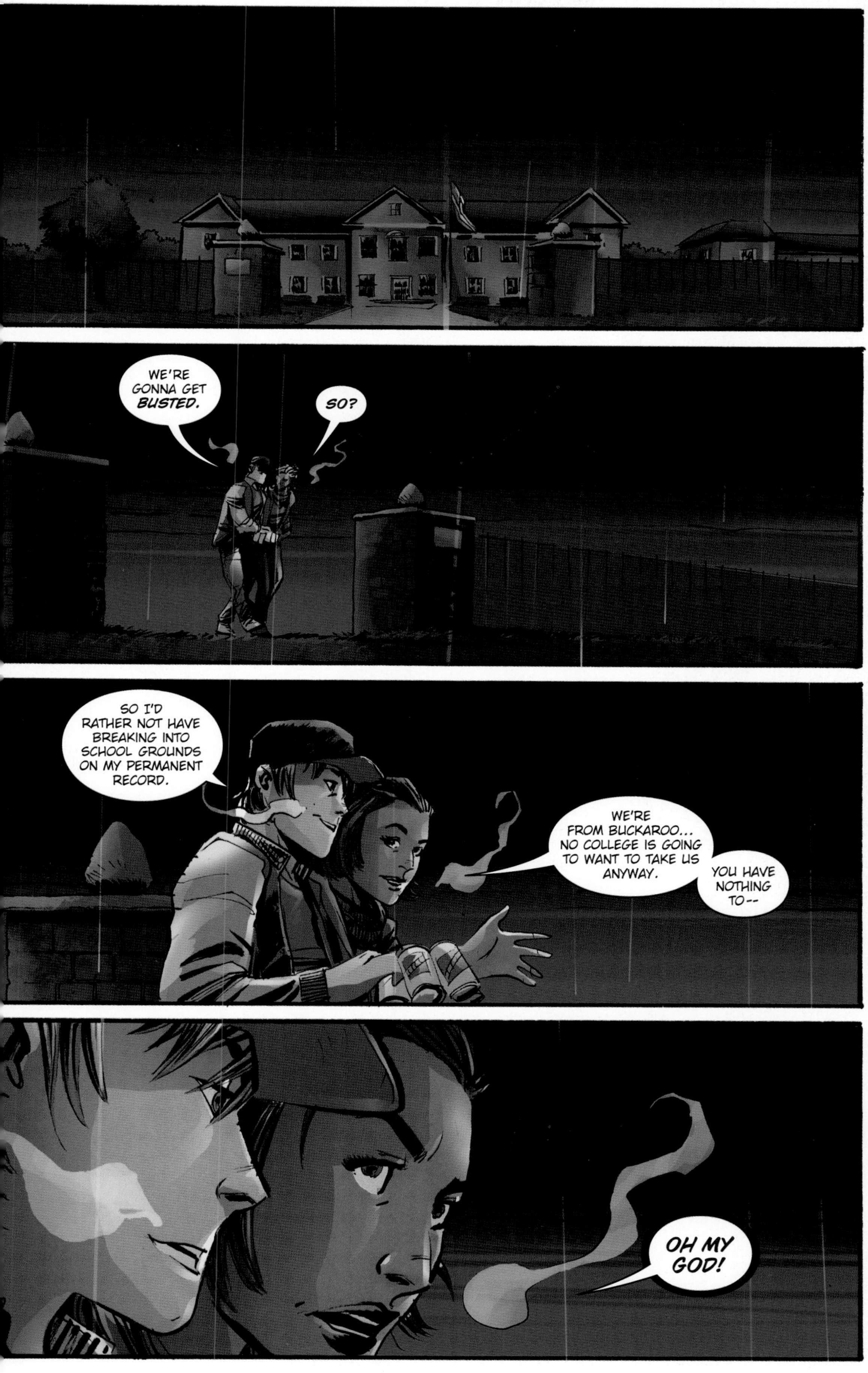
WE'RE GONNA GET *BUSTED.*
SO?
SO I'D RATHER NOT HAVE BREAKING INTO SCHOOL GROUNDS ON MY PERMANENT RECORD.
WE'RE FROM BUCKAROO... NO COLLEGE IS GOING TO WANT TO TAKE US ANYWAY.
YOU HAVE NOTHING TO--
OH MY GOD!

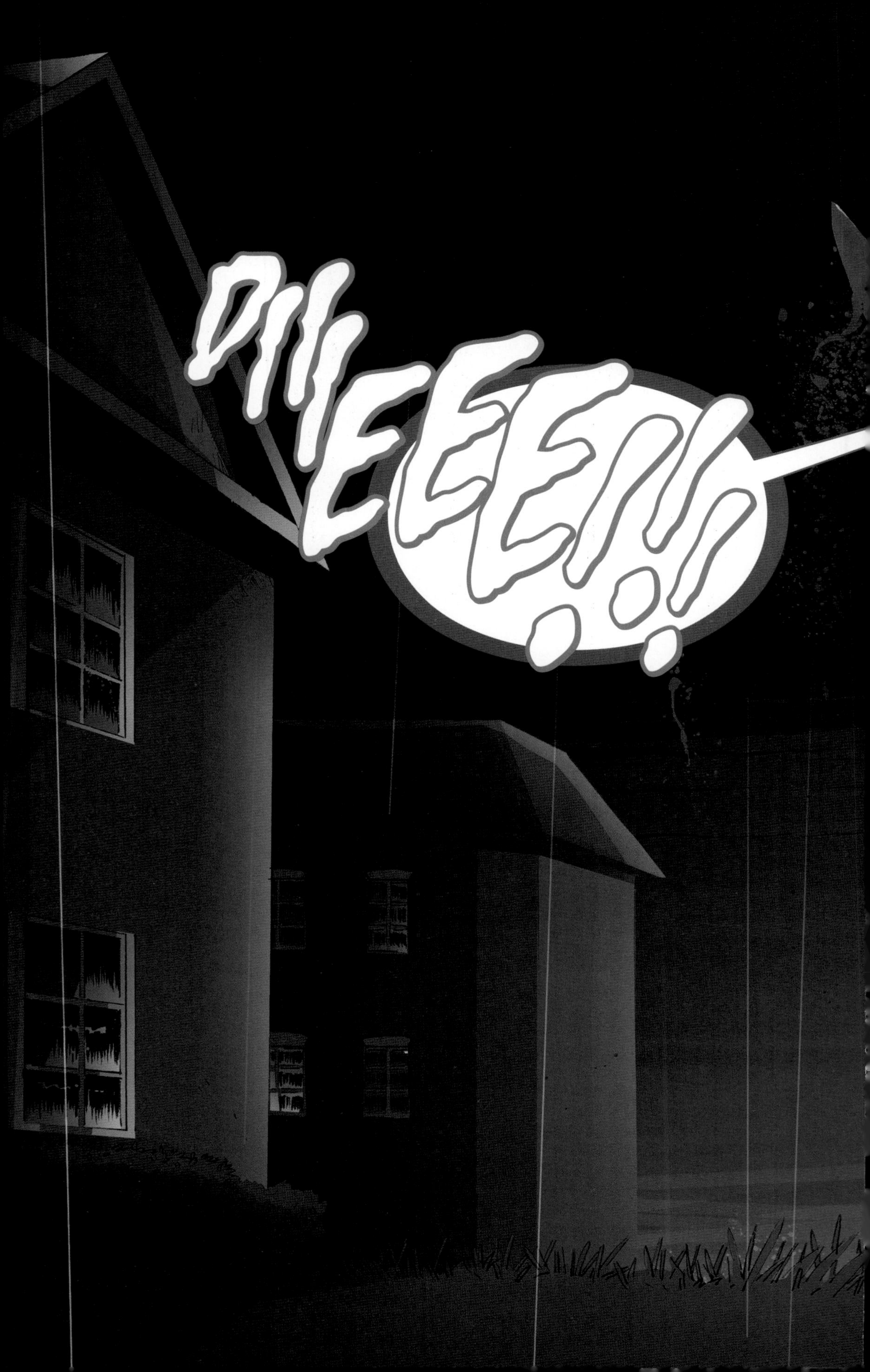
DIIEEE!!

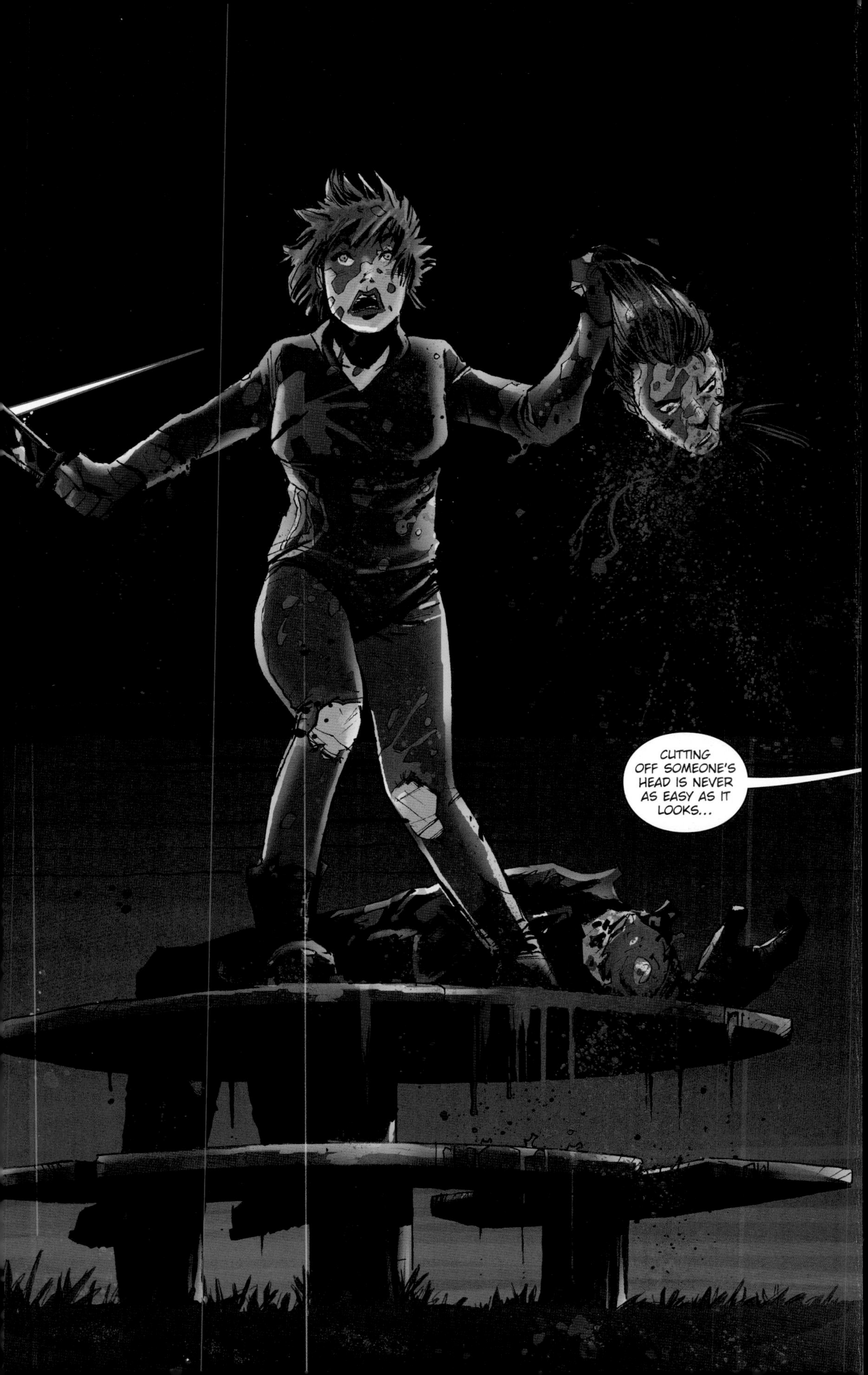
CUTTING OFF SOMEONE'S HEAD IS NEVER AS EASY AS IT LOOKS...

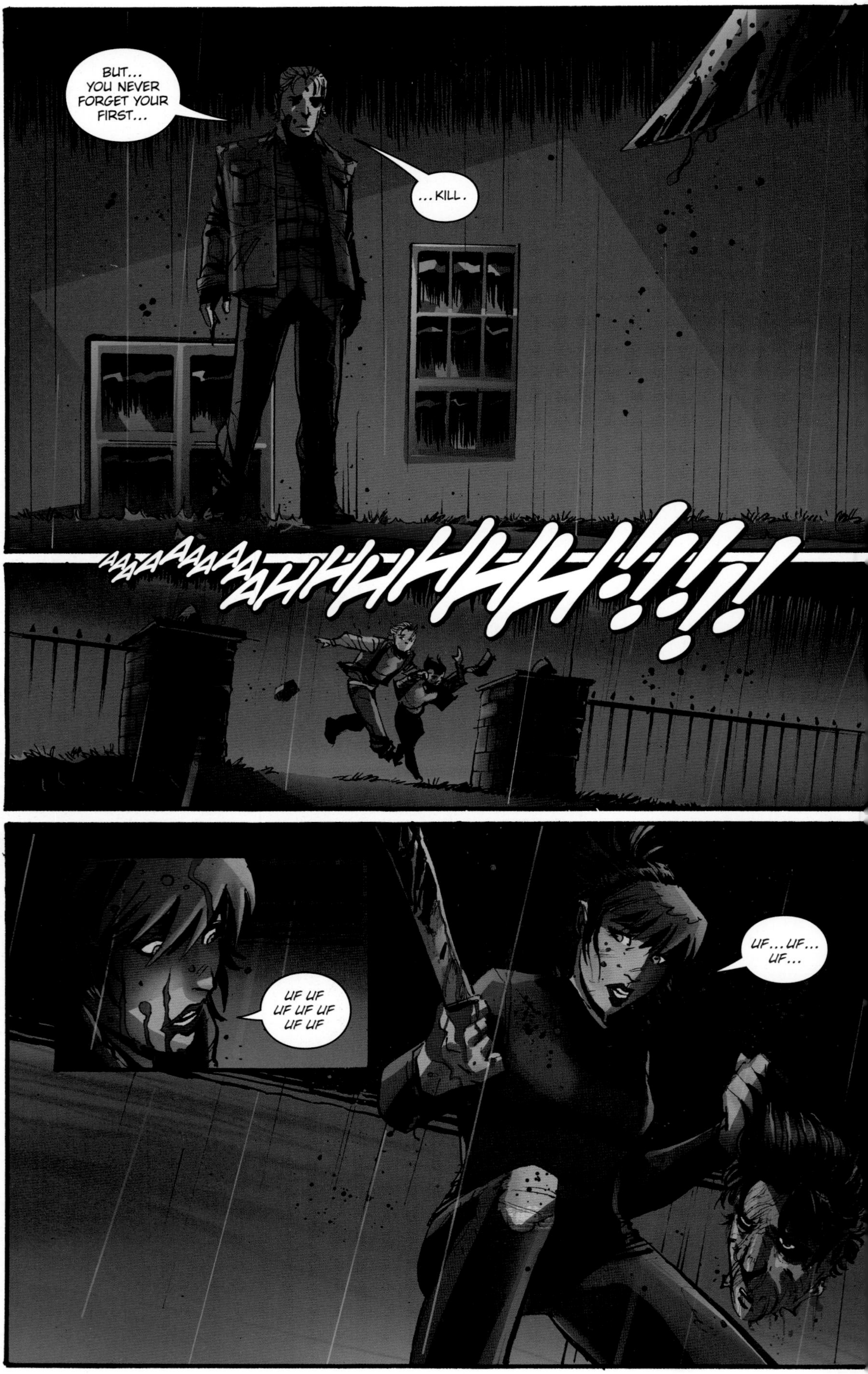
BUT... YOU NEVER FORGET YOUR FIRST...
...KILL.
AAAAAAAAAAHHHHHH!!!!!
UF UF UF UF UF UF UF
UF...UF... UF...

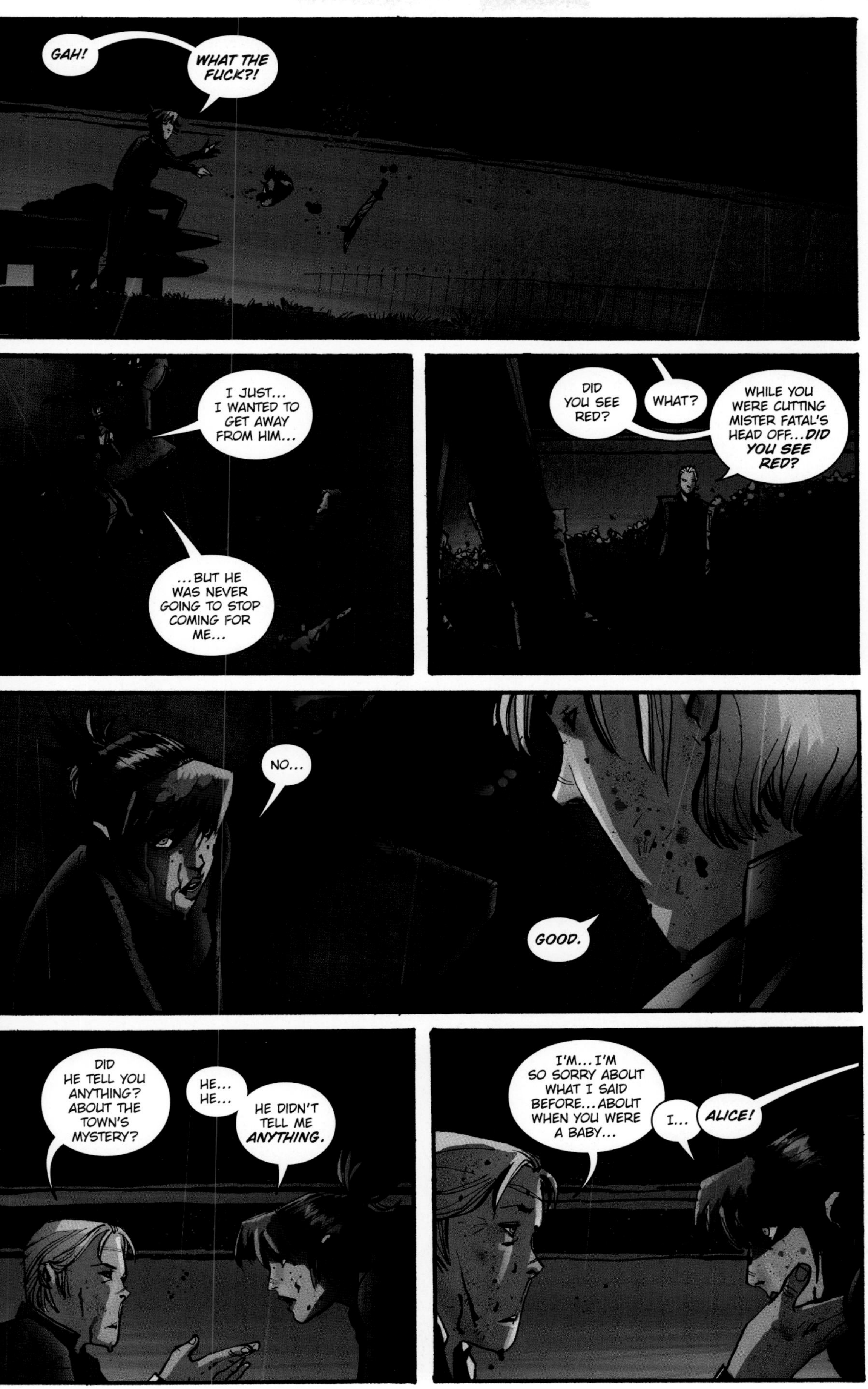
GAH!
WHAT THE FUCK?!
I JUST... I WANTED TO GET AWAY FROM HIM...
...BUT HE WAS NEVER GOING TO STOP COMING FOR ME...
DID YOU SEE RED?
WHAT?
WHILE YOU WERE CUTTING MISTER FATAL'S HEAD OFF...DID YOU SEE RED?
NO...
GOOD.
DID HE TELL YOU ANYTHING? ABOUT THE TOWN'S MYSTERY?
HE... HE...
HE DIDN'T TELL ME ANYTHING.
I'M... I'M SO SORRY ABOUT WHAT I SAID BEFORE... ABOUT WHEN YOU WERE A BABY...
I...
ALICE!

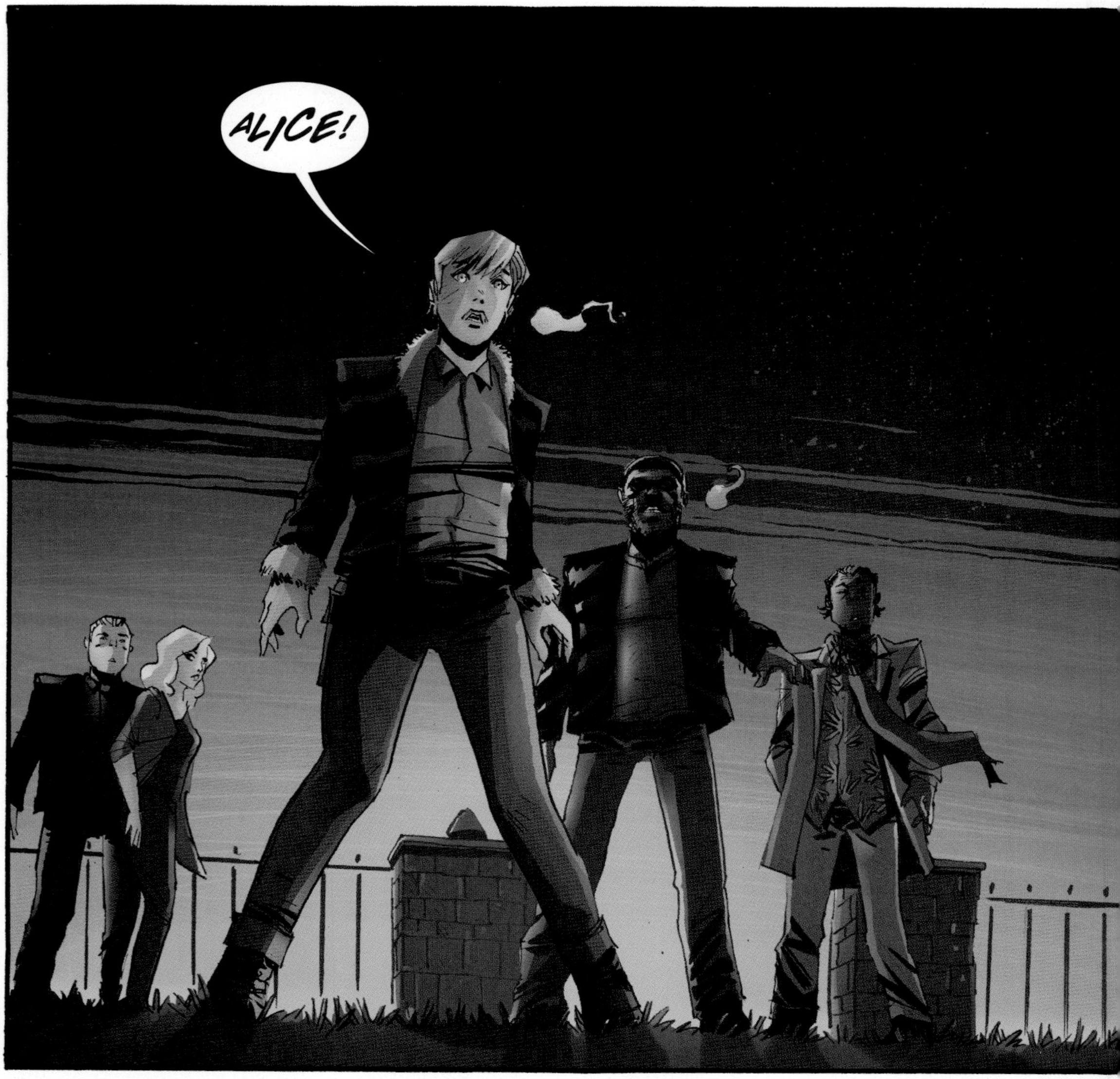
ALICE!

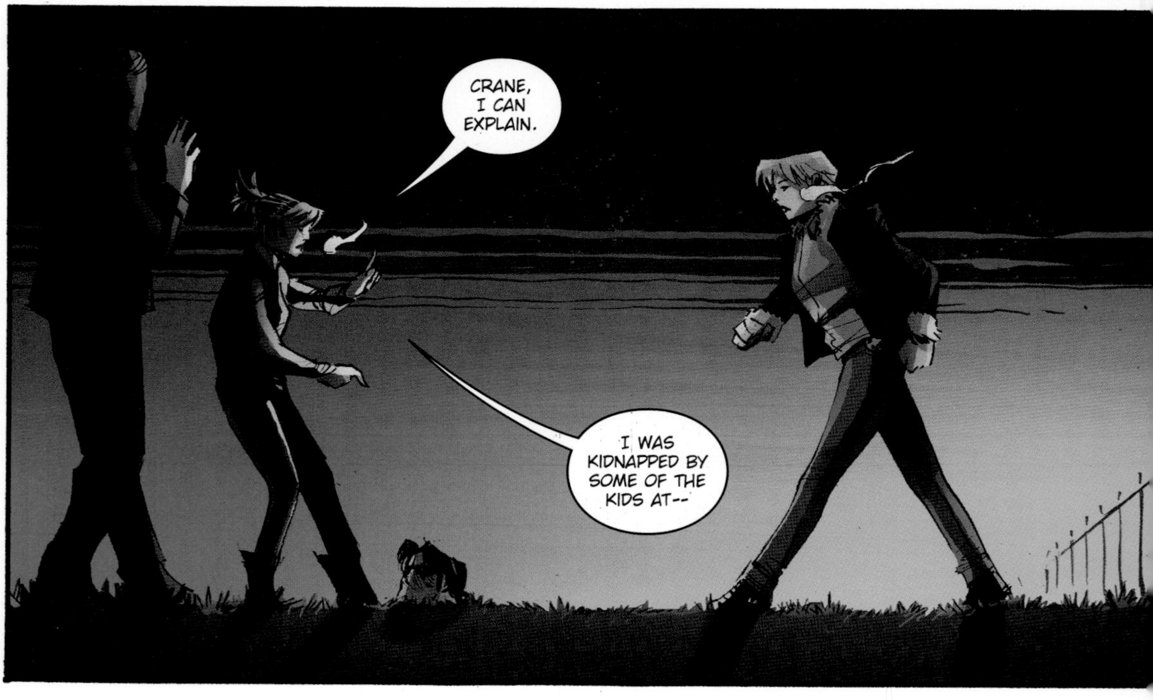
CRANE, I CAN EXPLAIN.
I WAS KIDNAPPED BY SOME OF THE KIDS AT--

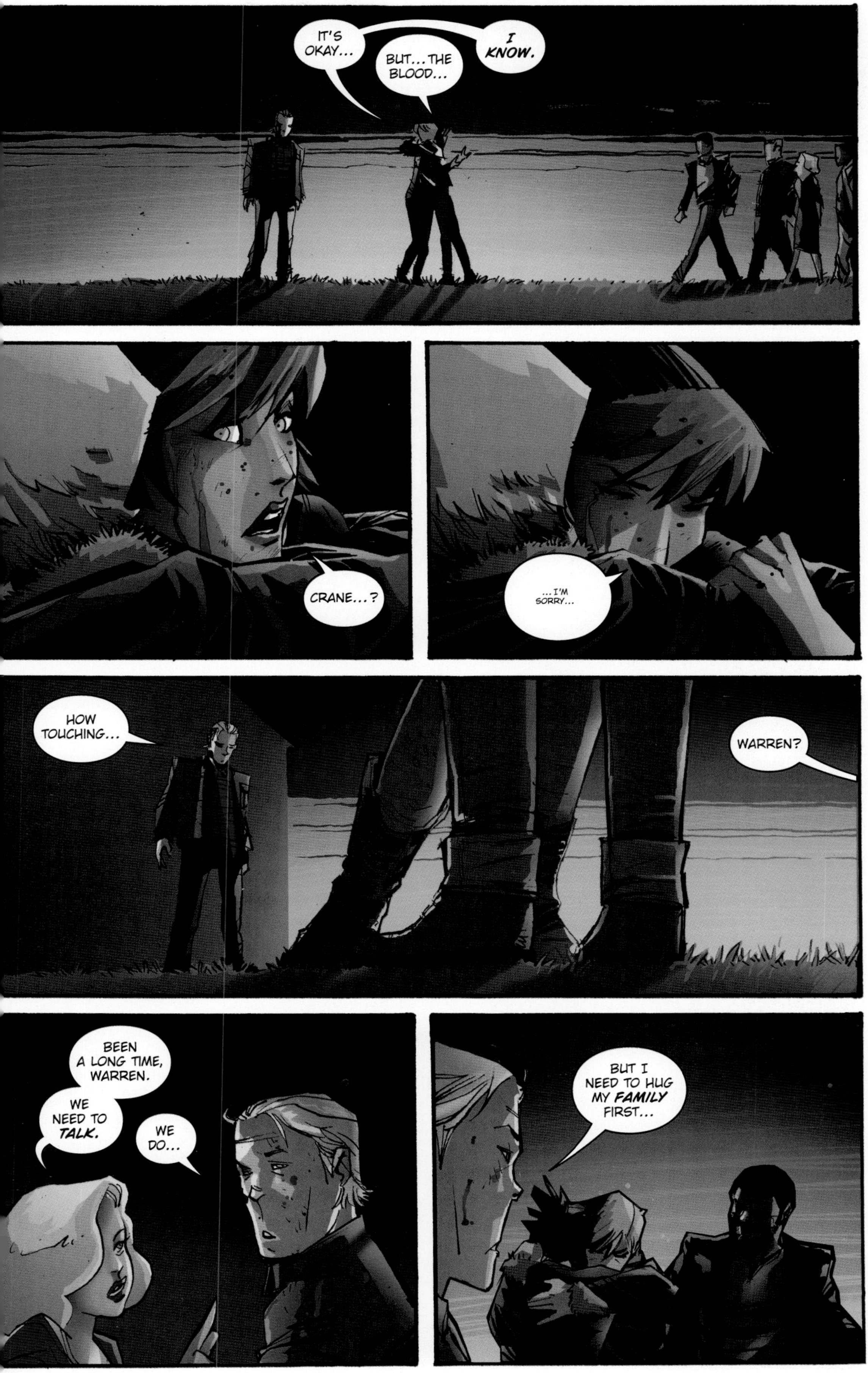
IT'S OKAY...
BUT... THE BLOOD...
I KNOW.
CRANE...?
...I'M SORRY...
HOW TOUCHING...
WARREN?
BEEN A LONG TIME, WARREN.
WE NEED TO TALK.
WE DO...
BUT I NEED TO HUG MY FAMILY FIRST...

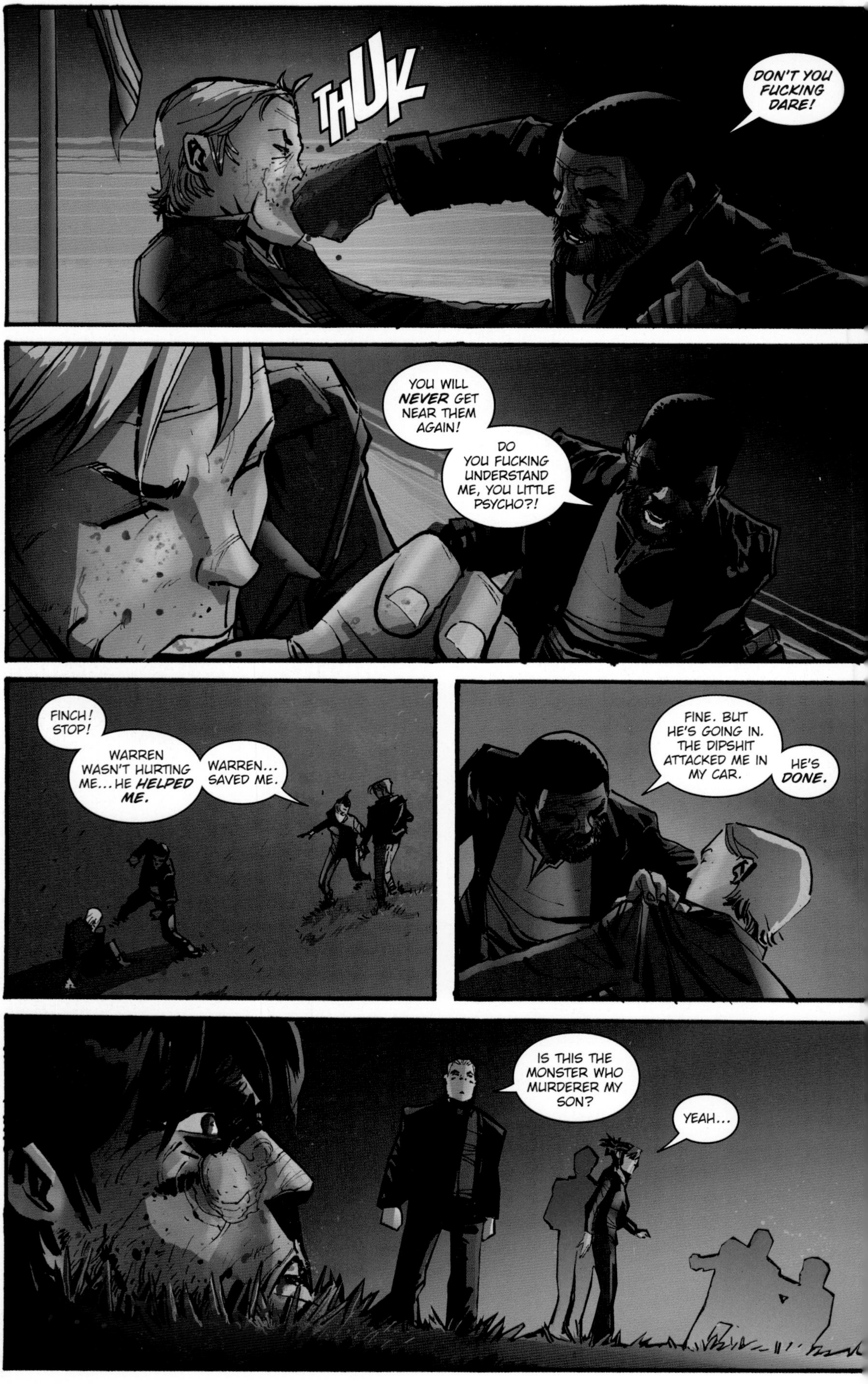
THUK
DON'T YOU FUCKING DARE!
YOU WILL NEVER GET NEAR THEM AGAIN!
DO YOU FUCKING UNDERSTAND ME, YOU LITTLE PSYCHO?!
FINCH! STOP!
WARREN WASN'T HURTING ME... HE HELPED ME.
WARREN... SAVED ME.
FINE. BUT HE'S GOING IN. THE DIPSHIT ATTACKED ME IN MY CAR.
HE'S DONE.
IS THIS THE MONSTER WHO MURDERER MY SON?
YEAH...

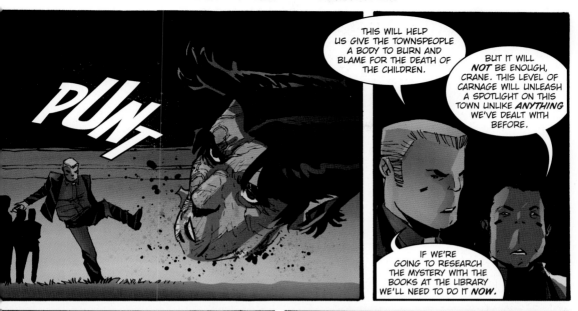

THIS WILL HELP US GIVE THE TOWNSPEOPLE A BODY TO BURN AND BLAME FOR THE DEATH OF THE CHILDREN.

BUT IT WILL *NOT* BE ENOUGH, CRANE. THIS LEVEL OF CARNAGE WILL UNLEASH A SPOTLIGHT ON THIS TOWN UNLIKE *ANYTHING* WE'VE DEALT WITH BEFORE.

PUNT

IF WE'RE GOING TO RESEARCH THE MYSTERY WITH THE BOOKS AT THE LIBRARY WE'LL NEED TO DO IT *NOW*.

WE CAN DEAL WITH THAT AFTER WE ALL GET SOME REST. JUST A FEW HOURS OF SLEEP.

I HAVE NO PLACE TO GO...

I WAS THINKING ABOUT THAT... YOU COULD TRY LIVING WITH *ME*?

THAT-- THAT MIGHT BE A LITTLE *WEIRD*.

ANY WEIRDER THAN THE REST OF THE STUFF THAT GOES ON IN THIS TOWN?

THE HAPPY FAMILY...

SMILES AND HUGS...

IF I DON'T GET TO HAVE THE HAPPY ENDING...

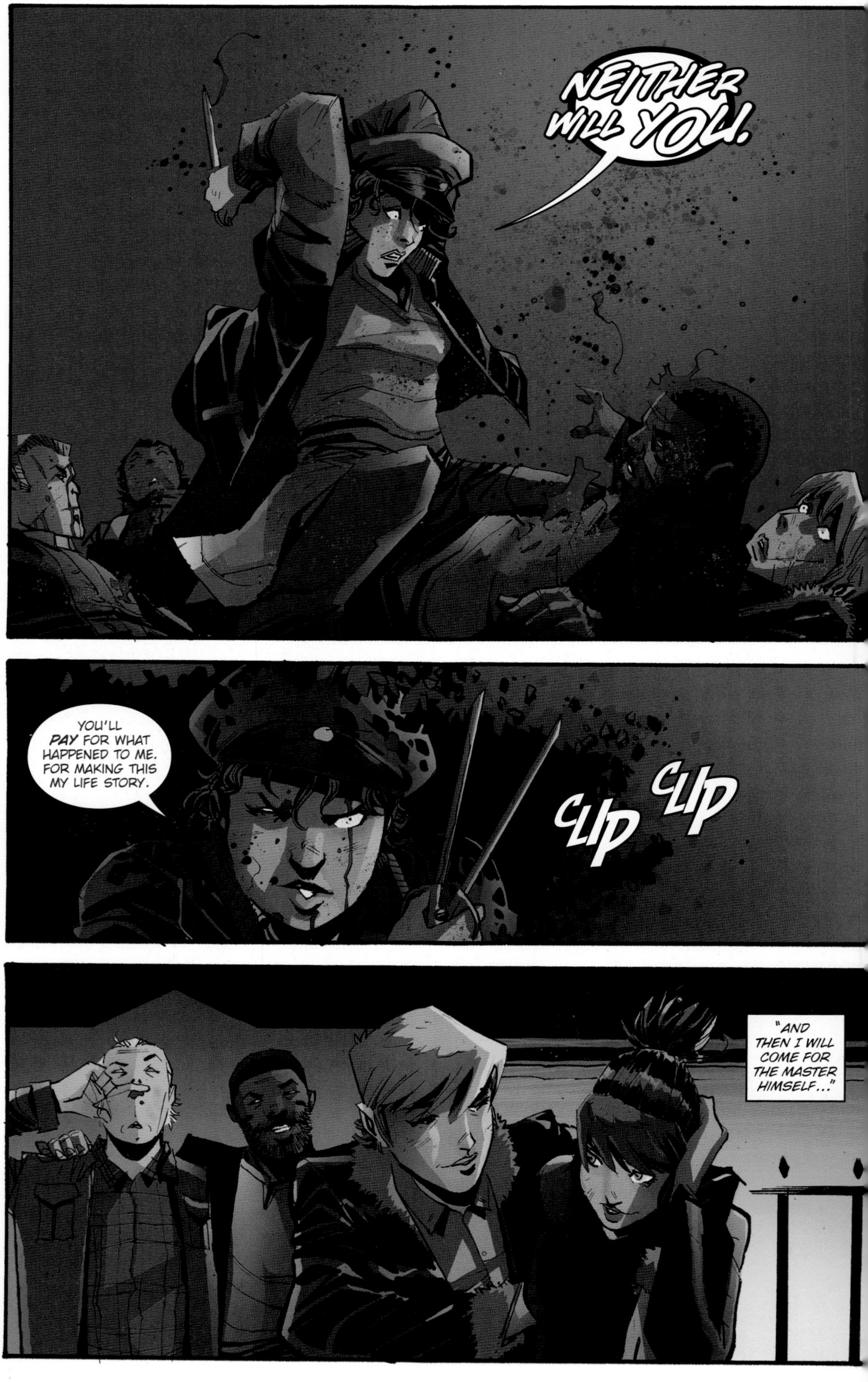
NEITHER WILL YOU.
YOU'LL PAY FOR WHAT HAPPENED TO ME. FOR MAKING THIS MY LIFE STORY.
CLIP CLIP
"AND THEN I WILL COME FOR THE MASTER HIMSELF..."

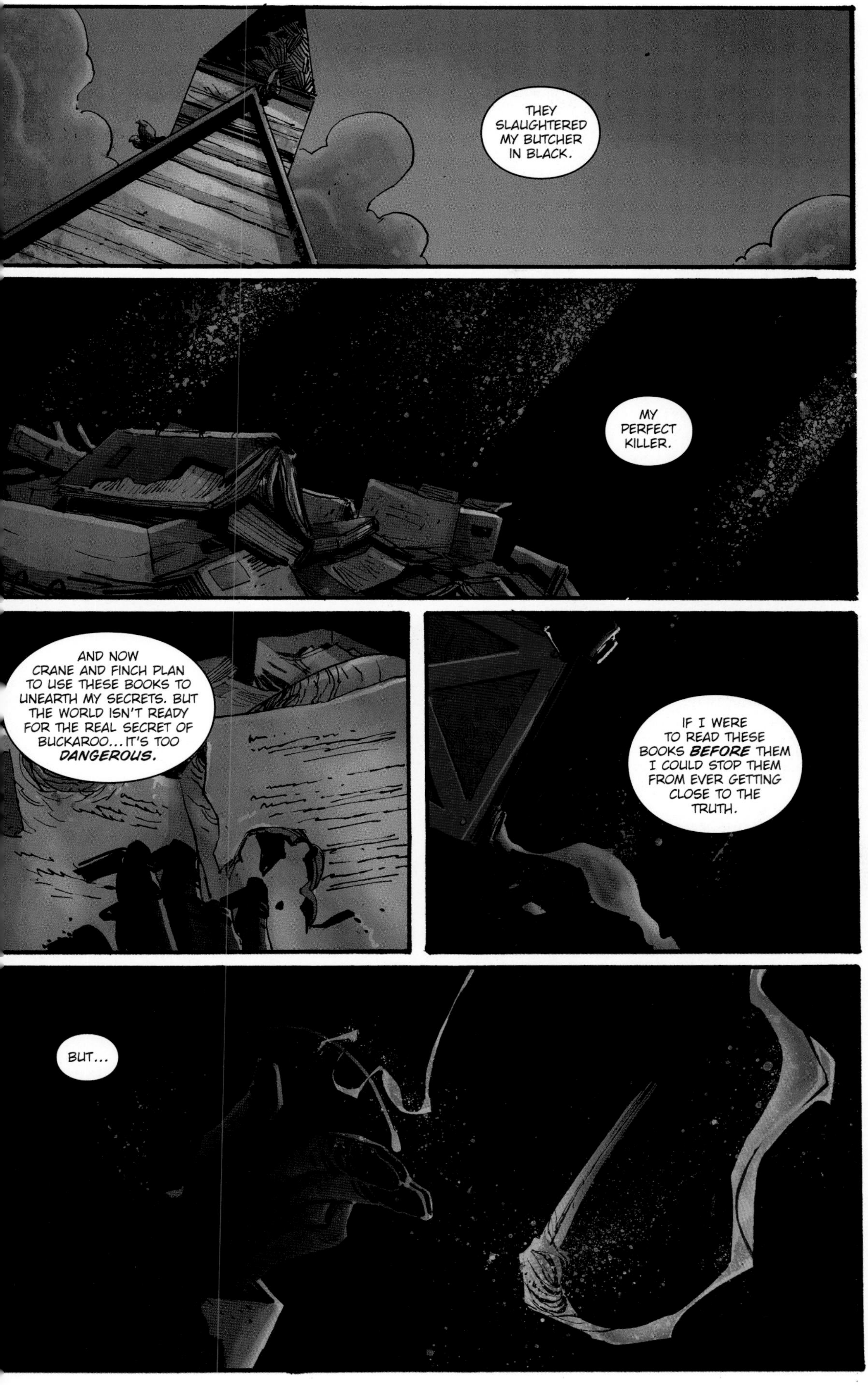
THEY SLAUGHTERED MY BUTCHER IN BLACK.
MY PERFECT KILLER.
AND NOW CRANE AND FINCH PLAN TO USE THESE BOOKS TO UNEARTH MY SECRETS. BUT THE WORLD ISN'T READY FOR THE REAL SECRET OF BUCKAROO... IT'S TOO ***DANGEROUS.***
IF I WERE TO READ THESE BOOKS ***BEFORE*** THEM I COULD STOP THEM FROM EVER GETTING CLOSE TO THE TRUTH.
BUT...

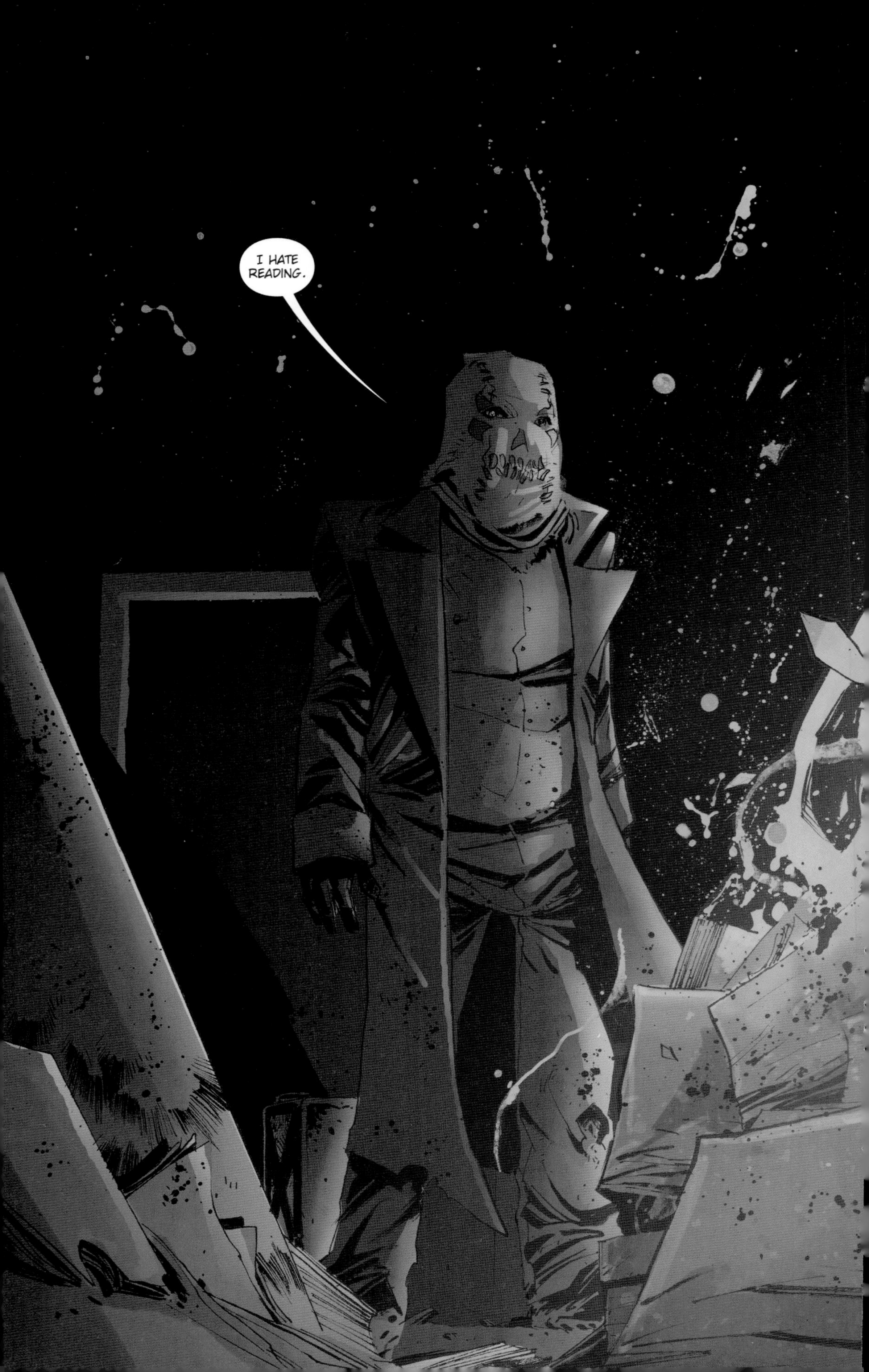
I HATE READING.

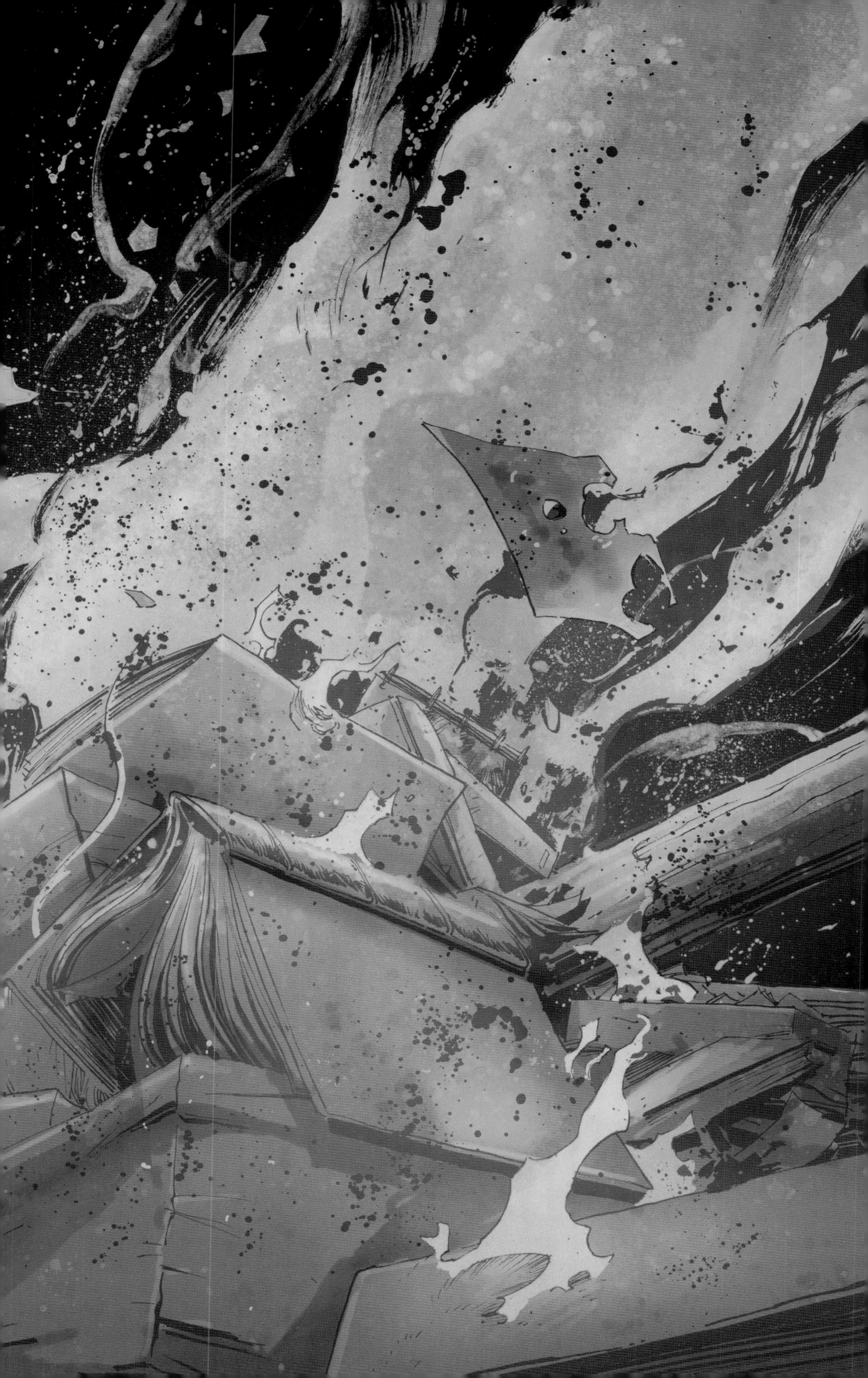

TO

BE

CONTI

NUED.

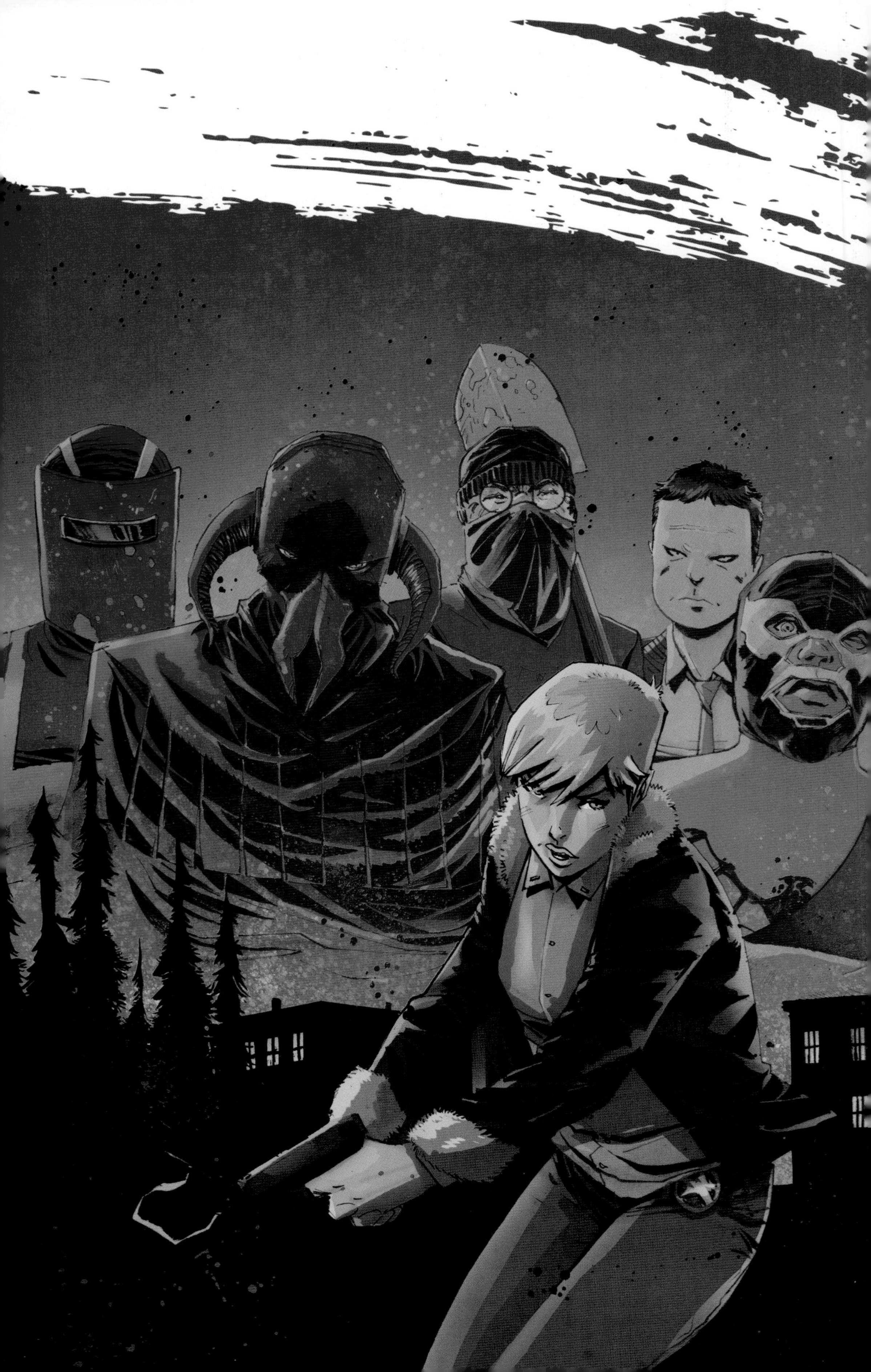

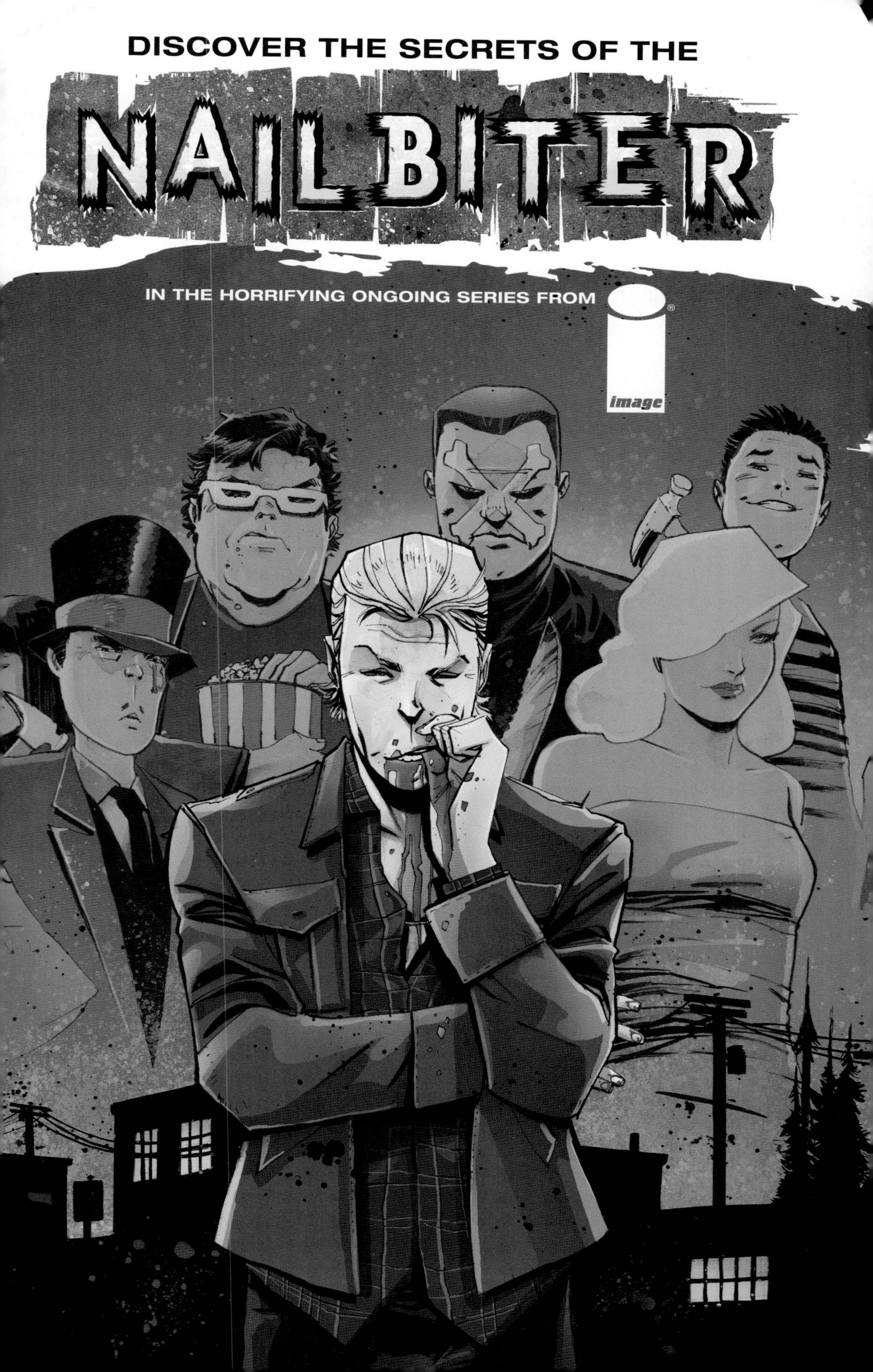
DISCOVER THE SECRETS OF THE
NAILBITER
IN THE HORRIFYING ONGOING SERIES FROM
image

IF YOU LIKED

NAILBITER

TRY THESE OTHER COLLECTIONS:

JOSHUA WILLIAMSON · GORAN SUDZUKA · MIROSLAV MRVA
GHOSTED
VOLUME ONE · HAUNTED HEIST

GHOSTED VOL. 1

Joshua Williamson,
Goran Sudzuka & Miroslav Mrva

144 PAGES SOFTCOVER
ISBN: 978-1-60706-836-5

GHOSTED VOL. 2

Joshua Williamson,
Davide Gianfelice & Miroslav Mrva

120 PAGES SOFTCOVER
ISBN: 978-1-63215-046-2

JOSHUA WILLIAMSON · DAVIDE GIANFELICE · MIROSLAV MRVA
GHOSTED
VOLUME TWO · BOOKS OF THE DEAD

WILLIAMSON · GIANFELICE · SUDZUKA · MRVA
GHOSTED
VOLUME THREE · DEATH WISH

GHOSTED VOL. 3

Joshua Williamson, Goran Sudzuka,
Davide Gianfelice & Miroslav Mrva

120 PAGES SOFTCOVER
ISBN: 978-1-63215-051-6

GHOSTED VOL. 4

Joshua Williamson, Goran Sudzuka,
Vladmir Krstic, Juan Jose Ryp &
Miroslav Mrva

112 PAGES SOFTCOVER
ISBN: 978-1-63215-317-3

WILLIAMSON LACI RYP MRVA
GHOSTED
VOLUME FOUR · GHOST TOWN

BIRTHRIGHT
WILLIAMSON BRESSAN LUCAS
VOLUME ONE
HOMECOMING

BIRTHRIGHT VOL. 1

Joshua Williamson,
Andrei Bressan & Adriano Lucas

128 PAGES SOFTCOVER
ISBN: 978-1-63215-231-2

BIRTHRIGHT VOL. 2

Joshua Williamson,
Andrei Bressan & Adriano Lucas

128 PAGES SOFTCOVER
ISBN: 978-1-63215-446-0

BIRTHRIGHT
WILLIAMSON BRESSAN LUCAS

image

PLEASE VISIT: **IMAGECOMICS.COM** for more information.
To find your local comic shop call **1-888-comicbook** or visit **www.comicshop.us**

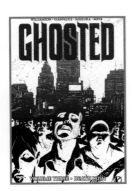